The Few

The Few

Cathy McSporran

FREIGHT BOOKS

First published 2015

Freight Books
49-53 Virginia Street
Glasgow, G1 1TS
www.freightbooks.co.uk

A CIP catalogue reference for this book is available
from the British Library

ISBN: 978-1-910449-34-9
eISBN: 978-1-910449-35-6

the publisher acknowledges investment from
Creative Scotland toward the publication of this book

Typeset by Freight in Adobe Garamond LT
Printed and bound by TJ International Ltd

For George, Louise and Gill –
Thanks guys, I couldn't have done it without you

And the Morrigan, goddess of war, appeared and said to the king: *If you dig up the head of Brandt, who sacrificed himself for this land, from its resting place, then the invaders will come. Already I see them, coming from the East. They will come with iron and blood, with eagles and wolves and ravens; and they will rain down fire upon you.*

But the king did not listen, and the head of Brandt was dug up and cast aside. For this is the nature of our wicked world: the sacrifice of one good man is never enough.

From *The First Lamentable Disclosure of the Island of Britain*

Characters

The Wizards

Maggie Ogilvie
Colin Ogilvie
Jannah Szymborska
Vincent William Walker
Alice Marianne Carrington

The Gothi

Lise
Albrecht
Petr
Hans
Manfred
Wolfgang
Werner
Lothar
Dieter
Franz
Harald
Joachim
Gottfried

20 Squadron
(Kestrel Squadron)

Arthur James Willoughby
Michal Capek
Harry Williams
Jonathan Penry-Smith
Nicholas 'Kiddy' Jones
Edward 'Scots Eddy' Paterson
Robert Edgar Fergusson
Christopher John Forbes
Paddy Draycott
Ben Solomon
William 'Tubs' MacKenzie
Rupert Robin Duffy

Prologue

The Black Sun

Berlin, May 1940

Lise soon realised she had nothing to worry about. Her stomach had been churning when she came into the vast, echoing chamber. No matter how often she assured herself that the Race-Soul would come to her – hadn't it always? – she had seen the eyes of the twelve boys settle on her, flat and sceptical, and she was full of fear. She was glad the underground room was so chilly; it meant there was an excuse for her hands and legs to tremble.

She had felt a little better when Albrecht came forward to lead her to her place. He had taken her hand and escorted her, their footsteps echoing, to the centre of the Black Sun painted on the stone floor. His hand was so warm and his smile so kind, his blue eyes so perfect, she had hoped he would take the place in the East, the one directly in front of her. The sight of him would warm her, make her strong again.

When the twelve boys had taken their places, however, standing around the Black Sun circle like numbers on a clock, it wasn't Albrecht who stood in front of her; it was Petr, with his usual impassive stare. She looked away from his cold eyes quickly, but not before the trembling, the *weakness*, started in her again. The boys were in place, and it was time to begin; but the more she needed strength, the more it eluded her. Why would the Race-Soul inspire her, when there was no steel in her heart? Why should the goddess think of coming to her?

But then the boys began the chant. The words were simple and familiar, straight from the sacred Edda, the precious tales of the old gods. *Possessor of the Slain, of Sessrúmnir, of the Gib-Cats, and of Brísinga-men; Goddess of the Vanir, Lady of the Vanir, Goddess Beautiful in Tears...* Simple – but so good, so pure! Lise lifted her eyes above Petr's scornful face to the fiery torches on the wall, but it was the image beside them that warmed her. The Führer's Cross, strong and clear on the flag adorning the plain stone wall – symbol of light and rebirth, of a people rising from the cleansing flames. The dear, the most blessed Swastika!

Now Lise forgot her own weaknesses. She forgot her imperfections, her pale but not golden hair, and her brown eyes – mud-brown, hateful! – as the power began to rise in her. All her imperfections would be purged, because now Freya was coming. Coming, as she always did, in rushing air and crackling light. Lise's white uniform blouse was pressed to her skin, her brown skirt swirled and lifted around her knees. The thought of the boys seeing her skinny legs would usually have horrified her, but now it just made her laugh. The boys' chanting voices coiled around her; and she became strong, stronger than she had ever been since the power first came to her, since she had known it as the Soul of the Aryan race. Now she was united with these twelve, these strong and pure young men, united in purity and in power.

And the goddess came to her.

Lise's hair, tightly plaited on her head, unwound itself and flew up in a cloud around her, sparking with amber light. She stretched out her arms and lifted, on tiptoe and then *up*, inches above the black and white floor. The boys, well-disciplined, continued to chant; but she knew their eyes were wide with excitement now, even Petr's. Lise laughed again, and reached upwards to the high, shadowed ceiling; the torches flared, the room was bright and stifling, and full of the presence of the goddess.

'Freya,' Lise said. 'She is here. Freya.'

Part One:

Blood, Toil, Tears and Sweat

The weak must be chiselled away. I want young men and women who can suffer pain. A young German must be as swift as a greyhound, as tough as leather, and as hard as Krupp's steel.

Adolf Hitler

Chapter One
Dunkirk

The English Channel, May 1940

'Mags, I don't feel very well.'
    'Sssh.'
    'But—'
    'Ssh. He'll hear you!'

If there was one thing Maggie and her brother agreed on these days, it was that they weren't about to let their father out of sight. They hadn't heard from *her* in months – busy with important war work, or so her last letter said – so now they followed their father whenever they could get away with it. In the shops, or outside the pub, or winding cables on the boat, Dad would look up and find his double shadow staring back at him with mute defiance. They weren't going anywhere, not unless he went too.

He always told them: they were all right, they were quite safe, nothing was going to happen. Maggie always smiled back, but wondered how he could have misunderstood so badly. It was *he* who looked at risk, *he* who looked like he couldn't take care of himself. 'He doesn't even know how many sugars he takes in his tea,' Maggie said to Colin, who understood perfectly. So they agreed: they would keep on following him.

So their father shouldn't have been surprised by what happened. But he was – he didn't think of it till after, when it was much too late.

The three were eating breakfast when the call came over the wireless. Gran was away seeing her sister; Dad had made breakfast so that Maggie could finish her homework. They were doing their best with the burnt toast and rock-hard boiled eggs when Dad suddenly jumped to his feet and turned up the wireless.

A beach in France – Dunkirk. Our boys. Trapped on the shore.

Waiting for boats. Our boats.

Maggie sat very still, as if that would make her father sit safely back down and stay there. But he drained his teacup, picked up the last of his toast and said, 'You two can do the washing-up.'

'You're not *going?*' said Maggie.

'You heard.' He was shrugging on his jumper. 'It's just across the Channel.'

'But you don't believe in fighting,' said Colin.

'This isn't fighting. It's rescuing people.' He finished lacing up his boots, and turned to smile at his children. 'I'll be back tonight. Maybe tomorrow. Tell your Gran.' He patted his son's shoulder and said, 'Look after your sister and your Gran till I get back.' Then he hugged his daughter and said, quietly but with rather more conviction, 'Look after them.'

Then he snapped off the wireless, and was gone.

Maggie and Colin stared at the remains of the breakfast table. Colin turned to his sister, his eyes huge and worried behind his glasses. 'Do you think we should…'

Maggie was looking at her fifteen-minute egg and her charcoaled toast. 'He can't even boil an egg,' she said.

This decided them. They jumped up and followed their father. From the front gate of the cottage, they looked down and saw the crowd gathering at the harbour. Beyond the harbour were the golden beaches, the pier and the big, white hotel: all deserted. It seemed everyone was at the harbour. The boats were alive with figures; the wharf was crowded with bystanders, mostly women with bright headscarves. Seagulls wheeled and screamed around the boats, but they would be disappointed; no fishing today.

Clutching their school satchels for cover, Maggie and Colin trotted down the path, their gas-masks bumping against their hips. The sea was flat and sparkling; to the East, France was a peaceful morning haze. 'Should be a calm enough trip,' Maggie said.

Colin nodded thankfully. They passed the church, Saint Michael's, the great square-towered Norman monstrosity that was far too big for the little village of Wardston. Then they were mingling with the crowd on the wharf. Maggie took Colin's hand and began to thread her way – slowly, casually – towards their father's boat.

They had the *Susan* in sight when a large heavy hand descended on Colin's shoulder. They looked up into a large heavy face under a blue domed helmet; the face said, 'Now then, young man. Not thinking of playing the hero, are we? Tagging along with your Dad?'

Colin stared open-mouthed at the policeman, a picture of guilt. Before he could say anything, Maggie put on her most sugary voice and said, 'It's all right, Constable Carter. I'll see he gets to school safe and sound. Boys are so *silly*, they just can't be trusted on their own!'

For a moment she thought she'd overdone it; but Carter's face had already softened. 'That's a good girl. You keep an eye on him.' He turned to Colin. 'You look after your sister and your grandma, now, you hear? You're the man of the house till your Dad gets back.'

Colin, who was ten years old and small as an eight-year-old, nodded solemnly. Maggie, nearly seventeen and as solidly built as her father, giggled and looked demurely at her feet. 'Come on, you big silly,' she said to Colin, and towed him away from the policeman, up Harbour Street towards the school.

After a hundred yards, Colin said, 'Are we really going to school?'

'Don't be daft.' Still clutching his hand, Maggie pulled him into Harbour Alley, back towards their father's boat.

That had been hours ago, and they'd spent most of that time crouching in the large galley cupboard. The cramp was bad enough. But now things were getting worse: either the weather had turned or they'd reached rougher water, because great humps of waves were lifting and dropping the *Susan* like a cork. And Colin, who could get poorly on a millpond, was starting to whimper: 'Maggie, I really don't feel well.'

'Sssh.'

'But Mags—'

'Ssssssh!'

'I think I'm going to be sick...' And then he was, splashing Maggie's ankles and filling the cupboard with stink. Maggie said a word her grandmother would have smacked her for, and pushed open the cupboard door.

She scrambled out into the cleaner air and the comparative brightness of the galley. Colin tumbled after her, mumbling apologies. Maggie was on her feet first, and her eyes cleared; and what she saw made her fall back, bumping against her brother.

Their father loomed in the hatchway; his face was terrible. 'What the *hell* are you two doing here?'

Colin pointed at his sister: 'She said you couldn't boil an egg.'

Maggie kicked him, but her father's gaze was already turning. 'It wasn't just me,' she cried, 'It wasn't just *me!*'

Before her dad could answer, there was a booming sound from above, like a big wave hitting the sand; the *Susan* rocked crazily, nearly throwing them off their feet. Dad snapped, 'Stay below,' and disappeared.

The two of them looked at each other in the dim, sick-scented galley. Eventually Maggie shrugged: how much more trouble could they get into? 'Might as well be hung for a sheep as a lamb,' she said, and followed her father. Colin was right behind her as she emerged onto the deck, out into the bright sunshine and a rolling cloud of smoke, and they saw what they had come to.

Dunkirk was burning.

Three huge cones of smoke towered over the beach like black tornadoes. Dull orange fire flickered at the bottom. Burning chemicals caught the backs of their throats – there was a mucky brown haze over the choppy sea and the dun-coloured sand. Maggie and Colin had seen the French coast before, on trips with Dad; they had watched the waves swishing across the bay, fanning out calmly onto the sand. But now the sea pitched and struggled under them, stirred up by boats. Dozens of them, large and small: from wooden rowing-boats to a great, shining steel destroyer, about a mile off, where the sun was breaking through.

Maggie glanced to starboard and almost screamed: there was a wall of iron a hundred yards off, too close. Another destroyer. Maggie and Colin looked up the metal wall, and saw an arm waving from amidst the gun-muzzles peeking over the side. Dad was waving back.

One of ours. Relieved, Maggie turned back to the beach, now only two hundred yards or so off. There were long lines of fence posts there, hundreds of them, forming straggling lines across the sand, each topped with a dull metallic sheen. Some of them stood in the sea, half-submerged, as if caught by the tide. They must be some kind of defence line, she thought, until she saw they were moving, each post shifting, making the line wriggle like a snake. They weren't fence-posts at all; they were men. Soldiers, standing in long, ragged lines across the beach.

Colin appeared at Maggie's elbow. 'What are they doing?'

'I think they're... queuing.'

Colin blinked. 'Like in the post office?'

Maggie couldn't help giggling; it was all so *polite*. 'They're just... waiting their turn—'

There was a droning sound overhead, nasal and unpleasant. The lines of men flattened themselves onto the sand. Something like a metal kite flashed overhead; Maggie and Colin looked up at steel wings marked with Luftwaffe black crosses. The fighter skimmed over them towards the shore. There was a rattle of popping sounds like fireworks, and little bursts of sand hurried up the beach in a zig-zagging line. The soldiers were moving, breaking out of their orderly queue, but they weren't quick enough. The zig-zag crossed the line of men, there was a haze of red, and some of the soldiers began to scream.

Colossal booming shook the boat: the destroyer's guns were firing. The German plane began to haemorrhage smoke, twisting and turning in the air. The men on the shore scattered, some up the beach and some down to the water, as the fighter struggled but kept its trajectory downwards, and then exploded on the beach in a cloud of smoke and sand and fire.

The men who'd fled down the beach were in the water now, pushing away from the flames and out to sea, as if they meant to wade to Dover. Some of them were up to their chests, and didn't seem to be stopping. They'd rather drown than burn, Maggie thought. She turned to her father, who was at the wheel, to point out the wading men; only then did she notice the change in the engine sound. Dad was turning the *Susan* around, away from the shore. 'Dad,' called Maggie, 'what are you doing?'

'Taking you two home.' He had to shout over the shots, the cannon fire, the roaring of the fires. 'What d'you think I'm doing?'

Maggie looked back at the men in the water. They had noticed her, in spite of all the noise. It was the last thing they expected to hear, a girl's voice; the last thing they thought they'd see, a girl's bright red plaited hair, shining even in the grubby cloud of smoke. They were pushing towards the *Susan* now, shrugging off their packs; they were stretching out their arms to Maggie. 'Dad, they're just there,' she cried.

He wasn't looking, deliberately not looking. 'I'm getting the two of you home.'

'We can't just leave them!'

'I told you to get below!'

The men were much closer now; Maggie could see their faces. 'No.' She hoisted herself up, threw one leg over the side. 'Dad, I'm getting them! I mean it!'

She didn't really mean it, of course; not really. But Colin started to wail, 'Don't, don't!' and Dad held out a hand to placate her.

'All right! Just get back down! And get below!'

Maggie obediently flattened herself to the deck. Her father left the wheel and reached overboard with both arms, tipping the *Susan* to starboard. He came up pulling something like a huge brown fish, dumped the gasping man onto the deck and reached over for another.

The boat tipped again, so low that a hand grabbed onto the side right above Maggie's head. She jumped up and held out her arms. A man's face, wide-eyed and staring like a frightened horse, looked back at her; hands grabbed onto her and she pulled, painfully, until the man rolled over the side and onto the deck. He lay there, panting and staring at her. Maggie heard Dad's voice shouting, 'Help the others!' The first man he'd pulled aboard was getting up, reaching over. Colin was only a few feet away, trying to pull an enormous man on board but being pulled closer and closer to the water himself. Maggie said to the man at her feet, 'Help the others,' and as he scrambled to his feet she lunged for Colin, grabbing the big soldier's arms just before they both fell backwards into the sea.

And then there were more and more of them, crowding onto the deck in their sopping-wet khakis, their eyes frantic and empty of thought. They piled into the galley, in a row on the bunk. They filled every inch: the *Susan* was riding so low in the surf that Maggie could reach overboard and put her hand right into the water. And still there were more.

'That's enough,' Dad said at last. He was looking at a man with a moustache, a man with extra patches on his shoulders. 'We'll capsize.'

The man nodded, and roared, 'That's it. You men in the water – off with you! Wait for the next boat!'

It was an upper-class accent, the voice of command; but even that wasn't enough. The gripping hands kept coming. The men who were safely in the boat shoved them off, unwrapping their clutching fingers or just hammering them with their fists. Still the reaching hands; now there were pleading voices, calling things Maggie couldn't hear and didn't want to. It wasn't until the officer shouted, 'Shoot the next man who tries to board!' that the clutching hands finally disappeared.

Wallowing impossibly low, the *Susan* heaved itself around and started pushing away from the beach. Maggie kept still, wedged against the port side by soaking, uniformed figures. Colin was over to starboard, tiny among the hulking men; Maggie smiled at him reassuringly, starting to feel reassured herself. The coast of Dunkirk fell away, five hundred, six hundred yards. A thousand.

The men's panting breath was slowing now; their faces relaxing, dull with exhaustion but human again. Quite a few faces were looking at Maggie and Colin. The officer – a major, Maggie saw, with a little embroidered crown on his shoulder – said, 'What the bloody hell are these children doing aboard?'

'Stowaways.' Dad glared at Maggie, who looked at her feet. 'Hid down below.'

'We just wanted to help,' Colin said. Some of the men laughed; one of them patted his shoulder. Dad ignored them, 'They're going right back to Dover.'

The major shook his head, 'Put them onto the *Grafton* with us.' He pointed at the destroyer. 'Then go back to the beach.'

'When I get my children home safe.'

'They'll be safe enough on the *Grafton*, man!'

Dad jerked his head towards the other destroyer, the one a mile off. Flames were blossoming from its hull. Things were falling into the sea, burning things. 'Dover,' Dad said.

'Dammit, man, this is an order!'

'I'm not in the army, mister.'

The major looked at the other men, who were looking away. Obviously Dover sounded good to them, but they weren't about to argue with an officer. Eventually the major said to Dad, 'Now look here. You've got one last chance before I commandeer this boat.'

'Do you know how to pilot it?'

'For God's sake, how hard can that be?'

'She lists to port,' said Dad, lying smoothly about his perfectly-maintained craft. 'Do you know how to compensate for that? Where to thump the motor if it goes belly-up?'

'You've – got one last—'

'Dover first.' Dad turned to look at the major. 'Drop off my kids. Then I'll go to and from your ship as often as you want.'

At that point the *Susan* sailed clear of the smoke, into the sunshine. They were nearly past the *Grafton*, looking into clean blue sky. There was the faint drone of a plane, somewhere far above, but no-one noticed because they could see the line of white on the other shore. The white cliffs.

The men cheered, and the major gave up. 'Very well. Dover—'

The cheering stopped and the drone became a roar, and iron wings painted with German black crosses flashed overhead. Something dropped about twenty yards off, and the *Susan* heaved to starboard as the sea erupted. Maggie saw Colin thrown sideways, saw his head smack against the side, saw the man beside him pull him upright. She was drenched in cold water as a wave broke over the starboard bow, but she was too wedged in place to move or to fall. She saw three men around her father clouded in a reddish haze; they, and her dad, who had been standing precariously balanced as he talked to the major, were thrown to starboard and over the side.

The *Susan* righted itself as the bomber skimmed upwards

and away, trying to shake off a British plane marked with RAF roundels – a Spitfire – that had swooped up behind it. Maggie shoved through the men around her to where Dad had gone overboard. She was ready to tease him – his boots flying up in the air like that, it looked so funny! She couldn't see him, though. He must have been too scared of the bomber to surface. 'It's all right,' she called. 'It's gone.'

Behind her she heard the major: 'Any sign of them?' She didn't hear the answers, though, she just reached down and splashed at the choppy water. What was he *playing* at? 'Dad! Come on!'

She was reaching for an upside-down metal helmet, which was bobbling along like a toy boat – Dad might be underneath it, trying to come up! – when the wailing sound began. A falling, screaming sound. The men beside her craned their necks up to the sky, like rabbits who've heard an eagle. Their eyes were wide again. A word went around them: 'Stuka.' It jumped from one man to the next – 'Stuka. *Stuka.*'

The major's shout cut them off as the dreadful wailing cry became louder. 'Get this thing moving! You there! The engine!'

Maggie was still scanning the water; she felt the tone of the engine change. 'No!' she cried, 'no, I haven't found him yet!'

No one seemed to hear. The major's voice barked again, 'Full speed! Steer for the ship!'

'No! Don't! My Dad—'

'Get us *moving*!'

The *Grafton*'s guns boomed again, but the scream of the siren got louder and louder. Maggie was still splashing at the water's surface, trying to swoosh a big piece of debris out of the way, when she heard someone cry out, a child's cry. She looked up for Colin, but it was one of the men beside her. She smelled urine. Now there were heavy splashing sounds; some of the men were throwing themselves into the sea, trying to swim away in their heavy uniforms. The man who'd cried out was standing up, pointing:

'Oh God help us!'

Maggie looked up. A plane was falling towards them. The fall was controlled: a dive-bomber. It was screaming as though it were being tortured, and it was pointed right at the *Susan*. It was small, with funny, fat little ankles, like a toy. But the men on the boat were scattering before it like swimmers from a shark. Its nose was grey like a shark's – it even had painted teeth around its nose. It was looking at her, grinning.

Maggie stood up. It was headed right at them; it was headed for the patch of water where her father had fallen. Where he was still waiting, obviously, still submerged – but he didn't know about the plane! Maggie stared at the Stuka, and gathered all her strength. Electricity crackled around her hair as it unwound from its thick plaits. Oblivious, Maggie focussed on the plane and screamed, *'Go away!'*, thrusting out both hands to ward it off.

The Stuka flipped over backwards, nose to tail, as if a gale-force wind had caught it. It scattered its little bombs, but they fell into empty water, and the fountains that roared up were harmless. The plane itself kept flipping, over and over, until it hit the sea in a massive burst of water, its wing scything into a packed rowing boat. There were more screams now.

'Mother of God,' the major said. He wasn't looking at the remains of the dinghy – he was staring at Maggie. She ignored him, and the screams, and turned back to the empty sea around the *Susan*. 'Dad! Dad!'

'Freya,' a voice beside her said. 'Freya. *Sie kommt.*'

It was Colin. He was beside her, staring at nothing. The side of his head was bloody. One of the lenses of his glasses was broken; his eye was cracked from side to side, staring into empty space. 'Freya,' he said. *'Die schöne göttin.* Freya.'

He was alive and in the boat; Maggie had already stopped listening to him, was looking all around. Maybe Dad had headed back to the beach? He would, surely he would? 'Dad! *Dad!*'

The engine was starting. The boat was moving away. 'No.' She turned to the man beside her, 'Wait!'

The man gazed back; it was the pity in his eyes that broke her. 'I'm sorry, lass,' he said.

'No! *Dad! Dad!*'

'I'm sorry,' the man said. He pulled her into his arms. 'There, lass, I'm sorry.'

She started screaming into his shoulder, as the *Susan* turned and made for Dover.

A thousand feet in the air, the man in the Spitfire looked down and thought: *Maggie. Her name is Maggie.*

Chapter Two

Conchie Kids

Wardston-Upon-Sea, South-East England
June 1940

Maggie climbed the last few feet to the top of the Mound, to the low standing stone. She turned at the sound of a car horn; the Land Army truck was still in sight, winding its way along the twisting local road. It was still close enough for her to see the mass of green jerseys and brown hats bouncing around in the back, even to hear a shriek of laughter in the still summer air. Maggie lifted a hand to wave, thinking the horn might have been for her, saying bye-bye. But it had been for the two sheep now scuttling off the road. The girls' faces were turned away towards their billet; they'd forgotten her already.

Maggie hastily dropped her hand. The other girls were all right though, she thought, resting her hand on the stone. None of them were local – most had been shipped in from London – so they didn't know about Mum or Dad or Colin or any of it. They were always at least civil to her, sometimes even friendly. Especially when they found she was always willing to finish digging a row for them, or lift a few extra sacks of spuds, so they could take a break for a chat and a ciggie.

Maggie didn't want any breaks. She could only sleep at night if she'd spent the day digging, lifting, pulling up or setting down – wearing out every muscle, hands and feet in the earth.

She sat down now, both hands flat against the ground, back against the standing stone. The stone was old and mossy, short and slightly skewed. Not some proud old monolith: it didn't even have a real name, although some people called it the Ward Stone. But it had always been there, on top of the Mound, the low hill above Gran's cottage. And Maggie had always come here, to breathe in the east wind from the sea and the west wind from the land, and let them carry some of the day's fears away.

She realised she had turned to watch the sea; everyone in the village, and in the countryside around it, was watching the sea. At the moment it was peaceful and glittering in the summer sunshine: empty. Maggie made herself look away, inland to the patchwork fields, the toy planes on the airstrip a mile away; to the school just outside the village, where she'd soon go to meet Colin, in case he'd had one of his turns again. She'd gone back to school herself at first, but it was no good: she'd just sat there in the stuffy classroom, the teacher's words inaudible above the pounding of blood in her ears, her breath coming short and her fingers prickling with pins and needles. After a while she'd just got up and walked out. The teacher's shouts, the other kids whispering, meant nothing. (There was no red haze, no flames, no boots flying up in the air... how could it matter?) She'd gone straight out to the village hall, asked for the forms; minutes later she was part of the Women's Land Army.

Then she'd gone home to face Gran's wrath. But Gran had just looked at her sadly. 'Your Dad always said you should stay on at the school,' she'd said. After a moment she added, 'Your mother would want you to as well.'

'If she comes and tells me to, I'll go back,' Maggie answered, knowing she'd won. They hadn't seen Mum in months. She sent letters, sometimes. Sometimes she sent books, with little notes telling Maggie and Colin to be sure to read them: weird, gory books, much like the ones she'd insisted on reading to them when they were little, full of magic and the Morrigan and buried heads that kept the Vikings away. Colin sometimes read them, but Maggie never bothered. Maggie repeated, 'If Mum comes back, I'll go back to school.'

Gran just said, 'You can go back when the war's over, then,' and that was that.

Now Maggie sat on top of the Mound, just for a minute longer. She let the breeze cool her forehead, and the stone cool her back through her green jumper and white shirt (clean and crisply ironed by Gran every day, despite Maggie's protests). Then she pushed herself to her feet, wriggling slightly in the Land Army brown breeches – they were a bit snug, she'd need to find Gran's old sewing machine and let them out a bit. Then she set off down the path that wound its way down the Mound.

She heard murmuring voices and smelled cigarette smoke just before the turn onto the Mound's east flank. Slightly annoyed – she always thought of the Mound as hers, although it was public land – she rounded the bend, head held high in case it was one of those idiots from the village. But it was two men in uniform, sitting on the grass beside the path, and looking out to sea. Not army uniforms – grey-blue ones, with little wings stitched onto the breast pockets. Pilots, from the air base. Maggie had seen them in the village. One was tall, golden-haired, confident, upper-class. Handsome: the village girls got all giggly and swoony when he went past. Maggie had once been on the Land Army truck when it passed him on the road, and what the other land girls said about him had made her blush to her ears. Maggie thought he was like a man on a recruitment poster: golden and handsome, but indistinguishable from the other golden and handsome poster-men around him.

He and the other pilot saw her, touched their caps politely, said, 'Good afternoon.' The other pilot's voice, softer than his friend's ringing aristocratic tone, was accented: almost Germanic. He'd appeared last year, Maggie remembered – the local kids had followed him everywhere, convinced they'd uncovered a spy, until they'd found out he was Polish. He wasn't so handsome: his face was a bit too thin, his nose a bit too big, his black hair was a bit straggly despite the severe military cut.She thought he looked like someone who'd been forcibly smartened up before being shoved into uniform. Dad would have approved. The Polish airman was frowning, as if he'd seen Maggie before and was trying to place her, but he didn't say anything else.

Maggie murmured 'good afternoon' in return, and carried on down the path. They didn't resume their conversation; she knew they were watching her walk away. When she was a good distance away – far enough that you'd think she was out of earshot, if you didn't know that sound carried oddly on the Mound – she heard the English pilot say, 'I don't think there can be anything in the world nicer than women's britches, do you?' There was a low chuckle in response. Maggie flushed angrily, picking up her speed and trying not to let her buttocks clench. She really would have to let these breeches out, as far out as they'd go. She hurried on downhill until Gran's cottage came into view.

The chimney was smoking: Gran was at home. Maggie went round to the back gate, as she always did, creaking it open and clicking it shut. She crossed the back garden, treading carefully on the duckboards; Grandad's fine gravelled path was long gone, as were his prize roses. Maggie still missed them, but the carefully-dug rows of earth had their own attraction: they meant there'd be spuds, carrots, peas, everything she and Gran and Colin needed. And they still had their morning eggs, of course; Maggie chook-chooked to the big russet hens as she went past their wire enclosure. They watched her hopefully for a moment, then lost interest when they saw she wasn't carrying the feed pail. Maggie passed the hump in the earth that marked the Anderson hut, the buried iron shed issued to everyone as an air-raid shelter. She carefully used the mud-scraper on the soles of her rubber boots, then opened the back door.

'It's only me,' she called before she'd even closed the door behind her, so that Gran wouldn't get her hopes up. She stopped to struggle out of her heavy boots, standing them carefully on the sheets of newspaper Gran had laid out for them. She could hear that Gran was in the sitting-room – the house was too small and the floorboards too creaky for anyone to move around undetected – so she padded in her stocking-soles through the kitchen and the tiny hallway into the bright front room.

Gran was standing against the east-facing window, dusting the windowsill. The sill was already spotless, so Maggie knew she'd actually been polishing the opaque candle-lantern, over and over, until the frosted glass was nearly clear. Every night, Gran would light it and put it on the windowsill. Constable Carter had told her that she shouldn't, as if the whole German navy was going to find its way across the Channel by homing in on Gran's little candle, but she lit it anyway. Couldn't stop herself, Maggie knew. Not until her son came home.

Neither of them showed any of this, of course. Gran smiled briefly as Maggie dropped a peck on her cheek. 'How're the spuds coming?'

'Nearly up.'

'Addison still working you hard then?'

Maggie snorted. Farmer Addison spent most of his time trying out his no-longer-boyish charms on the land girls. 'I work myself hard.'

Gran nodded approvingly. 'Ours'll be ready for lifting soon too.' There was a question in it; Gran had always ruled over the garden, but now Maggie was the spud expert. Maggie's face filled with pride, making her grandmother smile a little. 'Another week, maybe,' Maggie said.

'Right you are.'

Maggie was scanning the room, taking in the gleaming sideboard, side table and wireless, the spotless fireplace, the snow-white antimacassars on the chair-backs. There was nothing left to do; nowadays Gran worked all day without breaks too. 'Shall I get the tea on?' Maggie said.

Gran glanced at the clock. 'You should go and meet your brother.'

Maggie considered arguing. She was in the house, she was tired, Colin hadn't had one of his turns in a while... But then Gran added, with a little sigh, 'He was wearing your Dad's other jumper again this morning.'

Maggie, who was wearing Dad's old tie wrapped and knotted tight around her forearm, nodded in perfect understanding. But then she pictured Colin in the dark blue jumper, which was hopelessly baggy and reached to his knees, like a dress. It made him look... funny. She sighed too. 'I'll go and get him.'

Gran looked at the clock again. 'It's nearly four.'

'I'll go now.'

Maggie went into the kitchen and pulled on her brown brogues. She'd keep on the land girl uniform – she liked the freedom of the trousers, and it made her look years older, which was fine. She smoothed down her hair – a few tight, red curls had escaped from the single thick plait down her back, but there was no time to redo it now. Calling goodbye to Gran, she hurried out.

All the way down the path she looked at the sea, although it was still calm and empty. The beach was lined with looping skeins of barbed wire. A hundred yards out something stirred the water's surface: maybe a seal, maybe a mine. She passed the church and saw that the bell-tower was still padlocked shut: all over the country the bells had been silenced. They'd only ring if the invasion came. Maggie hurried by the harbour, looking away so she couldn't see the empty berth where the *Susan* ought to be. She kept going along the seafront, past the long sandy pleasure-beach on one side and the pastel-painted houses on the other. She could see the pier in the distance, and the Regent Hotel, but she didn't want to walk past them – there were soldiers billeted in the hotel now, and they sometimes called out things she didn't like. She turned uphill towards the school, winding through the narrow lanes past little groups of chattering kids. School had been out for a good few minutes now.

She headed into the cobbled town square, and looked around at all the familiar landmarks. The butcher's, the baker's, the post office and the bank. No sign of Colin. Mr Cromwell's sweet shop: Mr Cromwell was glowering at a crowd of overexcited children, but Colin wasn't among them. The Town Hall, another building far too big and grand for such a small town, a sandstone mini-castle; the pub, and then the bookshop. Still no Colin. The bookshop's proprietor, Mr Caplan, was just coming out of his shop in his hat and coat; he must be going visiting. He was a short man who held himself very straight, with big dark eyes that missed nothing. He lifted his hat politely as she went by. She smiled and nodded hello; Mr Caplan had remained a friend of Gran's, in spite of everything. But she didn't have time to stop. She hurried across the square, glancing inside the brick and corrugated iron surface shelter that (according to Dad, at least) wouldn't stop an airgun pellet let alone a bomb; nothing in there but a bad smell, someone had been using it as a toilet again. Just beyond the shelter, Simple Billy was sitting in his usual spot on a bench, feeding the pigeons; he called her name, but she just waved and hurried on. She had to find Colin.

In the centre of the wide square, Maggie stopped beside the statue of Queen Victoria, who sat frowning on her marble plinth among the flower beds. Maggie looked away quickly, because the statue made her think of Dad again. (He always used to point out the statue to them and say, *Doesn't she look miserable for a woman who owned everybody else's money?* It hadn't made him many friends.) Maggie couldn't see past the Queen's voluminous bronze skirts, but from the far side of the square she could hear what the Vicar always described as the merry laughter of little children. Maggie, only just turned seventeen, was young enough to remember what this particular kind of laughter usually meant. She quickened her pace.

Beyond the statue was a knot of boys. As she approached, one of them broke away from the group. Cheeky Charlie Chester, a well-grown lad with brown curls and freckles and a grin which made most adults – especially his parents – smile back no matter what he was doing. What he was doing at the moment was waving something blue in the air. He kept glancing down at the ground, while pretending to look at an invisible audience around the square. Maggie could hear him shouting, 'Anyone want a conchie-jumper? Eh? Eh? Fresh from a little conchie-kid, eh?'

Someone on the other side of the square, probably in the doorway of the Green Man, actually laughed. Charlie gave a bow, then turned away to toss the blue thing to one of the other boys. Which is why he didn't notice Maggie, not until she caught him by the elbow and spun him around like a dance partner. His mouth popped open in a little 'O'. Maggie grabbed him by his upper arms, and hoisted him up on tiptoe so they were eye to eye. 'What've you done with my brother, you little pig?'

Charlie gaped like a fish. There was more laughter from the Green Man: the drunks were impartial, at least. Maggie ignored them and shoved Charlie aside, paying no attention to his yelp as he tripped on the cobblestones and fell to the ground; she had just seen her brother. Colin was on the ground, struggling to his feet now the three other boys had let go of him. They backed away as Maggie advanced. Colin didn't seem hurt, although there was mud in his hair; his glasses were on skewed but they weren't broken (thank goodness, they couldn't afford to get the lenses replaced again). Maggie sighed and reached down. 'Come on, you.'

'You pushed me!' Charlie's voice was about an octave higher than usual. He waved his hand, which was grazed and lightly bleeding, under Maggie's nose. 'You hurt me! You can't do that, I'll tell my mum!'

He started to cry. Maggie turned her back on him. 'Come on, Colin.'

Colin pointed at the boy with the blue thing in his hands. 'Dad's jumper.'

Maggie turned a murderous look on the other boy, who quickly thrust the jumper towards her. She snatched it out of his hands and turned back to her brother; Colin seemed steady on his feet now, so she took hold of his elbow and started to steer him across the square. 'Let's go.'

'I'll tell my mum!' Charlie was shrieking now. He hurried after them, keeping a careful distance – the other boys followed. They ran and danced around Colin and Maggie, always a few feet away, like dogs snapping around a bull. 'You're a – a *bitch!*' Charlie was yelling. 'A conchie bitch! Your Mum's a – a – a *whore* and your Dad's a coward! Conchie! Conchie!'

'Ignore them,' Maggie told Colin. Colin nodded, trying not to cry. Maggie thought about stopping to box Charlie's ears, but she kept walking, towing Colin after her. 'They're idiots.'

They were almost out of the square when a figure loomed in front of them, terrible in a paisley-patterned headsquare. 'Just *what* do you think you're doing?'

Charlie hovered at the woman's elbow, a picture of affronted innocence. 'She hurt me, Mum! Look!'

Mrs Chester looked at his grazed hand, and gasped as if he were spouting blood all over the town square. 'Margaret Ogilvie, did you do this?'

Maggie didn't bother to lie. 'He and his friends were at my brother.'

'What's this?' Two more headsquares had appeared: Mrs Dawson the butcher's wife, and old Mrs Larkin. Mrs Chester pointed at Maggie. 'This – creature took it upon herself to strike my son!'

'You what?' said Maggie, hoping the other women would laugh.

But they turned their glares on Maggie, and set their lips in thin lines. 'Is that right?' Mrs Dawson placed a restraining hand on Mrs Chester's arm. 'Now just you calm down, Iris. Don't you stoop to her level.'

Mrs Larkin chipped in, 'Pretty free with her fists for a conchie's daughter, en't she?'

They clucked and nodded. Maggie stared at them, these women she'd known half her life. Then she straightened her back and lifted her chin. 'I wish I bloody had hit him,' she said. 'It's about time someone did.'

Mrs Chester's hand flashed out to slap her. Maggie didn't have time to lift her arm and block the blow, only to flick her wrist a little. But Mrs Chester's hand rebounded from her face. It seemed to bounce off thin air. Mrs Chester staggered back a step, and had to be steadied by Mrs Dawson. All three women stared and blinked. There was a moment in which they all considered what they'd seen – then swiftly dismissed it, and revised it into what they *must* have seen. Mrs Chester pointed at Maggie and shrieked, 'She hit me!'

Maggie snapped out of her own surprise, and tried to draw Colin away. 'Come on.'

'Maggie…' Colin tugged at her arm. Then his hand went limp, and his eyes lost focus. 'Freya,' he murmured.

Oh no… 'Colin, don't!' Maggie said. But of course he couldn't hear her. He was already sliding to his knees, his voice getting louder. 'Freya…!'

Maggie caught him before he fell, but his weight pulled her to her knees. 'Colin—'

'What's the matter with him?' Mrs Lawson's voice was clipped. 'What's he doing?'

'He's not well. He needs the doctor,' Maggie said, hoping this might get at least one of them to go away, 'go and get Dr Braithwaite!'

'What's this?' More people were arriving; faces stared down. 'What's that boy doing—'

Colin's voice rose. 'Freya! *Schöne göttin! Kürerin der Erschlagenen!'*

Maggie tried to muffle his voice in her shoulder. But he squirmed free. His voice was deeper, not his own; spittle flew from his mouth as his voice rose and rose. *'Die schöne Göttin ist in Tränen! Heil Hitler! Seig heil! Seig Heil! SEIG HEIL!'*

Chapter Three
In the Kaiserhof Hotel

Berlin, June 1940

Lise sat bolt upright on the fine leather settee, trying to keep her coffee cup level. One of the other girls (her name was Leni, or Lotte, or something) was wedged onto the settee beside her, talking and giggling with the boy on her other side. Her elbow kept bumping Lise; she'd already spilled coffee on the expensive leather and splashed Lise's skirt.

Lise shot her a look, but no one paid any attention. None of the boys had so much as looked at her since the twelve girls had arrived. She knew they had to treat them with some respect, of course; they were German girls with the finest blood. But the boys' voices had been getting louder, and their grins broader, since the new girls had walked in. And Lise was suddenly invisible.

She stared at her rich surroundings, to which everyone else seemed oblivious. The deep red wallpaper, the alcoves with tasteful nude statues of perfectly sculpted men and women; the simple, elegant settees and armchairs; the bone china coffee service embellished with tiny gold swastikas. Lise sipped her coffee as the hubbub of excited voices rose even further; she seemed to be the only one with any sense of where they were, of who had sat here.

The exclusive suites of the Nazi Party, which the Führer himself was known to use – and the others could hardly care less. These twelve young men and twelve young women had been brought together for a solemn duty to the Fatherland; and here they were, carrying on like silly children in a dance-hall!

Lise kept her spirits up by gazing at the picture on the wall. The painting was draped with burgundy velvet curtains and outlined with a heavy gold frame, but it was the image itself that held her attention. It was a reproduction of *The Standard Bearer*, her favourite painting of the Führer. He wore pure white armour, like a knight errant, and sat on horse back, proudly bearing aloft a flag of the Swastika. His profile was noble and dignified… and lonely, she thought: far above the foolishness of ordinary people. Alone in the world. Like her.

Lotte-or-Leni bumped her again, glanced sideways with the barest hint of apology. She was blonde, of course; they all were. They all seemed to be, at least; despite all the Führer's teachings on purity and natural beauty, some of them had quite obviously bleached their hair. A few were even wearing make-up. Not one of these girls was wearing the League of German Girls uniform – three were wearing the traditional dirndl, only their skirts were far too short, the bodices too tight and the lace blouses too low-cut. They looked like barmaids… and the worst of it was the boys either couldn't see this or didn't care. Even Albrecht seemed to have lost all his good sense. Earlier he'd made a remark about the girls' perfect, unspoiled natural beauty; Lise had choked on her expensive coffee, while the girls blushed to their already-rouged cheeks and stretched their artificially reddened lips in simpering grins. The girl Albrecht was paired with – Erika, her name was – had thrown Lise an unfriendly look, but then returned her perfect blue gaze to Albrecht. The twelve girls' already half-hearted attempts to be friendly to the skinny, scowling girl in the corner ceased completely after that. And the boys, even Albrecht, had remained oblivious to the whole thing.

Whores, Lise thought, *painted whores.* But the thought didn't sound like her own: it sounded like Freya. Lise had felt this other presence hovering at the edge of her mind ever since the Black Sun ceremony. But it couldn't be Freya, of course; Freya would know that these weren't whores – it was the Führer's will that good Aryans should pass on their seed. And that there was no seed finer (distasteful as the whole subject was) than that of these twelve boys. The girls were doing their duty.

And not all of them were happy about it, of course. The girls allocated to the younger boys looked distinctly crestfallen at their introductions; no doubt they'd been imagining god-like young supermen, but were faced instead with grinning boys in Hitler Youth shorts. And the girl allocated to Petr, Lise had noticed, was not joining in at all. She sat rigid beside him, while he stared in silence at the floor with his usual disdainful expression. Occasionally the girl would say something, trying to make conversation; he answered with a monosyllable. Lise couldn't help feeling a stab of pity. Imagine having to do *that,* with *him!* But she hardened her heart; the girl had her duty to do, and she would have to do it, like everyone else. And no doubt the rewards – the money and the accommodation and the preferential treatment – would be rich enough.

Lise heard the door open behind her, and then the boys were getting quickly to their feet. The girls, unsure, did the same; Lise managed to set her coffee down on the side table before the general upheaval tipped the whole lot onto her skirt. The boys' Youth Leader, a thin balding man in his thirties, hurried in. Lise thought she had never seen a grown man so excited; he was actually trembling. He clicked his heels and bowed his head to the girls, but was already saying: 'Ladies, would you excuse us please?'

The girl assigned to Petr was heading for the door before he'd even finished speaking. Petr didn't trouble to say goodbye to her.

Some of the other girls, the ones assigned to the younger boys, nodded goodbye and followed her quickly enough. But the others lingered, hovering in front of their respective boys. Erika, especially, was dragging her feet; she held out her hand for Albrecht to shake, but he kissed it instead. Erika simpered in a way that made Lise feel physically ill. Erika ignored the Youth Leader's scowls and kept hold of Albrecht's hand.

After thirty seconds there was no sign of anyone else moving, and the Youth Leader snapped a command at the boys. They came to attention immediately, eyes front; the girls were left looking at blank faces. 'Ladies, if you please,' the Youth Leader said.

Finally the girls got the hint and headed for the door, giving fluttery little waves and trying to catch the boys' eyes (successfully in some cases, to the Youth Leader's evident annoyance). Lise stayed where she was. The Youth Leader frowned at her, then appeared to remember who she was; he turned his attention to an inner door. Beyond it they could all now hear male voices, footsteps. The Youth Leader scuttled over to the door, almost falling over his own feet in his eagerness. He pulled the door open, came to attention and gave a full, stiff-armed salute as a man in uniform appeared in the doorway.

Lise was almost fainting with excitement. Was it, could it possibly be…? But no; the man in the doorway was not the Führer. He was small, moustached, with a round face and frameless glasses. Other uniformed men were around him, but it was to the round-faced man that all the boys snapped off a perfect, stiff-armed salute. Lise followed them a moment later. All thirteen stood rigidly to attention as the man came into the room.

Reichsführer Heinrich Himmler. Head of the SS. Here, with them!

He looks like a clerk, sneered the Freya-voice in Lise's head. She suppressed it quickly. If the Führer kept this man so close, he must be special indeed. Himmler nodded in acknowledgement of their salutes, and said in a quiet toneless voice, 'At ease, gentlemen. Miss.'

They dropped their arms. Lise hadn't a clue what to do next; so she watched Himmler and his entourage, hoping they wouldn't notice the coffee-stain on her skirt. Himmler was dwarfed by the men around him, tall men in black uniforms marked with silver skull insignia: SS officers. But they moved reverently a pace behind him; except for one man with white-blond hair and frosty blue eyes, who walked almost beside him. Himmler cleared his throat and said, 'You have met the young ladies with whom you have been matched.'

His voice was so uninflected it took the boys a moment to realise this had been a question. Albrecht answered, 'Yes, Herr Reichsführer.'

Himmler nodded. 'This is a most solemn duty. Donating a child to the Führer is one of the greatest services a German can perform for the Fatherland. It must be undertaken in all seriousness. Those good Aryan maidens must be shown every respect. You understand, gentlemen.'

Again, it was a question. Albrecht answered gravely, 'We are proud to do our duty, Herr Reichsführer.'

Himmler nodded again. Then he appeared to notice Lise. He asked, 'Is this the girl?' of the Youth Leader, who was hovering at his shoulder; the man nodded eagerly. Himmler moved forwards to Lise, the white-blond officer at his side. 'Miss,' Himmler said; he took her hand in his own small dry one, pressed her fingers to his dry lips. He didn't release her hand, but reached for her other one; held both her arms away from her sides so he could look her up and down. 'How old are you, Miss?' he said.

'N—' Lise cleared her throat and tried again, 'nearly sixteen, Herr Reichsführer.'

He seemed satisfied with the answer. Then he lowered his voice, but not so much that those around couldn't overhear clearly, 'And are your monthly courses healthy and regular, Miss?'

He couldn't possibly mean what she thought he meant. '…Herr Reichsführer?'

Himmler looked at the Youth Leader. 'Are they,' he asked.

The Youth Leader nodded obsequiously. 'The female Youth Leader assures me they are, Herr Reichsführer.'

'Good, good.' He beckoned to the white-blond man, who clicked his heels and bowed to Lise. Himmler said, 'You wish to do your duty to the Fatherland, Miss?'

'Of – of course, Herr Reichsführer…'

'This is SS-Führer Lange. You will be paired with him, as your brothers here are paired with the young ladies you met earlier.'

The man smiled down at Lise. He was twice her age. His features were as perfect as those of the marble sculptures around the room, but she could smell his sweat, his breath. Lise cringed backwards. 'But – but I thought I was to fight. With the boys.'

Lange laughed, but Himmler frowned. 'Your first duty is to give the Führer children. Sons. Sons with your unique abilities.'

'But—' She tried to speak calmly, but her voice came out high and shrill. 'But the boys need me. I'm the hub of the wheel. They need me. To fight the English.'

Lange took a step back, looking offended. Himmler was scowling now. He said, 'I understand your… modesty. But this is your duty. To the Fatherland.'

'I – I can't.' Tears, shameful tears, came to her eyes. She would rather fight, she would rather die. 'Please, don't…'

'A good German girl obeys orders,' Himmler snapped. 'Make up your mind to this. It must be done.'

Lise looked around for help; but most of the boys were behind her, Albrecht included, so she couldn't meet their eyes. Beside her was Petr, whose face was cold. But beyond him was the picture, the gold-framed picture. The Führer, chaste and untouched, like her. Lise gazed at him and found her strength. She stepped away from Lange. 'No! Not with him!' Her voice was still shrill and panic-stricken, but she kept going. 'If I have a child it will be with the Führer! No one but him! No one —'

Pain flared on her cheek as a muscular hand struck her. She sat down hard on the settee. Petr stood over her, hand raised for another slap. 'How dare you!' His face was twisted with scorn. 'How dare you speak so to the Reichsführer! How dare you speak that way of the Führer!'

Lise looked at the faces around her; all were tight with distaste. Even Albrecht had turned away, wouldn't meet her eye. The Youth Leader was stammering apologies to Himmler: 'She will obey, Herr Reichsführer, rest assured…'

Lise flinched as Petr bent over her, pushed his face into hers. He said, so only she could hear, 'You think you're better than those other bitches? You'll do what you're told. What you're good for.'

There was no help around her, only tall angry men. Lise cringed away inside herself, hiding from the anger and the disgust and the smell of male sweat. Lise hid.

But that left Freya, who was never far from her now.

And Freya rose.

Lise did not move. But something invisible picked up Petr and threw him across the room. He crashed into an armchair, which toppled heavily backwards. Lise stood up. Her neatly plaited hair unwound, crackling with yellow sparks. The air was hot and suffocating. Petr tried to get up; Lise nodded her head slightly, and everyone heard the smack of the blow that drove him back against the chair.

The room erupted with shouted commands. While the boys gaped in shock, the black-clad men drew pistols, pointed them at Lise. The round-faced man stood frozen and pale. Lise ignored them all. She stepped between two of the younger boys, who fell over themselves to get out of her way. She stared down at Petr as her power struck him, again and again. As his nose broke with a snap, her eyes began to glow like blue neon. As blood poured down his face she said, 'You will not touch me.' Two voices came from her mouth, one an intimate whisper, and the other an echoing silvery cry.

Petr stared back, defiant, in spite of the blood in his mouth. Lise's hair flew around her in a cloud. Himmler began to edge towards the door; the SS men were still shouting, moving closer to her. Still she ignored them. 'How dare you. How *dare* you…'

In that moment, anything could have happened. Then Albrecht stepped in front of Lise, blocking her view of Petr. He fell to one knee. 'Freya,' he said. 'Forgive us, Beautiful Goddess. Forgive us, Chooser of the Slain. Forgive us.'

Lise paused. She looked from Petr's blood-stained sneer to Albrecht's earnest, awe-stricken face. She said, with some scorn, 'Do you plead for him?'

'He is strong, Lady,' Albrecht said. 'He is a strong warrior. Let him serve you, Great Goddess.'

Lise inhaled, then exhaled slowly. Her hair settled down around her shoulders. Everyone in the room felt something die down. But when she turned to Himmler, her eyes were still molten blue. 'I will fight,' she said. Still her voice whispered and cried at the same time. 'I will fight for my beloved. My Führer. I will bring him England. Tell him this.'

Himmler paused. 'England?'

Lise smiled. 'England. My love-gift to him. My dowry. Hail to the victory to come! Seig heil! Sieg heil!'

Albrecht joined in, then the other boys. Then all the men were shouting, 'Seig heil! *Seig heil! Seig heil!*' while Freya's sweet, terrible laughter echoed around them.

Chapter Four

Arthur and Michal

'Seig heil! Seig heil!'

Colin's voice was loud in the village square. Maggie tried to lift him, to stand him on his feet, but his weight pulled her back down again. All around the village voices were exclaiming. There were more running feet, coming closer. The circle around them tightened. Faces loomed over them, staring and whispering.

Maggie shook Colin, screamed in his face, 'Colin, wake up!'

'Seig Heil! SEIG HEIL! SEIG HEIL!' Colin stopped suddenly, and slumped forward onto Maggie's shoulder. Maggie held her unconscious little brother and looked around for help, but the villagers stared back at her in silence. A week ago Maggie had seen Charlie goose-stepping down the High Street shouting, *'Achtung, Heil Hitler, Englisher swine!'* in a fake German accent; most of these people had laughed. But they weren't laughing now. 'He hit his head,' Maggie said, pleading, 'it's not his fault…'

'You nasty little brat.' Mrs Chester's face was livid white. 'Do you think that's funny? Do – you – think – that's – *funny!'*

'No, I told you—'

Mrs Larkin made a clumsy grab at Colin's hair. 'He ought to be leathered, that's what!'

'Don't you touch us.' Maggie's cheeks were flushing red. There were so many people in the circle now, they seemed to be using up all the air. 'Don't.'

Mrs Larkin's claw-hand grabbed at them again. 'Needs teaching a lesson!'

'Don't touch us.' Maggie's fingers began to prickle. The blood roared in her ears. *'Don't you touch us—'*

'What's the matter here?'

The voice was mild, but it carried. The upper-class accent made the crowd look around with a start. They stepped back; the English pilot from the Mound walked between them. His dark-haired friend was close behind. The two men looked down at Maggie and Colin. Maggie thought the Polish pilot looked angry, but the other man kept an expression of friendly concern. 'Is everything all right here?'

Mrs Chester pointed at Maggie again and declared, 'That young – woman hit my son!'

The blond pilot looked at Maggie, on her knees clutching her little brother; then at the tall, well-built Charlie, who suddenly looked uncomfortable. 'Really?' the pilot said politely.

Mrs Chester, oblivious to everything but her maternal outrage, repeated, 'She hit him!'

'It's all right, Mum,' Charlie mumbled, as the two pilots looked at him. When his mother drew breath to argue he hissed, 'Mum, don't *fuss!*'

The blond pilot nodded; that was the matter settled. He smiled down at Maggie and Colin. 'Do you need help, Miss?'

Mrs Larkin jabbed an accusing finger at Colin. 'He was talking German!'

'He hit his head.' Maggie was starting to recover. Colin was awake now, gazing around, looking dazed and pitiful. Maggie thought she saw a few guilty looks in the crowd. She pressed her advantage. 'He hit his head at *Dunkirk*. When we lost our *Dad*. When he went to *help!*'

The Polish pilot looked at her and opened his mouth; then he seemed to change his mind and kept quiet. His English friend beamed down at Colin. 'You were at Dunkirk? Brave little chap.'

Colin, who'd barely smiled in weeks, beamed back. The English pilot held out a hand to him; Colin grasped it and the man pulled him to his feet. The pilot ruffled Colin's hair gently. 'Scrambled the old noodle a bit, eh? Not surprising.'

Maggie could see people starting to believe it, saw them fall back and start to melt away. The anger went out of her; she closed her eyes for a moment, dizzy, and felt a touch on her elbow. The Polish pilot was crouching beside her. His eyes were kind. 'Are you all right?' he said.

Maggie nodded. She realised she was still kneeling on the cobbles; she got slowly to her feet, allowing the Polish pilot's hand to stay on her elbow, steadying her. She felt someone else pat her on the shoulder, and looked round at Charlie Chester's ingratiating smile. 'No hard feelings, eh, Maggie?'

Maggie smiled back sweetly, thinking: *I'll see about you later, you little sod.* Charlie grinned back even more broadly, but, out of the corner of her eye, she saw the dark-haired pilot suppress a smile. When she looked at him, though, his face was carefully bland. She narrowed her eyes; she'd have to watch this one. But her attention was drawn away, like everyone else's, when the English pilot spoke again. 'Well then,' he said cheerfully. 'Good, then. No harm done.'

Everyone saw that this was so. Maggie was to learn this, about Arthur: he assumed it was impossible for you to disagree with him, so no-one ever did. Now all the tension melted away into the warm summer air; the knot of people loosened, and most of the villagers started to amble away. The pilot turned his warm smile on Colin again. 'Perhaps you and this young lady should head off home.'

'Yes, sir.' Colin hesitated, speaking slowly; Maggie knew he didn't want the pilot to leave. 'I'm Colin Ogilvie. This is my sister Maggie.'

The blond pilot nodded seriously. 'I'm Arthur. Arthur James Willoughby.' He indicated the Polish pilot. 'That's my colleague, Michal Capek.'

Michal was smiling at Maggie, his hand still on her elbow. 'Shall we walk you home?'

Maggie thought his smile had become rather smug. She looked him in the eye. 'Not if you're just going to stare at my arse all the way there.'

The pilot's hand dropped. There was a chorus of gasps and tuts from the remains of the crowd. Maggie ignored them, holding Michal's gaze until he blushed. Arthur burst out laughing. 'Quite right. Teach us to be gentlemen, eh, Michal?'

'I am sorry,' Michal said. 'May we please walk you home?'

Colin nodded vigorously. Maggie thought about it. Being seen with pilots, actual heroic fighter pilots, could only make their lives easier in the village. And she was tired, suddenly, of having to fight her neighbours. 'All right,' she said. 'You may.'

Colin gave a little cheer, grabbed Arthur's arm and began towing him across the square. Maggie followed, Michal falling into step beside her. The villagers melted away, except for two girls who gaped at the sight of Margaret Ogilvie with a pilot. They gazed very obviously at Arthur, but he just smiled and nodded politely and returned his attention to Colin. He rarely talked to strangers, even before Dunkirk, but was talking away to Arthur as if he'd known him all his life. Maggie watched the blond pilot till they were out of the square, but he didn't seem to be doing anything except listening and nodding occasionally. 'How does he *do* that?' she muttered.

She hadn't meant to say it out loud, but Michal heard her. 'It is a sort of magic,' he agreed.

'It's... kind of him,' Maggie said. 'My brother... he's not, you know... I mean, it's kind. Of both of you. Thank you.'

'It is nothing,' said Michal. Maggie glanced sideways at him as they passed by the harbour. It probably *was* nothing, she thought, watching her brother gazing up at his new hero. Just two nice men, being kind to a pair of kids. She was suddenly aware that she was still wearing her sweaty work-clothes, that her hair was dishevelled and unfashionably long, that she was nothing like the village girls who attracted pilots from the airbase like bees to pollen. 'You don't have to come with us,' she said, 'thank you—'

But he was already talking over her. 'Why do they quarrel with you? The people of the village?'

After a moment, Maggie said: 'My Dad's a conchie.'

'A… conchie?'

'A Conscientious Objector. He doesn't believe in wars. Not after the first one.'

She looked him in the eye, waiting to see the look of contempt that meant she would walk away from him. But Michal just nodded and said, 'Then he is a brave man.'

Maggie's defiance collapsed. Suddenly there were tears in her eyes, so she looked out over the glittering sea, pretending to be dazzled. She said, 'He got – lost – at Dunkirk. He fell overboard.'

'And did he…'

'He'll be all right.' Maggie stared fiercely away from him. 'It was in the shallow water, he probably just waded ashore. He must've been captured. Or he's hiding somewhere.'

There was another pause. Maggie looked at her shoes: she didn't want to see his expression. After a moment he said, 'I am sorry.'

She shrugged. 'Thanks.'

'It is hard, not to know.'

Now she looked at him, and he stared out to sea. 'How d'you mean?' she said.

'To be apart. And not to know.' They were on the uphill path now. Arthur, ten yards ahead with Colin, looked back at them with a slight frown, but neither of them noticed. Michal said after a moment, 'When I left Poland, I left my mother and my grandmother behind.' Maggie waited. Arthur, still unnoticed, returned his attention to Colin. Eventually Michal said, 'They said it was my duty. I am a pilot. I went. I could not take them with me.'

They walked a few more steps uphill. After a while Maggie said, 'Have you heard anything from them?'

'Nothing. But then...' He shrugged: how would he hear anything? 'And they are strong.' He smiled. 'Like your father.'

She looked at him suspiciously. 'How do you know my Dad's strong?'

'Because his daughter is.'

Maggie thought, *oh please*: if Farmer Addison were to use a line like that on one of the land girls, they would laugh till they were sick. She glared at Michal; but he stared back, apparently utterly serious. She ducked her head awkwardly. 'What about your father?' she asked at last.

'He died when I was small.' He nodded at Maggie's murmur of condolence. 'I was brought up by my mother and grandmother.' They had left the village behind. A gentle cross wind caught them, blowing some of the tension away. Gran's cottage was in sight. Michal asked, 'Do you live here with your mother?'

'Not with *her*.' Maggie made an impatient sound. 'She left my Dad. She came and went a few times. We came and went, between here and Glasgow. But she went for good when the war started. She didn't agree with him. She's... not a conchie.'

'Where is she now?'

Maggie thought vaguely that she shouldn't answer, that Careless Talk Costs Lives. But she was already saying, 'Doing war-work. We don't know what. She knows about... history, and things. She writes us letters sometimes. Sends books.'

'Ah,' was all he said. Up ahead, Arthur and Colin had come to the cottage gate. Maggie saw Colin start to turn left, towards the back door, then remember that Arthur was company and wave him through the front gate instead. Arthur followed. Maggie said to

Michal, 'I think you're coming inside.'

'I think I am.'

They followed Colin as he proudly ushered Arthur through the front door. The little cottage was loud with men's heavy footsteps, men's voices. Maggie called quickly, 'It's just me and Colin, Gran.' Colin was already running into the living-room: 'Gran, this is Arthur, he's... oh.'

Maggie was at the living room door before she heard the murmur of female voices. Colin had stopped dead just in front of her; she moved him aside and stepped around him. 'Gran?'

Gran was in her usual chair. The good tea set was on the sidetable; three cups were filled, despite the rationing, with the best tea. Two young women in uniform were sitting on the couch; they rose as Maggie came in, Arthur and Michal behind her. The men took off their caps as Gran got slowly to her feet. 'Maggie, Colin,' she said.

'Gran?' Maggie could hear the blood pounding in her ears. 'What is it?'

Gran tried to smile. 'It's all right,' she said, although it obviously wasn't. 'These ladies...'

Maggie turned to them. Two women in Wren's uniforms. One of them, fresh-faced and chestnut-haired and pretty, said quickly, 'It's all right. It isn't bad news, nothing like that.'

Maggie looked at the other woman and didn't quite believe her. This one said nothing. She was mousey-haired and tall, so tall she stooped slightly; she was giving Maggie a flat stare that Maggie didn't like one bit. Maggie said, 'Who are you?'

The tall woman just stared at her. Colin came a little further into the room, and the tall woman switched her gaze to him. She didn't look like someone watching a child. She looked like someone watching a strange dog, wondering if it would bite. Maggie said abruptly, 'Gran, what do they want?'

'Maggie,' murmured Gran: manners had to be maintained. The

pretty, smiling Wren said, 'It's quite all right. You must be Maggie and Colin. I'm Laura. This is my colleague Vivian.' She glanced at Arthur and Michal; inevitably, it was to Arthur her gaze returned. 'Good afternoon…?'

Arthur stepped to the centre of the little room. 'Good afternoon. Is there a problem here?'

The pretty Wren, Laura, smiled. 'Why, not at all. It's good news.'

Maggie paid no attention, watched Vivian instead. The tall woman was ignoring Arthur completely. She kept shifting her wary gaze from Colin to Maggie and back again. 'Gran,' Maggie said urgently, 'Gran, what's—'

'Maggie.' Gran turned to her grandchildren. She was still trying to smile, still not succeeding. 'These ladies have come from London. They've come to take you to your mother.'

Chapter Five

London

There was silence in the living room, filled only by the slow tick of the clock. At last Maggie said, 'They've what?'

Colin's face was all smiles. '*Mum?* Where is she?'

Laura smiled back at him. 'She's in London. She wants to see you. She misses you—'

Maggie broke in: 'What do you mean, take us to her?'

Laura turned her smile to Maggie. 'She misses you very much. She asked us to come and get you.'

'Why didn't she just come herself?'

'Well, she's very busy, Maggie. War work.'

'So am I.' Maggie folded her arms. 'So am *I* doing war-work. I'm a land girl. And Colin's at school here.'

'I know that, but—'

'We're not going.'

Colin looked aghast. 'Maggie, it's Mum!'

'Then where is she? We don't know them,' she glared at the Wrens, 'and we're not just going off with people we don't know.'

Laura sighed. 'Maggie, your mother—'

'No!'

'We have our orders, Maggie.'

'Good for you. *We're* not in the army.'

Michal was murmuring something, to Arthur. Arthur said, in his most authoritarian voice, 'Ladies, may we see your orders?'

Laura seemed to struggle for a moment; but then she turned her sunny smile to him. 'I'm afraid we're not authorised to do that.'

Maggie took a step backwards, towards Michal. 'Then you're not *authorised* to take us away without—'

'Maggie.' It was Gran. Maggie subsided immediately; so did Arthur. Gran looked Maggie in the eye. 'Maggie, you need to go with these ladies.'

'But they're—'

'Your mother telephoned me, Maggie.'

'…She what?'

'She telephoned. While you were out.'

Colin was beaming again. 'You spoke to Mum?'

'Yes, love.'

'Are you sure it was her?' Maggie knew it was ridiculous; but Vivian was still staring at her, and she didn't like it. 'Are you sure?'

'Of course I'm sure.' Gran's voice was tart. 'Do you think I don't know my own daughter-in-law?'

'But Gran—'

'Not another word. Now go upstairs and change. I've put clean shirts on your beds. And wash your faces or your Mum will think I don't take care of you.'

Michal's voice cut in softly: 'Why is there such hurry?'

The tall Wren switched her gaze to him. 'That's our orders,' she said. A West Country voice, hard and chilly. 'To take these children to their mother.'

Colin whooped, 'We're going to London!' and charged upstairs. 'We're going to see Mum!'

Maggie followed. There seemed nothing else for it.

In her tiny bedroom, Maggie changed her shirt and re-plaited her hair as slowly as she could. But after Colin shouted, 'Mags, come *on!*' for the third time, she came downstairs. Michal was carrying two small suitcases into the hallway; Gran had already packed for them. He set them down and looked up at Maggie. 'Well,' he said.

'I've got to go, but…'

He took a deep breath. 'I have seen you before. I mean – I flew at Dunkirk.'

'Did you?'

'I saw you. And I knew… I knew you were…'

From the living-room, Gran called: 'Maggie?'

She had to go. 'I'll be back soon,' Maggie blurted, and went quickly past Michal into the living room.

Colin was bouncing up and down on the settee: 'We're going to see Mum! We're going to London!'

'Shut up,' hissed Maggie. Gran was trying to smile again, with even less success than before. Maggie said to her, 'We'll be back.'

Gran shook her head slowly. 'Not unless your mother says so.'

'I'm seventeen. I'll be back.'

Gran put her hand on Maggie's cheek, making her look at her. 'You'll go where it's safe. And that's final.'

'We have to go,' Laura the Wren said. The other woman was already at the open front door, waving at someone. An engine started up, and a car pulled up at the gate. It must have been parked round the corner, where they wouldn't have seen it as they approached the cottage. It was big and black, very fancy. The uniformed driver was getting out, opening the door. Vivian turned to Maggie, gestured with her head: out you go. Laura picked up the cases. 'We have to go,' she said again.

They left Gran standing helplessly at the front door, Michal and Arthur beside her. The car began to inch down the cliff road. Maggie and Colin waved through the back window till they were out of sight.

The car seats were expensive leather, hot in the afternoon sun. Laura was beside Maggie and Colin on the rear seat; Vivian sat opposite, directly in front of Maggie. Colin was bouncing up and down again. 'This is a great car! It must have cost a fortune!'

'Takes a lot of petrol, I'll bet,' Maggie said. Petrol was expensive, rationed: not to be used for just anything. She looked a question at Laura, who ignored it, and said brightly, 'We'll be in London in no time.'

The car crept through the village, winding through the narrow streets, past groups of people gawping. The villagers seemed to be coming out specially, just to see the big black car: just to see the Ogilvie children being taken away. Colin grinned and waved like crazy. Maggie ignored them, wondering what to do. Probably she shouldn't do anything, everything was all right, surely...

They were moving at a crawl around the town square when there was a tap on the window. Mr Caplan, the bookshop owner, was looking in at them. He stared suspiciously at the Wrens. They all heard his voice, muffled by the closed windows: 'What are you doing? Where are you taking those children?'

Vivian said to the driver: 'Drive on.'

The car moved away from Mr Caplan. Maggie reached out for the door handle, but Laura laid her hand, quite gently, on top of Maggie's. Then they were accelerating. Maggie turned and looked through the back window at Mr Caplan, who was saying something she couldn't hear. Then the car turned the corner, out of the town square, and she lost sight of him. Colin, who had turned to wave, said: 'What did Mr Caplan want?'

'I expect he was just saying bye-bye,' said Laura.

They passed the row of fishermen's cottages, and the big houses; soon they left the village behind. The car speeded up, but only slightly; it moved cautiously along the back roads. Five minutes later, they still weren't on the road to London. Maggie started to wonder if the driver was lost; all the sign-posts had been covered up since the start of the war, to confuse the Enemy. Colin must have had the same thought: 'This isn't the best way to London,' he said helpfully. 'You should've gone right back there—'

'We know,' said Laura reassuringly. 'We're going to collect someone first.' She smiled again. 'He's coming to London too. So we thought, two for the price of one! You know,' she laughed, 'is your journey really necessary, and all that!'

Colin laughed, a bit uncertainly. Maggie thought: *so why is* this *journey really necessary?* She looked out the window. Thick hedges lined the road on both sides. Through gaps on the right-hand side, there were flashes of metal. 'This is the air-base,' Maggie said.

'Yes. He's meeting us here.'

They were pulling up at a gateway, to the east. From the main road it looked like the turn-off to a farm track, but they turned onto a broad, well-maintained thoroughfare. There were sentry-posts on either side, a striped pole blocking the way through. Men in uniform stood outside. They were against the low evening sun, so Maggie couldn't see details: just two figures standing to attention and saluting a third. The third one returned the salute briefly, and started towards the car. The driver jumped out smartly, saluting and opening the rear door.

Laura said to Maggie and Colin, as the man approached, 'That's him. That's Major Fitzwilliam.' As an afterthought she added, 'He works with your mother.'

The man acknowledged the driver's salute, climbed into the car. 'At ease, ladies,' he said, to save the Wrens the awkwardness of trying to come to attention while sitting in a car. He shut the door behind him as they pulled away from the gate. He settled into the opposite seat, beside Vivian, then turned his attention to Maggie and Colin. 'Hello again, young man. Miss.'

It was the major from Dunkirk. The one who'd ordered Dad to turn back. The one who'd stared so hard at Maggie when the Stuka flipped over and cut into the ship's rowing-boat. He repeated, 'Hello again,' to Maggie and Colin, then glanced sideways at Vivian, nodding slightly. 'Yes, these are the... young people I met before. No question of it.'

There was no sound but the car engine speeding up. Colin was gaping at the major. 'Aren't you...? I mean – from Dunkirk?'

'That's right. Andrew Fitzwilliam.' He smiled affably and held out his hand to Colin. Colin shook it, too surprised to do anything else. Then the major reached out to Maggie. 'At your service.'

Maggie ignored his hand. 'What are you doing here?'

'Didn't the ladies tell you? I'm going to London with you. I'm a... colleague of your mother's.'

Colin looked from Maggie to the major and back. He had stopped bouncing. 'What do you do? With our mum?'

'Ah-ha, you know I can't tell you that.' He wagged a finger, laughed heartily. 'Careless talk costs lives, and all that—'

'What do you want?' Maggie was looking out of the window. The car was going much faster; they were finally on the road to London. 'What do you want with us?'

'My dear, I've told you.' He laughed again, but his face was wary. 'I'm taking you to your mother.'

'You've no right to just take us away.' Maggie's voice rose sharply, the Glasgow burr coming back into it. Her hand was on the door handle. 'You've no right!'

He shook his head. 'We have our orders.'

'We're not in the army!'

'My dear young lady, there's a war on. We're all in the army.'

Colin was staring at her. 'Maggie, what's...'

'Stop the car,' Maggie said.

The man shook his head again. 'We can't, my dear.'

'I don't feel well.' She made her voice small. 'I'm going to be sick. Please, stop!'

He looked at her levelly. 'If you're ill, we should get you to your mother right away. Please be patient, Miss.'

'Stop the car!' Maggie's fingers started to prickle. The sun was too hot, the car too airless. 'Now!'

'Miss Geraldson,' the major said sharply, to Vivian. The tall Wren said, 'Calm down, Maggie.'

'Let us out.' Maggie's fingers were tingling. A wisp of her hair came loose and wafted about her cheek, although the windows were closed and there was no breeze. 'Let – us – *out*—'

'Geraldson!' the major snapped.

Vivian leaned forwards abruptly, muttering something under her breath. Maggie's head began to swim. Her hands went numb. She fell back against the leather upholstery, as if she'd tried to stand up too quickly. Vivian held her gaze. 'Calm down.'

Colin looked from her to Maggie. 'What are you doing to my sister?'

'Why, she's not doing anything.' Laura's voice was soothing. 'How could she be?'

Maggie tried to sit up. But Vivian's pale eyes were all she could see, and she had to sit back again. It was like when the land girls had put gin in her tea as a joke, and she'd tried to stand up but couldn't. The land girls had laughed uproariously; but no-one in this car was laughing. 'Please,' said Maggie.

Vivian shook her head slowly. Laura said brightly, 'We'll be in London soon.'

The roadside hedgerows were already giving way to houses. Maggie could only turn her head, slowly, to look out of the window. They were leaving the clean air behind, heading into London, into the chasms of asphalt and stone. 'Please…'

The major was affable again. 'There, there, Miss.'

'I didn't mean it,' Maggie whispered.

'What's that, my dear?'

'The Stuka. The boat.' The rowing boat. Sights and sounds were coming back to her now; she was too weak to stop them. A broken plane, slicing into a crowded boat. 'The rowing boat.'

His eyes narrowed. 'The rowing boat?'

'I didn't mean it.' The screams. 'I did something. To the plane.

But I was just… I didn't…'

He was leaning forward. 'You did something?'

Colin whimpered as Maggie began to cry. 'I didn't mean it.'

The major tried to smile again. 'There, there. You mustn't worry.'

Laura leaned sideways to Vivian. 'Too much,' she murmured.

Vivian sat back slightly. Maggie blinked, reached up and rubbed at the tears on her face. The drunk feeling receded a little. Laura wound down a window, letting some air into the cramped car. Maggie took a deep breath, muttered to Colin, 'It's all right.'

'Nearly there now,' Laura said. 'Just think, you'll see your mother soon!'

'I don't believe you,' Maggie said.

Vivian frowned, sat forward again. The dizziness came back. Maggie could hear, dimly, as Laura sighed and said, 'Now that's just silly, Maggie, don't make such a *fuss…*'

'Maggie,' Colin said.

She shook her head at him wordlessly. Fresh tears spilled down her cheeks, as they drove into London.

The capital was baking in the June heat, stewing in the smells of cars and drains and people. The traffic was thick, considering petrol was so restricted; taxis and buses jostled with trams, and the car moved slowly through the unwashed streets. A park slid past, most of the grass bleached pale. They passed under an unexpected shadow: a barrage balloon, looming over the road. The air coming through the window was tepid and felt second-hand. Maggie thought: *now I am going to be sick,* and closed her eyes.

The next thing she knew, someone was shaking her arm. She could hear Colin calling, 'Maggie, *Maggie!*' She opened her eyes. Faces, Vivian and Laura, were close to hers. Laura said, 'She's awake.' She sat back. 'There, Colin, she was only asleep. Don't worry.'

Vivian sat back too. Maggie looked around. The queasy motion of the car had stopped. They were parked on a side street, the door open; the air coming in was not much fresher. The major was on the pavement peering in, his body blocking the doorway. Colin was opposite Maggie – he looked a lot younger than ten. 'Mags? Are you all right now?'

'She's fine,' Laura answered for her. 'Let's get inside.'

Slowly and carefully, Maggie got out of the car into the airless heat. They were outside a terraced house in an elegant crescent. Rows of holes, like empty tooth-sockets, lined the low walls, marking where wrought-iron railings had been removed for the war effort. Steps led up to a polished front door and a discreet metal plaque, like an expensive doctor's surgery. As Maggie staggered a little, Vivian took her arm, and the major put one hand under her other elbow. 'Up here, my dear,' he said. Ignoring her attempt to shake him off, he walked her up the steps. Maggie could hear Laura's soothing murmur as she led Colin after them.

The door opened before anyone could ring the bell. A blonde woman in uniform – another Wren – saluted, smiled. The major and Vivian led Maggie inside without pausing. They were in a narrow, uncarpeted hallway, lined with heavy oak doors; the far end opened up into a grand staircase. A grandfather clock ticked solemnly at the foot. Their footsteps were loud on the bare floor boards as they crossed to one of the doors; the new Wren opened it, smiled at Maggie. 'You can wait in here.'

The major let go of Maggie's arm, turned to the new Wren. Vivian propelled Maggie through the door, Laura close behind with Colin. The room beyond was light and bright, wallpapered expensively; a sitting room with elegantly curved furniture and an art nouveau fireplace. The refined effect was spoiled by the heavy, coarse, black-out curtains hanging by the tall windows. There was a second door at right angles to the first, but Vivian was between it and Maggie. The door closed behind them.

Vivian steered Maggie towards a chair by the fireplace. 'Sit down.'

Maggie nodded. But before she reached the chair her legs buckled and she sank to the floor, only half held up by Vivian's large hand on her arm. 'I can't…'

She heard Colin's frightened exclamation, and Laura's sigh. 'Told you it was too much,' she said to Vivian. Then to Maggie, loudly and brightly, 'I'll just get you a glass of water,' and she hurried out.

Maggie, kneeling on the fireside rug, heard Colin shout her name.

'She's fine,' said Vivian.

'What are you doing to her?' Colin's voice was shrill. 'Get away from her!'

Vivian tried unsuccessfully to pull Maggie to her feet. 'Calm down, Colin.'

'You let her go!' Colin grabbed Vivian's free arm and tugged at her. 'Get away from my sister!'

'I said calm down!' Vivian pushed Colin away. Maggie felt Vivian's attention leave her, just for a moment. Maggie clenched her fists, thought about the Stuka, and *pushed* out the way she had then; this time at Vivian. Vivian gave a cry and lifted a hand, but she wasn't quick enough. Something invisible shoved her, hard, and threw her out of the room. The door slammed behind her.

Maggie, staggering to her feet, pointed at the door. 'Lock it!'

Colin fumbled for the key, turned it. The handle began to rattle; there were angry shouts from the hall outside. Colin turned to stare at his sister. 'Mags, what's going on?'

'I don't know,' Maggie said. Then she jumped, and Colin backed away from the door. Something was battering against it: something that sounded much bigger than a fist. A furious voice shouted, 'Open this door!'

'Come on.' Maggie grabbed Colin's hand and pulled him towards the second door. If it had been locked, that would have been that; but it opened. Maggie ran through another high, elegant room, this one with its furniture stacked high. There was another door opposite, this one ajar. They went through, and were out into a corridor. Uncarpeted stairs led upwards.

Maggie paused, but there was nowhere else to go. She said, 'Come on,' and they clattered upstairs, terribly loud on the floorboards. They emerged into a corridor, thickly carpeted in blue. Turning left would take them to the main staircase, Maggie thought, where they'd surely be seen; but she could hear raised voices to the right, so she pulled Colin left. Sure enough, they burst out onto the main staircase. Sunlight fell on them from the skylight. The carpet ended on the main landing, and their feet clattered on the bare wood.

'Stop there!' The major was in the hallway downstairs, staring up at them. Laura emerged from the doorway they'd first gone through; someone, presumably Vivian, was right behind her. Maggie tightened her grip on Colin's hand and ran upstairs, onto the next floor. A mahogany door was in front of them. As footsteps began to pound up the stairs, Maggie threw open the door and pulled Colin inside.

They were looking directly at a row of west-facing windows, a bank of dazzling light. Someone was in the room, a dark figure silhouetted against the windows. A woman in a fitted skirt – probably another Wren, Maggie thought. Maggie turned away from the glare; there was another door, to the left. She cried, 'You leave us alone,' to the new Wren, and pulled Colin away to the left.

'What are you doing?'

They both stopped at the voice. The woman came towards them. She was slim, beautifully dressed in a figure-hugging suit. Her hair, gleaming red in the yellow-gold light, was smooth and wavy. Her brown eyes were wide with surprise. 'Colin? Maggie?' she said. 'What are you doing?'

They stared at her. Maggie, finding her voice after a long silence, eventually said: '*Mum?*'

Part Two:

The Skull of Brandt

When an opponent declares, 'I will not come over to your side,' I calmly say, 'Your child belongs to us already... What are you? You will pass on. Your descendants, however, now stand in the new camp. In a short time, they will know nothing else but this new community.'

Adolf Hitler

Chapter Six

The Ministry of Ungentlemanly Warfare

'Mum!' Colin pulled away from Maggie, ran across the room, and threw himself into his mother's arms. *'Mum!'*

Maggie followed. She couldn't help it; she caught hold of her mother's sleeve and clung to it. 'Mum…'

Miriam Ogilvie, her son still wrapped around her, looked at her daughter in amazement. 'What's the matter?'

'I didn't think you were really here,' Maggie muttered.

'Why ever not?'

Before she could reply, the door crashed open. The major burst in, Vivian and Laura behind him. Colin's grip on his mother tightened; Maggie, without thinking, stepped behind her. The trio in the doorway stopped, relaxed. 'Ah, Mrs Ogilvie,' the major said. 'I see you found them.'

Their mother was starting to smile. 'Yes, I have.' She looked down at Colin, whose face was still pressed into her lapel. 'And they seem somewhat… concerned.'

Colin looked up at her, returning the smile. 'We didn't think you were really here.'

His mother frowned; as usual, she turned to Maggie for an explanation. 'Why would you think that?'

Because you sent complete strangers to arrest us, Maggie thought;

but she just shrugged sullenly. She realised she was still clinging, childishly, to her mother's arm. She let go and stepped back, watching her sidelong, studying the mother she hadn't seen in months. Miriam was, as usual, beautifully dressed – today in a light brown skirt and jacket that must have cost more clothing coupons than most people saw in a year. Her hair was set in flawless collar-length waves. Maggie reflected that if *she* ever cut her hair that short she'd look like a ginger dandelion-clock, but her mother's dark red hair was, as always, smooth and perfect. Her pretty, clever face was immaculately made-up, her lips matte and scarlet. She was now looking down at Maggie's trousers, still grubby from lifting spuds. 'What on earth are you wearing?'

'I'm a land girl now,' Maggie mumbled, moving away hastily as her mother began to brush dried mud from her knees. 'Don't.'

Miriam looked up at her. 'You mean you're not at school?'

The major interrupted. 'Mrs Ogilvie, shall we…'

'Yes. Thank you.' With a look at Maggie that meant *later*, Mum turned her attention to the major. 'I'll introduce them to the others now.'

The major nodded. Miriam smiled down at Colin again, gently loosened his grip on her so she could take him by the hand. 'Come with me,' she said. She reached out her other hand for Maggie, but Maggie stepped away again. After a moment Miriam touched her fingers to Maggie's elbow and said, rather less warmly, 'Come on.'

She drew them to the door, fashionable heels clicking on the floorboards. Colin walked beside her, swinging their joined hands happily; Maggie, after a pause, followed a step behind. The major and the two Wrens drew back to let them past. Maggie glared at Vivian, daring her to say something so she'd have the chance to snarl back. But Vivian just looked at her impassively; she and Laura and the major fell in step behind Miriam as she led her son and daughter out into the corridor. 'Up here,' Mum said.

Up here was up another flight of the grand staircase. The carpet had been lifted, but the striped wallpaper was expensive and the landing window was made of richly-coloured stained glass. Colin was looking around curiously. 'Mum, what's this place?'

'It's special.' Miriam squeezed her son's hand affectionately. 'It's a very special place, where we're doing important things to help win the war.'

'It looks like someone's house.'

'It was. But they're lending it to us. While they're away in the country.'

'What are you doing here?'

'Ah, you'll see—'

'Did you know,' Maggie said, 'that we lost Dad?'

Her mother turned to her. For a moment her face was bleak. 'Yes. I know.' Then she took a deep breath, smiled again. 'We'll talk about it later, Maggie.'

Maggie was about to say something else, but her mother and Colin were already clattering on up the staircase. Maggie had to keep moving to stop the three behind walking right into her. They all climbed on, passing through pools of evening sunlight tinted red and blue by the stained glass; until they came to another gilded door, two storeys above the first. Miriam Ogilvie stopped with her hand on the doorknob. She smiled at her children, conspiratorial, like she used to when she took them to see Santa Claus. 'Now,' she said, 'there are some people I want you to meet.'

There was something on the other side of the door. They both felt it, suddenly. Both rocked back on their feet. Colin said, 'Oh.' Maggie said, 'Don't open it.' She wanted to be at home, in Gran's house under the Mound. She wanted life to be simple again. 'Don't open it!'

'You see?' Miriam was looking past them, triumphantly, back down to the major and the Wrens. 'They can feel it. With no training at all! They know they're there!'

'You were right,' Laura agreed. All three were smiling and

nodding as if they'd won a bet. Maggie reached out to catch hold of her mother's wrist, to stop her turning the doorknob. But Miriam was already opening the door: 'Come on, you two. Nothing to worry about.'

She went inside, leading Colin after her. He hesitated on the threshold, but followed his mother. Maggie watched him being drawn into the room, looking small and fragile, and followed close behind.

The room was large, and tinged gold with the last of the evening light. It was empty of furniture except for a large, loose circle of chairs, expensive but mismatched: carved oak dining chairs, pale brocade armchairs, even a pine kitchen bench. Only three seats were occupied. The three people sitting there looked around and stood up.

Maggie's first feeling was relief. They were just kids, no older than she was. A tall skinny boy about sixteen; a small fair-haired girl, and a girl with black hair, both a year or so younger. Miriam Ogilvie led Colin to them, into the circle, as if she were about to make formal introductions. But she abruptly let go of his hand, and stepped back out of the circle of chairs. Colin was left looking at his empty hand; without thinking, Maggie came forward and took it.

Her hands started to prickle. Strands of hair wafted around her face in the still room. She looked again at the three young people in front of her, and nearly sank to her knees as she saw the late sunlight flare up around them. The skinny boy muttered under his breath, the blonde girl gasped and the other girl swayed as if she were about to faint.

Maggie looked at them again. The blonde girl was short and a little plump, with small blue eyes. Her eyebrows and lashes were pale enough to look white, making her face look naked and vulnerable. She wore a white blouse. The pallor of her seemed to flare up over her head and around her shoulders, a wavering halo around her. The flare was divided into three, as if three pale faces were standing over her. The girl was gaping at Maggie and Colin. 'Oh, my goodness,' she said, in an accent even more upper-class than Arthur's. 'Oh, *my*.'

The boy was whip-thin. His mousey hair was cut short around his sharp, knowing face. He scowled from Maggie to Colin, pushing his chin out as if he were about to ask what they were looking at. Maggie thought something dark stood behind him, something shaped like a tall stocky man in black, with his hand pressed down on the boy's shoulders. Lying at the boy's feet was what looked like another figure, smaller, with long hair trailing on the floor. But the shapes wavered; Maggie blinked hard, and they were only shadows.

The dark-haired girl still looked wobbly on her feet. She had flawless olive skin, a wide mouth, glossy black hair and huge dark eyes. She was the prettiest girl Maggie had ever seen; and, Maggie thought, the most frightened. Then it seemed to Maggie that other people must have stolen into the room without her knowing, because there was a small crowd around the dark girl. A man and a woman, black-haired like her; a girl about twelve, fair-skinned and deep honey-blonde. Behind them were others: men, women and children. At least five, maybe more.

Maggie closed her eyes, kept them closed for a few seconds. When she opened them, there were just two girls and a boy standing in front of her, no-one else. There might still have been some strange wavering at the edges of her vision; but that was surely just a trick of the evening sun. She turned to her mother. Her voice came out hoarse and angry: 'Who are these people?'

Miriam, the major and the two Wrens were standing behind them, outside the circle of chairs. Miriam's face was flushed. 'They're like you,' she said. 'They have power.'

'What?'

The blonde girl interrupted. Her face was as excited as Miriam's.

'Join hands,' she said. She grabbed the dark-haired girl's hand, reached out for the boy's. 'Come on.'

'You what?' The boy's Cockney voice was sharp, but he didn't move his hand away. 'What for?'

'Just join hands, quickly!'

She grabbed his hand. After a moment the boy shrugged, stretched out his other hand to Maggie. She was already reaching out towards him; but she caught herself just in time. 'What are you doing?'

'It's all right, Mags.' Colin tugged at her other arm. He looked delighted, like it was his birthday. He turned to the dark-haired girl. She couldn't keep from smiling back, and didn't resist when he took her hand.

Maggie felt the other boy's bony fingers catch hold of hers, and then they were standing in a joined circle. She cried out as something warm pulsed through them. Her hair lifted around her face, the plait unravelling. She stared into the startled eyes of the three strangers. But they weren't strangers; she knew their names. 'You're Alice,' she said to the blonde girl. 'And you're Vincent,' she said to the boy, and turned to the other girl, 'and you're... Hannah?'

Colin laughed happily. 'No, it's Jannah.'

The dark-haired girl inhaled sharply, but she didn't let go of his hand. The blonde girl – Alice – laughed back at Colin. 'And you're Colin and Maggie.'

'Our mother must've told you that,' Maggie whispered.

'No, she didn't,' Alice said.

'A circle of power.' Miriam's voice was low, awe-stricken. Maggie turned to her, but her mother was looking at Laura and Vivian and the major. 'Did you see that? Without any ritual whatsoever? Did you *see*?'

The boy – Vince – pulled his hand away from Maggie's. 'What the bloody hell is going on?'

'We're drawing down power.' Alice was almost dancing on the

spot. 'We didn't have to chant or erect a temple or *anything.*'

Vincent stared at her. 'You what?'

'No consecration ritual.' Alice was grinning at Miriam, who was smiling indulgently back. 'Not even an athame, nothing!'

'Mum,' Maggie said, 'what's going on? What are we here for?'

Miriam turned her triumphant smile to her daughter. 'You're here because you can do magic,' she said.

An hour later the lights were on. The Wrens and the major had quietly left the room, after swathing the windows with blackout curtains so none of the dangerous light could escape onto the darkened streets. Nightfall hadn't made the London air any cooler; Maggie wanted to take her jumper off, but she knew her shirt's armpits would be sweat-stained by now. So she just rolled up her sleeves, uncovering Dad's tie in the process. She wondered if her mother would say anything, but Miriam didn't seem to notice.

Maggie put her empty plate aside. The five of them sat around the circle, chairs pulled closer together in a conspiratorial huddle. Miriam was in the sixth seat. The Wrens had brought ham sandwiches – thick and juicy, with real butter. They'd all had some; Vince had eaten all of his, one arm wrapped around his plate like a convict, and was currently working his way through the ones Alice didn't want. Maggie had eaten too, remembering she should have had her tea hours ago. But now the food was sitting heavy in her stomach. She was listening to her mother talk, and wanted to be very far away.

'Magic,' Miriam was saying. 'Some call it witchcraft. Or power. It's in all of us. But in some, it's very strong.' She paused for effect. 'And in you five, it's the strongest I've ever seen.'

Maggie looked around the circle. The black-haired girl – Jannah – cleared her throat anxiously. 'We are strongest?' she said. Her voice was soft – her accent sounded Eastern European, a lot like

Michal's. 'Have you seen many? Who are also strong?'

'Some. The ladies you met earlier. Especially Vivian.' Maggie recalled nearly fainting in the car, while Vivian's pale eyes stared her down. She squirmed at the memory. Miriam's voice went on: 'And myself, of course. There are others, with different skills. We've formed a group.'

'A coven?' asked Alice. She and Colin were still pink-faced. 'Is it a coven?'

Miriam looked pained. 'That's an old-fashioned word. It's not really like that. We're part of a new unit. The Special Operations Executive. It's just been set up. By Mr Churchill himself.' She paused – waiting for the gasps of awe, Maggie thought. Alice and Colin duly obliged, so she went on, with a laugh: 'It's for – unusual forms of warfare. Some of the old generals call it the Ministry of Ungentlemanly Warfare.'

Vince looked up, his mouth still full of sandwich. 'Warfare?' he echoed.

'In a manner of speaking. We find people with special talents. And you all have those, don't you? You can do things. Things just happen around you, isn't that right?'

Colin was almost bouncing with excitement. 'I can hear things. Things people say far away. That's right, isn't it, Mags?'

'No, you're just good at guessing,' Maggie said.

'I'm not. You know I'm not. And you can do things too. You can make things move! Just by looking at them!'

'No I can't.'

'Yes, you can, Maggie. You know you can—'

'Just shoosh, will you!'

Alice interrupted before he could reply: 'I can do it too! I've moved books, and, and my bed in the dorm at night, and I once pushed a senior girl without being near her! I truly did!'

Jannah and Vince were looking at each other, their faces wary. At last Jannah said, 'Yes, I too. I can do those things. Can you?'

Vince shrugged. 'Maybe.'

'You all can,' said Miriam triumphantly, before Maggie could break in. 'And we want you to use your skills. To find something that will keep us all safe.'

Vince frowned. 'Find what?'

'A skull,' Miriam said. She was fishing in a leather satchel beside her chair. 'A head.'

Maggie thought: *oh no, not that…* But sure enough, Miriam was pulling out an old leather-bound book. One that made Colin give a happy cry of recognition. '*The Skull of Brandt?*'

'That's right.' Miriam beamed at him, and added to the others: 'This is a story I used to read to Maggie and Colin when they were little.'

'Mum,' Maggie hissed, 'no-one wants to hear a bedtime *story…*'

'It's not just a story,' Miriam said. 'It's real.' She opened the book, raised her voice over Maggie's protests. 'Now, listen…'

Long ago there was a wise king of Britain, whose name was Brandt. In those days there was war in Britain; the peoples of the East came across the sea to invade, again and again. One day Brandt met them in a great battle, and was victorious over them, so they fled back into the East. But everyone knew they would return.

Brandt himself was injured in the battle, and lay among the dying in the field. Then the Morrigan, the goddess of war, appeared to him. She said to Brandt: 'Go to the island-valley of Avilion, and be healed of your grievous wounds. Then you will live to fight another day.'

But Brandt said: 'War has brought death to my people. I know a way to bring them life.' And the Morrigan vanished. Brandt called to his men, who wanted to tend to his wounds and save his life. But Brandt refused, and told them: 'You must sever my head, and bury it under the White Hill of London. While it remains there, no invader will ever land on Britain's shores.'

Brandt's men wept, but they did as he asked. They cut off his head, and took it to the White Hill. The stories say that the head came back to life just as they were about to bury it, and it said: 'Turn my face towards the East, to the lands of the Saxons and the Angles and the Germans, so they may never set foot on our shores.'

Brandt's men did as he said, and buried his head on the hill. Later they built a tower on the hill, and set crows and ravens to guard it; this is the Tower of London. Then the Morrigan slept; and while Brandt's head remained below the White Hill, no invader ever set foot on the shores of Britain.

Centuries later, Britain was ruled by a king called Arturus. He was a great warrior, but proud and foolish. He heard the story of the head of Brandt, and it displeased him. He said: 'It is I who safeguard Britain against invaders, and yet the people say it is the head of Brandt, and the kings of other lands scorn me because of it. And so I shall dig up the head, and all shall see that I defend this land.'

And so Arturus went to the White Hill with his men, and had Brandt's head brought up from the earth. Then the Morrigan appeared to Arturus, and she said: 'If you uncover Brandt's head, the invaders will come, and you will set me free in this land.'

But Arturus told her: 'It is I who defend this land against invaders.'

And the Morrigan said: 'Already I see them, coming from the East. They will come with iron and blood, with eagles and wolves and ravens; and they will rain down fire upon you.'

But Arturus said: 'Let them come, for I shall drive them out. And now let the skull be destroyed.' But the Morrigan laughed, and she took the skull and vanished.

And so the invaders began to come across the sea from the East, from the lands of the Saxons and the Angles and the Germans. And Arturus bitterly regretted the uncovering of Brandt's head, and called for the head to be buried again under the White Hill. But the head was gone, and they never found it again. And the Morrigan ran free in the

land of Britain, and fire and ruin came with her, until the invaders
conquered Britain and made it their own.

Miriam closed the book. In the heavy silence that followed, Maggie stared at her shoes and thought sourly: *Some mothers just read their kids fairy tales.* Colin and Alice sat back and sighed. But Jannah looked more worried than ever; and Vince was looking at Miriam with disbelief. 'Mum,' said Maggie, 'why are you reading us *stories?*'

'I told you. It's a true story.'

Alice was nodding vigorously. 'It's an ancient mythic motif. The self-sacrifice. The sacrificed king. The head as protective talisman. There *must* be something to it. Every culture has a variant—'

'It does,' Miriam interrupted her mid-flow, 'and this one is real. The head is real. We think it's still here. It's buried somewhere in London.'

Vince shrugged. 'So what if it is?'

'If we find it, and we place it just right, it could help us fight the war. It could stop the Germans invading.'

There was a long silence. 'Mum,' Maggie said at last, 'that's – that's—'

'This power is *real*.' Miriam's whisper filled the room, echoed in their heads. 'You know it is. Maggie, you used it to throw a German bomber out of the sky.' The others' heads swivelled towards Maggie; she stared at the floor and wouldn't meet their eyes. 'You all have that power. You can use it. To help your country. To win this war. What do you say?'

'We'll do it.' It was Colin. 'We'll help win the war.'

Miriam turned her warmest smile on him. 'That's good. Good boy. Alice, what about you?'

'Of course.' Alice was almost quivering with pride. 'I'll do it.'

'And you, Jannah?'

'If I can help…' Jannah hesitated, took a deep breath: 'If I can help. I will do it.'

'Wonderful. Vincent?'

Vincent shrugged, then laughed. 'Why not. Let's show the Jerries what's what.'

'That's the spirit. And Maggie? Will you help us?' Miriam turned to her daughter. 'Will you do this? Maggie?'

Chapter Seven

In the Wewelsburg

'No,' said Maggie. 'I won't.'

Everyone stared at her. 'What d'you mean, you *won't?*' Vince said after a moment.

'I mean I won't do it.' Maggie folded her arms. 'I won't fight her war for her.'

'It en't just *her* war!'

'Maggie,' said Miriam sharply, 'stop being silly.'

Maggie stood up. She pointed at Colin. 'He's *ten*. He's a *kid*.' She waved a hand towards Jannah and Vince and Alice. 'They're, what? Fifteen?'

'I'm sixteen,' snapped Vince.

'Sixteen. So what? They're kids. *We're* kids, and you want us to fight your war for you?'

'Maggie, sit down.'

'We're not fighting. We're *not in the army*.' Miriam pressed her lips together and said nothing. Maggie's voice rose to a cry: 'You wouldn't ask us this if Dad was here! You wouldn't dare!'

Miriam stood up; Maggie couldn't stop herself flinching. Without taking her eyes off her daughter, Miriam said: 'Would the rest of you excuse us, please?'

'Mum,' said Colin.

'Right now, Colin, please.'

Vince cast a contemptuous look at Maggie and walked out. The two girls went after him, Alice looking bewildered, Jannah drawing Colin after her. Maggie didn't want them to go. But despite the heat rising into her face, she made herself look at her mother. 'I'm doing what Dad would want,' she said. 'I'm not going to war. There can't be a war if no one takes part.'

'You're being ridiculous,' snapped Miriam. 'No one's sending you to the trenches.'

'It's still war.'

'Nonsense. I'm asking you to use your natural abilities. To help your country—'

'I don't have any abilities,' Maggie mumbled.

'You know that's not true.'

Maggie felt her eyes prick with tears. 'All right. So what. That doesn't mean any of *this* –' she pointed at the book in her mother's hand 'matters a bit.'

'It matters in a way you can't understand.'

'Oh come on. So I can… move things around a bit. But a magic head? The *Morrigan*, for Pete's sake?'

'The gods are powers within us.' Miriam waved her hand dismissively. 'They're part of us. We make them in our own image. So, yes, the Morrigan is very real.'

She dropped the book onto her chair. It fell open at a picture, a colour plate. A female figure against a burning horizon, her hair falling in blood-red waves all around her. Claw hands clutching a white skull. Eyes wholly black; a dark maw of a mouth, stretched wide in a scream. It had given Maggie nightmares all through her childhood. 'Rubbish,' she said, and reached for Gran's phrase, '*codswallop*.'

Her mother sighed, as if it was all just too tiresome. 'All right,' she said. 'You're right. I forget how young you are. I'd hoped you'd understand by now.' She paused, but Maggie said nothing. Miriam turned away. 'You can go home.'

Maggie let out a sigh of relief. But Miriam wasn't finished. 'Home to Glasgow.'

'What?'

'Well, not Glasgow, obviously. Somewhere in the countryside around it. Helensburgh, maybe.'

'That's not home!'

'You mean you want to go back to your grandmother's?'

'Of course!'

Miriam shook her head. 'Don't be silly. That's right in the path of the invasion.'

Maggie stopped in her tracks. 'Invasion? You think it's... real? What they say?'

'Real? Of course it's real. Hitler has already laid his plans. It's to happen this summer.'

Maggie stared at her, aghast. 'I didn't think it would really happen...'

'If you think that, then you really are too immature. You and your brother will go to Scotland.'

Maggie shook her head. 'What about Gran?'

'Your grandmother can be evacuated too, if she wants.'

'She'll never leave.'

'That's up to her.'

'She's lived there all her life! Her family's always lived there!'

'Things are different now.'

'Me and Colin are all she's got now, we can't go all that way away!'

'Well.' Miriam shrugged. 'You can stay here, under my supervision, if you choose. Or you can go to Scotland. It's up to you.'

So that was it. Do what I want, or I'll pack you off like a parcel. Maggie's fingers began to prickle. She stared at her mother; Miriam gazed back, a little pale under her make-up, but calm and composed.

Tears began to run down Maggie's face. 'I hate you,' she said. 'I wish we'd lost you instead of Dad.'

Without waiting for a reply she ran to the door, wrenched it open and fell through into the hall before her mother could call her back. There was no one on the landing, but she could hear voices downstairs. So she headed up. She thought she heard Colin call anxiously, 'Maggie?' but she blundered on, blind with tears.

She turned left on the next landing up, expecting another door. But instead there was a wall of thick black fabric: blackout curtains. The curtains were securely pulled together, but Maggie could still feel a breath of outside air coming through them. She pulled one aside, and found full-length French windows, one ajar. Slightly cooler air brushed her overheated face. Not caring where she was going, Maggie pushed the glass door open and stumbled through.

She emerged into the London blackout. London hadn't been so dark for a thousand years. But Maggie was used to unlit nights in the country; she stopped dead and waited for her eyes to adjust. The sky was still hazed with sunset, and a half-moon hung above it. After a minute she could see clearly enough.

It was a wide patio, a rooftop garden. Dark wooden chairs lined the parapets, some set around outdoor tables. Tubs of flowers, some intense colour that was grey in the half-light, were set here and there. Maggie jumped as a shape turned slowly just beyond the right-hand parapet; but it was only a barrage balloon, being winched silently into the sky, its half-inflated tail-fin rippling.

Maggie stood alone in the middle of the roof garden, her face still hot, her hands prickling, feeling like she was about to explode. She drew in a ragged breath, then let out a frustrated cry, like an angry dog. Something – the power, the *magic*, she couldn't deny it now – whooshed out of her in all directions. It was stronger than it had ever been, scattering the wooden chairs like bowling pins. It sent the barrage balloon spinning; she heard a shout of alarm from below, as the balloon crew struggled to control it. Maggie tipped her face back, and let her anger fly upwards, into the summer sky.

At once she knew she'd made a mistake. Something was whispering, something new, different, too far away to hear. Something flickered at the corner of her eye, but when she turned it was just the moon. A half-moon: rising in the West; a planet below it, gleaming like a diamond pendant. Maggie closed her eyes and shook her head.

But the whispering was louder. The words were unclear, but the sense of it wasn't: *What's this? What's this?* She opened her eyes again and was dazzled by the moon, the light danced and wavered. She blinked rapidly, but the light didn't fade. It was squirming, changing: taking shape.

Maggie took a step back as the light formed into three figures at the far end of the garden. No faces, no features; just figures of yellow light. But two were men, she saw, or boys. And the one in the middle was slender and feminine, with bright hair billowing all around it. The whispering was louder, clearer: *What's this? Who are you? Who?*

'Close your eyes,' said a voice at her elbow. Maggie jumped, spun round to see Jannah beside her. Jannah's face was pale, her eyes deep and dark. 'You must close your eyes, quickly,' she said.

Maggie screwed her eyes shut, swaying slightly. Jannah's hand fell onto her arm, a light touch but warm and solid. Maggie found she didn't want to open her eyes again, she really didn't… Then the fear made her angry, and she defiantly opened her eyes wide.

The three figures had vanished. Jannah was gazing at the spot where they had stood; she nodded. 'I think they are gone,' she said.

Maggie drew breath to say she'd been seeing things, it was just the moon. But what came out was: 'Who were they?'

'I do not know.' Jannah shook her head. 'But I have seen them before. Sometimes I see more, perhaps ten, twelve. But always the three. They are the most…' she made a gesture, searching for the right word, '…most important.'

'I've never seen them before,' Maggie whispered.

'But you will see them again. We will all see them.'

'How do you know?'

'I see the future, sometimes,' Jannah said simply. 'Although it is not easy. There are many futures, the future can change. Perhaps you will see too, through me.'

'I can't see the future!'

Jannah shrugged. 'Now you can see what I see. The circle of power…' she spread her hands, shrugged again. 'We are all together now, I think.'

Maggie stared down at her pale, sad face. 'Downstairs I saw people around you,' she said. 'A man, and a woman. And a little girl.'

Jannah's eyes opened wide. 'You saw them?'

'I – thought I did. And other people too.'

Jannah nodded. 'My parents. And my sister. My family.'

'Where are they?'

'They are still in Poland.'

'You're from Poland?'

'I escaped. They did not.' Her voice dropped to a whisper. 'They were taken away. To a…' she shook her head, looking for a word, 'a camp.'

Maggie wondered if Jannah had the right word. A camp didn't sound bad… but Jannah's face was suddenly sick and drawn. 'Why did they take them away?' Maggie said.

Jannah's looked away. Her voice was the tiniest whisper. 'We are Jews.'

Maggie blinked. She remembered the image of the little girl, who couldn't have been older than Colin. What could a twelve-year-old girl possibly have done? 'Is that all?' she said.

Jannah just looked at her. Maggie dropped her gaze. She was thinking how it would feel, having to flee to a strange country and leave Gran and Colin behind, and Dad, and, yes, Mum too. She remembered the scene downstairs, how badly treated she'd felt; now she went hot with shame. 'I'm sorry,' she said.

Jannah nodded and looked away again. Maggie said after a moment: 'Do you believe all this stuff about the skull?'

'Yes,' said Jannah. 'I believe.'

'You really think it'd make a difference? An old skull?'

'Yes,' Jannah said again. 'Objects can have power, yes?'

Maggie nodded. 'All right. I'll help you find it then.'

For the first time Jannah smiled. 'Thank you.'

They both looked out over the darkened city. After a moment, Maggie put an arm around the younger girl's shoulders as if she were Colin. 'It's all right,' she said. 'They won't get you here.'

Jannah's smile flashed again. 'You will prevent it?'

'Yes,' Maggie said, making herself sound confident. 'I will prevent it.'

Wewelsburg Castle, Western Germany – June 1940

The thirteen *gothi* came back to their surroundings, to the mundane world. But the candles still blazed high, and the air still crackled. Thirteen faces were flushed with the heat, and with triumph. Their power ran as high as their confidence, as their joy to be here, at the new centre of the world.

They opened their eyes slowly to the stone-faced walls of the

Hall of the Generals. The walls were unadorned, with not even a Swastika flag; bare except for the multitude of candles, which were starting to droop under their high flames. The light shone through the twelve high, uncurtained windows. All of the Wewelsburg blazed out: to the forests and the villages around, to the countryside, to the whole world.

They were actually here, in the Wewelsburg. At the centre of power of the SS, Heinrich Himmler's chosen ones. At the spiritual heart of the Third Reich: the Führer's Camelot, the axis of Hitler's new world.

The twelve boys took a moment to return to themselves. Some of them had risen a few inches above the marble floor as the power flowed through them. This power, they knew, came from the Aryan Race-Soul, the collective will of the Master Race, of which they were prime specimens. Now they settled again, each at one arm of the Black Sun wheel on the floor. No crudely painted symbol, not here. The Black Sun, the triple Swastika, was cast in greenish-black marble, set flawlessly into the smooth floor: purpose-built.

In the centre of the marble mosaic, Lise's white satin shoes alighted on pure gold. The twenty-inch disc, embedded in the heart of the Black Sun, flared reddish-amber as she touched down, gracefully, not staggering to keep her balance as the boys had. Lise's hair flowed loose. She wore a white dress of some expensive silky stuff, which lifted and swirled around her. A tight red sash hugged her waist. She was smiling radiantly, her eyes still distant: still burning sapphire-blue. The boys gazed at her with varying degrees of lust and awe. Even Petr, still scornful that the prime centre place should be occupied by a mere female, had to admit her appearance was... striking.

They knew she would not speak to them, not yet; so they turned their attention to one another. To their triumph. A routine survey of the enemy defences had yielded, at last, something truly interesting. 'Well,' said Albrecht. 'It seems we have competition.'

'It's to be expected.' It was Hans, one of the younger ones; a studious boy. 'There's a lot of Aryan blood in the English.' They all shook their heads at the folly of the British: making war on their Aryan brothers! 'Some of them must be inspired by the Race-Soul, it stands to reason.'

'But there are only five of them.' Albrecht sounded almost disappointed. Five wouldn't make for a fair fight. 'And three of them girls.'

'And one of *them* a Jewess,' said Petr.

There was an uncomfortable silence. They all knew Jews were the Enemy; but she'd just looked like a frightened girl. And they were supposed to protect girls, weren't they? 'How do you know she's Jewish?' said Hans at last.

Petr sneered. 'You only have to look at her.'

There was another silence. 'If she's a Jewess, how can she have the same sort of Power as us?' one of the younger boys said uncertainly. 'I thought the Power came from the Race-Soul.'

Petr waved the question away impatiently. Who knew what sort of Jewish trickery the girl was using? 'Nevertheless.'

'Perhaps the Power doesn't always come from the Race-Soul,' Hans said thoughtfully. 'Perhaps there's something else...'

'She must have some Aryan blood then,' Albrecht interrupted, as Petr made a mental note that Hans's speculations were becoming... unsound. 'Anyhow, brothers – we have opponents. Taking England will not be as straightforward as we thought.' Some of the others started to look alarmed; but then he added: 'But of course, we have what they do not. We have the blessed Goddess. We have Freya.'

They all looked at Lise. 'Lady,' said Albrecht reverently, lovingly, 'what would you have us do? We are your loyal knights. Speak, we implore you.'

The blue eyes focussed, came to rest on him. Lise began to laugh. 'Five children,' she said. 'Five English children, lost and alone. Do you think they have any idea of the traitor in their midst?'

Chapter Eight

Sandbag City

Piccadilly Circus, July 1940

Dear Gran,

Here we are in London! We are quite safe, you are not to worry because there are no bombs. Everything is going on as normal here –

A particularly loud blare of traffic made Maggie look up. A double-decker bus had been swinging around the Circus at speed, but had pulled up short when two boys nipped in front of it. The driver thrust his head out of the window, shouting at them. The boys stuck two fingers up and ran off.

Vince laughed, leaning forward from his vantage point on the top step. The major was scowling, though. 'Those children should have been evacuated,' he growled.

He had been speaking to Laura and Vivian but Vince answered cheerfully: 'They probably was evacuated. But lots of kids've come back now. No bombs falling.'

Maggie looked around Piccadilly Circus. They were on the steps of the octagonal traffic island in the middle of the Circus, eating the lunchtime sandwiches the Wrens had brought with them. Vince was right: there were a lot of children and young people around. All day they'd seen stern posters – *Don't do it, Mother! Keep them in the country!* – but no one seemed to be paying attention.

In fact, she thought, there wasn't that much sign of the war at all. Piccadilly Circus looked just the same as ever, stewing in the clammy air. Black cars nosed their way around the roundabout; buses and trams lumbered along beside them. The neon signs were still in place on the towering fronts of the buildings: BOVRIL. SCHWEPPES TONIC WATER. GUINNESS IS GOOD FOR YOU! Presumably they weren't switched on at night, but no one had thought to take them away. Crowds pushed and bumped on the narrow pavements: women with shopping baskets, men in bowler hats – hardly anyone carried a gasmask. A woman in a dusty black hat sat on the bottom step a few yards away selling flowers. All business as usual.

The major was scowling. He sat with the Wrens, as far from Maggie and the others as he could without being out of earshot. He and Laura and Vivian were out of uniform, in civilian clothes; Maggie thought that just made him look even more military than before. He was glaring at the children in the crowd like an angry sergeant-major. 'Good God, they're everywhere. It's damned irresponsible. Have they *all* come back?'

Again, he was talking to Laura and Vivian, but it was Vince who answered. 'Most of them.' He pointed to the top of the steps and laughed. 'All 'cept him, of course.'

They all looked. The podium in the centre of the Circus, where the statue of Eros was supposed to stand, was empty. The boy archer, like a lot of other public statues, had been removed to an underground shelter for its own safety. *Unlike us,* thought Maggie. She glanced around their little group: Vince stretched out confidently on the top step, Jannah sitting beside him; herself and Colin by their feet, sharing the last bottle of lemonade; Alice below them again, halfway between Colin's feet and the trio of adults. They looked exposed. Maggie realised the signs of war were there after all. The concrete pillbox across the street, so shored up with sandbags one of its walls seemed to be built out of them. The tin hats on so many of the passers-by; the drab-coloured siren suits, baggy as a baby's coveralls. One tin-hatted man, plump and moustached and wearing a yellow arm-band, gave them a hard stare as he walked past. An air-raid warden. Vince made a rude sound in his throat. 'Bleedin' little Hitlers,' he said.

'They are doing their duty,' snapped the major. 'As we all must.' *As we're completely failing to do now, you mean*, Maggie thought. The search was not going well. Maggie returned to her writing pad:

We have met some people of our own age. There is Jannah, she is a refugee from Poland. There is Alice, she goes to a big private school with her three sisters, but she is on her holidays now. And there is Vince. He is from London. He is a thief.

She stopped, scored out the last part and wrote:

Vince is from London. He is very good at finding things.

She looked at Vince, who was surveying Piccadilly like a king from his throne. That was Vince's special skill, they'd discovered (Alice called it 'dowsing', which it seemed didn't just apply to water.) Apparently, ever since the blackout began, Vince had been finding his way into other people's houses and making off with their stuff, or bumping into them in the street and finding out what they had in their pockets. The major had been watching Vince like a hawk ever since he'd found this out. No, Maggie thought, scoring out the last sentence, it would be best not to tell Gran all that much about Vince. She settled for:

Vince is from London, and so he knows his way around. And now, we are —

She stopped. What *were* they doing, exactly? She tuned back to the conversation. Alice, who never seemed to relax, was arguing earnestly with the major. 'We're doing our best. We can't just press a button, you know. Magick doesn't work that way.' Alice always referred to their power that way: 'Magic-*k*'. You could hear the extra K at the end. 'We need the proper atmosphere.'

'Yeah, atmosphere,' agreed Vince lazily, winking at Jannah, who giggled softly. 'And more grub.'

The major's face went redder than before. Laura put a soothing hand on his arm, and passed Vince the last cheese sandwich. Vince crammed it into his mouth as quickly as possible. Maggie looked at his skinny frame and reflected that whatever he'd been stealing before they met him, it hadn't been food. Alice was still shaking her head. 'We can't do it just like that, you know. We're witches, not plumbers.'

Was that what they were? Maggie shook her head to clear it. If she was a witch, you'd think she could make herself think clearly, even in this heat. You'd think she wouldn't be boiling in the land girl uniform trousers she still insisted on wearing, in spite of the expensive frocks her mother had bought for her. 'Don't think you can be a witch and wear trousers,' she mumbled.

Vince had objections too. 'Me and Col ain't witches.' He nudged Colin companionably with his foot. 'Witches are women. We must be… wizards, or something.'

Colin nodded. Maggie shrugged. *Witch* had an unpleasant ring to it. 'We'll all be wizards, then.'

After a moment, Alice nodded too. 'All right, if you like. Witch and wizard mean the same thing, after all. They both mean wise one. They come from the same root word, *wyse*, from the Old English, you know…'

It was turning into one of Alice's lectures. Maggie tuned out, closed her eyes, and tried to imagine she was at home. But closing her eyes didn't help; she could still hear the cacophony of traffic, still smell petrol and sweat and the fusty, gritty odour of the omnipresent sandbags. A pang went through her as she caught a whiff of something floral, something like grass and fresh air. She opened her eyes and realised it was coming from the flower-seller's baskets. She got up abruptly and went to the foot of the steps, ignoring the question Laura called after her. The flower-seller smiled up at her as she leaned over the cut flowers, inhaling the green, damp smell. Her eye fell on a splash of bright orange-red: a rose. Just like the ones grandad used to grow. 'That one, please,' she said.

The woman drew the rose out carefully and handed it to her. 'That's thruppence, dear.'

Maggie paused. She had only a few pennies left. 'Oh, that's…'

'I'll get it.' Alice was at her elbow, her purse open. Before Maggie could object, she'd thrust a shilling at the flower-seller. 'They're lovely. One for me too, please. No, no,' she waved away the three pennies Maggie was trying to put into her purse, 'it's all right. I've got more than you. I'll pay.'

Maggie turned away, more offended than if Alice had stolen her money. But Alice was right behind her. 'I think we should talk,' Alice whispered, 'the five of us alone.'

Maggie sighed, torn between annoyance and pity. Alice sometimes reminded her of the smallest piglet in Addison's sow's litter: always trying twice as hard, but still never getting the attention she wanted. It was a hot day, so annoyance won. 'Not now, Alice,' she said, and went back to her place on the steps. Tucking the flower into her top button-hole, she picked up her notepad again:

I hope we will be able to come home soon. In fact we will have to come soon, as the potatoes will need lifting and that is my job! I hope you are well and you are managing all right without us.

If you see Michal from the airbase, tell him –

Tell him what? And why was she even bothering to write this letter at all? As soon as she handed the letter over for posting, it would go straight to Miriam; and Miriam would tell her it wasn't 'suitable' and refuse to send it. Maggie tore the page out of her notepad and screwed it up angrily, shoving it into her trouser pocket. Ignoring the looks the others were giving her, she took out a souvenir postcard of Piccadilly Circus, and wrote – *Here we are in London. We are doing fine. Hope you are well. Hope to see you soon. Love, Maggie and Colin.*

She stabbed a full stop onto the card, and stood up. If they had to be here, they could at least be *doing* something. 'Shall we get on?' she said.

The other four – other four *wizards*, she supposed she'd have to learn to say – looked at her resentfully. They were hot and footsore, not in a great hurry to move. But the major stood up too, brushing crumbs from his immaculately-pressed trousers. 'Yes, indeed. Let's try again, shall we?'

Alice shook her head. 'We can't do anything here.' She raised her voice over a blaring car-horn. 'We need somewhere quieter.'

'I know somewhere.' Vince got up, offered a hand to Jannah and pulled her to her feet. He kept hold of her hand, casually, until she gently disentangled herself. 'Come on then,' he said, bouncing down the steps and across the road, heading south. Laura called after him, 'Wait, Vince.' But he just waved as he dodged expertly through the traffic. Then he stood on the other side, tapping his foot with exaggerated impatience, as everyone else straggled after him.

When almost everyone was across the road, Vince led them south down the broad sweep of Regent Street. He wove effortlessly through the throngs of people. Sometimes he would run lightly up and down the wide steps outside the great buildings; occasionally he would even reach out and run his fingertips over the elegant stonework, with a Londoner's fierce possessive pride. The others followed in a ragged line. Maggie kept hearing the major's rumble of impatience as other pedestrians flowed between, separating them. Maggie ignored him and kept hold of Colin's hand. Colin had started objecting to hand-holding, at least when Vince and the two girls were watching, but today he submitted without a word. He looked pale and quiet; the heat didn't agree with him, Maggie thought. 'Are you all right?' she said.

Colin just nodded, looking ahead, trying to keep Vince in view. Maggie could see the older boy clearly enough. He was tall and hatless, easy to spot in the bobbing mass of trilbies and metal helmets. Still, she almost missed it when he turned sharp right, steering easily through the milling crowds on the corner. Maggie hurried after him, raising a hand to signal to the others behind, although she knew her red hair made her visible a long way off. Ignoring the major's bellows to wait, she towed Colin down a much narrower street after Vince.

The street ended, after just a block, in a wide square. Vince had been right; it was much quieter. There were far fewer people, hardly any traffic. This was London as Maggie recalled it from visits before the war, with Dad and Mum and Colin: pockets of quiet amidst the uproar. Here fine Georgian buildings, fronted with columns and painted white and vanilla, sat back decorously from the square, which held a tiny park. Low, warm-coloured stone walls surrounded it; they had the gap-toothed look that meant the railings had been taken away to be melted down. Trees towered over the walls all around the square. They were in full summer leaf; this must have provided cover for the lawn, because the grass here wasn't bleached-out, but still green.

Maggie followed Vince through the empty space where wide wrought-iron gates should have stood. Just inside the park were a few wooden benches, which held a handful of people: two young office-girls eating sandwiches, an elderly couple sitting side-by-side, a mother with a chunky toddler on her lap. A smooth pathway led past the benches to the square's centre, where there was a tall white stone plinth. Empty. Another evacuated statue.

Maggie suddenly had the feeling she'd been here before. She ignored the path under her feet and stepped onto the grass, relishing the faint earthy smell that rose to greet her. She led Colin across the inner pathway that traced a circle around the absent statue; the two of them joined Vince at the foot of the plinth.

Vince stretched out his arms expansively as the rest of their little party gathered around him. 'What d'you think?' he said. 'S'perfect, right?'

'It is quiet,' Jannah agreed, since he obviously wanted praising. She was eyeing the gold inscription on the side of the plinth. It said, in big Latinate capitals, GVLIELMVS. III. 'What does that mean?' she asked.

The major glanced at it. 'William the Third,' he explained. 'The statue's of King William the Third.'

Jannah looked at it in bemusement, obviously wondering how GVLIELMVS could possibly mean William. It was Latin, Maggie thought, wondering how she knew… then she remembered: Mum had told her. They *had* been here before. She recalled the statue too: a man sitting proudly on horseback, with a flowing cloak and floppy hair like a poet. 'King Billy,' she said. 'On his horse.'

'With the molehill,' Colin said.

Everyone looked at him. 'You what, mate?' said Vince, when nothing else was forthcoming.

'The molehill.' Colin stared up at the plinth, eyes wide and serious behind his glasses. 'King William. He died when his horse tripped on a molehill and threw him off. The statue,' he pointed upwards, 'has got the molehill on it.'

God, that was right. Maggie remembered now: recalled Mum pointing out the sculpted bronze lump under the horse's hoof. It wasn't just the statue of a man; it was a statue of his death. Morbid, she thought, taking a step back onto the grass. 'Well,' she said, 'shall we—'

'Of course. Of course!' Alice was so excited she hadn't noticed Maggie was speaking. 'The death of a king!'

'What?'

'The death of a king!'

Vivian interrupted softly. 'He didn't die here, Alice.'

'But it's an effigy. Of a king's death. People have been *looking* at it! For *years!*'

Vivian nodded, as if all this made perfect sense. 'It might be worth a try,' she said. 'The five of you – form a circle—'

'Not down here.' Alice pointed at the top of the plinth. 'Up *there!*'

Everyone looked up. The plinth was ten feet tall, with smooth sides. 'Up *there?*' Maggie echoed.

'Yes. It's the focal point...' Alice at last seemed to realise what she was saying. 'Oh. We may need a ladder.'

'Nah, we can do it.' Vince was full of energy again. 'Give us a bunk-up, mister.'

The major scowled. But Vivian caught his eye and nodded firmly, so he joined his hands into a cradle and held them out. Vince set one foot on them; the major hoisted, Vince put his other foot onto the major's shoulder (none too gently), and up he went, nimble as a monkey. He grinned down. 'Now you, Jannah.'

The major stepped back hastily, obviously too embarrassed to lay hands on a girl, and gestured Vivian forward instead. Jannah climbed with a lot less confidence, but with Vivian pushing her up and Vince catching hold of her hands she was soon on the plinth.

After that it was the work of a moment to hand Colin up. Then Alice, whimpering – Maggie guessed Physical Training was not Alice's favourite subject – was pushed and pulled into position.

Maggie hauled herself up without too much struggle, her arms strong from digging up spuds. She straightened up. The podium, although long enough and wide enough for the bronze horse and its rider, seemed cramped with all five of them on it. But still, it was exhilarating to be so high up. Maggie looked around, suddenly aware of the summer sky. It had been nothing but a narrow strip above the high-sided streets, but over the open park it was a high blue dome, like it ought to be. There was even a hint of a breeze.

'Now,' Alice said. 'Stand back-to-back. Join hands.'

They all did, keeping carefully back from the edge. Maggie took Colin's hand on one side and Alice's on the other, but she wasn't paying much attention. They'd been trying the same thing all day, in a multitude of different places: holding hands and waiting for something to happen. The major and the two Wrens hanging over them, watching hungrily for the least flicker of power. But it was like trying to strike a wet match; they'd tried over and over again, but still, nothing.

She raised her face to the breath of wind, even though it brought a stale sort of smell that was probably the Thames. Laura and Vivian and the major seemed a long way down, their upturned faces small and rather absurd. Maggie looked away from them. There was blue sky above her and green all around; for a moment, it was like being at home. 'All right,' she heard Alice say. 'Everyone concentrate.'

And then, something happened.

Suddenly, the wind was strong. It rushed across the grass, set the trees nodding and hissing. Maggie felt heat surging through her, running from Alice's hand on the left into Colin's on the right. Her hair whipped up around her. Warmth pulsed into her hands, now from both sides at once: churning, making her stomach heave.

She cried out as she swayed, was aware of the others doing the same, buffeted by the wind. And by the energy trying to push itself through them.

'Clockwise,' hissed Alice. 'Think *clockwise*.'

Maggie concentrated: imagined stirring a bowl of water, down from her right and up to her left. *Clockwise*. The others must have been doing the same, because suddenly the warmth was flowing smoothly and comfortably, from her left hand to her right. They gripped each other's hands as the power – the magic – coursed easily through them like electricity through wire.

'Faster,' murmured Alice. Maggie thought, *Faster*, and pictured a Catherine wheel spinning. Yellow sparks, whirling. All day they'd been trying to no effect; now the power took off and flew like a kite in the wind. Maggie was dimly aware of the Wrens' and the major's upturned faces, but she closed her eyes and thought again: *faster, faster*. She imagined the Catherine wheel turning until the glow became a solid circle, so fast there was no sign of movement. The heat inside her stopped pulsing, became a constant glow. Maggie opened her eyes.

The world was changed. There was a sort of twilight over the buildings, the wall and the road. The grass and the trees were darkened too: dull and drab, as if the sky were overcast. But the people... shone. The two office workers on the bench had turned into shapes of light. The old couple were transformed too, full of yellow fire. The mother glowed saffron; the child on her lap was brightest of all, shining like a flame. Maggie could see people outside the square's wall, all pulsing golden-orange glows, as if she could see the warm life in them.

'My God,' Alice whispered. 'Witch-sight.'

Maggie turned to look at her and the others, and caught her breath. The other four flamed with life like the people below. But their light flared out beyond their own bodies, far beyond their own skin. Orange and yellow fire rippled out all around them.

There were white haloes around their joined hands. Maggie heard Vince laugh delightedly, and the golden brightness leapt as if he'd blown onto a fire.

'What can you see?' The voice came from below their feet, distracting their attention and making their light dim for a moment. It was one of the two Wrens; Maggie didn't know which one, and didn't much care. She glanced down to shoosh them. The three adults, like the people in the square, were full of the golden-orange glow. A little of the wavering light went beyond their own shapes, she saw; Vivian rather more than the other two. Although none of the three shone nearly as bright, Maggie noticed proudly, as the five young people on the statue's plinth. Maggie looked away from them: and saw what lay beyond. 'Oh,' she said, 'oh, *look*.'

A pathway of light lay across the grass. It cut across the little square, passing right through the plinth. It was yards across, and it glowed with the same light that surrounded them now – only much brighter. Maggie's eyes watered, blurred. She thought she could see movement on the shining path: figures moving. People walking along it, like it was a busy road. People in strange costumes – there were suggestions of long skirts, robes, even, she thought, furs and skins. People leaving some of their brightness behind, treading it into the ground. Dozens of people walking this line –

'What can you *see*? Answer me!'

The major's bark cut through her thoughts like an axe. She looked down at him, saw his red face staring back up excitedly. The flame around him dipped and vanished. Maggie swore and looked away. But the pathway of light faded, went out. She heard a cry of disappointment from Alice, a curse from Vince. Maggie's eyes watered again, painfully.

When she opened them again, the square was in normal daylight again. The light around the people was gone. The world was ordinary again.

Vince glared down at the major. 'What the bloody hell did you do that for?'

'Mind your language, young man!'

'You stupid, stuck-up git!'

'Did you hear what I—'

'Colin?' Maggie said sharply. Colin's hand had tightened on hers. All the colour had gone out of his face. 'Are you all right?'

'Freya,' Colin said. *'Schöne göttin.Kürerin der Erschlagenen.'*

'Colin!'

He swayed. *'Die schöne Göttin ist in Tränen.'*

Maggie pulled her fingers out of Colin's grip, and grabbed onto his right arm. 'Help me,' she said to Vince, who was on Colin's other side. She crouched down, just as Colin toppled forward. He was going to pull them both off the edge. Then Vince was beside her; he had grabbed Colin's right wrist. Colin fell heavily, nearly pulling their arms out of their sockets; they held him dangling, until the major reached him and threw his arms around him. He lowered the unconscious boy to the ground.

Maggie scrambled down the smooth sides of the plinth, dropping the last five feet and landing jarringly on the solid path. She pushed past Vivian and Laura, lifted her brother into her arms. 'Colin?'

His eyelids fluttered. 'Freya,' he said. *'Schöne göttin. Freya.'*

Vivian inhaled sharply. 'Did he say *Freya*?'

'He's just having one of his turns,' Maggie snapped.

Vivian ignored her. 'That's German. Laura, you know German – what's he saying?'

Colin's voice rose. *'Schöne göttin. Freya. Die schöne Göttin ist in Tränen.'*

'*Bright goddess,*' Laura translated. '*Goddess beautiful in tears. Freya.*'

There was a thump behind them as someone else descended from the plinth. 'That's the Edda,' Alice said.

Maggie glared at her. 'The what?'

'The Edda. Old Germanic verse about the gods. The Nazis think it's sacred...' She appeared at Maggie's elbow; her voice trailed off when she saw Colin's pallid face. 'Colin?'

Colin had gone limp. Vince and Jannah appeared behind Alice. 'Is the little one all right?' Jannah said.

Laura, Vivian and the major didn't seem to hear. They were staring at each other. 'There's another group of witches,' Laura said. 'A German group.'

'And they're channelling a goddess,' Vivian said.

The major swore. 'Mrs Ogilvie has to be told about this. Now. Go and find a telephone.'

Laura and Vivian left, almost at a run. The major looked around, noticed a small crowd gathering. All the people from the park benches – the office workers and the old couple and the mother – were converging on them, muttering curiously. The major swore again. 'There's nothing to see here,' he snapped. 'The boy's been taken ill...'

He got up, went to talk to the crowd, leaving the five young wizards together. Colin's eyes started to flutter. Vince snapped his fingers in front of Colin's face. 'Col? You with us, mate?'

Colin's eyes finally opened. 'Mags?' he croaked.

'It's all right.' She realised she'd been holding her breath, let it out in a whoosh. 'You just had one of your turns.'

'I heard them talking, Mags. It was coming out of my own mouth, I couldn't help it...' His voice faded to a hoarse whisper.

Alice rummaged in her gas mask carrier, handed Maggie a bottle of lemonade. 'Here, give him something to drink.'

Maggie nodded her thanks, put the bottle to Colin's lips. Then she looked around for the major; but he was still talking to the small crowd. 'No, madam, there's no need for a doctor. The boy's just a little... well, the heat, you know...'

'Silly old bugger,' Vince said.

'We need to get away from them.' Alice's voice was cold, unlike any tone they'd heard her use before. 'Right away.'

'What do you mean?' Jannah said.

'We need to get away from them, away from all of them. They're distracting us. We need to be alone.'

'They will not leave us alone.'

Alice shrugged. 'Then we'll have to run away from them.'

Vince grinned. 'Now you're talking!'

'That would be foolish,' Jannah said. She looked at Maggie for support. 'Do you not think so?'

Maggie looked from Colin's peaky face to the major's back. She thought how he and the two Wrens had been very interested in what Colin was saying, but not bothered to check he was all right. And when their mother heard what happened, would she be any different? Maggie didn't think so. 'Yes,' she said. 'Let's get away from them.'

Chapter Nine
The Shining Path

Night-time silence fell on the ministry building. If Maggie had walked into the large third floor room, the one where she had met Alice and Vince and Jannah, she would hardly have recognised it. The chairs had been cleared out, the carpet rolled back, and the curtains firmly drawn against the darkness. Seven-branched candelabra, tall enough for a cathedral, stood against every wall. The blonde Wren moved between them, lighting the thick creamy candles with a taper. The swish of her long white robes was the only sound in the hushed room. An incense burner hung from the ceiling; white clouds tumbled from it slowly, thickening the air and making the candlelight hazy.

A pentangle – a five-pointed star – had been chalked carefully onto the bare floorboards. Three robed figures stood around it, motionless and silent; a fourth occupied the star's centre. No one moved but the blonde Wren, who now lit the last candle and snuffed out the taper. She crossed to the east side of the room, where an altar swathed in dark blue cloth stood against the far wall. Above it hung a white satin banner: the banner of the East, printed with a cross and a Tau and a six-pointed star. The small altar was laden with gleaming objects. The blonde Wren lifted a heavy gold disc like a large coin; holding it reverently in both hands, she steered her way, clockwise, around the pentangle. She took her place beside the curtained windows, at the tip of the star's south-western point.

Only then did the others move. The major, who was standing at the pentangle's northern point, paced clockwise around the star to the altar; he picked up a short sword, and moved clockwise back to his place. Then Laura moved away from the chalked star, out from under the black flag of the West with its scarlet cross and white triangle; she collected a silver chalice from the altar, slowly made her way back to the pentangle's western point. Finally Vivian stepped out from under the white banner of the East: took a painted wand from the altar, returned to the pentangle's eastern point, and waited.

They all waited. Their white linen robes hung limp in the airless room; silver embroidery glimmered in the diffuse light. Then all at once, like well-rehearsed dancers, they lifted the precious objects in their hands, and raised their eyes to the figure at the pentangle's centre.

Miriam Ogilvie was absolutely still. Her long white robe, thick with gold embroidery, shimmered; her dark red hair was loose about her shoulders. She was staring at the huge gilded mirror which stood at the pentangle's fifth point. Her own dark eyes stared back at her, motionless. For a long minute, the others waited.

Then Miriam drew a deep breath. She raised her right hand, her long, wide sleeve sliding back from her bare arm. From the folds of fabric emerged a silver double-sided dagger: an athame. Miriam raised the dagger in front of her face, its tip inches from her forehead. When at last she spoke, the word vibrated around the room: '*Ateh.*'

She moved the athame downwards, level with her navel. One of the others exhaled as a pale line of light trailed after the dagger's point and hung in mid-air. Miriam said: '*Malkuth.*' Then she raised the knife to her right shoulder: '*Ve-Gevurah.*' The others sighed as she moved the athame again, tracing a faint yellow light to her left shoulder: '*Ve-Gedulah.*' She moved the knife to her breast, to the centre of the cross of light that had formed in front of her; she clasped her left hand over her right: *'Leolahm. Amen.'* The Cabbalistic Cross flared briefly, then faded out.

Miriam closed her eyes for a moment. When she opened them she turned swiftly, her gilded robes glittering, to the east: to Vivian. Vivian lifted the wand in her hand: a slim hazel wand, carved with spirals and painted blue and silver. Miriam raised the athame and pointed it at the wand.

'Before me, Air.' Her voice was no more than a whisper. Then it echoed back from every corner of the room: *'Raph-ae-el.'*

The wand quivered; the silver symbols shimmered. A faint breeze lifted Vivian's sleeves and wafted across the circle, swirling the incense. Miriam spun around to the west, to Laura and the silver chalice. 'Behind me, Water,' Miriam whispered. Then she said, and the word vibrated: *'Gab-ri-el.'*

The silver goblet flashed like sunlight on a stream. Now the breeze was cool and fresh and damp. Miriam turned again, to her right: to the north, where the major stood. The major lifted up the sword. It was made of silver and gold, symbols traced on its pommel in red-gold and copper. Miriam pointed the athame at it and said, 'To my right hand, Fire. *Mich-ae-el.'*

Flames burst out of the sword's tip. The major flinched but kept his grip on the gold pommel as fire enveloped the silver blade. Warm air swept over them all. Miriam turned again, robes flaring out around her, to her left: the south-west. The blond Wren held up the golden disc: a pentacle, etched with a five-sided star. Miriam said: 'To my left hand, Earth. *Au-ri-el,'* and the room was full of the rich smell of turned soil.

Miriam turned at last to the final point of the pentangle: the south-east. The direction of Germany. She gazed into her own dark eyes in the mirror. 'Spirit all around me,' she murmured. Then the others raised their voices with hers: *'A-don-ae-i!'*

A pinpoint of light appeared at the centre of the mirror. It grew, turned into a swirling glow. The others gasped aloud; but Miriam kept her gaze on the light. 'Yes,' she said. 'Show me.'

The glowing circle expanded, still turning, growing wider with each turn. In the centre was an image, blurred and opaque, as if they were looking through frosted glass. Miriam raised her voice: 'Show me!'

The image sharpened. It was still out of focus, but now they could make out a room: a round chamber, with high windows and some kind of circular design set into the marble floor. Figures moved across it. Light and quick figures: young figures.

Vivian made a groaning sound. Miriam glanced at her, to silence her. But Vivian was swaying where she stood. She stared ahead, her eyes unfocused. She began to mumble: her gruff voice had turned light, youthful. *'Was, nehmen Sie an, tun sie jetzt grade?'*

German. Miriam nodded at Laura, who translated: *'What are they doing now, do you suppose?'*

Vivian's voice changed: became deeper, more confident. *'Sie schlafen wahrscheinlich. Wie gute kleine kinder.'*

Laura translated: 'They're probably sleeping, like good little children.'

Vivian laughed. No sound came from the mirror; but the figures there were obviously laughing. One of them, the tallest, was talking – his lips moved silently in the glass. Vivian began to speak: *'Sie werden nicht begeistert...'*

Laura spoke over her: 'They are not inspired. They have no great cause, as we do. That is why they cannot succeed.'

One of the others in the mirror stepped forward, interrupting. Vivian's voice changed. Its tone was flat, ugly. Laura translated: 'What about the Jewess? She will stop us if she can.'

'Das kann sie nicht.' The confident voice was back. 'She cannot stand against destiny. She cannot fight against *Freya.'*

The blond Wren hissed. Miriam ignored her and kept her gaze on the mirror. The figures there had all appeared to be male; but now they stood back, and an obviously female shape came forward, light skirts fluttering around her.

The female figure began to speak. Vivian staggered slightly as her voice cracked in two. There were two voices speaking, one high and one low, although no one else in the mirror-room seemed to be talking. Laura, her voice shaking, translated: 'There is nothing to fear. They will do as we expected them to do, they – but—'

Laura broke off, aghast, as the double voice coming from Vivian's mouth began to speak clear, slightly accented English. 'But who are you? Spying on us? Who?'

The female figure in the mirror was staring straight at them. The round chamber and its inhabitants faded out; they were replaced by two glowing points of sapphire light. Neon-blue eyes. Vivian swayed as the echoing voice came out of her mouth: 'I see you! I *see* you!'

Miriam shook herself, managed to speak. 'Who are you? What do you—'

The double voice was growing louder: 'Don't you know better? At your age? Don't you know it's rude to *spy?*'

'*Ateh.*' Miriam raised the athame to her forehead, drew it quickly down to her navel. '*Malkuth.*' A faint line of light appeared as the protective cross began to form. But before she could lift the double-edged blade to her shoulder, it snapped in her hand like dry wood. Vivian burst into peals of girlish laughter. 'What are you doing with that little knife? What is that trash you are all holding?'

Hot, dry air gusted through the room. It seemed to be coming out of the mirror. Miriam and the others staggered back, their robes swirling around them. Vivian's eyes snapped wide open, but the terrible voice was still spilling out of her mouth. 'Look at you all! Don't you look *silly!*'

Miriam reached out to the mirror, but the gale-force wind rocked her back on her heels. The banners of the East and West flapped wildly, then came loose from the ceiling and flew like runaway kites until they hit the far wall. The blond Wren shrieked as the incense burner was pulled from its chains and crashed to the floor. The candelabra tottered and fell onto the bare floor boards, extinguishing the candles as they fell. Now the only light came from the swirling glow in the mirror. Miriam struggled to stay on her feet, her loose robe moulded against her body. She threw away the broken knife, touched her right shoulder with her finger tips. '*Ve-Gedulah.*'

'Oh, won't you all put those silly toys down?' The blue eyes in the mirror flashed. The sacred regalia, the wand and the chalice and the sword and the pentacle, were wrenched from their holders' hands and went spinning across the floor. 'Your children may be silly, but even they don't use that rubbish! Are you so old and worn-out that you actually *need* such things?'

There were other voices now, boys' voices, a dozen of them: laughing. The room was full of the laughter of children. Gleefully mocking laughter, sounding like a class with an inadequate teacher. Miriam reached up to touch her left shoulder; the glowing line vanished instantly, but she cried out: '*Ve-Gedulah!*'

'Oh, very well. We're going.' The voice was starting to sound bored. 'We know our manners. We must respect the wishes of the old.'

Vivian was staggering, barely keeping her feet. Blood started to run from her nostrils. Her eyes darted wildly from side to side, but still her mouth moved. 'But we shall see you again, yes? You too must learn respect. You must learn to respect Freya!'

Vivian fell to her knees. The mirror flashed bright blue, then cracked across with a sound like gunfire. Miriam, still on her feet, brought her hands to her breast and cried out, '*Leolahm, Amen!* Leave us alone, be gone!'

There was a last girlish giggle, and the blue eyes vanished. Vivian toppled forwards as the light in the broken mirror winked out. The room fell into darkness. There was no sound but harsh breathing, and muffled sobbing from one of the Wrens.

Then a tiny light flared. The major stood, cupping his hand

around the lit match. He crossed quickly to the wall and snapped on the light. In the hard electric glow they could all see the devastation: the toppled candelabra, the banners lying crumpled on the floor. The dark-blue altar cloth had been blown across the room, revealing the altar as just a crude wooden table. And the regalia, the wand and the chalice and the sword and the pentacle, were scattered against the far wall. Miriam ran to gather them up; but then she paused to look at them, lying on the wooden floor, as if she were seeing them for the first time. *Silly toys*, that's what the voice had called them. Useless things, rubbish...

She turned at a groan behind her. Vivian was struggling to sit up. Blood smeared her face and was spattered all over her white robe. Laura cried out and ran to her, followed by the major and the blond Wren. They sat her up, tipped her head forward. Laura pinched her nostrils closed. Vivian struggled weakly for a moment, then gave herself over to her friends' care as the nosebleed began to slow.

Miriam took a deep breath, stood up straight. She looked at the blond Wren. 'Go and check on the children,' she said.

The blond Wren, who was still holding Vivian upright, looked at Miriam and shook her head slightly: she didn't want to leave her. Miriam's voice rose: 'The children. My children and the other three. *They* know about them, *they've* seen them! Go and check on them, now!'

The blond Wren shifted her share of Vivian's weight into the major's arms, scrambled to her feet, and left the room at a run. Miriam went to the others, almost tripping over a piece of her robe the wind had ripped apart. She knelt down in front of Vivian. 'Listen to me, Vivian.'

Laura murmured a protest, but Vivian opened her eyes. She brushed Laura's hand away, raised her sleeve to wipe her face. 'Mrs Ogilvie.'

'A goddess,' Miriam said. 'I'm right, aren't I?'

Vivian nodded. 'Freya.'

'Freya?' asked the major.

'The Viking goddess,' Vivian said. 'Goddess of love and war.'

'Love *and* war?' He looked at Miriam and Laura for confirmation.

'That's the Vikings for you,' muttered Laura, and she and the major laughed shakily.

Miriam and Vivian didn't laugh. 'That girl,' Miriam said. 'It's goddess-energy. She's channelling a goddess.'

'Poor kid,' Vivian said.

Miriam shrugged impatiently. 'Poor us.' She stood, looked around. 'We need to prepare.' She nodded towards the door, towards the upstairs rooms, where she'd put the five young wizards to bed hours before. '*They* need to prepare. There's so much they need to know.'

Footsteps pounded down the stairs. The blond Wren burst in, her face as pale as Vivian's. 'They're not in their beds,' she said. 'I can't find them anywhere. They're gone.'

The bus bumped its way slowly through the darkened streets. Maggie tightened her grip on the rail as they swayed around a corner. She was reminding herself firmly that she was seventeen now, she could do what she liked. She tried to suppress the part of herself thinking, *Mum's going to kill me.*

The others didn't seem to share her misgivings. Alice sat calmly in the seat in front of Maggie, her blue eyes determined. Jannah sat beside Alice looking worried, but Colin sat trustingly by Maggie; and Vince didn't seem to have a care in the world. Of course, Maggie thought, they wouldn't be the ones getting into trouble: she would, it was always the oldest.

She looked around the bus's lower deck. The seats were worn and threadbare. The windows were criss-crossed with strips of brown tape: blast tape, to stop flying glass. Maggie couldn't see a thing. The windows were coated with grime on the outside anyway – if dirt was blast-proof, this would be the best armoured bus in London – and the strips of tape made it even harder to see out. In lots of places people had peeled back the tape at eye-level, ignoring the stern notices all around: *I trust you'll pardon my correction, That stuff is there for your protection.* Someone had pulled the tape right back from Maggie's window anyway, and had written on it in pencil: *I trust you'll hear my explanation, I can't see the bloody station.* Even so Maggie couldn't see a thing, and wouldn't have known where she was going even if she could. She asked Vince: 'Is it much further now?'

'Nah, just a couple more stops,' Vince said carelessly. He didn't even glance out of the window. Vince always knew where he was going. He was sitting sprawled casually across two seats, as relaxed as if he were in his own front room. The bus's only other passenger, an old man in a coat and flat cap, turned to scowl at him sometimes. Vince seemed to have that effect on people. Vince ignored him, was too busy turning round in his seat to smile at Jannah. 'All right, Jan?'

Jannah did not look all right. Her face was tense and sallow in the artificial light. 'I still do not think that this is a good plan,' she said.

Alice shook her head. 'It's the only thing to do, Jannah.'

'Yeah, Jannah.' Vince grinned at her. He sat up, kneeling on the seat to face her, so his feet were jammed against the chair behind. 'Don't worry. I'll look after you.'

The old man was glaring at Vince's feet on the upholstery. 'Did no one ever tell you to keep your mucky feet off the furniture?'

Vince didn't look at him. 'No, mate, you're the first.'

Colin giggled. The old man's face flushed. 'You cheeky little sod.'

'Get lost, grandad,' said Vince.

Time to get off. Maggie stood up and rang the bell. 'We can

walk from here,' she said.

The bus ground to a halt, and Maggie pulled Colin off the rear platform. The old man was shouting something after Vince, who waved and jumped down onto the pavement, Jannah and Alice close behind. The bus revved up and trundled away, leaving them in the dark. They stood blind for a moment, eyes adjusting. Alice whispered, 'Oh my goodness, I can't see a thing.'

'What's the hold-up?' Vince was walking away – Maggie could just see his face like a white balloon bobbing in the darkness. Something pale waved at them: his hand, beckoning. 'Come on!'

'We'd better hold hands,' Maggie said. She had been talking to Colin, but Vince said, 'Good idea,' and his hand grabbed towards the greyish shape that was resolving into Jannah. Then he was pulling Jannah away; Maggie grabbed at her, felt the rough wool of her sleeve, before Jannah's sweating fingers closed on hers. Maggie squeezed them reassuringly, tightened her grip on Colin's hand and let Vince tow them away, leaving Alice to catch hold of Colin's other arm. 'Wait, not so quickly!' Alice wailed, but they were already being drawn away into the gloom.

Vince pulled them sharply round a corner. Maggie could now make out shapes, railings and walls. Then her feet were on soft ground: grass. A breath of wind blew, and the dark blurs above became swaying tree-branches. They were in the little park. After a few moments a white shape loomed in front of them: the statue's plinth. 'Up we go then,' said Vince.

The others peered upwards. It was one thing to climb the plinth in daylight; now they could barely see the top. 'We should've brought a ladder this time,' Maggie said. She was annoyed to hear her voice quaver. 'I mean, it would have been better.'

'Scaredy-cat,' Vince jeered.

Maggie bristled. 'You go up, then.'

'Don't mind if I do.' Vince rubbed his hands together, bent his knees and jumped, grabbing onto the top of the plinth. He hung there: 'Give us a bunk-up, then!'

Maggie and Jannah grabbed a foot each and pushed. Vince scrambled up, turned around and reached down. One by one, they clambered up, more hesitant than last time. Once she was at the top, Maggie was even more reluctant to stand up. The ground was lost in the dark, and in her imagination it was a very long way down. But she wouldn't have Vince laughing at her, so she clambered to her feet. 'What do we do now?'

'What we did before.' Alice's voice was calm now, determined. Maggie felt Alice's plump little hand taking hold of hers. 'Form a circle.'

'What about Colin? What if he…' Jannah didn't have the English words, '…is – ill again?'

'He'll be fine. Join hands.' They were back-to-back now, holding hands. Maggie tightened her grip on Colin, drawing him back from the edge. 'If you're going to faint, tell me—'

It happened suddenly this time. The wind hit them hard out of the darkness, making Jannah cry out in fright. The trees hissed and thrashed around. Maggie's hands were hot, her stomach heaved. She thought quickly, *clockwise*. The warmth began to pulse smoothly, left to right.

Power circled obediently around the joined hands of the little coven. Maggie shut her eyes on the blackness. She could hear Alice murmuring something – a spell? '*The world is charged with the grandeur of God… it will flame out, like shining from shook foil…*'

Not a spell: a poem. One of Gran's favourites, Maggie knew it at once. She joined in: '*It gathers to a greatness, like the ooze of oil crushed… Why do men then now not reck his rod… Generations have trod, have trod, have trod…*'

Maggie stopped, forgetting the rest. But it didn't matter; the others were repeating it now, '*Generations have trod, have trod, have trod… have trod, have trod, have trod…*'

Maggie opened her eyes. The world was bright with witch-sight, the twilight hanging over the buildings and the trees. The shining path stretched across the grass. It led west, towards the river. Figures walked along it as before, in robes or in suits or in rags and skins. *Generations have trod, have trod.* Figures full of light, part of this ground forever, for those who had the eyes to see.

'Come on,' Alice said. She pulled her hand away from Maggie's. Maggie tried to grab it back, not wanting to break the circuit. But the path stayed in place, and the figures still walked. Maggie looked at the other wizards, glowing on the marble plinth. Alice shone particularly bright, almost white with determination. 'Let's go,' she said, and lowered herself fearlessly over the side of the plinth.

The others hurried after her, after her brightness. They stepped onto the shining path. Maggie felt warmth bloom through her body, as if she'd just heard wonderful news. Light was in her and all around her. She lifted her hand, laughed as she watched the glow stream through her fingers. She looked at the others and laughed again. They were all light and fire. They could do anything.

For a while they just stood, watching the silent, radiant figures walk past. They saw a cluster of men in monk's robes, their lips moving in a chant, holding up a crucifix that shone bright gold. A group of people in black and white, the women's heads covered, mouthing songs. Then a file of men and women in white; their long robes were embroidered with archaic-looking symbols, but the women had modern hairstyles and some of the men wore glasses. They sang too, as they moved in procession along the shining path.

'Let's go,' Alice said again. They turned and followed the white-gold robes. Their footprints shone like molten copper for a moment, then faded into the path's haze of light. They didn't hold hands as they moved; they didn't have to, the power flowed in and out, warm as sunshine. On they went without a word, treading the path after the robes and long skirts and skins.

On they went in a ringing silence. The little park, the street and its buildings, went past like a dream. Once a man in a tin helmet and a siren-suit – an air-raid warden – crossed right in front of them, full of the red-orange glow of life, blind to everything in the London blackout. They stopped and held their breath, but he passed on oblivious, and vanished into the twilight.

'Ah, look,' whispered Jannah, as they emerged from the street and the Thames opened out in front of them. Another path – wider, brighter – cut across theirs at right angles, following the line of the river. The path they were walking went straight over the river-bank, out across the water; the faint lines of a crude wooden bridge stretched out over the Thames, fading out into the half-light. Up ahead some of the walkers, the monks with the golden cross, stepped out onto the bridge and melted away. The more recent figures, the robed ones with the glasses and the Olympic-waved hair, paused, then wheeled around to the left and set out again.

Alice led the coven to the centre of the crossroads. Maggie thought it was like wading waist-deep into a river, feeling the current push against her. She turned to the left. There was a light in the distance, a dull orange glow. Alice moved towards it; but then fell back, lifting a hand to point, staring to the right.

Another group was moving towards them. There were no rich embroidered robes here. The five figures were short, dressed in dull shades, in rags overlapped with tatty fur. But they were so bright, so clear. Their mouths were open, but they weren't singing; they were wailing. The other figures on the shining path had all been silent, but Maggie and the others could hear their wordless voices, their high, thin keening.

Colin covered his ears with his hands. Maggie pulled him back as the group drew closer. There were four men: bearded, in rough tunics. Their hair was long and uncombed, pulled back into thick matted locks. Their arms and chests were bare, their wrists knotted with leather cords. Inky blue shapes were daubed on their foreheads. They were young, Maggie realised, not much older than she was.

A woman walked in front of them. A girl, Maggie corrected herself, no older than Jannah. Her long, loose hair was poppy-red, dark at the roots. Her arms were covered in elaborate traceries of blue-black; a staring eye, wonderfully detailed, had been painted on her forehead. There was a copper torque around her neck. Her feet were bare. Her mouth was open, howling.

The four men held a stretcher of skins at shoulder-height, like coffin-bearers. Maggie heard Colin whimper as he saw what the men were carrying. A severed head: bearded, long-haired, dead eyes glassy and torn skin ragged around the stump of the neck.

Maggie and the others stood back, watching as the group walked past. Vince pointed at them, shaking, but said nothing. Jannah was crying silently. Alice's lips moved, tried to form words, finally croaked out, 'Brandt. The head of *Brandt*.'

Maggie moved to put her hand over Alice's mouth, to shush her. But the five figures hadn't reacted to Alice's voice. They were only images, Maggie thought, they couldn't hear, they were only pictures. She watched them move away, forced herself to speak. 'We should…' her voice failed, she cleared her throat and tried again – '…we should follow them.'

'S'right,' mumbled Vince. No one else spoke. They just stood watching Brandt's men carry his head away. In the end Maggie took hold of Colin with one hand and Jannah with the other, and nudged Alice and Vince along the path as if they were nervous sheep. This got everyone moving at least. They followed, slow as a funeral, after the five keening figures in furs and skins.

Along the Embankment they walked, along the broad shining path. Sometimes other figures emerged, faintly, in all manner of long skirts and cloaks and robes. But the five they were following were so bright, the rest faded out like over-exposed photographs. Maggie and the others passed under the elaborate lamp-posts, unlit in the blackout, but clear to them in their witch-twilight. The river moved sluggishly. Brandt's people kept their halting pace. At last Colin said, in quite a normal voice, 'Do you think they're a coven too?'

Alice cleared her throat. 'I think so. They're young. Powerful,' she added with an unmistakable note of satisfaction, 'like us.'

Vince was looking at the scarlet-haired girl who led the group. 'Is she the boss, then' he whispered.

'Oh, I think so.' Alice sounded even more satisfied. 'The women usually are.'

Vince snorted in displeasure. 'That right?'

'Oh, yes, it's—'

'What is that?' Jannah's voice was worried again. 'This… wall?'

Vince didn't even have to look. 'Tower of London, innit.'

They fell silent, watching Brandt's people move towards the dark bulk ahead. The familiar turrets of the tower shimmered in the twilight. Sometimes they looked solid; sometimes they wavered, the lines blurred, before they reformed again. Maggie didn't want to look at it. It was the Tower of London, the Bloody Tower. She didn't want to see what walked the path there. The shining line led straight to a high dense stone wall; she was relieved when the five figures ahead of them simply walked through the wall and vanished.

They stood for a while. The witch-sight held; the night sky over the river was twilit. Even so, the world seemed duller, less vivid without the five they'd been following. Maggie was aware of the smell of the river, the sound of a bus rumbling in the distance. 'Well,' she said, 'what do we do now – '

There was a smell like copper; a feeling like electricity crawling on their skin, raising the hair on the backs of their necks. The wind was hot and dry, so sudden and strong it sent them staggering. Light blazed from the wall, a ruddy glow as if the stones were burning. A figure, solitary, carrying something solid, walked out through the wall onto the path.

It was the girl, the girl with scarlet hair. She was older, Maggie saw, maybe ten years older; her clothes were even more ragged. Her hair was still red, but the black at the roots was tinged with grey.

One of her teeth was missing. They could see that at once, because her mouth was open, wide open.

A shriek split the silence. The girl was screaming, howling. She held up both hands, clutching something bone-white. A skull, with strands of long hair still attached to its smooth crown. Light poured from it, but the five young wizards could barely see it, because the girl was at the centre of a firestorm. She burned like a coal in a furnace. She lit the night.

And her eyes, oh her eyes. They were blank, and wholly black, but outlined with white-hot light. Maggie turned away, but still saw them. She grabbed Colin, and whoever was on her other side – Vince, she didn't care – and fell to her knees, dragging them both with her. She clapped her hand over Colin's eyes. 'Don't look. Don't look at her!'

She shut her eyes, but could still see the girl's eyes in the darkness, burning. So she opened her own and stared at the ground, at the crack in the pavement, keeping her gaze fixed to it. The others were kneeling around her. Maggie saw the girl's feet – bare, soles bloody – walk past. She felt those dreadful eyes sweep over them, lift and pass on.

After a long moment, Maggie looked up. The poppy-haired girl was walking the path. She didn't turn, thank God, but kept walking along the bank of the river. The twilight wavered and pulsed around her fiery light.

Maggie looked up at her companions. Jannah was sobbing and shaking. Vince was ghastly pale, swaying where he knelt. Alice had lost the little colour she had had. Maggie thought Alice must be crying too, because her nose was running; but then she saw it was blood, oozing from both nostrils. And Colin? Maggie turned to him urgently; but although he was pale, he was quite composed. He said, matter-of-factly: 'That was the Morrigan.'

Vince shook his head. 'It was her. It was that same girl we saw before.'

'Yes,' Colin conceded, 'but it was the Morrigan as well.'

Alice wiped her nose impatiently. 'We need to follow her,' she said.

'No,' said Jannah.

'We don't have a choice.'

She was right. Maggie took Jannah's hand. 'Come on.'

They followed the burning girl, at a distance. She followed the path that ran beside the river. She seemed to have a hundred voices, all screaming. Her howls drilled into their ears. Jannah kept sobbing. More blood splashed onto Alice's blouse, no matter how often she wiped her face. Maggie fought to keep calm; but she thought that if the figure ahead turned round, and she had to see those eyes again, she would run. She would leave the others behind – even Colin, yes, even him – and run.

Then the girl – the Morrigan – turned right, away from the river. She followed an intersecting path. Her howling rose to a piercing shriek. The light around the Morrigan intensified; she screamed as if she were on fire. Then she vanished.

Jannah gasped with relief. Maggie loosened her hand, which she realised was gripping Colin's painfully tight. The shining path wasn't gone, though. It led to a bank of light, a broad tower hundreds of feet high. The structure's façade seemed ornate, but their eyes were too dazzled to see clearly. The place was the end-point of countless shining paths, which criss-crossed an open square. Countless figures, in all sorts of clothes and costumes, walked towards the convergence of the paths, to the tower of light.

'That's', Vince's voice was high and hoarse. He cleared his throat and tried again. 'That's Westminster Abbey.'

'That's where the skull is,' Alice said.

The shining paths vanished. They were back in the dark, everyday, wartime world again. The tower of light was now in darkness.

Westminster Abbey.

Chapter Ten

The Traitor

The abbey's great door squealed as Maggie eased it open. They all froze, waiting for adult voices to order them to stop. Maggie counted to thirty, her hand on Colin's shoulder to stop him running inside. But nothing happened. After a moment Alice pushed past her; Vince muttered something and followed. Maggie eased through the barely-open door, drawing Colin after her. At last Jannah, still reluctant, followed the others inside.

They stopped after just a few paces. Every footstep echoed as if they were wearing iron shoes. The vast open space of the nave amplified every sound. Maggie looked around carefully in the artificial light, barely recognising what she saw. She'd only ever been to the abbey in daylight, when the stained glass windows filled its vast spaces with light and colour; when the footsteps and murmurs of a hundred tourists echoed around the huge stone pillars and rose up to the sky-high ceiling. Now the nave had the grubby, utilitarian look of the rest of wartime London. The walls had been stripped of the ancient flags and banners, spirited away for safekeeping, presumably, with the city's statues. The windows were boarded over with yards of rough planks; the only light came from yellowish gas lamps. The lingering scent of incense and chilly stone mixed with a gritty smell, as they tiptoed forwards, Maggie noticed there were piles of sandbags under the covered windows.

From somewhere inside came the murmur of adult voices and the hiss of a tea-urn. Vince nodded, whispered: 'There's a fire-watch station.'

Maggie looked around. 'Where?'

'In the Pyx Chapel.' When the others looked at him blankly he gestured impatiently to the north-east; Vince could never quite believe no one else shared his encyclopaedic knowledge of London. 'You know. Through the cloisters.'

Alice nodded and started forwards. Evidently the cloisters were some distance away. 'Come on, then,' she said. 'But quietly.'

They crept forwards, up the wide aisle. Stone columns rose on either side, vaster than tree trunks; the ceiling was lost in the dim lighting. A black tombstone, smooth and shiny as water, was set into the stone floor; automatically they steered around it, not wanting to step on anyone's grave. Up ahead they could see polished wooden seating to the left and right: the choir. Beyond that must be the high altar, but it was lost in the gloom. Jannah whispered timidly, 'Where do you think the skull will be?'

They stopped again, staring at the vast space around them. Narrowing the search down to the abbey's precincts no longer felt like such an achievement. 'Well,' Alice said at last, 'Brandt was a king. It's probably in a king's tomb.'

Vince turned to glare at her. 'Half the kings of England are buried here. Which one?'

'I'm not – sure…'

'Henry the Seventh? Edward the Confessor? Elizabeth bloody Tudor?'

'I don't *know!*'

'Keep it down!' Maggie waved at them frantically. The adult voices in the distance had stopped. They all froze in the middle of the wide aisle. After a moment, the voices started up again. The five wizards remembered to breathe. 'So now what?'

Colin began to murmur in a sing-song voice, 'They buried him among the kings, because he had done good toward God and his house.'

'Shoosh, Colin.' Maggie was thinking: *we'll have to go back. Tell Mum what we've found out. It would be enough, wouldn't it?* 'We'd best get going.'

'Yes,' said Jannah, turning back to the door.

'No.' Alice was shaking her head. 'We can do this. It's for us to do…'

'Greater love hath no man than this,' Colin said.

Alice blinked. 'What are you talking about?'

'Unknown and yet well known,' said Colin. 'Look, Maggie.'

They all turned to look at him. He was crouched beside the black tombstone set into the floor. His finger was running along the gold script carved into the black marble. He read aloud: 'Unknown and yet well known, dying and behold we live.' He looked up, his eyes huge and solemn behind his glasses. 'Look, Maggie.'

Maggie went over to him, read the first part of the inscription. 'Beneath this stone rests the body of a British warrior unknown by name or rank.'

'It's the grave of the Unknown Soldier.' Vince's voice was impatient. 'So what? He wasn't a king.'

'No.' Alice's voice rose with excitement. 'No, but he was a sacrifice.'

'He died in the Great War.'

'Look.' Alice was staring avidly at the middle of the tombstone. 'Listen to what it says about him. He gave the most that man can give, life itself. He sacrificed himself.' She took a deep shuddering breath. 'The Skull's here!'

'Don't be a twit,' Vince said. 'The Unknown Soldier's only been here since 1920 or something.'

'Why do you think they put him here?'

'What?'

'Why do you think they put the whole *abbey* here?'

'Eh?'

'The ground!' Alice pressed her hand against the black marble, as if she wanted to push all the way through to the earth beneath. 'The ground!'

Vince shook his head. 'She's gone off her nut.'

'No.' Maggie was thinking about the Mound. The stone. The ground kept things. Places remembered. 'She's right. It must be here.' She stepped forward onto the grave, balancing carefully on the glassy marble. She took Colin's hand, reached out to Alice. 'Come on.'

Alice eagerly joined her on the tombstone, grabbing Vince and hauling him forward. He shrugged, reached out to Jannah, whose arms were wrapped around her chest as if she were cold. After a long moment she came slowly forward, reaching out to Vince on one side and Colin on the other. 'I do not think this ground should be disturbed—'

Her hands touched the two boys', completing the circle. The power slammed through them all, tightening their clasped hands. Jannah cried out as white light engulfed them, arcing up from the tomb like a searchlight. Maggie tried to pull her hands away, but they were locked into Colin's and Alice's. Alice's grip was getting tighter. Maggie tried to shake her off: 'Let go!'

'It's all right.' Alice was smiling, her blue eyes rapturous. 'Just look. *Look.*'

Maggie made herself be calm, still. Now she saw there were figures in the light, distinct but outlined in gold. Two young men in uniform, climbing out of a deep trench into a blasted landscape. Maggie could hear no sound, just a buzzing in her ears as the power pulsed from hand to hand around the circle. But the two men reacted to something they heard, turning suddenly. Then one stepped swiftly in front of the other. His chest exploded in a red mess, and he fell back into the arms of the man behind.

The scene shifted. Now the dead man lay on a stone floor, pale and stiff, dressed in a fresh uniform. He was surrounded by other uniformed bodies. An older man was looking from one to the next – a faint aura of power glowed around him. The older man muttered a few words. The dead man lit up in a blaze of white. The older man nodded, pointed at him, mouthed: *That one.*

The scene shifted again; to the abbey, to the very spot where Maggie and the others now stood. People were approaching slowly, carrying the dead man's coffin, which blazed white. The dead man's body was set in place in the abbey, secured by the familiar slab of black marble.

But the wizards had seen how the grave was glowing long before the coffin was in place. The Unknown Soldier's light met and merged with it: masked it. So anyone who looked with the Sight would see the poor dead boy with the ruined chest, but not what lay beneath.

The vision ended. The five wizards staggered back from the grave, gasping as if they'd been underwater. The light vanished. Jannah wobbled and fell to her knees. The gold Star of David, worked loose from under her collar, gleamed dully; her hand rose towards it, dropped back down as she fought to calm herself. 'It – it—'

'What the bloody hell do you kids think you're doing?'

They jumped, looked around. A man in a siren suit and tin helmet emerged from the choir, glaring at them. 'How did you get in here?'

Maggie stuttered, 'We – the door was—'

Alice stepped forward. 'Ah, good,' she said. Her patrician tones rang out. 'We need to use your telephone, my good man.'

The man stopped in his tracks. 'Here, miss, you can't—'

'We need to use it *now!*'

Miriam, Laura and the major were there in minutes. They burst through the great door and ran to Maggie and the others, their faces bright with excitement. 'Is it here?' Miriam's voice was high and girlish. 'Is it—'

She noticed the man in the siren-suit, still hovering disapprovingly by the choir. Miriam's face returned to its usual impassive mask. She strode quickly to the man, rapped out a few words; the major followed, producing papers. After a moment the man retreated sulkily back the way he'd came.

Laura turned to the five wizards. 'Where is it?'

They pointed wordlessly at the grave. Laura frowned. 'That's the Unknown—'

'We know. It's underneath,' Alice said.

'Where?'

'Down,' Colin said solemnly. 'Way down.'

Laura smiled. 'Then we'd better be going down,' she said.

They made their way into the depths of the abbey. The gold leaf and high ceilings gave way to plain empty passages and staircases. They emerged into a windowless stone chamber whose ceiling was barely higher than their heads.

Then it seemed the five wizards' work was finished. Miriam and the major appeared with men in uniform, workmen with tools, all crowding in. They found a switch, and a bare light bulb filled the room with a yellow glow. They were all talking at once, pointing at the ceiling, pointing at the floor. Maggie and the others found themselves crowded back against the stone walls.

Finally the major's patience evaporated. 'Clear the way,' he barked, and everyone backed away from the centre of the room. Silence fell as Miriam came forward, staring at the empty, slightly uneven, paved floor. She stretched out her hand to one of the uniforms; he scurried forwards and handed her a carpet bag.

The five young wizards craned over other people's shoulders to see. Miriam was drawing something out of the bag: a blue-and-silver wand. 'Air,' she murmured, *'Raphael.'* A thick silence fell as she reached into the bag again; Maggie stood on her tiptoes to see. Miriam pulled out a gleaming silver chalice, placed it carefully on the floor opposite the wand. 'Water. *Gabriel.'*

The chamber was getting warm. So many people, Maggie thought, using up all the air; after the vast heights of the nave, the room's ceiling seemed stiflingly low. Now Miriam was taking a linen-wrapped bundle from the carpet-bag and, unwrapping it: a short sword. She set it on the floor, at right angles to the wand and the chalice. 'Fire. *Michael.'*

Finally she took out a golden disc etched with a five-pointed star. Maggie had begun to sweat. She glanced at the others, who were pale and queasy-looking; only Alice looked happy, eyes bright and excited. She let out a sigh as Miriam put the gold disc in place opposite the sword; murmured along with Miriam, 'Earth. *Auriel.'*

Maggie's fingers started to prickle as the four objects trembled in place. Then, as if they'd been magnetised, they moved: came together, so fast there was a crack, like snapping wood. Fiery light spread through them. Miriam breathed: 'That's it. It's here.'

'We could've told her that,' Vince muttered. Everyone ignored him.

Miriam was pointing at the worn flagstone. 'Dig,' she said, and men with tools scurried forward like worker ants. They produced a crow bar and levered up the square slab of stone, revealing the raw earth underneath. Hands passed them shovels and they began to dig.

There was no sound for a long time but the bite and slice of shovels in the ground. Maggie lost track of time – it could have been hours, in the heat and the smell of gritty earth. Eventually the major, fidgeting in the tense silence, said, 'How long do you think—'

It was like an oven door opening. Maggie rocked back on her feet; Jannah made a whimpering sound in her throat. One of the men, who were now up to their waists in the earth, said: 'There's something here.'

Alice said thickly, 'That's it.'

Vince stepped forward from his place against the wall. Sweat was running down his face. 'We'll fetch it out,' he said.

The major scowled and shook his head. But Miriam watched Vince thoughtfully as he walked forward, Alice at his heels. After a moment, Miriam waved the men out of their path. 'Yes,' she said. 'The five of you.'

Maggie glanced at Jannah, who looked haggard and sick. *She needs to be out of here, in the fresh air,* Maggie thought. They needed to get this over with. 'Come on,' Maggie said. She took Jannah's hand, then Colin's, and they moved forward to the pit.

The hole was only three feet deep, about six feet square. They peered down into it. There seemed to be nothing but the dark earth. Vince was about to jump in when Alice cried out, 'Be careful.' Vince hesitated, and Maggie looked again. There was something set into the pit's floor, the very top of a grimy sphere; like a giant potato still buried in the ground. Alice lowered herself carefully into the hole, keeping her feet well away from the centre. 'Come on,' she whispered.

Vince climbed down after her. Maggie made herself follow, with Colin and Jannah close behind. They knelt in a circle. With trembling fingers, Alice reached out and began to brush earth away from the buried sphere. Vince began to do the same. Sweat dripped from his face, splatting into the earth like rain. The adults around were a silent, staring presence.

Alice and Vince cleared the earth away from the thing in the ground. It looked like a buried football, until Alice gently dusted the earth away from its eye sockets. Maggie jumped when she felt something pressing into her shoulder; her mother was passing her a little brush, round and bristly like a shaving brush. Maggie looked at it stupidly, then she understood. She waved Vince and Alice's hands away, used the brush to sweep the burying earth aside.

The skull emerged. Strands of Maggie's hair began drifting in front of her face; she knew if she tried to push them back they would crackle with electricity. Behind her Miriam said something, something like *Be careful*, but Maggie ignored her. She could hear the breathing of the five around her, smell their sweat. Finally, the skull was clear. It wasn't much to look at: yellowed, missing its jaw bone, with only a few peg-like teeth. But they knew, they knew what it was. Alice took a deep shuddering breath. 'Now,' she said. 'All together.'

Slowly they put out their hands, placed their fingertips onto the curve of the skull. Maggie had expected it to be hot, but it was cool and gritty. Alice muttered, 'Lift,' and they scooped their fingers underneath and lifted it up. It was surprisingly light. They held it up like a communion goblet, and heard a sort of ecstatic groan pass around the room behind them.

Then Jannah jerked backwards, pulling the skull away from the others. Maggie reached out a hand to her, thinking she was falling, but the other girl shrugged her off. Jannah clamped her hands around the skull, palms pressed against the bone. She didn't seem to be exerting much pressure. But the skull cracked with a retort, like gunfire. Fault lines appeared across the brown bone surface; the skull caved in like an Easter egg, collapsed into a dozen pieces.

There was a scream behind them. Maggie's hair fell limp around her face; the sweat under her collar went cold as the heat began to lift. Maggie and Vince and Alice and Colin stared at Jannah. Maggie's first thought, idiotically, was how stupid Jannah must be feeling. How clumsy, to have broken the thing by mistake.

But Jannah's expression told her how wrong she was. Jannah was still ghastly pale, her dark eyes huge. But she looked at the others and her face split into a wolfish grin. 'And that is that,' she said. 'It is done. *Heil Hitler. Sieg heil.*'

Chapter Eleven
Mother and Daughter

They all stood there like statues. Miriam let out a wail as if she'd seen her child's head split open. No one else moved or spoke. Jannah, standing up in the raw earth, poured words into the appalled silence. 'Now you know. It is no good to fight. The Führer will come.'

Vince whispered, 'Jannah—'

'Why do you fight? The English are Aryans too. The Germans are your brothers!' Jannah laughed. Drops of sweat were running down her face. 'We are all brothers and sisters! The Führer has said so! The Führer will come here, I have seen the future! The Aryans will be united—'

'But you're a Jew!' Alice burst out.

'I'm not a Jew!' Jannah's face twisted. 'How can you have believed that? My family are good Aryans. My family...we are all of good Aryan blood. Pure! Pure as any of you!'

Alice's face froze. 'I'm not Aryan,' she said. 'I'm Jewish.'

Jannah faltered. 'You cannot be.'

'My mother was Jewish. That means I am too.'

'But you are...' Jannah gestured weakly at Alice's blonde hair, her blue eyes. 'You are—'

'Jewish.'

Jannah stared at her, swaying where she stood. But only for a moment. Then her face hardened and she looked away. 'Dirty Jew,' she said.

Alice hit her in the face, so hard she staggered backwards. The slap echoed around the room, and finally everyone moved. Maggie grabbed Alice's arms before she could lunge at Jannah again. Alice fought like an angry cat; Vince had to step in front of her, wrap his arms around her and throw his weight against her. Behind them Miriam snapped an order; soldiers grabbed Jannah and dragged her out of the shallow pit. Maggie couldn't help but flinch as they twisted Jannah's arms up behind her. Jannah was staring back at her, dark eyes huge in her bloodless face, as they pulled her towards the door. 'Maggie! Help me! Colin! Vince! *Vince!*'

Vince swallowed hard but didn't look at her. He murmured into Alice's shoulder, 'There, there, easy now. Easy.'

'Maggie!' Jannah was gone. The fight went out of Alice, and she sagged against Vince. He went on holding her; Maggie's arms were still around both of them. Colin, still sitting on the edge of the pit, sobbed aloud. Miriam half-jumped, half-fell into the pit. She ignored her weeping son, crawled to the broken pieces of the skull. She gathered up the fragments, cradling them in both hands. 'It can be mended,' she said. 'Can't it? Can't it?'

She was staring at Maggie. Maggie looked at the remains of the skull. She felt nothing; the power was gone. The skull was only a few pieces of bone. She shook her head, unable to meet her mother's eyes. Miriam let out a heart-broken howl. Maggie swayed against Alice, didn't know she was doing it till she felt Vince's hand on her arm. 'Don't you faint, girl,' he muttered. 'Don't you pass out on me.'

Maggie looked up at her mother's face, then looked away again thinking, *It's not my fault!* To give herself something else to focus on she said, 'Alice? All right now?'

Alice took a deep breath. She looked over Vince's shoulder at

Miriam, nodded towards the remains of the skull. 'I'm sorry,' she said, 'the power's gone out of it.'

'I know.' Miriam's voice was choked. She looked into the stricken faces of Vivian and Laura and the major. 'It's lost. It's lost. We had it in our hands, and it—'

'Mum.' Colin's voice was high but clear. 'Where are they taking Jannah?'

Miriam looked at him as if she'd just remembered he was there. 'They're taking her away,' she said hoarsely.

'What's going to happen to her?'

'She's a traitor.'

They all knew what that meant. Maggie said shakily, 'You shouldn't hurt her.'

'I said: she's a traitor.' Miriam was in control of herself again. She stood, gathering the pieces of the skull. To Laura she said, 'Come. Bring the children with you.'

'Don't hurt her,' Maggie said. 'She's – one of us – we're joined—'

Miriam took no notice, made for the door. Alice gently pushed Maggie and Vince away. Her face was as cold as Miriam's. 'She's a traitor. Come on.' She looked at Laura, who was hovering tearfully at their elbows. 'What are you waiting for? Take us away from here!'

In the grey light of dawn, they emerged from the abbey. Laura ushered Maggie, Colin, Alice and Vince into a waiting car. Miriam had already left. There was no sign of Jannah.

No one spoke as Laura drove them back to the ministry. The silence was broken only by the occasional hiccupping sob from Colin. Maggie hugged him and murmured to him, glad of the distraction. Alice's face was like stone. Vince looked as if he was going to cry like Colin. 'I don't believe it,' he said at last. 'Why'd she do it?'

'I think they've got her family,' Maggie said. 'Her parents and her sister—'

'She did it because she's a Nazi,' Alice snapped. 'It's what they do.'

'What will they do to her?'

'They'll shoot her.'

The car pulled up outside the ministry. Alice was the first out onto the pavement. 'She's a traitor,' she said. 'Forget about her.'

They followed her inside and up the echoing, uncarpeted staircase. *Sleep,* Maggie was thinking, *it'll all seem better after we've slept...* but as they were passing the large room on the first floor, Miriam's voice came from inside: 'In here.'

They filed in. Miriam stood, arms folded, beside a big man with blonde curls; the major hovered at the man's elbow. Maggie stared at the big man and blinked; for a moment she'd thought... but no, his face was unfamiliar. He was looking at the four of them with keen interest, but Miriam's face remained grim. 'Yes,' she told the man, 'here they are.'

He and Miriam exchanged a look Maggie couldn't read. Then he nodded to her and left without a word; the major hurried to open the door for him, then followed. When they were gone Miriam said, 'All of you, go to bed.'

They were already turning gratefully to the door when Miriam added, 'Not you, Maggie.'

The other three paused for a moment; but under Miriam's gaze they trooped out, giving Maggie pitying looks. Maggie was left standing in front of her mother like a naughty schoolgirl in front of the headmistress. Miriam turned to her slowly. Her make-up was still perfect, Maggie noticed, but underneath she was ghastly white. 'Do you know,' Miriam said, 'what this means? Do you have *any* idea?'

Maggie shook her head dumbly. Miriam took a step towards her. 'How could you not know you had a traitor in your midst?'

'Me?' Maggie's voice rose to a shriek. 'How was *I* meant to know?'

'She was one of you. Part of your coven.' Miriam had begun to pace up and down. 'Why didn't you sense it?'

'She told us…'

'Never mind what she told you. You should have known!'

Hot tears pricked Maggie's eyes. She stared at the floor. 'I'm sorry.'

She heard her mother sigh impatiently. 'You were right. You are only children.'

'I'm not—'

'I asked too much of you. But done is done.' She sighed again. 'It's time you went home.'

Maggie nodded. Yes, it was time. Back to Gran's; the potatoes would need lifting…but Miriam was still talking. 'Yes. Back to Glasgow, where you should have been all along.'

'What?'

'We've talked about this, Maggie. You'll go back to Scotland, to a place I know near Helensburgh—'

'We need to get back to Gran's!'

'Don't be silly. The South Coast is much too dangerous.'

'But it's where Gran is.' *And the Mound,* she thought. And Michal… 'She'll never leave the cottage.'

'I told you, that's up to her. But the two of you are going somewhere safe.'

'What about Alice and Vince?'

'They can both go home. This…experiment has obviously failed. You simply are not mature enough.'

Maggie stared at her for a long moment; then she stood up straight. 'I'm going home,' she said.

'What do you mean?'

'I'm going home. To Gran's.' She turned on her heel and headed for the door. 'Goodbye, Mum.'

'Maggie! Come back here!'

Maggie kept walking. When she was out on the landing she began to run upstairs, taking the wooden steps two at a time up to the third floor and into the bedroom she'd been sharing with Alice and Jannah. She burst in to find Alice sitting on her own bed, Vince and Colin on Maggie's. No one sat on Jannah's bed. All three stared at Maggie. 'What's happening?' said Alice.

Maggie went to her bedside cabinet. 'I'm going home. Back to Wardston.'

They all gaped at her. Vince said, 'What about the rest of us?'

'You're being sent home.' Maggie pulled out her little suitcase. 'Sent somewhere *safe.*'

'So how come they're letting *you* go back to the coast?'

'They're not letting me.' Maggie pulled her few spare clothes out of the cabinet and started jamming them into the case. 'I'm going anyway.'

'I don't want to go back to my school!' cried Alice. *It's the holidays*, Maggie realised, *but her family's left her at her school.* It said it all. Alice stood up. 'I won't go back!'

'And I en't going back to my stepdad's.' Vince's voice trembled for a moment. Maggie remembered the man in black she'd seen looming behind him, and the woman lying at his feet. Vince shook his head. 'I en't going back neither.'

Maggie looked from one to the other. 'Get your ration books then,' she said. 'You're coming with us.'

Vince grinned. 'You're on.' He clapped his hand onto Colin's shoulder. 'Get your ration book, Col, we're going to the seaside.'

Maggie looked at her little brother, suddenly doubtful. He was only ten. 'Colin? Do you want to stay with Mum...or...'

'I'm coming with you.' He was already following Vince across the corridor to their room. 'Of course.'

Maggie was left with a babbling Alice. 'Are you sure? Oh dear. Won't your grandmother mind? Are you sure we should—'

Maggie closed her suitcase. 'Get packing, Alice.'

A few minutes later they were clattering downstairs. Maggie fully expected Miriam to step out in front of them, but she didn't appear. No one did, until they were nearly at the front door. Then Vivian stepped out of the front room, into their path. 'Where do you think you're going?'

Maggie, still powered by anger, didn't even have to think about it. She flicked a finger, and Vivian was propelled out of the way and into the wall. Maggie stared at her defiantly, but Vivian was smiling; she looked pleased. She reached over and opened the front door for them. 'Good luck,' she said.

The four tumbled out into the hot summer sunshine. Vince was shaking his head. 'Glad to be out of that,' he said. 'They're all bleedin' mental.' He paused as Alice nudged him; then he obviously recalled that one of 'them' was Maggie and Colin's mother. 'No offence,' he added.

'None taken. They *are* mental.' Maggie glanced up at the ministry building. The morning sun blazed off the windows, so she couldn't see if anyone was watching them. 'Let's go.' She looked at Vince. 'Can you take us to the train station?'

'Course I can.' Vince could take them anywhere. 'Can you give us money for the tickets?'

Maggie stopped dead. For a moment she thought they'd have to go back inside and ask for money. No, she'd walk to Wardston first… but Alice patted her pocket. 'I've got enough for all of us. And I've got enough to give your grandmother, for having us.'

'Don't offer her money!'

'Why ever not?'

'Just don't…'

They followed Vince round the corner and left the ministry behind.

From the first floor window, Miriam watched them go. The door opened behind her; the big man with blonde curls came in quietly. The major was at his heels, but the man waved him away.

When they were alone, the big man crossed the room to Miriam. As he walked, the air around his face flickered and wavered. His blonde curls vanished to leave a shiny bald scalp. His features shimmered and began to change. By the time he stood beside Miriam, his face had changed into the most famous face in Britain. Most people would have turned to greet that face with great deference. Miriam just glanced at it and said, 'The *glamor* spell's wearing off, Winston.'

'What a pity.' The voice was famous too. The man put his hand where the blonde curls had been. 'I did so enjoy having hair again.'

'I'll get Vivian to recast it before you leave.' She was still looking out of the window. The two stood in silence for a moment, watching the four young wizards walk away. Miriam's face wore a tender expression which would have surprised Maggie very much. Churchill said, gently, 'She's doing as you thought she would? She's going back to Wardston?'

'Of course. Tell her to do something and she'll do precisely the opposite.' She snorted. 'Stubborn. I don't know where she gets it.'

Churchill waited; but this didn't seem to be a joke. 'They're very powerful,' he said at last.

'They'll have to be. They'll be right in the thick of it.'

'Indeed.'

Miriam kept her gaze out of the window. 'And you're still searching? For… their father?'

'Yes. Nothing yet, I'm afraid.'

'Because that would help to motivate them, you know. To think there was hope.'

'Yes.'

Miriam nodded. In silence, she watched her son and daughter turn the corner and vanish. Then she whispered, 'It won't be them, will it, Winston? Not one of them?'

Churchill was silent. All over the country, mothers were asking the same thing: *not my son? Not my daughter? Please, not them?* 'They're powerful,' he said again. 'Like you.'

Miriam drew in a ragged breath. 'And they have work to do.'

The train journey was long and hot. The carriage smelled of upholstery and sweat. Maggie dozed, and dreamed of being at home on the Mound, surrounded by an overpowering scent of roses. She was kneeling on the grass beside someone in a white dress, someone who was whispering to her, telling her important and secret things. But when the train juddered to a halt and Maggie was jolted awake, the memory melted away. She opened her eyes to find Vince hanging out of the window, scanning the station platform. 'This it then?'

Maggie glanced outside. The sign that said *Wardston-Upon-Sea* had been taken down in 1939, but she knew where they were. Colin was already opening the carriage door. 'This is it,' he said.

They scrambled out onto the platform. A sea breeze found them as they left the station, cooling the sweat on their faces. Maggie inhaled a good lungful: home. 'This way,' she told Alice and Vince. Colin was already leading them. They passed the big houses, then the fishermen's cottages, and came to the town square. They passed the butcher's, the baker's, the florist and all the rest. They passed Caplan's bookshop, where Mr Caplan's little granddaughter was playing in the doorway with her inseparable friend the butcher's daughter. The little girls waved absently and went back to their game. Simple Billy sat on his bench, but he was absorbed in feeding the pigeons and didn't look up. All so familiar; nothing had changed. Maggie felt she'd been away for an age.

The square was busy, full of children skipping and running, and clambering on the corrugated iron roof of the surface shelter. Around the statue of Queen Victoria was a clump of boys. When Colin checked his stride and fell back, Maggie realised that in the middle of the gang – inevitably – was Charlie Chester. He saw Maggie and Colin and grinned. 'It's the conchie kids!'

'You what?' The soft hissing voice was Vince's. His face had gone hard. Maggie put a hand on his arm: 'Leave it, Vince.' Vince was looking at Charlie as if he were committing his face to memory. Charlie's grin faltered. But when Maggie, Colin, Vince and Alice walked past he regained his courage and shouted at their backs, 'Bye-bye, conchies!'

'Who's that little gobshite?' Vince said.

'Charlie.' Maggie nudged his arm. 'And stop swearing. We'll be at my Gran's soon.'

They climbed the cliff path. A sea breeze found them, ruffling their clothes and lifting strands of their hair. Vince was gazing out to sea, rapt, stumbling occasionally on the rutted track. At last he said, 'So that's the sea then?'

They all looked at him. 'Haven't you seen it before?' said Alice.

'Never been out of London.'

No one knew what to say. Eventually Alice asked, 'What do you think of it?'

Vince pondered. 'Big,' he announced at last.

Alice giggled. It was the first time she'd smiled since Jannah. 'Big?'

'Very big,' said Vince.

She was still giggling, snorting and snuffling with laughter, when they reached the cottage gate. Two adult-sized bicycles leaned on the wall outside. Maggie eyed them warily – she knew all the bicycles in the village, and had never seen these before. Alice stopped laughing. 'Visitors?'

'Looks like it.' Maggie pushed open the gate. Then they all heard a man's voice, coming from somewhere behind the cottage. Without another word, Maggie walked quickly around to the back garden, the others falling into step behind her.

A man was in the garden, turned away from them, bent double

over the potato patch. He looked as if he'd be tall standing up – slim-built but muscular, with long legs. In fact, if Michelangelo's David had put on brown corduroy trousers and bent over a potato patch, this was how he might have looked. Alice said faintly, 'Oh, my goodness.' Maggie started to laugh. 'Hello, Arthur,' she called.

The figure stood up and turned. Even out of uniform, in grubby old working clothes, the pilot looked like a recruitment poster: the doughty Englishman. Digging for Victory. There was a single smudge of earth on his right cheek. Apart from one golden curl hanging over his forehead, his blond hair was immaculate. He beamed at them. 'Good morning!'

'Arthur, what are you doing here?'

'Helping with the potatoes, of course.' He called over his shoulder, 'Hi, Michal, see who's here!'

Michal appeared in the back doorway. His worn-out clothes were a size too big for him; his face was dirty and his hair stuck up around his head. He looked like an urchin. Maggie crossed the garden in a few strides, as if she were going to throw her arms around him, but stopped short and stood in front of him. 'Hello,' she said.

He smiled. 'Hello, Maggie.'

She started to laugh again. 'So have you joined the Land Army too?'

'Ah.' He spread his arms, looking down at his clothes. 'You look better in uniform than I do, I think.'

They stood smiling at one another, oblivious to Arthur, who stared at them, his own smile faltering slightly. Then a small figure appeared behind Michal in the narrow doorway. 'Don't just stand there, Michal dear—'

'Gran! Gran!' Maggie and Colin rushed to her, crowding Michal out of the doorway, throwing their arms around her like much younger children. When they finally let her go she tried to look stern – 'What are you doing back here?' – but her pink cheeks and teary eyes gave her away. 'You shouldn't be here, you shouldn't…'

Then a wailing noise rose in the air, making Maggie's scalp crawl. 'What's that?'

Gran nodded to the west. 'It's from the airbase,' she said.

Arthur and Michal weren't smiling any more. Arthur was already moving towards the gate, towards the bicycles. He nodded briefly to Alice and Vince, who fell back out of the way as he went past.

Michal turned to Maggie. 'We must go,' he said.

Part Three:

The War in the Air

The Battle of France is over. I expect that the Battle of Britain is about to begin… The whole fury and might of the enemy must very soon be turned on us.

Winston Churchill

Chapter Twelve

Angels Five

They were at the foot of the Mound, veering crazily around the path, when the siren stopped. By that time they could hear the hum of aircraft overhead. Still distant. Arthur skidded to a halt, one foot planted on the grass verge. 'Ours or theirs?' he said.

Michal paused only briefly. 'I cannot tell. Hurry anyway.' He took off along the road.

They cycled at full-pelt, skimming over the tarmac between the high hedges. The morning traffic was light; the roads remained empty, shimmering in the hot sun. The drone of engines overhead increased steadily, filling the enclosed roadways. Eventually it mingled with the wail of the all-clear, but the two pilots, sweating under their heavy work clothes, pedalled on until they reached the airfield's main gate.

They had just skidded to a halt at the barrier when the engine drone built to a roar and the aircraft passed directly overhead. Many would have dived for cover, but Arthur and Michal knew the sound of those engines: Spitfires.

Three Spitfires flashed past in V-formation, low enough for them to feel the whoosh of the downdraft. Black smoke trailed from the leading Spit – not great gouts from the engine, thin wafts from the top of the craft. Fire in the cockpit. They pedalled faster.

The Spits disappeared from sight, over the roofs of the hangars and main buildings, landing gear lowering. In the distance, Michal and Arthur could already hear the jangling of the base's fire engine.

The guard, grim-faced, was raising the barrier for them. Arthur said to him, 'Who was that, do you know?'

'Don't know, sir.' The guard spread his hands helplessly. Arthur nodded and followed Michal, who was already past the barrier and cycling up the base's main road.

They passed the turnoff to the barracks, and kept going towards the airfield. The dispersal hut blocked their view of the runway, but they could see black smoke rising over the low wooden building. They rounded the corner and braked sharply. A cluster of men in blue-grey uniforms were sitting in deckchairs and armchairs in front of the hut: most of 20 Squadron's pilots. They were in their shirt-sleeves; books and newspapers and games of cards lay, ignored, in front of them. A few faces peered through the dispersal hut's hatch. No one looked up at Michal and Arthur's arrival; their attention was fixed on the airfield.

The three Spitfires had landed. Two had only a couple of ground crew attending them, climbing on the wings to inspect the Perspex bubble over the cockpit. But the third, a hundred yards from the others and still leaking smoke, had drawn a crowd. The fire engine, several Land Rovers, and a swarm of men in uniform surrounded it. Fitters and riggers climbed on the Spit like children in a playground; one had detached the smoke-stained Perspex canopy and was passing it to others on the ground. The base ambulance stood a few yards away, its two-man crew waiting. From their deckchairs, the pilots watched silently.

Arthur turned to the nearest man: Flight-Sergeant Williams. Harry Williams' big face was impassive, his heavy dark brows furrowed – but that was his usual expression. He noticed Arthur, jerked his chin and grunted a greeting – highly eloquent for Williams. Arthur looked back at the stricken Spitfire, trying to read the pilot ident painted on the plane's flank; but the fuselage was covered in soot. 'Who is that?' Arthur said.

'Fergusson,' said Williams.

The Squadron leader. Arthur shook his head slightly. 'Fire in the cockpit?'

Williams nodded.

'How bad?'

'Don't know yet.'

Arthur turned to watch. There was movement in the cockpit now. A murmur of relief went around the pilots as the occupant stood up – *he's still standing, can't be that bad* – and clumsily lifted a foot out onto the wing. He was holding his hands out in front of him, palms turned inwards, like a surgeon who's just scrubbed up. Even a hundred yards away, they could all see his hands were an angry red. One of the fitters, balancing on the wing, reached out to take him by the elbow; riggers held the plane steady as the pilot jumped heavily to the ground, his knees buckling slightly. The two medics took an arm each and walked him to the ambulance, slamming the doors behind them.

As the ambulance pulled away, bell clanging, the crowd around the blackened Spitfire began to disperse. Three men walked slowly towards the hut. The middle one, a head above the others, was immediately recognisable: Flight Commander Owens, blond moustache drooping, his flushed face unsmiling. On either side were two pilots – Harrison and Draycott – new boys who still hung about with parachute packs and life jackets. Clearly they'd just emerged from the other two Spitfires. Harrison had a smear of blood on his forehead. Draycott's pallid face was streaked with tears; the assembled pilots looked away tactfully. Without looking up, the two disappeared into the dispersal hut. Before Owens could follow, Arthur touched his arm and said: 'How bad is Fergusson, sir?'

Owens grunted. 'Burns to the hands. Second-degree, they

reckon. He'll recover.'

'Will he fly again?'

'Eventually.'

Slowly, the pilots relaxed back into their chairs. It wasn't good; but it could have been a lot worse. Owens turned away to the hut; then he seemed to remember something, and turned back to Arthur: 'Willoughby.' He looked around for Michal: 'Capek, you too. I'm sorry, you fellows, your leave's cancelled for the day. Had to send three chaps out on a recce an hour ago, so we're down to nine.' He lowered his voice and nodded towards the dispersal hut. 'Don't want to send those two up again for an hour or so.'

'Understood, sir.'

'You're Blue One. Capek—' he looked around, couldn't see Michal and turned back to Arthur, 'tell him he's Blue Two. And Arthur,' Owens looked him in the eye, 'you're acting Squadron Leader.'

'Yes, sir.'

Owens disappeared into the hut. Arthur stood silent for a moment. Then he turned to the nearest man – Williams – and sighed. 'Can't a man enjoy his day off around here?'

Williams shrugged. 'Complain to Adolf.'

The door of the dispersal hut banged open. Flight-Lieutenant John Penry-Smith, clutching a mug of tea, wandered out and lowered his lanky frame into a tattered armchair. He looked at Arthur and Michal in their muddy gardening clothes. 'What ho, everyone, the land girls are back.'

'Michal.' Ignoring Penry-Smith, Arthur looked around for his friend, and found the Polish pilot staring up into the sky. Frowning, Arthur followed his gaze. There was nothing there but the three Spitfires' vapour trails, frayed and dispersing across clear azure blue. 'Michal,' Arthur called again. 'Did you hear Owens? The spuds will have to wait. Maggie too, I'm afraid.'

'Maggie?' Penry-Smith, lounging bored in his armchair, looked at Michal and said a bit more loudly, 'That fierce little redhead Michal likes? Is she back?'

'She is,' said Arthur.

'The one in the britches? With the very tight—'

'You're wasting your time, Penry,' Arthur said. 'He's not listening.' Michal was still staring up. 'Michal?'

'Something is coming,' Michal said.

Penry-Smith shook his head uncertainly. 'It was a false alarm, old man. Just our chaps coming back.'

Everyone else was silent. They knew about Michal's hunches. Then everyone jumped as, in the dispersal hut, the phone began to ring.

No one moved or breathed as the ringing cut off. Through the hatch came Owen's voice: 'Dispersal... yes... right.'

They heard the clatter of the phone going down. Owen's face, then his uniformed arm, appeared in the hatchway. He grabbed the rope of the large brass bell hanging on the hut's wall. The ringing clanged out into the silence. 'Squadron scramble!'

Before Owen's words were out, every man was on his feet. Books and papers and cards flew everywhere. The pilots began to run across the turf towards the waiting Spitfires. The ground crew were in attendance; already the engines were roaring into life. Arthur ran into the hut, Michal close behind him. They pulled open their lockers, dragged out their parachutes, flying jackets, life jackets. Struggling into the heavy fleece-lined flying jackets, they hurled themselves out into the sunshine again.

All the others, even in their heavy flying boots, had already covered several hundred yards and were almost at their planes. Ground crew scrambled and shouted; the growl of more and more engines added to the roar. The warm air was full of the scent of trodden grass and the reek of fuel. Michal ran; Arthur followed.

Within a minute of the scramble bell, Arthur was at his Spitfire. The engine was humming, and the little plane trembled like a racehorse. The airscrew was spinning, a blurred disk on the Spit's long elegant nose. Arthur's fitter was just levering himself out of the cockpit onto the wing. The rigger, seeing Arthur still struggling into his life jacket and chute, fastened him into them like a mother dressing a child. 'Thanks, Benjamin,' Arthur said.

'Give'em hell, sir,' said Benjamin.

'Fully intend to. Thanks, Sanderson.' Arthur clapped the fitter's shoulder as he passed him on the wing, their combined weight making the Spitfire's frame dip to the side. Sanderson dropped to the ground; Arthur lowered himself into the cockpit.

He was surrounded by the rumble of the engine, by the smell of fuel and leather. The single-seat cockpit was so small and snug, the instruments and joystick so close, he felt he was wearing the Spitfire like a coat: like an extension of himself. Every time that same feeling came to him, that fierce rush of joy: *whatever happens now, I fly a Spitfire.*

No time to glory in it, of course. He pulled on his leather helmet, fitted the goggles over his eyes. He connected up the oxygen, then the radio, wrapping the mask around his mouth. From the corner of his eyes he could see other planes starting to edge forward. He was behind the others; he hurried through all the instrument checks. Then he hurried through them again, because you couldn't afford to miss one. Fuel? Okay. Ammunition? Fine. Then he fastened himself into the harness, pulled the straps around his shoulders and legs, pulled tight. From the ground Sanderson shouted above the growl of the engine: 'All right sir?'

Arthur closed the cockpit canopy, sliding the smooth Perspex dome into place. Outside Sanderson and Benjamin were standing by the chocks. Arthur waved the signal; the rigger and fitter pulled the ropes and the wedges slid away from the Spitfire's wheels. The two men touched the tips of the Spitfire's graceful curved wings, as much for luck as to keep the plane steady. As they stood clear, Arthur released the brake and eased open the throttle. The Spit began to move.

Arthur steered carefully over the turf. He was aware of Michal, his main wingman, on his immediate left and Penry-Smith's Spit manoeuvring into position to his right. The other six formed up behind them, in two V's of three. Following Arthur's lead, the planes bumped and trundled across the airfield, nosing north-east into the wind. When they were all in place they halted, poised for the off. Arthur took a deep breath and flipped on the radio transmitter.

'All right, squadron Kestrel.' 20 Squadron's radio call sign. 'This is Kestrel Leader. Here we go, gentlemen.'

He released the brakes and began to roll forwards. Faster and faster; bumping and jolting across the turf. From the corners of his eyes he saw Michal and Penry-Smith keeping pace with him. More and more acceleration; the tail rose. Then the wheels. The bumping and jolting vanished.

The Spitfire was airborne.

Back in the cottage, an argument was hotting up.

'But we're supposed to take cover,' Alice was saying. 'There's going to be fighting overhead. That's what we do. That's the *procedure.*'

'Sod that!' Vince noticed Maggie's glare – Gran was only in the kitchen, well within earshot – and lowered his voice. 'To hell with that. I'm not hiding away while other people fight. Let's get out there!'

'We can't. We're – civilians.'

'So was our Dad.' Maggie's abrupt tone stopped them dead. She looked at Colin, who nodded firmly. She nodded too. 'Let's go.'

'Hello, Wardston. This is Kestrel. Kestrel Squadron airborne. Over.'

With Arthur's calm, reassuring voice in their ears, the eight other pilots lifted into the sky behind him. Michal smiled to himself: it was amazing, how just listening to Arthur made everyone feel better. Michal glanced to the right as he tugged on the hydraulic lever that raised his Spitfire's wheels. He had to make adjustments to keep station with Arthur, who was climbing steep and fast. Behind them the others were following suit. They all knew they needed height.

There was a crackle from the radio, and the voice of the ground controller came through loud and clear. 'Kestrel Leader, this is Wardston. Vector two-five-zero, Kestrel. Bandits eight plus, at angels five. Over.'

'Wardston, this is Kestrel.' Arthur had already begun to swing around. They had been heading north-east; they needed to be south-west. More than eight enemy planes, coming in at five thousand feet, heading for – what? 'Steering two-five-zero. What's their target, Wardston?'

More radio crackle. After a moment: 'Kestrel, this is Wardston. They're coming in over the Channel, Kestrel. We think they're after the radar station south of Wardston village. Over.'

'Thank you, Wardston. On our way.'

The nine Spitfires arced around, making height all the time. The countryside rolled past below, fields of grass and wheat, a patchwork of green and brown and yellow in the bright summer sun. To their left was the sparkling sea. In a moment they'd pass Wardston village. Michal, almost involuntarily, glanced down to the garden where he'd left Maggie. There was the cottage, tiny and neat like a model from a train set; there was the little brown garden. There was the green hump of the Mound, topped with a shard of granite: the Stone.

And on the slope of the Mound, slogging up the winding path, were four figures. The leader's bright red hair blew around her head. Michal felt his stomach clench when he saw her out in the open – she should be inside, under cover, what was she *doing?* As if she'd heard him, the figure turned. Her face was just a tiny pale blob, but it seemed to look directly at him. Then the Mound was past; Michal turned his attention forwards.

At seven thousand feet they evened out. The squadron, in perfect formation, thundered through the clear, still air. There were no clouds but a high, thin canopy of cirrus, more than ten thousand feet above. Perfect flying weather. Perfect bombing weather too. Michal checked above, below, behind, to left and right. His shirt was already chafing the back of his neck – he'd forgotten to pick up his silk scarf from the locker – but he turned his head again and again anyway. Control hadn't reported any other aircraft in the vicinity, but Control didn't spot everything. It was the one you didn't see that got you, everybody knew that.

The sea vanished as their course took them over land. A carpet of green, no farmland; the country was wilder here. That didn't mean there was nothing of interest, of course. Up ahead, spindly towers stood against the clear sky. Arthur's voice came over the radio: 'Kestrel Squadron, this is Kestrel Leader. Radar station at 12 o'clock. Keep your eyes peeled, gentlemen, our customers are around here somewhere.'

They closed in on the radar station. The four metal-frame antennae, like skinny Eiffel Towers, were perched on the edge of a cliff. They didn't look particularly large, until you realised the tiny wooden boxes at the base were actually buildings: the operators' huts. Beyond the antennae, the sea glittered. And in the blue dead ahead, a cluster of black dots. A casual observer might have thought they were a swarm of flies.

The pilots knew better. In his radio headset, Michal heard Penry-Smith mutter: 'Christ on a bike.'

Arthur's voice was as calm as ever. 'Wardston, this is Kestrel. Bandits sighted at 12 o'clock. A few more than eight of them, I'd say.'

'This is the Stone you were telling us about? The Ward Stone? It's incredible! What a locus of power! Do any ley lines converge on it? I've never felt anything like—'

'Give it a rest, Alice. Mags, what do we do now?'

'Join hands. Like before. No, not like that. With the Stone in the middle.'

'Kestrel Leader, this is Wardston.' Arthur thought that Control sounded faintly embarrassed. 'Confirm twenty-four bandits, coming in at angels five. Bombers with fighter escort. They're still over the Channel. Target confirmed as the radar station. Over.'

'Wardston, this is Kestrel. We can see them now.'

The radar station flashed past. Arthur saw tiny figures moving at the base of the antennae: station people hurrying to their shelters, or running to man the guns. *Hope they know the difference between us and them*, Arthur thought. The squadron members were easing apart, giving each other fighting space. Then the land vanished altogether, and they headed out over the sea.

The swarm was bigger now, closer. A formation of twelve big planes, much larger than the Spitfires. They seemed to ride heavily in the air. Bombers. Hovering above were a cluster of planes almost as small and light as the Spits. Fighters: there to protect the bombers. Now the dots were growing wings, taking on shape and detail. The bombers had straight wings and nose-cones glazed like greenhouses: Junkers 88s, most likely. The smaller planes had boxy, oblong wings: definitely Messerschmitt 109's. The only German fighter with a chance against the Spitfire.

Now the Messerschmitts were descending, trying to move in front of the bombers. *They've seen us.* Time for final combat checks – Arthur glanced at the control column, making sure the gun button was set to fire. When he looked up the German fighters were close enough to count. There were twelve of them; *and only*, Arthur thought, *nine of us.* When he spoke, however, his voice was warm and steady, almost amused: 'This is Kestrel leader. Moving to engage. We've got height on them, gentleman, and we're coming out of the sun. Let's send them for a swim, shall we? Tally-ho!'

He aimed at the nearest Messerschmitt, and dived.

Behind him, the squadron's immaculate formation splintered apart. Arthur, with no idea where his friends were and no way to help them anyway, focused on the German fighter rising to meet him. He kept a straight course towards it; risky, you never flew straight in a fight, but he held his course. Five seconds. Ten. The Messerschmitt levelled out, its nose pointed straight at Arthur's Spitfire. It was no more than a thousand yards away: Me109s, for all they looked so square and clumsy, were nippy little bastards.

Not as nippy as a Spitfire, however. Arthur threw the plane into a dive, as steep as he dared. For a horrible moment he thought the engine was going to stall and cut out, but the motor roared on and the plane held its course. *Good little Spitfire, that's a good girl.* Arthur passed under the Messerschmitt; its dull green wings, marked with black crosses, flashed past and were gone.

Which left him where he wanted to be: diving straight towards the first bomber. The Plexiglas cockpit and nose of the bomber flashed like newly-washed windows. He was coming at them out of the sun. Arthur, gambling that none of the German fighters had had the chance to turn yet, kept his downward course straight. In seconds he was close enough to see the two figures inside the cockpit, the single figure behind the clear nose-cone. He felt an abrupt stab of pity, but it didn't stop him.

He fired, six times, in short bursts. Tracer raked across the 88s cockpit and nose. Plexiglas shattered; inside, the figures flailed. Arthur thought he saw a splatter of red. Then he was under the bomber, for an instant in its dark shade, then out into bright sunshine again. He glanced into his mirror, looked above and all around him. No enemy fighters; they hadn't had time to turn. The attack had only taken a few seconds. No sign of his wingmen, either – Michal and Penry must have been distracted elsewhere. Arthur pulled into a tight turn, arcing up and back towards the action.

As he turned he saw the bomber, the one he'd just hit, begin to droop nose-downwards. Smoke streamed from its cockpit. With no one left to control it, the big plane toppled into a headlong, spinning fall. On its underside there was movement – the crew-hatch under the nose was opening. Arthur took aim; but when the little figure appeared, it was nowhere near any weapons. In fact, he was clambering out onto the fuselage. In an instant the slipstream whisked him clear, and a few seconds later a white parachute bloomed against the blue sky. Arthur raised the Spitfire's nose so it would pass well above the open parachute. Then he headed back to the battle.

'Now concentrate. Let the power flow. Vince, find them. Find where they've gone.'

'How?'

'Just concentrate. You can do it. Concentrate…'

Chaos, Arthur thought. No other word for it. He was slightly below the main action now. Planes big and small zoomed and dipped everywhere, in all directions. Smoke and exhaust trails criss-crossed the sky. The radio was a babble of shouts and shrieks: *'Watch, 109s behind you'* – *'oh shit shit shit'* – *'look out, two o'clock, break, break!'* Arthur turned his head to check all around – behind, below, above, to both sides – clear. He was still lower than the rest, he realised, as he pointed the Spitfire's nose upwards. Not ideal, but at least the reflected glare from the sea was reduced. And from underneath they might not see him coming.

The scene above him made slightly more sense now. The fighters, both Messerschmitts and Spitfires, were swooping in all directions, but the bombers were still more or less on course. Their formation had been broken – his own forward attack had seen to that – and one of them had black smoke pouring from its port engine, but the 88s were still heading for the radar station. The radar station: if they knocked that out, Control wouldn't be able to see anything coming. Couldn't have that. Arthur checked all around again, then chose the nearest bomber and turned towards it.

Before he reached the 88, smoke began to billow from its starboard engine. A Spitfire was clinging to its tail, Arthur realised, just a hundred yards or so behind. It was Harry Williams; he was still firing, and sparkles of tracer fire were dancing across the bomber's tail. He was locked onto his target, completely focussed. And he hadn't noticed the Messerschmitt on *his* tail. Before Arthur could shout a warning, the Me109 fired. Holes appeared on Williams' starboard wing; black smoke began to belch out of his engine.

Arthur closed in on the fighter behind Williams, got it in range and fired. He saw the pilot spasm in the cockpit; saw the engine light up as it burst into flame. There was an eye-watering flash, and a blast he heard even above the noise of his own engine, as the Me109 exploded against the bright blue sky. Arthur jinked left to avoid the flaming debris. Just a few hundred yards beyond he saw William's Spitfire tipping into a headlong dive, drawing a thick line of smoke behind it. The plane was doomed, but he could see Williams still moving in the cockpit. *Come on, Harry, bale out.* Williams was pushing at the hatch, trying to get it open.

But after a few seconds, Arthur could tell that William's Perspex hood was stuck tight. If it was going to open, it would have done it by now. *Oh, Harry.* Arthur could only watch as the crippled Spitfire spiralled away towards the ocean, with Williams still struggling inside.

'That's it! They're there! Bloody hell! Can you see?'

'Yes, we can see. But what do we do? It's *chaos!* Complete *chaos!*'

'Hush, Alice. Look there! That plane, the one falling! We've got to get him out!'

Arthur was about to turn away – nothing more he could do – when he saw William's cockpit canopy move. More than move. It bulged for a moment; then the whole canopy was just torn away, as if a giant hand had pulled the plane apart. Arthur stared. That didn't happen to Spitfires. It couldn't.

Then Williams was out of the plane. He hadn't climbed out, or even fallen – he'd popped out like a champagne cork. Even hundreds of yards away, Arthur could see the astonished expression on his face. Then, as he began to fall, Williams recovered enough to scrabble at the cord of his parachute. He pulled. The white mass of the parachute was pulled out of the pack; but it stayed tightly folded at the end of its cords. It hadn't opened. Williams continued to fall.

Then the wadded-up parachute spun several times. The kinks in the cords were unravelled, and the parachute puffed open. Williams was drifting slowly downwards, his defective parachute suddenly working perfectly. Arthur was still staring. That couldn't happen either. It –

Out of the cacophony over the radio, Michal's voice came through clearly. 'Arthur! Behind you!'

Chapter Thirteen
Nine O'Clock High

Arthur didn't hesitate. He didn't even look back. He threw the Spit to the side, into a half-roll. As the plane responded, he turned and glanced over his shoulder; a Messerschmitt was right behind him, no more than fifty yards away. It was locked onto him. And it was his own fault; he'd let himself be distracted. He'd been staring into space like an amateur. And now he was going to die for it.

He swooped downwards, towards the dazzling brightness of the sea. The 109 followed, keeping pace with him. Now Arthur saw the guns flash on the German fighter's wings, and sparkles zig-zag along his own port wing. He was hit. This must be the end. His poor mother and sisters, he thought, another dead idiot in the family. In sheer desperation, he forced the Spitfire into a tight turn, expecting at any moment to feel the gunfire thumping into him again. *Just let it be quick,* he thought. *Oh God, don't let me burn.*

After five long seconds, he realised nothing was happening. He glanced over his shoulder again. The 109 was still there, but not right on his tail; it was off the starboard side now, making a much wider turn. Notes from his training came back to him – an Me109 couldn't turn as sharply as a Spit. Without conscious thought he'd done the one thing that would save him. Not just save him. In fact…

He pushed the Spit into the tightest spin he'd ever tried. He wouldn't have been surprised to feel the little plane struggle in protest, but it followed his movements perfectly. *Good girl.* He actually laughed aloud; now he was right on the tail of the same Me109. *Let's see how you like it, you bugger.* He fired.

The Messerschmitt pilot was too quick for him, though. Instantly the German fighter dropped into a steep dive; Arthur's shots didn't connect. The temptation was to dive right after him; no doubt exactly what the 109 pilot wanted, knowing quite well that a Spitfire would stall at that sort of angle. *Crafty bastard.* Arthur straightened up. The Me109 was dipping into a steep zoom-climb – probably hoping to lure Arthur into following. At which point of course the German fighter would be much higher, and could turn around and come at him out of the sun. *Yes, very crafty. But not today, my friend.* Arthur let the Messerschmitt go, and turned back to the main targets: the bombers.

The Junkers 88s were almost at the radar station. There were only seven of them now – the others brought down or driven back – but seven would be more than enough to destroy the station. Between Arthur and the bombers was a whirling mass of fighters, with gunfire flashing and sparking on almost all of them. Arthur patted the Spit's dashboard for luck – *come on, old girl, hang in there* – and flung himself into the melee.

Arthur spun and turned, weaving his way through the hurtling planes. He checked around him constantly, below and above and beside and behind. He took deep breaths to stave off the dizziness – just a minute, wasn't he high enough for oxygen? He flicked his face-mask's oxygen toggle and took a few deep breaths. And all the while he zigged and zagged and rose and fell. You never, ever, flew straight. A Messerschmitt clung on his tail for a while, so he had to lose height, throwing it off in a sharp turn. But it couldn't get a fix on him and, eventually, he left it behind.

When he levelled out from the turn, he couldn't see any of the bombers. Was he that low? No; he was too high. He looked down. The bombers' path had tilted downwards. They'd started the bombing run.

Arthur swung after them. He'd keep pounding them, if the Me109s didn't stop him. But he knew how well-armoured the rear of a German bomber was. You needed to hit them from the front and, even if he could get there in time, that's where all the 109s would be.

He was too late. But there was nothing left to do but try. He plunged downwards.

'Look! They're heading for those big tower thingies!'

'Big tower thingies…? That's a radar station, you dozy mare! We've got to stop them!'

Arthur swooped down behind the nearest 88, got it in his sights, and opened fire. His tracer sparkled along the tail fin. Useless: it was barely scratched. Arthur fired again; he wanted to keep firing, really pound the bugger...but he already knew what had to be behind him. A glance over his shoulder showed an Me109 right on his tail. He half-rolled away; maybe he could lure it out of the way, give one of the other Spits a chance to get close. By the time he'd straightened up he was a thousand feet below. He looked behind: nothing. The Me109 hadn't been drawn away, it was sticking close to the bomber. Damn. He turned and angled up.

By then the first four 88s were over the radar station. Arthur saw the bombs detach from beneath the Junkers' wings and tumble down. The air was still; the bombers were as low as they dared, and their aim was good. On the cliff top, tiny figures were running for cover. The ack-ack gunners were sticking to their post, blasting away, but weren't making much impression. The 88s tore past above them, already in an upward climb. The bombs continued to fall, slow and almost leisurely; several were right on target for the spindly towers.

Then it happened. The bombs slowed down and down, as if they were getting lighter. When they were no more than a hundred yards above the station, they seemed to bounce as if they'd hit a trampoline. Then, light as shuttlecocks, they flipped back out to sea. When they were away from the towers, they became heavy again. They plummeted into the water, landing in the shallows below the cliff, and exploded in a mucky spray of seawater and sand.

The blast jolted Arthur's Spitfire; he had to fight for a moment to keep steady. When he'd straightened out again, the four remaining Junkers 88s were nearly over the radar towers. A Spitfire swooped down to meet them head on, two Me109s on its tail. The Spitfire swayed and turned like a swallow. It was Michal. Despite the German fighters clinging on behind him, Michal fired into the cockpit of the middle 88, then – with only split seconds to spare – lifted his nose and skimmed over the incoming bombers. The Me109s followed. Smoke began to stream from the middle 88's cockpit. But it maintained its dive, and released its bombs when the others did.

The two bombers on either side went into a steep climb, but the middle one kept descending. Some of its crew must have still been alive in there, struggling to keep the 88 steady, but it was losing height all the time. Two Spitfires that had been buzzing around it, looking for a chance, peeled away from the descending bomber; it was obviously finished. Arthur put it from his mind and steered upwards, forcing the Spitfire into a steep climb. *Come on, girl. Just a bit more for me now –*

Then he saw it happen again. The bombs had reached about a thousand feet; and then they simply bounced away. They went further out to sea this time, so the explosion blasted only water into the air. Arthur was too high to feel the jolt; and he had his eye on an Me109 that was suddenly flying straight. It was so close Arthur could see the pilot's head, which was turned in the direction of the explosion. He was staring at the mysterious leaping bombs, just as Arthur had stopped to gawp at Williams' miraculous, self-opening parachute. Arthur thought, *Gotcha.* He zoomed in on the Messerschmitt's port side, aimed at the canopy, and fired.

The 109 pilot spotted him an instant before the shots connected. The man must have had the reflexes of a cat, because he half-rolled away. Arthur saw his tracer fire sparking along the rear fuselage, however, until – most satisfyingly – it blasted into the swastika painted on the tail fin. Half the fin was blasted to pieces. The

Me109 continued to roll away, but was struggling. Arthur followed it, and fired again.

Nothing: just the thud-thud of an empty case. Arthur swore. He was out of ammo. He hadn't even noticed he was getting low – another beginner's mistake. Now that crippled Me109 – the one he'd been looking forward to finishing off – was suddenly more dangerous than he was. He turned away as sharply as he could. With a bit of luck the 109 pilot hadn't noticed he was firing empty. He turned and dived. If anyone followed, all he could do was try to shake them off.

He was at less than a thousand feet when he realised nothing was following. In fact, he was alone. He checked all around, checked again – something might be underneath him, or coming out of the sun. Nothing. Below, the sea sparkled innocently. In the west, the Junkers, Messerschmitts and Spitfires were shrinking to toy-size in the distance. Apart from them, the sky was clear and empty. The battle had moved on, leaving him behind.

He started to climb, to follow the others over the cliffs, after the fleeing bombers. But then he forced himself to level out again. There was nothing he could do. He was out of ammo, and – he checked the gauge – yes, he was getting low on fuel. It was time to go home.

The battle was over, for him at least. The whole thing had taken less than ten minutes.

Arthur took a couple of deep breaths. He was drenched in sweat, he suddenly realised, under his heavy flight jacket. The cockpit was stifling, and the sun beat down through the Spitfire's Perspex hood. Some fresh air, that's what he needed. Fresh air and a bath —

'Kestrel, this is Wardston. Do you read me, Kestrel? Over.'

How long had Control been calling? He'd been too distracted to notice. Arthur took another breath and answered, 'Wardston, this is Kestrel Leader, over.'

'Kestrel. Nice to hear from you.' Control sounded relieved.

'Be advised, Kestrel, Edey and Jacko Squadrons are coming at you – angels seven, vector three-one-oh. Confirm, two Hurricane squadrons coming your way. Watch your fire, Kestrel. Over.'

Hurricanes. British fighters. Slower than Spitfires, but still more than capable. They'd take on the surviving Junkers and Messerschmitts. Bring them down, probably, now that Kestrel Squadron had worn them out and half-crippled them. He wanted to shout at Control, *They're ours, you bastards…*Instead, he kept his voice level. 'Thanks, Wardston. Heading for home now. Over.'

'Welcome back, Kestrel. Out.'

Arthur made his voice light. The rest of Kestrel Squadron would still be in hot pursuit, he knew. They wouldn't want to abandon the chase; but, by now, they would all be as low on ammo and fuel as he was. 'This is Kestrel Leader. Home time, gentlemen. Let's leave some for the Hurricanes; it's not their fault they're slow.'

Radio crackle. 'Kestrel Leader, this is Blue Three.' Penry-Smith. 'Good to hear your voice, Arthur. Heading home.'

No one else replied. They could be caught up in the battle; or they could have been shot down. No way of knowing, and nothing he could do about it anyway. 'Blue Three, this is Kestrel Leader. Heading home.'

But there was something he had to do first. Arthur tipped the Spitfire into a slow, curving descent. Making wide lazy circles like a falcon, he scanned the shimmering surface of the sea. Nothing. The glare from the water made his eyes stream. He kept going anyway; he was low on fuel, but there'd be enough for this. He was less than a thousand feet up when he spotted something grey-white. He circled closer. Yes, there it was: an open parachute, floating on the calm water like a giant jellyfish, trailing its cables. Nothing attached to it, however. *Come on, Harry…*

And yes: there was something, a few hundred yards away. Something bobbing in the water. Not just bobbing – waving. A tiny arm was gesturing at him. Arthur swooped down to no more than a hundred yards, until he was sure. It was Williams. So many pilots who baled out over the Channel went straight to the bottom, but Williams had evidently got his life-jacket inflated in time. *Good man, Harry.* Arthur spoke into the radio: 'Wardston, this is Kestrel Leader. We have a man in the water about a mile off the radar station. I repeat, one of our men is in the water, just off the radar station. Over.'

'Kestrel, this is Wardston. Understood, Kestrel Leader, we'll ring the coastguard.'

Arthur dipped a wing to show Williams he'd seen him, then began his ascent. The air was clear; inland, the swarming planes were reduced to the size of insects. Arthur, still reluctant to leave them, made himself steer for home. He watched carefully as one of the insects grew bigger, sprouted wings; but it was a Spitfire. It followed Arthur along the coastline, north towards Wardston. When it was a couple of hundred yards away, it meekly took up position off Arthur's port side, as if the formation had never been broken. Arthur spoke into the radio: 'Blue Three, welcome back. Heading home, Penry?'

'Kestrel Leader, this is Blue Three. Out of ammo and nearly out of juice, Arthur. Not much choice really.'

'Blue Three, this is Kestrel—'

'Bandit, nine o'clock high.' The jolly note was gone from Penry's voice. 'Coming in over land.'

Arthur looked up, to his left. About a thousand feet above, a small plane was approaching in a hurry. A Messerschmitt. 'I see him. Get ready to run for it, Blue Three.'

'Roger, Kestrel Leader... No. Wait. He's got one of ours on his tail.'

Arthur looked up again. Another plane took on shape, directly behind the German fighter. A Spitfire. It was less than a thousand yards from the 109's tail. The Me109 was trailing smoke, but was still going over 300 mph. It flashed over Penry-Smith and Arthur, ignoring them completely. Then the Spitfire passed over them too. It had been hit at some point: the leading edge of its port wing was as ragged as a tomcat's ear. But it pressed on with the chase. Within seconds, both planes were over the Channel.

'Just look at that maniac.' Penry-Smith's tone was admiring. 'What's that mad Polish bugger up to this time?'

'That's Michal! Stay with him!'
   'What about the bombers?'
   'Never mind that, just stay with him!'

The Me109 was struggling. Michal watched it carefully. He was dimly aware that the Spit's cockpit was full of the smell of coolant. Leaking? He checked the glycol – seemed okay, the temperature was a bit high, but he thought it would hold. He was over the sea now. Probably wiser to turn back. But he focussed on the Messerschmitt.

Arthur's voice spoke in his ear. 'Blue Two, this is Kestrel Leader. Looks like you've been hit, Blue Two. Suggest you turn back. That 109's finished, Michal, let it go.'

Michal studied the Me109. It was less than nine hundred yards away by now. It was losing height, and leaking black oily smoke. Arthur was undoubtedly right: the plane was finished. Even if it managed to land, it would be beyond repair. But Michal lined it up in his sights.

The plane didn't matter. The Nazi pilot inside did.

Eight hundred yards. Now the voice in Michal's ear was Penry-Smith's. 'Blue Two, this is Blue Three. You've definitely been hit, Blue Two, your port wing's like a bloody Swiss cheese. That Jerry's going down, Michal, come home and leave the poor sod alone.'

The poor sod. Michal shook his head. How sentimental the British pilots could be, about the Nazi airmen who invaded their country's skies every day and tried to kill them. *Our opposite numbers,* they called them. Like the whole war was one big game of cricket. He'd seen his British comrades with captured Nazi pilots; slapping their backs, offering them cigarettes, even buying them drinks. Once a British airman had told him, *They're really no different from us, you know,* and Arthur had had to drag Michal away.

Seven hundred yards. It was because the British didn't *know,* of course. They'd only seen the Nazis as downed and captured prisoners, frightened and bedraggled. They hadn't really seen them. But if swastika'd tanks ever rolled through the streets of London, when swastika'd planes bombed British towns and villages flat, *then* the British would see the Nazis as they really were. Six hundred yards.

Five hundred. The Messerschmitt's pilot had given up all attempts to duck and weave. He was flying straight. Panicking, hoping sheer speed would get him away; in fact, making himself an easy target. An inexperienced pilot: probably young. Michal took aim. Four hundred yards – perfect. He fired.

The 109's tail-fin was blown apart. Rudderless, the German fighter fell into a spin. As Michal flashed past overhead, he could see the pilot wrestling to open the cockpit canopy.

'Look, there! Pull the pilot out!'
　'Eh? That's a German plane, Maggie.'
　'I don't care, just pull him out!'

There were no other planes for miles around, so Michal was still watching the Me109 when the canopy was ripped open and the occupant was yanked out. Michal thought: *Maggie*. The 109 maintained its headlong fall. Then a fireball flashed against the blue sky, as the engine ignited and the plane exploded.

Michal blinked to clear the after-image. The smoking wreckage of the German plane was plunging to the sea. But floating above, there was a patch of white. The Nazi pilot had baled out; his parachute had opened, and he was floating calmly, thousands of feet over the Channel.

Michal throttled back, reducing speed, and steered into a wide turn. He checked fuel – low, but there'd be enough. He banked smoothly downwards, until he was level with the figure hanging from the parachute a few thousand yards away. He aimed the Spitfire's nose at the Nazi airman and, taking his time, steered directly towards him.

The radio buzzed into life in his ear. 'Blue Two.' It was Arthur. 'Blue Two, return to base. You've been hit. You brought him down, Michal, now leave it.'

Michal shook his head again. All the British – even Arthur – they thought it was about bringing down the plane. After that, the game was over. But it was the pilot that mattered. The pilot, who could be rescued, who could make his way home to the Fatherland. What did a Messerschmitt matter, without the Nazi airman inside? Michal had the open chute in his sights now. He was closing in.

Arthur's voice again: 'That's an order, Blue Two. Return to base.'

Michal ignored him. The pilot was in the circle of the Spitfire's gun-sight. His face was a pale dot, turned towards the approaching Spitfire. He could see Michal coming. He could see his death coming. Michal thought: *That's right. That's how it feels.* Closer now; closer. He could almost see the Nazi's expression, see him realise he was going to die. *That's how it feels. That's how my mother feels. Every day.* He put his thumb on the firing button.

The man was struggling in his chute now, actually trying to swing out of the way. But there was nothing he could do. *That's how it feels.* No more than a hundred yards away now. Arthur was saying something, but Michal didn't listen. He was thinking:

That's how it feels. Now, remember it.

With only fifty yards or so to spare, Michal took his thumb off the firing button and steered down and to starboard. He flashed underneath the Nazi airman, glimpsing the white circle of the chute and – for an instant – the soles of the man's feet. The right foot was pale and bare; the German had lost one of his boots. Michal watched in the mirror as the pilot tried to spin himself around, so he could keep Michal's Spitfire in sight. There was nothing he could do to defend himself, of course, if Michal came back; but he couldn't help looking anyway. *That's how it is. You can't help looking, when death is coming. That's how it feels. Remember it.*

Michal swung in a wide arc, turning his head to watch the parachutist, considering. His slipstream had blown the man towards the British coastline. He would still come down in the sea, though, maybe a mile or two offshore. He'd probably drown. In spite of himself, Michal thought about flying around the man again, pushing him a bit closer to land. It was the memory of that dangling foot, bare and vulnerable, that did it. Maybe he would go around him once more...

No. He was low on fuel, and his wing was damaged. He was running a risk every moment he stayed airborne. And he wouldn't keep running that risk for a Nazi. The man might well drown, but he might be lucky – a fishing boat might pick him up.

'He's going to land in the water. Pull him in, onto the beach.'

'Aw, bloody hell, Maggie—'

'Just do it!'

Michal saw the parachute's downward drift change. Suddenly the man was heading straight towards the British coast, as if a strong wind were blowing him; but there was no such wind. He looked as if he'd been snagged on a fishing-line, and someone was reeling him in.

Michal thought: *Maggie*. Not just Maggie: her little brother, Colin. And the other two. He'd seen them in the cottage garden. *Alice. And Vince.* No one had told him their names; he'd only seen them for a moment. But he knew they were Alice and Vince.

Michal followed the fast-moving parachute. It was still descending, but by the time the descent was concluded, the pilot was on the beach below the radar station. Michal reduced his height. The Nazi was standing up to his thighs in water, fumbling with the straps of his parachute. The chute was drifting on the surf, trying to tug him back out to sea. The man tipped his head back and watched Michal pass by overhead. His mouth was hanging open. He was so dazed he didn't even try to take cover.

Michal thought: *Maggie.*

It was all he could think for the rest of the day: *Maggie.* When he landed back at the base with only a few gallons of fuel to spare. When the ground crew threw up their hands in horror at the state of his Spitfire. When he collected his bicycle and tried to ride away towards the Mound, until Arthur grabbed his shoulder and reminded him he was still on duty.

It was the longest afternoon of his life. Sitting in the sunshine outside the dispersal hut, waiting for the order to scramble again. Waiting in vain; the sky was suddenly empty. A whole afternoon playing cards, trying to ignore Penry-Smith's efforts to annoy him, eating corned beef sandwiches from the NAAFI van and drinking endless cups of tea. All the while thinking: *Maggie.* Sometimes *Colin, Vince, Alice*; because they were waiting too. They were watching the skies too.

Sunset, and permission to stand down, came like a release from prison. He was on his bicycle and away without a word to anyone. Along the twilit roads to the foot of the Mound. He left his bicycle and ran, around the winding path to the top.

All four of them were still there. Maggie and Alice were sitting on the ground, propped up against the Stone. Colin and Vince were on their feet, pacing. They all looked tired, but they all looked up at Michal and grinned. Alice said: 'I *knew* he could sense us.'

Michal stared back at them, still gasping from the run. He had no words for what he wanted to ask, in English or in Polish. 'What,' he managed, 'what did you…'

Vince laughed. 'We're your new secret weapon, mate,' he said. 'We're going to win the war.'

In London, crouched in a small room deep underground, Jannah couldn't help smiling too.

Chapter Fourteen

The World's Centre

Wewelsburg Castle, Western Germany

The Wewelsburg was lit up like a diamond in a jeweller's window. The castle was unique: a triangular keep, with a tower at each of its three corners. It stood proudly on its hilltop, surrounded by trees. Each tower was floodlit, and lights shone in the windows. Its sandstone walls were pale yellow in the artificial light. In the valley below the castle were the lesser lights of the village. Only at the very foot of the hill was darkness; the clump of shabby huts, where the forced-labourers slept, was not lit by night.

On the flat roof of the round North Tower, torches burned. There was movement there. No air traffic was allowed over the Wewelsburg, but a pilot flying overhead would have seen an extraordinary sight – a circle of twelve boys, with a girl in a red dress in the centre, and all thirteen were floating a dozen feet in the air. They hung suspended in the night sky, the boys' white shirts bright in the firelight, the girl's skirts a swirl of crimson.

At last, they descended. They sank until they were just a few inches from the floor; then the twelve boys stepped down easily and gracefully onto the rooftop. Lise spun downwards as light as thistledown, her skirts twirling around her. She opened her eyes, which flashed electric blue, before settling to her normal brown.

Slowly, the twelve boys opened their eyes. There was a pause as they came back to the here and now. At last, Albrecht said: 'So, it seems our British friends still have their power.'

The others looked sombre. The four British children – *wizards*, they called themselves – were not as incapacitated as they had hoped. In fact… 'They seem to be getting stronger,' Albrecht added.

Hans nodded thoughtfully. 'I thought they'd lose their power when the traitor was removed and the circle was broken.' Then he added what the others were thinking, but didn't want to say: 'Reichsführer Himmler thought they would. But he was… wrong.'

They avoided each other's eyes. Heinrich Himmler, wrong? Surely not… 'It must be because the traitor is still alive,' Albrecht said firmly. 'She hasn't been killed, so the circle isn't truly broken.'

They all thought of the vision they'd seen earlier: the Polish girl Jannah, sitting alone in a tiny room, weeping. 'Perhaps that's why the British haven't killed her,' Hans said. 'They're afraid to break the connection.'

Petr thought: *Because they're weak, more likely.* He could imagine what must have happened: the pretty Polish girl had looked up at her captors with big sad eyes, and they'd been too gutless to do what ought to be done. That was why the British would lose the war: only National Socialism gave a man backbone. 'Our people might as well get rid of the girl's family now,' he said. 'The sister looks like she might be racially pure enough to be worth hanging onto, but the parents can be disposed of.'

Albrecht shook his head. 'Our people won't do that. They promised the girl that her family would be safe if she co-operated. Keeping a promise is a matter of honour.'

Lise looked at him admiringly, while the other boys nodded agreement. Petr looked away. How naïve could they be? The German High Command, bound by a promise to a Pole? Hardly.

He shook his head, but contented himself with saying: 'The British wizards still have their powers, certainly. But if they keep on using them so incompetently, we have nothing to worry about.'

'That's true,' said Albrecht. 'They should have focused on the bombers, but they wasted their time pulling men out of cockpits and following individual pilots. The older boy has the right instincts, but he lets himself be dominated by the others. By the girls.'

They all smiled contemptuously. At first they'd been more worried about the older boy – what was he called, Vince – than about any of the others. They'd expected him at least to take the lead, as was only natural for the oldest male in the group. He looked as if he had good blood; and what they knew of his past suggested he had the strength to be a real threat, since he'd so regrettably decided to use that strength against them. But so far, he had proved unimpressive. Petr said, 'We needn't be too concerned about a man who lets himself be ruled by women.'

'Unless those women are divinely inspired, of course,' said Albrecht, smiling and bowing slightly to Lise, who giggled and smiled back. Albrecht added, to Petr: 'You're right, though. The older girl seems to be leading the group now. What's her name, Maggie? Magda?'

'The red-haired one?' said Petr. 'The Jewess?'

There was a silence. Eventually Manfred, one of the younger boys, said uncertainly, 'How do you know she's Jewish?'

Petr looked at him. 'By her hair.' Hadn't he seen the films, the pictures, the Party information leaflets? 'That curly red hair, it's Jewish.'

There was another silence. The others thought about the Jewish people they'd seen, who had looked – they had to admit it – more or less like everybody else. 'I thought Jews were supposed to have black hair,' Manfred said at last.

'Sometimes they do.'

'And besides, there used to be this Jewish family on our street, and they had sort of brown hair like mine,' Manfred persisted. 'Some of them were nearly blonde.'

Another boy added, 'And my sister's got red hair. She's not Jewish. She's not,' he added defensively as some of the others burst into jeering laughter, 'she's been racially defined, she had her head measured and everything. She's Germanic all right, she's just got red hair.'

Petr stared him down. 'Not any red hair. Just hair like – that.'

Manfred was still trying to understand. 'And what about that British wizard girl? Alice, isn't it? She's got blonde hair, but says she's Jewish.'

'She's lying,' snapped Petr.

'Why would she lie about being Jewish?'

Petr shrugged. 'All right then, she says she's a half-Jew. They can sometimes have blonde hair. They're still Jews.'

Hans smiled. 'So what you're saying is that Jews definitely have red hair, except when it's black? Or brown, or blonde?' A few of the younger boys laughed. Encouraged, Hans went on, 'And non-Jews can have red hair, so long as it's not Jewish red hair?'

'That's not—'

'Isn't that Magda or Maggie or whoever Scottish anyway? I thought they all had red hair there?'

Petr looked away. Hans thought he was funny. He'd have to be careful, Petr thought. It wasn't always good, to think you were funny. But he just said, 'It doesn't matter. She's leading the group. And all she cares about is keeping her Polish fancy-man safe.'

Lise sighed. 'It makes no sense to me,' she declared, 'why any girl would choose a Pole when there are better men around.' Poles were dirty, lazy and stupid, everyone knew that. It flashed across her mind that the pilot Michal didn't seem to be any of those things, but she pushed the thought away quickly; his Polish traits would surely come out in the end. 'And his friend is obviously so much more Aryan,' she added. 'You can tell it at a glance. What's his name – it's a bit like Albrecht…' She caught Albrecht's eye and blushed prettily, 'Arthur? Why doesn't the silly girl want to be with him instead?'

'It's probably because the Polish airman has the power too,' Hans said absently. 'Maybe she wants to have a baby with him. The child of two wizards would be very strong.'

There was silence. 'Are you sure?' Albrecht said. 'About the Polish pilot?'

Hans was still musing to himself. 'Strange, isn't it, that a Pole should have the power and his Aryan friend should not… if the power truly comes from the Aryan Race-Soul…'

Albrecht interrupted, 'Hans, are you sure? That the Polish pilot has the gift too?'

'Of course.' Hans looked surprised. 'How else do you think he could sense what they were doing? It's not very strong in him, but it's enough for that.'

There was silence. A psychic coven, directing a psychic fighter pilot? That could be very unfortunate. Albrecht nodded. 'We must tell Reichsführer Himmler. The Polish pilot should be disposed of, we'll advise him of that.'

A shiver of pleasure went through them all. They were actually giving advice to Himmler! And he would listen! Albrecht nodded again. 'We'll advise that the Luftwaffe should target the whole squadron. The British wizards have clearly formed a bond with them. Perhaps with them out of the way, they'll become more… reasonable.'

Lise sighed again. 'It's so silly, isn't it, that they have to carry on this fight! That people have to die! People with Aryan blood!'

Albrecht smiled at her. 'Don't think about that,' he said gently. 'Think of what we're fighting for. Show us again. Show us, lady. Show us how it will be, when National Socialism triumphs!'

Lise smiled. She lifted her arm and turned in a sweeping circle.

Her eyes blazed sapphire-blue. 'Close your eyes,' she said.

The boys obeyed. When they opened them again, the night was gone and they looked out into daylight. The glamour spell had created bright golden unwavering sunshine, beautiful and unreal as a Hollywood film. The land around the castle was emerald green. The labour camp had vanished without a trace. The sprawling village had been replaced by an orderly block of white villas, landscaped with manicured lawns and neat little streams. The castle itself seemed to have been extended; a vast circular wall, the same glowing gold as the castle, skirted the hill. It was hung with banners, with Swastikas and Black Suns.

The boys smiled with pleasure; but the best was yet to come. The Wewelsburg was the hub of a dozen straight white roads, all leading inwards to the castle. On each road moved a procession. On one was a group of girls in white dresses, carrying flowers; on another, boys in shorts, marching in perfect time. A legion of brownshirts; a legion of black-clad SS officers. And men on horseback, like fully-equipped knights, their horses draped in red and black.

On the North tower, the *gothi* boys exclaimed and pointed as tanks rolled in perfect formation towards them. German planes, Messerschmitts and Stukas and Junkers 88s, flew overhead, dipping their wings in salute. All the legions on the roads sang a chorus by Wagner in perfect unison and harmony. Crowds lined the roads, cheering and throwing flowers. In the block of white villas, well-dressed people stood in doorways or leaned out of windows. They waved; the marchers on the roads saluted as they passed.

On the roof of the tower, Manfred whispered in awe: 'Is that Wewelsburg village? Is that what it will be like? When…'

'When the Thousand-Year Reich comes.' The musical voice of Lise – of Freya – surrounded them. 'When the Führer's vision comes to pass.'

Albrecht pointed to the white houses on the site of the village. 'The old village will be replaced,' he explained to Manfred. 'These will be homes for high-ranking SS officers.'

Manfred paused. He'd met some of the current villagers; he quite liked them. 'Where will the villagers go?' he asked.

'They'll be given lands elsewhere,' Albrecht said. 'Good lands. Somewhere in the new Greater Germany.'

'What about the people down there?' Hans said. He was pointing at the beautiful, empty green field where – back in mundane reality – the forced-labour camp stood. 'Where will they go?'

Albrecht frowned. 'Back where they came from, I suppose.'

'Where *did* they come from? What—'

'Come.' Freya's voice called them. They forgot everything else. 'Come and see it,' she said. Lise, eyes electric-blue, was rising into the air.

All twelve rose obediently after her. They floated to fifty feet, to a hundred. The Technicolor vision spread out below them. The roads and the emerald grass formed a huge sun-wheel below them. The golden triangular castle was lodged in the circle's heart like the tip of a spear. The whole thing was a reverse image of the Black Sun, white on green. 'The Black Sun,' Albrecht cried.

'Holy emblem of the German people,' agreed Freya. 'This place will be the heart of the Führer's empire.' Her heart swelled with joy. 'When we enter into sacred marriage, he and I, this will be our dwelling place. The centre of the new world.'

They stared in awe. Some were moved to tears. They stayed hovering there for over an hour, gazing at this glorious vision. Their bodies, stuck in the mundane night-time world, became cold and chilled in the evening air. But none of them noticed.

Wardston Air Base, South-East England

The bar in the officers' mess was full of laughter. The whole of Kestrel Squadron, minus only Michal and Williams, sat around the long battered table. The mess steward, affronted by the presence of non-officers, was angrily polishing glasses behind the bar, tight-lipped with disapproval. The pilots took no notice. Empty beer glasses thronged the scratched wooden table-top. Every man held a full glass.

Penry-Smith was holding forth: '...So he's got his chute open, but now the poor little Kraut's just hanging there. Crapping himself, you can practically see it running down his leg. He's watching Michal charging towards him. Thinks his number's up. Then at the last minute, the mad Polish bastard jinks to one side and goes right past him. Misses him by inches, I'm telling you. Then the slipstream just picks the man up and wafts him all the way to Blighty. I've never seen anything like it. Must have been two miles at least. Next thing the Jerry knows, he's standing on the beach below the radar station, trying to empty the shit out of his trousers before the Home Guard show up to arrest him. Priceless.' Penry-Smith wiped the tears of mirth from his eyes. 'Good old Michal, always value for money.'

The pilot beside him, Scots Eddy Paterson, drained his glass. 'Where is Michal, anyway?'

Penry-Smith shrugged. The man opposite, a new boy known as Kiddy Jones, piped up: 'Took off on his bicycle, as soon as we were stood down. Heading for the village, I think.'

'Oh ho.' Penry raised his eyebrows. 'Off to the lovely Maggie,

I'd say. D'you know Maggie, Eddy?'

'Aye, I think I've seen her right enough.' Eddy's Aberdeen accent always seemed to get stronger when he was talking to Penry-Smith. 'That wee red-haired lassie?'

'That's her. One of your lot, isn't she? Scottish? On her mother's side or something?'

'Aye, I think so.'

Penry-Smith leered. 'And how do you feel about one of your countrywomen being rogered by our Polish friend?'

Eddy shrugged. 'Better than a stuck-up English nancyboy like you.'

Before the laughter died down, the door banged open. A cheer went up; it was Flight-Sergeant Williams. He was dry, and wearing his second-best uniform, but his hair was sticking out in all directions, clogged with sea-salt. Arthur caught the mess steward's eye, signalled for more beer. Williams dropped into a chair, muttering an acknowledgement of the others' greeting. Arthur said, 'How was your swim, Harry?'

'Ruddy freezing.' Williams took the beer from the steward, ignoring the man's frosty expression, and took a big gulp. He looked around the table, counting heads and checking faces, then frowned and looked at Arthur. 'Michal?'

'Safe,' Arthur assured him.

'Safe in the arms of Maggie,' said Penry-Smith. 'Remember her, Harry?'

Williams thought for a moment. 'Ginger hair?' he offered eventually. 'Big tits?'

'Keep it respectful, Williams,' Arthur said sharply.

Williams mumbled an apology. Penry-Smith made a stern face at him. 'Yes, watch that rough Northern tongue of yours, Flight-Sergeant. You're among officers now.'

'Up yours. Sir,' said Williams.

'That's better. Bit of deference at least.' Drunk on beer and euphoria, Penry-Smith turned to Arthur, a sly look on his face. 'So when are we going to meet that little poppet of yours, Arthur? The one in the picture?'

Arthur gazed at him levelly. After a moment's silence, Scots Eddy put down his glass and said, 'Okay, I'll bite. What picture?'

'The photo by Arthur's bed. Big silver frame and everything. Portrait of the most delectable little WAAF you've ever seen. Think of Vivien Leigh, only blonde.'

'Are you a married man too, Arthur?' asked Eddy, who had a wife and two children back in Aberdeenshire.

'No.' After a pause Arthur added, 'Not yet.'

'Engaged then?'

'Yes.'

Arthur kept his stare fixed on Penry. The others were quietening down, starting to get the hint, but Penry-Smith ploughed on. 'What's her name?'

'Sylvia.'

'And she's a WAAF? Where's she stationed?'

'I can't tell you.'

'Fair enough. Careless talk and all that. But can't she get a transfer here? Keep you company?'

'No, she can't.'

At last, even Penry-Smith seemed to catch on. 'All right. No offense, old man, just asking.'

Arthur kept his gaze on Penry-Smith. At last he said, 'You getting a round in, Penry?'

'All right, all right.' Penry-Smith was waving to the steward when the door opened again. They all sat up a bit straighter as Flight-Commander Owens appeared; you didn't stand to attention in the mess, but some habits were too deeply ingrained to ignore completely. 'Sir,' said Arthur as Owens strolled over to them.

'Gentlemen.' Owens looked at Flight-Sergeant Williams and Kiddy Jones, who was a sergeant-pilot. 'My eyes must be deceiving me,' Owens said mildly, 'I can't possibly be looking at two non-officers drinking in the officers' mess, can I?'

'No sir,' Penry-Smith said promptly. 'Perish the thought, sir. Figments of your imagination, sir.'

'Indeed. Must be something I ate.'

'Too much cheese,' suggested Williams.

'Quite. Look, you chaps.' He sighed. 'I'm sorry, but I'll have to cut into your free time again. You'll need to be on night-readiness tonight.'

They all groaned. Scots Eddy said, 'What about 24 Squadron? I thought they were on tonight?'

'24 Squadron took a bit of a pasting this afternoon, I'm afraid.'

The pilots fell silent. They knew most of 24 Squadron. Arthur said, 'How bad?'

'Five planes lost in total. One forced landing, pilot's okay; two bale-outs, both in hospital. The other two men didn't make it.'

After a long pause, Arthur said, 'Who?'

'Timmy Price. And George Herrick.'

Arthur nodded. Owens sighed again, and patted him on the shoulder. 'You'll all be bunking down in the dispersal tents tonight, Willoughby. Make sure everybody knows. As like as not you'll have a quiet night.' He left without another word.

No one spoke. Arthur signalled towards the bar. The steward, who had overheard the conversation, appeared in moments carrying a tray with eleven small glasses and a bottle of whisky. Arthur poured and passed out the glasses in silence. When everyone had a glass, he raised his. 'Price and Herrick,' he said, and drank his whisky in one.

'Price and Herrick,' the others echoed, and drained their glasses. Arthur gave them another five seconds to sit in silence; then he set his empty glass down firmly. 'Right, gentlemen. You heard the man. We're camping out tonight. Just like being in the Scouts again.'

'All due respect, sir,' said Penry-Smith, 'but I'm fairly shit-faced.' He waved at the empty glasses on the table. 'So are the rest of us. And what about Michal?'

'Black coffee all round.' Arthur signalled to the steward again. 'And don't worry about Michal. I'll get them to telephone him. I know where he'll be.'

Michal and Maggie lay in the grass, on the still-warm earth. The Mound was in near-darkness. Behind them, light still rimmed the western horizon. If they sat up they would be facing out to sea, into darkness. The sky was black; high cloud covered the moon and stars. In peacetime the lights of Wardston would have been shining below, but the village was blacked-out. The rest of the world had vanished. Michal could hear nothing but the rhythmic hiss of waves on the beach below, and Maggie's breathing. He could smell the sea, the grass and – from the potato fields to the north – a whiff of manure. He could smell the earth, still warm from the hot summer sun. And Maggie, of course. She didn't wear artificial perfume; she smelled of soap and clean sweat and something warm and spicy in her hair. She smelled of herself.

Michal lay on his back, his arm around Maggie, who lay beside him. Her arm was across him, her face rested on the rough cotton of his shirt. It occurred to him that he was still wearing his grubby old gardening clothes, and that he hadn't had a wash since this morning; but Maggie didn't seem to mind. She hugged him against her, body warm against his side. His arm was getting cramped, but he wouldn't have moved it for the world. She was murmuring to him: 'Magic. I know how it sounds, but it's true.'

'I believe you.'

'I'm – I don't know – a wizard. Or a witch, or something.'

'You are too pretty to be a witch.'

She laughed, and lifted herself up so she could kiss him again.

After a blissfully long time, she pulled away. He felt her tense up a little; he waited. At last she said uncertainly: 'Michal?'

'Yes?'

'When you...shoot the planes down. And the pilots get killed.'

'Yes.'

'Is it hard? Don't you mind it?'

He thought about lying to her; decided against it. 'No. No, not now.'

'Did you mind before?'

'Yes. Before. I am my mother's son.'

'Your mother?'

'Yes. She used to believe as your father believed.'

'A conchie?'

'A pacifist. Yes. But she changed.'

'Why did she change?'

'Because the Nazis invaded. She said, "We must fight them now." I said, "Why now?" She said, "Because they are here." I was a pilot. I tried to drive them out. I could not. So she said – "Go to England, and try again from there." So I did. I left her and my grandmother and came here. My mother is a teacher of languages, so my English is good. I joined the British air force. They do not like to take Polish men into squadrons of British pilots, but they made exceptions for me.'

'Because your English is so good?'

'Yes.' Also because, as the recruiting officer had told him: *Right now we need mad, trigger-happy bastards like you, Capek, so welcome aboard.* But he left that part out. 'Because of my English. And because I make so many kills.'

He felt her flinch. 'Kills?'

'To shoot down a plane is called a kill,' he explained gently. 'Not to kill a man.'

She nodded. 'I saw you with that German pilot. After you brought down his plane. You looked like you were going to shoot him. But you didn't.'

'There was no need. He was parachuting over British water. Over Britain.'

'What if he was parachuting down over France? Over German territory? Would you have shot him then?'

Again, he thought about lying; again, he decided against it. 'Yes. I would.'

They lay silent for a long time. Eventually Michal said, 'The British pilots say the Nazis are their opposite numbers. I say they are a wolf that attacks my home and my family. When a wolf attacks, you shoot it. It is not a game. You do not enjoy it. But you shoot. And if you cannot shoot, you pull out its teeth and its claws. One by one. The Nazi pilots. If we pull them one by one, then some day the wolf will not be able to bite.'

'Oh.' He wondered if she would shrink away from him. But she stayed where she was. After a while she said quietly, 'I don't know if I could kill someone.'

'I know you do not.' *But you will find out, I think.*

There was a long silence. He didn't want to talk about killing any more. He was relieved when she laughed softly and said, 'I didn't think you'd believe me. About the magic. It sounds mad.'

'Not to me. It is in my family too, I think.' A lot was making sense to him now. 'My aunt. She could make things move. Without touching them.' He frowned. 'But when she did, it made her nose bleed. Her ears sometimes. So she stopped. She was not... strong, I think.'

And here they were again: back at blood and death. He rolled over and gathered her into his arms. 'I do not want to talk of this.'

Her mouth was against his; he felt her smile. 'What do you want to talk about?'

'I do not want to talk.'

When the voice started calling, far away, he prayed it was a night-bird. *'Miiiichaaal...?'* Or a hallucination. *'Miiiiichaaaaal...?'*

Or a ghost, anything. *'Miiiiii-chaaaaaal…!'* But eventually Maggie disentangled herself. 'I think that's Colin.'

He thought, *not now…* But she was sitting up. 'Colin? Colin?'

'Maggie?' Colin's voice echoed upwards. It sounded like he was halfway up the Mound, on the path below them. '…Is Michal still there?'

'Colin? Where are you?'

'I'm down here.' Definitely, right below them. 'Gran sent me to find Michal. Vince said I shouldn't come all the way up… in case you two… umm…'

With all the patience he could muster, Michal called: 'What is it, Colin?'

'Michal? There's a phone call for you. At the cottage. It's the airbase. They say you've to come, right now…'

Chapter Fifteen

Night Flying

Michal cycled carefully through the blacked-out countryside. His bicycle lamp was covered in paper to reduce the light to a faint glow. He went slowly, keeping his ears open for oncoming cars, which might not see him and his bike until it was too late. There was no need to worry, though – the road was silent and empty. So were the skies. Not a single sign of enemy aircraft – but still, he'd had to leave Maggie's arms to sleep in a tent and wait for them. Maggie. Who was a wizard. And she was his girl now. Maggie. He was murmuring to himself as he rode through the airbase gate. The guard looked at him, startled, from his dimly-lit sentry hut, but said nothing.

Michal found his way to the dispersal hut more by memory than by sight. The hut was in complete darkness, of course, its hatch covered by a black-out curtain. There were dim lights a few yards away, though, and beside the lights were rows of greenish-black humps. Tents. The squadron's usual sleeping quarters were half a mile away, and pilots on night-readiness had to sleep as close as possible to their planes; hence the little camp-site a few hundred yards from the Spitfires. Michal heard the murmur of voices, saw figures seated outside the tents in deck-chairs or on the ground. A hurricane lantern stood outside each tent, wrapped in paper like

Michal's bicycle-lamp. Tiny red lights moved and winked; Michal could smell smoke from pipes and cigarettes.

When Michal's eyes had adjusted to the dim light, he left his bike and made his way past the other pilots. They had been talking quietly, but they started laughing and wolf-whistling as Michal walked by. Even in the low light they could see how grass-stained his clothes were; clearly, he'd just been lying on the ground. 'Welcome back, lover boy,' Penry-Smith called.

Michal ignored them. At the end of the row of tents, he found Arthur and Scots Eddy sitting on camp-chairs. Eddy took his pipe out of his mouth and grinned up at Michal: 'Evening, Romeo.' When Michal stepped further into the glow from the lantern, and Arthur and Eddy could see the dazed look on his face, Eddy burst out laughing. 'My God, man, what did she do to you?'

Michal took no notice. 'Arthur, I must speak to you.'

Arthur wasn't smiling. 'Oh?'

'We must speak in private.'

Eddy said amiably, 'I know when I'm not wanted.' He got up, winked at Michal, and strolled away. Michal sat in his chair and waited until he was out of earshot. 'I must tell you.'

'Tell me what?'

'About…' He thought about it. *Hello, Arthur, my girlfriend is a wizard.* 'About Maggie.' *She can do magic. And she is my girl now.* He laughed. 'She…'

Arthur looked away, into the lantern. His expression was cold. 'I don't think I want to know.'

Michal stopped, bemused. 'No, I must tell you. She—'

'Very well then.' Arthur's voice became hard and clipped. 'I'll tell *you* something. I have a friendship with that girl's family. She has no father to say this, so I will. Maggie is young, and I think very poorly of any man who would take advantage of her.'

'What?'

'You may be unaware of it, but there is a strict code of behaviour here. There are things a decent man does not do outside of marriage.'

'Arthur—'

'In this country, we have standards.'

In this country. 'Is that so?'

'There are certain customs and traditions here.'

It was too much. He knew he shouldn't say this, but… 'So I should treat her as you treat your girl? Your Sylvia?'

Arthur stared at him. 'Be careful.'

'I should do as you do?' He'd been called away from Maggie, for this? 'I should never write to her? I should never see her? I should not care if I am with her or if I am not? Is this the British way?'

Arthur was on his feet. 'You can't…'

Michal got up too, and walked away. He walked past the other pilots, who had fallen silent. He wanted to keep walking, away over the fields. Instead he went into the dispersal hut, briefly letting its light escape, and slammed the door behind him.

The other pilots turned to look at Arthur. Penry-Smith said, 'Trouble in paradise?'

'Shut up, Penry-Smith.'

They left Arthur alone for the rest of the evening. After a while he went into his tent, without another word to anyone. Michal never emerged from the hut.

Maggie dreamed she was strolling on the Mound. She knew it was a dream: the grass was the colour of emeralds, like grass in a child's painting. The air didn't smell of grass, or the sea, or manure from the fields; it smelled of roses, a heavy scent like perfume. She was on her way to the top of the Mound. Something was waiting for her at the top. Someone was walking at her side –

'Maggie! Maggie!'

She thought: *Shoosh, Colin.* She wanted to see who was beside her, in the dream. She wanted to see what was at the top of the Mound.

'*Maggie!*'

She made an indignant noise and opened her eyes. She couldn't see a thing in the darkened bedroom. Alice stirred beside her. The two of them were sharing Dad's bed – sleeping space was restricted in the tiny cottage. They had stayed awake late that night, talking about Alice's three taller, sportier and prettier sisters, whom Alice's parents obviously considered much more of a credit to the family than Alice. Afterwards, Maggie had lain awake even later, getting angry on Alice's behalf, while Alice herself slept peacefully on her side of the bed. Now Maggie blinked up in annoyance at the pale shape that must be Colin's face. 'What *is* it, Colin?'

'I had this dream, Maggie.'

She sighed and pulled the covers back. 'Do you want to get in with us?'

'No, it was a *real* dream, Maggie.'

There was the scrape of a match, and a flare of light. Alice lit the candle by her bedside and said, 'Colin? Are you sure?'

'It was real.' His face was pale. 'They're coming here, Maggie. For Michal.'

Michal awoke suddenly, his stomach lurching. The room was too bright. He was sitting in an armchair in the dispersal hut; he'd nodded off where he sat. He looked around. It must be the middle of the night; the rest of the squadron would be asleep in their tents. No one else was in the hut but the telephone orderly, who was looking at him curiously. 'Are you—'

The phone rang. Michal thought: *They're coming for me.*

The orderly grabbed the receiver. 'Yes… right.' He hung up, sat forward and pulled the hatch's black-out curtain aside. He leaned out and started ringing the bell. 'Squadron scramble!'

Michal was sweating. He leapt up and ran outside. He had to get somewhere safe, underground. In the blackout he turned towards the base and set out to run.

He slammed into someone. A hand grabbed his arm and dragged him into the light. It was Owens. 'What the hell are you doing, Capek!'

Michal doubled up and vomited. Owens shook him. 'Do that on your own time, man! Get to your plane! Go!'

He thrust Michal in the direction of the tents. The other pilots had already crawled out, grabbed their lanterns and were running for their Spitfires. Michal wanted to run in the opposite direction, but habit and training carried him along with the others. He went past the tents, following the bobbing lights ahead. In the blackness engines roared into life; lights began to appear, red and green and white and pale blue. The ground crew were readying the Spitfires.

Michal ran past the other planes and their pilots and crew. When he reached his own plane, he doubled over again. *They are coming for me.* He retched. He heard a voice say, 'Are you all right, sir?' and felt a hand on his shoulder. His fitter: right now he couldn't even remember the man's name. When Michal didn't reply, the fitter pulled him upright and started fastening all the straps on his parachute and life jacket. Michal stood, unresisting. He looked at his Spitfire, which was well-enough lit at close range by the lights on its wings and tail and over the ident letter, and saw the blue exhaust jets ignite. It was ready to go; he would have to be too. He spat to get the taste out of his mouth. The fitter steered him up onto the wing. 'In you go, sir.'

He dropped into his seat in the cockpit. The interior light was bright after the darkness. What now? For a panic-stricken moment he didn't know. Then he remembered: cockpit checks. Come on, he thought, you know this. Gyros... trim... pitch... fuel... straps... helmet, radio. Lower the canopy. One more check around – everything okay. Now the nod to his ground crew – they pulled the chocks away.

The Spitfire rolled forward. Michal felt it respond, and began to feel better. He was in control. He was in his element. His stomach began to settle as he followed the plane in front of him, focussing on its white tail light, the red light on its port wing and the green to starboard. Nothing much else to be seen, but he told himself that didn't matter. The Nazis wouldn't be able to see either.

The Spitfires trundled across the airfield, heading for the flare path. Michal told himself that the sortie would probably be uneventful anyway. That had been Kestrel Squadron's experience of night missions so far. He remembered how Penry-Smith had described night flying to Kiddy Jones: *You can't see the Hun and he can't see you. So you go up, you fly around in circles until you run out of juice, then you land and go back to bed. Complete bloody waste of time.* Usually they couldn't find the enemy in time to engage them. Generally, Michal found it frustrating, but tonight it would suit him just fine.

In front, Arthur was ready for take-off. Arthur was approaching the flare path, the two rows of dimly-lit lamps lining the runway. Arthur steered between the rows of lamps. The white light behind his cockpit flashed out a short sequence: he was Morse-coding his identification letter, so the night-flying officer knew who he was. There was an answering green flash from the officer's Aldis lamp – all clear. Arthur accelerated down the flare path; his Spitfire's lights lifted into the air.

Michal was right behind him. He lined up at the flare-path, Morsed his ident letter, got the green flash and opened up the throttle. The Spitfire responded, speeding down the path between the lamps, lifting smoothly into the air. Michal corrected for swing, and followed Arthur's tail-light. He was beginning to feel ridiculous for panicking so badly. It was, after all, highly unlikely that the Luftwaffe would come all the way across the Channel just to target Michal Capek. He eased into position off Arthur's starboard wing.

The rest of the squadron were forming up around them. There was someone – he looked sideways – on his starboard: Scots Eddy. Eddy sat in a little dome of soft light: the cockpit lights were the brightest things in the sky. Michal could just make out the outline of Eddy's plane. Beyond that, blackness. The moon and stars were still masked by cloud. He glanced backwards, saw the green and red and white lights of the rest of the squadron as they moved into place; behind and below them the flare path, now narrow and dimly lit. He looked ahead. Nothing.

He focussed on the control panel. When you flew in darkness, instruments were what kept you alive. He kept a watchful eye on the little plane-picture on the artificial horizon, making sure it stayed level. Checked height, checked rate of climb. Glanced again and again at Arthur's starboard wing on his left, Eddy's port wing on his right. For the moment, his quarrel with Arthur was forgotten. If he lost track of Arthur and Eddy, he'd be alone in the blackness.

They climbed steadily. Arthur's voice spoke in his ear: 'Wardston, this is Kestrel Leader. Kestrel Squadron airborne. Please advise vector and altitude, Wardston. Over.'

'Kestrel Leader, this is Wardston. Your vector is one-nine-oh. Twelve plus bandits approaching from the south, Kestrel. Angels seven. Over.'

Twelve enemy planes, at seven thousand feet. Coming from the south? Michal scanned his mental map of Southern England. Where were they going? Arthur must have had the same thought: 'Understood, Wardston. Any idea of their target? Over.'

'Not sure yet, Kestrel Leader.' Michal thought Control sounded nervous. 'Their current route would take them right over Wardston.'

Michal went cold. *They're coming here.* But Arthur's voice was sceptical: 'Must be a lot more targets on the way, Wardston. They might be having another pop at the radar station. Over.'

'Still unsure. Keep your eyes peeled, Kestrel. We'll let you know when there's more. Over.'

Keep your eyes peeled. Michal stared out into the darkness until his eyes watered. They were reaching seven thousand feet now, surely they'd see something soon... But, nothing. Michal swore softly. They'd all heard rumours that the scientists were working on a way to fit fighter planes with radar. It couldn't come a day too soon. In the meantime, they would keep on blundering about like moths.

Unless they saw carpets of fire on the earth below, of course. When the bombs had fallen and exploded, you saw the bombers, lit up by the fires they'd made on the ground. But by then it was too late. Michal scanned the sky ahead, looking for the pin-prick gleams of cockpit lights and navigation lights. Still nothing. He had forgotten his hopes that they'd pass by the bombers in the night; he wanted them now, before they let their bombs fall.

The radio spoke in his ear. 'Kestrel Leader, this is Wardston. The bandits have passed over the radar station, Kestrel. Repeat, the radar station doesn't appear to be the target. They're still coming your way. Over.'

'Understood, Wardston.'

'Kestrel Leader, they're flying inland now. We might be losing them soon.' Michal cursed again. The British radar system tended to lose planes when they went inland. After that, Control relied on lookout reports from the Observer Corp. Who, of course, couldn't see in the dark any better than a Spitfire pilot. 'They're coming your way, Kestrel. Keep trying for visual contact. Over.'

Michal could hear other pilots muttering, too. British radar couldn't pinpoint the planes; but the German radio-beam system, the *Knickebein*, could steer the bombers right to their target on the ground. Arthur's voice cut into the murmuring: 'Right, gentlemen, you heard. They're coming our way. They may be in the dark, but they've got cockpit lights and navigation lights just like we have. So fan out and look. They're there, and we'll find them.'

The squadron eased apart, so their lights wouldn't dazzle each other. Michal stared ahead. Whatever Arthur said, he knew where the Nazi bombers were going. They were going to Wardston. To the airbase. His panic was gone; cold fury had taken its place. Because right next to the airbase was the village. The Nazi planes were at seven thousand feet, their bombing wouldn't be accurate. Very easy for a few bombs to go astray.

Very easy to hit the cottage. Where Maggie, and her brother and her grandmother and her friends, were. Where even now they must surely be asleep, not suspecting a thing.

The London blackout had been dark but blackout on the Mound was close to true darkness. Maggie, trousers and boots hastily pulled on over her nightclothes, climbed the path as quickly as she dared. She kept tight hold of Colin's hand. She didn't have to hold onto Alice and Vince, she could hear them behind her. She thought the whole country must be able to hear them.

'Colin, mate, are you sure about this?' Vince had not appreciated being woken in the middle of the night. 'I mean, they can't be coming just for Maggie's boyfriend, can they? Makes no sense.'

That was just what Maggie was thinking, now her initial panic had worn off. But Alice was determined: 'Colin has the power just like the rest of us. Of course he's sure.'

'Oh, come on. Just look at it out here. Black as a coalminer's arse. Not exactly top bombing conditions, are they?'

'You said yourself the German bombers can find their targets in darkness. By the Knicknack system.'

'It's Knickebein, you dozy cow, not—'

'Stop calling me names!'

Maggie snapped, 'Pack it in, you two!'

When they fell silent, they could all hear the sound of engines overhead. It was faint, but it was getting louder. Maggie said, 'Vince, are they ours or theirs?'

'Dunno. Too far away.'

But they were coming closer. Maggie scanned the black sky: she couldn't see a thing. The four of them were right out in the open. She wanted to scuttle back to the cottage, or to burrow into the earth like an animal. But she said, 'Let's get to the Stone,' and started to run uphill.

By the time they reached the Stone, the planes sounded much closer. They stood around the Stone, and joined hands; they didn't need to, not here on the Mound, but they held onto each other anyway, for reassurance. Maggie closed her eyes and tried to steady her nerves. When they formed the circle on the Mound, they never knew quite what they were going to get. 'Here goes,' she said. 'Concentrate…'

The magic hit them at once, hard, as it always did here. It went through them like pain or love or fear. For a moment, Maggie was struck by vertigo, her stomach churning. But she said to herself: *Clockwise.* The others must have been thinking it too, because in an instant the power was flowing obediently around the circle, through their joined hands. Tamed, at least for now. Maggie opened her eyes.

The witch-sight came to them easily. Suddenly the world was in twilight and they could see the landscape again: the village and the sea and the airbase, dark grey, misty shapes in the half-light. Down in the village, one point of glowing yellow moved across the town square: an air-raid warden perhaps, or Constable Carter on his beat. Everyone else must be inside, asleep.

And of course, they could see one another: four figures full of orange-yellow fire, each surrounded by a wide wavering aura. Their joined hands glowed. There was, as always, the desire to just stay still and look in wonder at what they were really made of.

But there was no time. They had to concentrate on the ley lines. The shining paths. They had to focus. *Generations have trod, have trod, have trod…*

The ground beneath their feet began to glow. The summit of the Mound, for about ten feet around the Stone, lit up like a lamp. As the four wizards watched and concentrated, the path that spiralled up around the Mound began to gleam golden-yellow. A circular track was unheard of, Alice had told them: ley lines were always straight. But so many generations had trod, had trod: so many souls had walked or run or processed up the Mound that they'd left their mark. The four wizards could see the shapes of these walkers all around them, in robes or trousers or skirts or furs, bright and translucent. But they turned their attention away, and looked out over the countryside.

The land was a network of straight, shining paths. They crisscrossed the ground as far as the eye could see. Some were narrow, and a dull golden-orange like heated wire. Some were much wider and brighter; a few, the major thoroughfares, were a hundred yards wide and shone almost white. Where they crossed they burned especially bright: Maggie and the others had already noticed that the airbase had been placed precisely on one of these intersections. On other crossing-places there was usually a small church, or a mound, or a little copse of trees. There was also, as often as not, an Observer post, or a checkpoint, or an ack-ack gun placement. Someone had arranged the country's defences with great care.

They gazed out at the web of energy lines. Figures moved along every path: in single file along the thin tracks, in crowds along the wide ones. From almost any other site in the country, that would have been all they could perceive: silent, spectral walkers. But they stood on Wardston Mound, at the top of the spiral path. So other things came to them too, crowding in all at once. The four wizards concentrated, gripping each other's hands hard. This was the worst part, when it all came flooding in; this was when Alice's nose often started to bleed. There were so many voices. And thoughts, and feelings.

This time, because what you put into the lines was so often what you got out, the note of them all was: *Fear*.

Not panic, not quite that. More like wariness. Gradually though they made sense of the cacophony of sounds and sensations, allowing some voices to fade into the background and others to become distinct. Where there was speech, they allowed voices speaking English to come to the fore. They heard prayers –

Dear Lord, keep us and protect us – they heard barked orders and instructions – *Keep your eyes open, Corporal, I don't care how bloody dark it is* – they heard whispered conversations – *Mummy, will the bad Germans come tonight?* One voice was particularly heartfelt, and familiar: Mr Caplan, down in the village, reading the Torah to his grandchildren – *The Lord is my strength and song, and He is become my salvation; this is my God, and I will glorify Him; my father's God, and I will exalt Him…*

Some of what came to them was more vague. Thoughts: *I'll show them Jerries if they come, I'll show them what's what… We're right in the invasion path, we shouldn't be here… What'll we do if the German soldiers come, don't let them get my daughters, please God, not them…* Feelings: perspectives. Impressions of a fear of *this*, a fear of over *there*.

Gradually, patiently, the four wizards narrowed it down – to fears focussed outwards across the sea, fears of something coming from the east. There was so much apprehension and anger there, but they narrowed it down to – ah, yes. Only the most recent, the thoughts in very modern English. From the Twentieth Century.

Terrors exclusive to the last forty years: terror of enemy aircraft. Fear of attack from above.

Along the lines came the collective anxiety, and anger, and prayers, of a million people watching the skies. With a few came images that must be from the first war: visions of big silver Zeppelins, caught in the searchlights, dropping their primitive bombs. But most of the pictures and thoughts and emotions came from the here and now. The feelings weren't just of apprehension, though; there was hope and trust, too. Trust in…

The four wizards looked up. The plane engines they'd heard were loud, right overhead. In the gloaming of witch-sight they could see a dozen winged shapes thousands of feet above. Maggie frowned. 'Vince, are they—'

Vince laughed. 'It's all right. They're Spitfires.'

… hope and trust in the RAF. The fighter pilots. Above all, the men in the Spitfires.

Alice was smiling. 'Maggie, do you think Michal's up there?'

Maggie shrugged. Even if she could tell one Spitfire from another, the planes were too far up. 'I don't know.'

'Find out.' Alice looked thoughtful. 'He's got the gift too. See if he's there.'

'How do I do that?'

'Just try.'

Maggie closed her eyes. She felt awkward, thinking about Michal with the others watching her, but she tried. Michal. How he looked. How he smelled. How his mouth felt… his warm body… *Michal…*

'Maggie?'

Suddenly the cockpit was full of the scent of her. He could hear her voice: *Michal… Michal…* He could almost feel her breath on the back of his neck. It was as if the Spitfire had become a two-seater, as if she were sitting behind him, and if he turned around he would see her face.

Someone spoke to him on the radio: it was Eddy. Michal didn't listen. He said again, 'Maggie?'

Michal. I'm here.

'I can hear you.'

Look, love. Close your eyes, then look…

He closed his eyes, and opened them again.

He was suddenly in twilight. He looked to his right, and he could see the wing of his Spitfire; he could see Scots Eddy's plane, clearly enough to make out the ident markings. And he could see the glow in the cockpit. He almost cried out: the glow was Eddy himself. He was full of amber light; it was what he was made of. Eddy was looking over at him – lighter yellow shading rippled through the amber. He was watching him, saying something. Beyond Eddy, Michal could see two more darkened Spitfires, and two more tawny lights inside them. Kiddy Jones and Harry Williams were both golden glows in their own cockpits, each made of different shades of amber and orange rippling in different complex patterns. Each unique. Michal laughed out loud.

He heard Arthur say, 'Michal?' and turned. He drew in a breath. Arthur too was full of light; it was so dazzling Michal could barely see the plane Arthur sat in. It was golden white like the sun. Arthur lit up the sky. Michal looked again at Eddy and Jones and Williams. They were beautiful, radiant: but not like Arthur. No wonder everyone followed him so readily. He shone like a star.

Michal. Michal, can you see them?

Yes, oh yes. He could see –

The German planes. They're coming here, Michal.

For a moment the twilight wavered, but it held. Michal ran his eyes over the instruments, a reflex reaction. Then he looked ahead. In the grey distance was a shoal of darker grey shapes. Points of amber light glowed in their heads. Their charcoal-coloured bodies were long and thin. He remembered the nickname: Flying Pencils.

Dornier 17s. German fast bombers.

Michal spoke into the radio. 'Bandits sighted. One o'clock low. About a thousand feet down. Two miles away.'

There was silence as the rest of the squadron looked out into the darkness. Eventually Arthur said, 'I don't see them.'

'I see them. Twelve Flying Pencils. No fighter escort.'

Penry-Smith's voice cut in: 'I can't see a bloody thing. Are you sure?'

'I am sure. I see them.'

After a moment Arthur said, 'Then get ready to take us down, Blue Two. Wardston, this is Kestrel Leader. Bandits sighted. We're moving to engage. Kestrel Squadron, dim your cockpit lights and follow Blue Two. Michal – after you.'

Michal was easing forward, taking position ahead of Arthur. 'Follow me,' he said. No – what was the phrase? 'Tally-ho!'

He swung into a dive, aware of the rest of the squadron following him. They swooped down on the Dorniers. Michal was tempted to lunge into an even steeper descent, but he restrained himself; the others were flying almost blind, he had to let them keep up with him. He looked over the bombers, and singled out the one in the lead. He'd never gone after a Dornier before. They were slim, elegant planes: fast, he'd heard. Both the nose-cone and the cockpit were entirely glazed. In the bomber he'd targeted, he could plainly see four golden-yellow lights behind the Plexiglas. A four-man crew. They sat still and untroubled.

He was just in firing range when he heard Arthur cry, 'I see them!' The bombers' cockpit lights were lowered, but now the rest of Kestrel squadron were close enough to see their navigation lights. At the same time, he saw the four bright figures in the lead Dornier jump into movement; they'd spotted the Spitfires. Michal knew he'd have to make these shots count. He opened fire.

One of the golden lights faded quickly to a dark orange. Another one, in the cockpit, simply winked out. Michal, who would usually have been delighted by such a successful shot, stared in shock. As he watched, the darkening orange light dulled to a dirty brown, then went out. Just died away.

It distracted him for only a moment, but that was enough. There was a shockingly loud bang to his right, and a bright flash. The Dornier had returned fire; he'd been hit. There was another flash; when Michal's eyes cleared, the witch-twilight was gone and he was back in the dark. He felt the Spitfire shudder; one moment it was running smoothly, the next it was bucking like a wild horse. There was a hissing sound; Michal could smell something sharp and acrid. Red light flared as fire leapt on his starboard wing. He tried to half-roll away, but the Spitfire wouldn't respond.

Time to get out.

'I'm baling out,' he said before he disconnected the radio and pulled off his mask. It took him an age to undo all the straps, fumbling with the catches, remembering not to loosen his parachute harness while he was at it. Trying not to watch the fire grow outside the cockpit. At last he was free, and he pushed at the hatch. It opened at once, sliding back neatly. Cold air gusted into the cockpit, drawing tips of flame in with it. Michal tried again to steer the Spitfire into a roll, throwing all his strength into it. This time the plane responded, flipping upside down. Michal, no longer strapped in, tumbled out of the cockpit.

The Spitfire carried on, while Michal fell clear. It was quiet without the roar of the engine. He felt for the parachute's rip-cord. If the chute didn't open, then he was dead. He remembered his training, remembered sitting in a warm classroom while the instructor pointed to numbers on a board and said things like, *Don't be in a hurry to open your chute. Let yourself fall clear first. Remember, you only fall a thousand feet in five seconds!* He tried to count to ten, he really did. But he had to know if he was going to die today. He crossed himself as he'd done as a child, and pulled the cord.

The chute rustled out of its pack and slipped into the sky. Then came the bruising jolt as the straps yanked him upwards. The parachute was open. His fall was cut short, and he began to drift. Michal sagged into his harness with relief. He crossed himself again, because it couldn't do any harm. Then he just waited. There was a burst of flame below as his abandoned Spitfire hit the ground.

Michal floated slowly down. It had seemed quiet without his own engine, but now he was very aware of other engines. The low rumble of the bombers, the lighter tone of the fighters, swooping and zooming all around him. This was why he should have waited longer: he was still in the middle of the dogfight. He watched the spectacular explosion as a Dornier blew up, and hoped that the other Nazi airmen had better things to do than go after him. After all, he carried no light, so he was invisible.

But suddenly there was blue-white light all around him. He could see wisps of smoke drifting in front of his eyes. He looked down; a round white light was glaring up at him. A searchlight. Someone on the ground, at an ack-ack station maybe, had seen the explosions and was trying to see what was going on. Michal wanted to scream, *Point it away! Get it on the bombers!* But the light didn't move. The fool operating it hadn't noticed him.

But one of the bombers had. When the searchlight finally swept away from him it picked up one of the Dorniers. And the bomber had swung around and was coming towards him. The crew couldn't know he was the one who had discovered them. They must just be targeting enemy pilots. The bomber had a couple of Spitfires behind it, but it was staying ahead of them; Dorniers really were fast. All Michal could do was hang there, watching the big bomber coming towards him like a shark towards a bather. *This is how it feels. It's like this...*

Michal?

He said her name aloud. 'Maggie?'

Michal! No!

The Dornier shuddered. He thought he saw movement in the cockpit. For a moment, impossibly, the fuselage seemed to bulge; then the bomber exploded in a dazzling fireball. The men inside must have been killed instantly.

Michal felt himself being whisked away. He thought it was the blast from the explosion, but when the tugging sensation remained constant, he realised it wasn't. Something invisible had caught hold of one of his parachute's cords, and was drawing him gently but firmly away.

Dreamily, he watched the battle go on without him, lit up by the sweeping searchlight. Michal tried to count the Spitfires: they were too fast for him to be sure, of course, but he thought all eleven of them were still in the air. He saw two more bombers explode, however, and one go down in flames. They hadn't brought a guard of fighters with them, he realised, because they didn't think Spitfires could find them in the dark. They were undefended, and it was a rout. He should feel like gloating; but the memory of that golden light winking out kept coming back to him.

He drifted on. He could see now, he realised; only dimly, but he could make out the ground below. It wasn't the magical twilight – just the first sign of dawn. The fields, a patchwork of greys, became more distinct as they got closer. When he passed over Wardston village, that unseen but persistent hand still drawing him in, he realised where he was going. He saw the Mound, a dim hump above the village. He saw the Stone, and the little group standing around it. They were just letting go of each other's hands.

When he was just above the Mound, three of the four figures detached themselves and went to the path. They started to walk down; the tallest stopped and made a suggestive gesture with his arm, but the other two dragged him firmly away. The last figure left the Stone and came to meet Michal as he touched down. Her hand was stretched out towards him – it dropped as he landed on his feet, not with the usual jarring drop-and-roll, but light as a feather.

Maggie ran to him. Even in the dullest light, her hair was bright and glorious. She was laughing and crying at once. 'You're all right,' she said.

'I am – fine.'

He was still trying to struggle out of his parachute harness when she threw her arms around him. He was unsteady on his feet; they both fell to their knees. 'They were going to kill you,' she said. 'So I killed them. I did it.'

'You had to.'

'I thought I was going to lose you.'

'You didn't. You won't.'

She clung to him. 'Michal.'

'Maggie.' He gave up on escaping from his parachute, and took her in his arms. The two of them fell gently to the ground.

Chapter Sixteen

The Rufus Stone

Wewelsburg Castle, Western Germany

The morning sun shone over the Wewelsburg. A typical German summer day. But the thirteen watchers on the North Tower did not appreciate it. When they opened their eyes, they hardly dared look at each other. Some of the younger boys were trying hard not to cry.

At last Lise sighed. 'Those men,' she said. 'Those good German airmen! Lost!'

'Not to mention the planes,' said Hans. 'All because a Pole has the same powers we do.'

'It's his fault,' Manfred agreed. 'That Polack. Our bombers would never have been brought down so easily. If it wasn't for him. He… cheated.'

Some of the others nodded vigorously. But Albrecht shook his head. 'The Polish pilot is nothing,' he said. 'All the pilots count for nothing. If they were left to themselves, the Luftwaffe could overcome them easily enough. It's *them*. The four wizards.'

Petr said flatly, 'Reichsführer Himmler will be displeased. With us.'

It was what they were all thinking. But one of the boys – the one with the red-haired sister – protested: 'It's not our fault! We didn't know they could do – that!'

'Do you think the Reichsführer will care about excuses?' Petr knew, all too well that the Reichsführer was not a forgiving man. Petr had been making some covert explorations, these last few nights. It was easy, with his powers, to get into locked offices, to see secret writings. And now he knew a lot more about the Reichsführer's plans; now he knew just how far Heinrich Himmler was prepared to go with those who weren't an asset to the Fatherland. 'It's our function to know such things,' Petr told the other *gothi*. 'This is why we have been given all of our privileges. If we fail, we will be discarded.'

They shivered. What would happen if they were no longer useful? Hans shook his head. 'Perhaps we're failing because our assumptions are wrong. Perhaps our powers are not exclusive to the Aryan race.'

There was an appalled silence. 'Of course they are,' cried Manfred. 'The Führer says so. Everyone says so!'

'Then why do non-Aryans have the powers?' He laughed. 'Come on, think! Think about it, all of it—'

Albrecht cut in smoothly. 'Come now, we're all tired. Petr, you're being too negative. We're not beaten yet. If the four British wizards are the problem, then they are the ones we must target. Directly. Face to face.'

Manfred gasped. 'You mean... fight them?'

'That's just what I mean. Battle. We take the war to them.'

'Go to England?'

'Yes,' he said. 'To England.'

They smiled at him. England! Battle! At last! 'When?'

'As soon as we can.'

'How? I mean, how will we get there?'

Petr interrupted. 'We take to the skies.'

Manfred faltered. 'Are we good enough? To do that?'

'Of course we are. And Freya will help us.' Petr bowed, stiffly, to

Lise. 'Won't you help? My lady?'

Lise beamed at this reverence from Petr. Her eyes began to shine blue. 'Of course I will!'

'Then let us fly.' Petr rose a few inches. 'Let us prove to ourselves what we can do!'

They all rose into the air, buoyed up on Freya's sweet laughter. The power filled them. They rose on a rush of ecstasy. When Petr broke out of the circle and swooped away alone, the others faltered for a moment. But he didn't fall, and neither did they. So they all leapt and spun, around the tower, around the castle, like swallows. Every one soaring and diving in a joyous world of his own.

Afterwards, no one could agree on exactly what happened. It seemed that no one even saw it happen. But they all heard a dull cracking sound, as if something solid had hit the castle wall. They all came to investigate, swooping around the tower and sinking towards the ground, as yet no more than curious. Then they looked down and saw Hans, lying on the flagstones at the foot of the castle. Halfway up the stone wall was a red stain. When they came closer, they saw the puddle of scarlet mess under his head; they saw his dead, staring eyes.

Lise saw this. She saw that Hans' head was a slightly different shape. Because it had been cracked, like a coconut, and the pieces had slipped a bit under his scalp. She caught a smell from the body – a raw, meaty smell. Lise closed her eyes and shrank away, deep inside herself. Freya rose to the surface.

After that, there was only Freya.

Now, with exquisite grace, Freya descended to the stones where Hans lay. 'Ah!' she cried to the others. 'Come and see! The first of the fallen! How beautiful!'

The others landed around her, uncertainly. She waved her hand towards the roof of the castle. The Swastika flag detached itself from the flagpole, and floated down. Carefully, it draped itself over Hans' body. His blood soaked into the flag.

'See!' cried Freya. 'His precious blood! How honoured he is! The first to fall for the Fatherland!'

She began to weep. She was Freya, goddess beautiful in tears; her tears were drops of molten gold. They fell onto the flag and set hard, into smooth precious nuggets glinting in the morning sun.

Albrecht fell to his knees. He was weeping too – ordinary tears – but he gazed at Freya. 'Lucky, how lucky he is,' he cried. 'To die so beautifully! With the tears of a goddess on his winding-sheet! May we all die so well!'

The others, most of them sobbing too, knelt around them. Now that the corpse was covered up, and adorned in shining gold, their queasiness had passed. Their friend had died for his race and his Fatherland. It was enviable. It was sublime!

Petr knelt quietly behind them all. He kept his head down, so no one would notice there were no tears on his face. He looked at the body. He hadn't meant to kill the fool, of course. Not that. Merely to hurt him: a little push against a hard wall. To incapacitate him, so he couldn't keep tainting the air with his poisonous speech. But, well, he was dead and that was that. He must have been weak anyway, or he couldn't have been killed so easily.

Petr was determined not to be troubled. Remorse was a weakness, the Führer was quite clear about that. The strong had no need of it; and Petr was strong, he knew – the strongest. In any case, this was probably a blessing – how much longer could they have borne the presence of one whose thinking had become so unsound? He'd had to be sacrificed, for the good of the group.

So Petr kept his head bowed and said nothing. He would never be able to say anything. Reichsführer Himmler would not understand: he would see the loss of Hans as the waste of a precious resource. It really was most regrettable. Now that he knew how the Reichsführer's mind truly worked, Petr was sure that if Himmler could fully understand what he had done, he would applaud him for it.

It was late morning when Michal got back to the airbase. He'd phoned earlier from the cottage, spoken to Owens; he wouldn't be on readiness till four in the afternoon, thank God. Owens congratulated him on sighting the Dorniers, and told him he must eat a lot of carrots. Michal, too tired to ask what he was talking about, had just agreed with him and hung up.

He went straight to the living quarters, and managed to avoid meeting anyone else. Until, that is, he made his way to the small room he shared with Arthur. There was Arthur himself, sitting on his narrow bed, gazing at nothing. The silver-framed picture of Sylvia stood in its usual place on the bedside cabinet. Michal noticed, not for the first time, that the photo was placed outwards to face the room, not inwards where Arthur could see it before he turned out the light. Arthur stood up when Michal appeared. 'Ah. Hello.'

Michal nodded warily. Arthur cleared his throat. 'Owens said you were on the way back. You're all right?'

'Yes.'

'Good, good. Fancy a cup of tea?'

'Yes. Thank you.'

Arthur went to the door and shouted for his batman: 'Wilkinson, two teas, please.' He closed the door, glanced at Michal, and took a deep breath. 'Look, old man. I'm sorry. For the things I said. I mean. I know you, ah. I know you respect Maggie and all.'

Michal sat down heavily on his bed. 'Yes. I do.'

'Of course you do. I went over the line. I apologise.'

Michal sighed. They couldn't hold grudges; there were things you didn't want to be your last words to someone. 'I am sorry too.

For what I said. About your fiancée.'

'Well, you had a point. I have been neglecting the poor old girl. I must telephone her, or write her a letter or something.' Arthur waved his hand dismissively. 'Soon as I get the time.'

He sounded like he was talking about his mother. Michal thought about trying to get through the next few days without being with Maggie: impossible. 'Do you know Sylvia – well?' was all he could think to say.

He knew by the sharp glance that Arthur had misunderstood him. But before he could rephrase the question, he saw that Arthur was staring at the floor, and blushing like a girl. 'Not…that way. You know. We've never. *I've* never. I mean, it's understood that, you know…You wait to be married.'

Michal thought: *You and I might not live long enough to be married.* 'No, I mean, have you known Sylvia for a long time?'

'Oh! Oh. Good heavens.' Arthur's blush had intensified. 'I see. Yes, we've known each other since we were babies. Our families are great friends, you see. Distantly related, in fact, on my father's side. It's always been understood that Sylv and I will get married someday. When the time comes. Keep it in the family, you know how it is.'

Michal had no idea how it was. Clearly, the ways of the British upper classes were very strange. He gave up trying to understand, and decided to fall back on formality: 'I wish you both every happiness. When the time comes.'

'Thanks, old man.' He cleared his throat again. 'Right. Well—'

There was a tap at the door: Wilkinson had arrived with the tea. When he was gone, Arthur sat down on his bed and looked across at Michal. 'We got all but two of those Flying Pencils last night, by the way. Congratulations on spotting them. You must have been eating your carrots.'

Michal blinked. Carrots again. 'I am sorry?'

'Carrots. Help you see in the dark, you know.' He spoke lightly, but he was giving Michal a fairly hard stare. 'How did you do it?'

Michal shrugged – time to change the subject. 'I do not know. But there was no more action? After the Dorniers?'

'Spot of bother on the way back. Nothing serious. But the Flying Pencils, how did you see them?'

Michal sighed. 'Arthur. Maggie and her friends…'

He broke off, hearing loud voices and heavy footsteps in the corridor. The door burst open, and in came Scots Eddy, closely followed by Harry Williams and Kiddy Jones, all three clutching mugs of tea. 'Michal!' said Eddy, as they all crowded into the little room, 'Wilkinson said you were here. Thought you could sneak back in without coming to see us, eh? How are you, laddie?'

Michal sighed. The airbase had all the privacy of a beehive. 'I am well, Eddy.'

Williams and Kiddy sat on either side of Arthur, while Eddy sat down beside Michal, ruffling his hair. 'Well done on those Dorniers, Michal. The rest of us couldn't see a damned thing. You've been eating up your carrots, haven't you?'

'Yes,' agreed Michal. 'I eat many carrots.'

'Thought so. Owens says he'll make sure we all get them for dinner from now on. If we could all see like you, we wouldn't need radar.'

Time to change the subject, again. 'You had a spot of bother? After I baled out?'

'Oh yes, wait till you hear – '

He broke off as someone else appeared at the door: Penry-Smith. Eddy, Williams and Kiddy laughed and cheered. Eddy said, 'Here's the very man! Hurricane Penry!'

Penry-Smith sat down next to Michal. 'Sod off, you lot.'

Michal looked at Eddy. 'Hurricane…?'

'Shot down a Hurricane, didn't he.' Eddy wiped away tears of laughter. 'On the way home.'

'It was dark,' protested Penry-Smith. 'We had no warning there were friendly planes about. Silly bugger just came at me out of nowhere, of course I shot him.'

'But the pilot?' said Michal. He didn't think they'd be laughing if a British pilot had been hurt, but you never knew. 'He was not injured?'

'No, baled out and came down right in our back yard. I saw him in the mess earlier. There wasn't a scratch on him. Foul-mouthed bugger, though, you wouldn't believe some of the things he called me.'

Williams choked on his tea, and Kiddy leaned around Arthur to thump him between the shoulder-blades. Penry-Smith shook his head ruefully. 'I'm going to be Hurricane Penry till the day I die, aren't I?'

'Poor old Penry,' said Eddy solemnly. 'You've shot down a dozen Messerschmitts, but no-one calls you Messerschmitt Penry. You've shot down half a dozen Junkers 88s, but they don't call you Junkers Penry. But...' the others joined in, '...you shoot down *one Hurricane*...'

'I hate you all,' Penry-Smith announced calmly. 'Come on, Michal looks like he needs his rest. Anyone for a spot of lunch?'

'Right you are, Hurricane,' said Eddy. 'Coming, Arthur?'

'In a minute.' Arthur sat still while the other four filed out. When they were well out of earshot he said: 'Michal... those Dorniers...'

Michal was too tired. 'Arthur. We will talk later.'

Arthur looked at him for a moment, then nodded and left without another word. Michal stretched out on the bed fully clothed, and was asleep in seconds.

In the cottage garden, Maggie pushed the spade down into the ground and levered the slice of earth upwards. At the same time, she grabbed the plant firmly and pulled, then drew the whole thing clear. Lots of spuds clung to the roots. A good crop. And it was good to be doing something solid and simple: lifting her own spuds, from her own ground.

Vince didn't seem to share her pleasure. 'We shouldn't be spending our time on this,' he grumbled, tugging fitfully at a potato plant that he hadn't worked loose enough. 'Haven't we got valuable war work to do or something?'

'This is valuable war work,' said Alice, twisting a pea pod off its stem. Alice had proved surprisingly proficient at basic gardening. Apparently, at her school she had to do all sorts of menial chores, including digging up vegetables. It seemed the more expensive the British private school, the more Spartan the living conditions. She snapped open the pod, plucked out the peas, and dropped them into the bowl Colin was holding for her. 'We're digging for victory. So stop whingeing.'

'Is that what we're doing?' He nodded at the pea pod in her hand. 'What are those then?'

'They're peas, silly.'

'Are they?' He winked at Maggie. 'Always thought they came out of the sea.'

'No you didn't.'

'Straight up. I did. Told you I'd never been out of London.'

'...Really?'

He looked at her for a moment; then burst out laughing. Alice threw a clod of earth at him. 'Vince!'

'Had you going there, didn't I? No, I en't that ignorant. My mum's got a vegetable patch. She grows peas and things.'

His voice had become a little wistful. Alice said gently, 'Why don't you write to your mum?'

'Can't. She'd tell *him* where I was.'

Maggie remembered the hulking figure in black she'd seen standing behind him on the day they'd met. 'You mean your stepdad?'

'Yeah. Him.'

'Is he that bad?'

Vince shoved his spade deep into the ground. 'Bloody Mosleyite, isn't he.'

'What's a Mosleyite?' said Colin.

Alice said contemptuously: 'A British Nazi.'

'That's right.' Vince was staring at his spade, not looking at anyone. 'One of Hitler's little English bully-boys. He goes out and… smashes shop windows and things. You know. If the shopkeepers are…'

'Jews?' said Alice.

'Yeah.' He finally looked at Alice. 'That's him, that's what he does. That's not me.'

'I know.' Alice sighed. 'Does he try to make you – do what he does?'

'You mean, does he try and turn me into a good little Nazi? Oh, yeah. He's been doing it all my life.' He stamped his spade savagely into the earth. 'Now I don't take nothing more to do with him.'

Alice shook her head. 'Why on earth did your mum marry a man like that?'

'Unwed mother, wasn't she. My real dad was a sailor. He went off. Suppose after that she thought she couldn't be choosy. Poor cow.'

'She still shouldn't have… Colin?'

Colin had dropped the bowl, spilling green peas all over the turned earth. He was swaying. His eyes were unfocused behind his glasses. Maggie threw down the spade and ran to catch him as he folded at the knees and sank to the ground. Maggie laid his head on her lap and eased off his glasses. 'Colin? Can you hear me?'

Alice knelt beside him. Vince hovered anxiously: 'Shall I get your gran?'

'No. Best not. It's one of his… turns. He might—'

Colin opened his mouth wide and began to scream. '*Mama! Mama!*'

It didn't sound like his voice. It sounded female, and it sounded familiar. Maggie put her hand over his mouth, but he wrenched his head to one side and the wailing cries went on. '*Mama! Ah, nie, nie! Tata! Tata!*'

'What the hell's he saying?' said Vince. 'Is that German again?'

Alice shook her head. 'It sounds more like Russian. Or Polish…'

'Jannah.' Maggie said what they were all thinking. 'It sounds like Jannah.'

Gran appeared at the back door of the cottage. 'What's… Colin? What's the matter?'

'*Ah, Mama, Tata… Nie… Mama…*' Colin's cries trailed off into awful sobs. His eyes were still blank and unfocussed. Gran hurried towards him. 'What happened?'

'He's just having one of his turns,' Maggie said. 'Vince – help me lift him, we'll take him inside.'

She and Vince carried Colin inside and laid him down on the sofa. The sobs were trailing off now. Gran gently pushed Vince aside and bent down to feel Colin's forehead. 'He feels cool enough.' She sounded relieved. 'I'll ring Dr Braithwaite anyway.'

'I don't think you need to, Gran.'

'Oh?' Gran gave her a hard look. 'I think I'll be the judge of that, thank you.'

Gran disappeared into the hall, to the telephone. When she was gone, Vince whispered, 'What was he saying? *Mama, Tata?*'

'I think it's *Mummy, Daddy,*' Alice said.

Vince's voice shook slightly. 'D'you think it was Jannah?'

'It sounded like her.'

'Then what's…' He trailed off.

No one wanted to say it. Eventually Maggie took a deep breath: 'I think they've killed her mum and dad.'

They fell silent. They could hear Gran's voice, murmuring into the telephone. At last Vince said, 'How would she know? I mean – would we all be able to tell? Things like that?'

No one knew how to answer. Gran came back into the room. 'Doctor's on his way,' she said. She put her hand on Colin's forehead, smoothed his hair away from his face. He was quiet now, his eyes closed. He seemed to be asleep. Gran said: 'Alice, dear, would you make some tea? Vince, you can help her.'

Alice and Vince trooped out of the room. Gran touched Colin's cheek again; he was still sleeping peacefully. Gran turned to Maggie. 'Right, my girl,' she said. 'I think you'd better tell me what's going on here.'

Maggie hesitated. But no: Gran had a right to know too. 'Gran,' she said, very gently. 'Gran, we – I mean… Gran, I'm a wizard.'

Gran snorted. 'Well, I know *that*. You're your mother's daughter, aren't you?'

Maggie's mouth dropped open. 'You *know?*'

'I've got eyes, haven't I? I meant, what are the four of you doing up on the Mound? What have you been doing, up at the Ward Stone?'

A black car bumped along the narrow road into the heart of the forest. It was a big car, heavy; armoured, in fact. Not too flashy, though; it looked old and in need of a wash. Not a car that would attract too much attention.

All around lay the New Forest, in its summer green. Trees leaned over the road, brushing the car roof with trailing branches. The car's passenger windows were half-open, and a fresh breeze cooled the interior. The passenger himself was enjoying a rare taste of the English countryside, and an even rarer moment of peace and quiet. Winston Churchill leaned back on the comfortable leather seats, listening to a lark trilling somewhere high above. The driver – excellent fellow – watched the road and didn't try to make conversation.

It didn't last, of course. Soon they were at the edge of a large clearing, where the road came to an end. Another, smaller car was parked there. Three people stood beside it: Major Fitzwilliam, and the Wrens, Vivian and Laura. They had been looking anxiously towards the centre of the clearing, but they turned as the large car came to a stop. The major came forward to open the passenger door, and stood to attention as the car's occupant clambered out. 'Mr Churchill,' said the major, 'welcome.'

'Good morning, major. Ladies.' Churchill looked around. 'Is Mrs Ogilvie here?'

'She's at the Rufus Stone, sir.'

'Ah. Excuse me, then.'

Churchill set out across the clearing. In its centre, Miriam Ogilvie stood beside a three-sided standing stone coated in black iron. The Rufus Stone stood about five feet high; each of its three sides bore an inscription in white lettering. The one closest to Churchill read:

> HERE STOOD
> THE OAK TREE,
> ON WHICH AN ARROW
> SHOT BY
> SIR WALTER TYRRELL
> AT A STAG,
> GLANCED AND STRUCK
> KING WILLIAM
> THE SECOND,
> SURNAMED RUFUS,
> ON THE BREAST,
> OF WHICH HE
> INSTANTLY DIED
> ON THE SECOND DAY OF AUGUST
> ANNO 1100

Churchill looked at the Rufus Stone. Its iron casing was Victorian, but the stone itself was much older. 'Blasted ugly thing, I've always thought,' he said.

Miriam, one elegant gloved hand resting on the stone, smiled slightly. 'It marks the death of a king, Winston. It doesn't have to be pretty.'

William 'Rufus' the Second. There were stories about him, and about his death. 'I heard he sacrificed himself for the good of the land,' Churchill said. 'A willing sacrifice. There's no truth in that, I suppose?'

'No such luck. He really did die in a hunting accident, I'm afraid. You shouldn't believe everything you read.'

'It's still a place of power, though?'

'Yes. Oh, yes.'

After a moment's pause, Churchill said softly: 'You got my message? Our – enquiries about your children's father?'

She nodded. 'There's no more news, I suppose?'

'None, I'm afraid. Our people in Dunkirk can't investigate further without attracting attention. If it's him, we'll just have to wait till he wakes up.'

'I understand.' Miriam looked as if she were about to add something; but then shook her head, and was all business again. 'We'll soon have a full coven. Twelve, plus myself. Everyone will want to be part of this.'

Churchill looked around the pleasant clearing. 'Who will you bring here? Who's coming to join you?'

'The usual people. Vivian and Laura, of course. Major Fitzwilliams.' She nodded towards the little group standing at the edge of the clearing. 'And Gerald, definitely. Perhaps Sybil…'

'Aleister?'

'Definitely *not* Aleister. Arnold, though. And Dorothy, of course.'

Churchill nodded. 'What are you going to do?'

'A Cone of Power,' Miriam said at once. 'A Spell of Influence. To persuade Hitler to abandon the invasion. We'll start with that. Then it will depend on what *they* do.'

'Your son and daughter and their friends?'

'No. They're already doing more than we ever could. The others.'

'You mean the German children.'

'Children.' She made an angry gesture. 'They're hardly children. I doubt they're even human any more. They're *gothi*, Nazi necromancers. And one of them is channelling a goddess.'

'How the devil do we combat that?'

Miriam stared at the Rufus Stone. 'If needs be, I'll try to call down the Morrigan.'

Churchill looked at her: her dark auburn hair, pale skin, red lipsticked mouth. He could imagine her all too well as the Morrigan. 'I've heard you don't come back, from the Morrigan.'

She shrugged. 'Then I won't come back.'

'We don't want to lose you,' he said gently.

She smiled at him. 'You know that doesn't matter. Only they matter. My children, and the other two. What happens in Wardston – that's what matters now.'

Gran poured the tea, and Maggie added the milk. Colin was asleep upstairs. Alice and Vince had been sent away, and they had looked glad to go – Gran announced they all had *Some Explaining To Do*, and they'd jumped at the chance to escape. Maggie finished her explanation, and waited for Gran to speak.

After a long pause, Gran sighed. 'So it's that type of thing you're doing. Magick. Magick with a K at the end. Just like your mum used to do at the Ward Stone.'

'Mum? Mum used to do magic here?'

'Of course. That's how she met your dad, didn't you know? She came here to see the Ward Stone, and the Mound. They're famous in – certain circles. The ones your mother moves in. How else do you think a woman like her would meet a man like your dad? Her with her university education. And him just a fisherman.' Gran shook her head. 'Who'd have thought it, the two of them?'

Maggie had sometimes wondered about that too. 'Why did they get together?'

Gran shrugged. 'He fell in love with her. And she knew…'

'She knew what?'

A note of bitterness crept into Gran's voice. 'He lived on the Mound. Born and raised on it. That he was part of it. Just like you are now.'

'I wasn't born on it. And I haven't always lived on it.'

'Doesn't matter. Still part of it, aren't you?' Maggie nodded. 'That's what I thought. Your mother knows that too, that's why she sent you back here.'

'She didn't send me here! She tried to send me to Scotland!'

'Is that right? Well, well.'

Maggie was still thunderstuck. 'I can't believe you just – know, that we're…'

'Gifted? That's what your mother calls it.' Gran smiled sadly and looked into the fire. 'Not always a gift you'd wish on someone, is it? That's what your Dad used to say.'

'Gran.' Maggie took a deep breath. 'Gran, we think Dad's alive. We think me and Colin would know – if he died.'

Gran smiled. 'I hope you're right, pet,' she said.

Wewelsburg Aerodrome, Western Germany
August 1940

The cars inched their way across the aerodrome. It was another hot summer day. The heat shimmered on the wide expanse of concrete in front of the hangar. The sun gleamed dully on the metal fencing that surrounded the aerodrome, guarding this highly secret and special operation. From the first car's cool interior, Albrecht saw lines of men in overalls; he knew most of the ground crew had been dismissed for the day, and only a few essential, carefully selected men had been permitted to remain. Albrecht smiled. These worthy German workmen were about to receive a rare privilege.

Albrecht looked out of the car's back window. The four other cars were still following, creeping slowly across the concrete in single file. He could see the other *gothi* in the passenger seats; some of the younger ones were literally bouncing with excitement. They were very eager, naturally. Albrecht still considered, however, that he was the most honoured of the eleven young men, since he was the one highest in favour with Freya.

She had even condescended to let him share this car with her. He looked at her admiringly. 'What a shame you must cover your beautiful eyes,' he said.

She smiled. 'I must keep them hidden from lesser men. For now.'

Albrecht nodded. She was right, of course; these ordinary men couldn't behold her in all her glory. One day her light would shine all over Germany, as she stood by the Führer's side. But for now... 'As you say, my lady.'

The car was pulling to a halt. The line of overalled men stood to attention. There were uniformed men too – Luftwaffe officers. One of them – clearly the aerodrome's commandant – was hurrying forward to open the door. He snapped off a stiff-armed salute as Albrecht climbed out. 'Heil Hitler!'

'Heil Hitler!' Albrecht returned the salute, then turned back to the car. Behind him, the other cars had stopped and the other boys were spilling out. Albrecht bowed and handed Freya out into the sunshine.

Albrecht heard a few of the men inhale sharply. The commandant looked pale and nervous, as did the junior officers around him.

Well, no doubt they were anxious to please; Albrecht didn't blame them for being overawed. Freya was looking particularly beautiful today, in a white sheath dress and high heels, her hair swept upwards in an elaborate chignon. She looked like a film star – and like a film star, she wore dark glasses. Her eyes were totally obscured.

The commandant had started to sweat, but he bowed his head and clicked his heels, perfectly correctly, to Freya. 'Miss. Gentlemen. You are all most welcome.'

Albrecht nodded. 'Thank you, commandant. Is everything ready?'

'It is… sir.'

Freya condescended to speak to him in person. 'Then show us,' she said. Her double voice was loud in the motionless air. There were more sharp intakes of breath, which Freya did not lower herself to acknowledge. 'Take my friends to their chariots.'

Sweat was rolling down the commandant's face, but, again, his response was impeccable. 'This way, if you please.'

Albrecht offered his arm to Freya; she laid a slim white hand on his sleeve. Her touch made him remember, briefly, the thoughts he'd once had about this girl, when she *was* just a girl, only Lise… But that time was over. He was called to a much greater destiny now. 'Shall we, my lady?'

They set off, towards the great aircraft hangar. The ground crew stood rigidly to attention as they passed. Albrecht smiled at them graciously, but Freya paid them no mind. The other boys followed after them; they took their cue from Freya, and ignored the men haughtily. So they didn't see how the ground crew leaned away from them, how they sagged with relief when the *gothi* had passed. One of the men even crossed himself, earning a sharp look from his superior. The *gothi* walked on, oblivious.

The commandant stopped at the hangar doors. He gestured to two of his junior officers to open them. One ran to the door; the other stopped, and clapped a hand to his face as his nose began to bleed. The commandant barked an order, and the man stumbled away. Another officer took his place, and the great hangar doors rumbled open.

The boys cried out in excitement. The commandant turned to Albrecht: 'Shall we leave you now?'

Albrecht nodded. The commandant and his officers snapped a salute and then hurried away. Albrecht watched them narrowly; they seemed very eager to go. In fact, he was starting to suspect that they did not quite appreciate the great honour they were receiving. Perhaps they needed to be re-educated; he would have to speak to Reichsführer Himmler about it.

But for now, he turned to the other boys, smiling benignly. They had resisted the idea, the idea of requiring transport, at first. But Albrecht had been determined. Hans' death had convinced him – and the Reichsführer – that they should have some kind of armour, some kind of metal shielding. They were powerful, but not invulnerable. The others had complained; but only until Albrecht had told them what their transport was going to be. 'Brothers,' he said to them now. He gestured into the aircraft hangar. 'Our chariots await.'

The boys ran into the hangar, where eleven aircraft waited for them. Messerschmitt 109s. Fighter planes. The kind that featured in all the newsreels and comic books, fighting heroically against the British Spitfires. They would ride into battle like knights of the air. Now each boy chose a fighter, squabbling amongst themselves although all eleven planes were the same. Each boy scrambled up the short ladder and leapt into the cockpit. The hanger echoed with delighted shouts as they flicked switches on and off, peered through gunsights and hammered on the firing buttons, some of them making bang-bang noises while they did so.

Albrecht listened indulgently, giving them a moment to settle down. Sure enough, disappointment soon started to set in, as the boys realised that the planes wouldn't simply fly at the touch of a button. When Albrecht felt they were calm enough, he called to them. 'Brothers. Machinery alone won't carry us into battle. We fly also by the Power. The glory of the Aryan Race-Soul. The Aryan people need us, my brothers, and we shall not fail them!'

Cheers echoed around the hangar. Albrecht sensed movement just behind him. He turned, and found Freya sitting on the plane's fuselage behind him. She sat side-saddle, her legs crossed daintily in her close-fitting skirt. She had removed her sunglasses. Her eyes blazed neon-blue. 'Look, my Albrecht,' she said. She placed her hand gently on the plane's camouflage-painted skin. The dull green and brown paint faded where she touched it, to be replaced by a stormy black shot through with blue and purple and silver. The new shade rippled out from her hand, until it covered the entire plane.

Albrecht smiled with pleasure. But Freya wasn't finished. The Messerschmitt's stencilled ident letters were replaced by other symbols, each drawn in black against a scarlet circle: the *Todesrune*, the ancient Germanic rune of death; and the Black Sun.

Freya turned and pointed to the aircraft's tail. On its upright fin a picture was forming. A golden-haired woman in white, riding on the wings of a storm. A Valkyrie, a warrior-maiden riding into battle.

The other boys were watching, standing on the cockpit seats and exclaiming. Even Petr was swept up in the moment. Now all the planes were losing their camouflage coating and turning cloudy blue-black. On eleven planes there appeared the sacred death rune, and the Black Sun. Pictures were forming on tail fins, a different image for each one: an eagle descending on a bolt of lightning; a raven clutching something bloody in its claws; a wolf with red eyes and a red gaping maw.

Albrecht laughed delightedly. All were creatures sacred to the ancient Germans, of whom the *gothi* were the true descendants. So when the *gothi* fell upon their enemy, they would do so not just with their people behind them, but with all of their ancestors too. With the soul of the Aryan Race. He placed his hands on the Messerschmitt's controls, his feet on its rudders. Power streamed out of his fingers, flowing into the fighter, into every inch of it, until he hardly knew where he ended and the plane began.

Although the engines were silent and the turnscrews were still, the planes rose into the air. With a shout of pure joy, Albrecht steered out of the hangar and up into the blue sky. Freya stayed perched effortlessly behind him, laughing. The others followed. Within minutes they were all soaring, twisting and turning; powering straight up, or straight down, or even hovering on the spot like a hunting hawk. There was nothing they couldn't do.

On the ground, the Luftwaffe officers and crew watched silently. One crewman doubled up and vomited. No one rebuked him for it.

Part Four:

The Battle of Wardston

We have before us an ordeal of the most grievous kind… You ask, what is our policy? I can say: it is to wage war, by sea, land and air, with all our might and with all the strength that God can give us; to wage war against a monstrous tyranny, never surpassed in the dark, lamentable catalogue of human crime.

Winston Churchill

Chapter Seventeen

At Readiness

August 1940

The four wizards lay on the Mound in the breathless heat. The sun was low behind them, but the day didn't seem any cooler. Colin was asleep; he could nod off wherever and whenever he felt like it. Maggie couldn't remember when she'd last had an untroubled night's sleep. She was having dreams, dreams of an overpowering scent of roses, but she could never remember them in the morning.

Lying in the warm grass, she looked up at the flawless sky. There were no clouds, but there was plenty of white: aircraft vapour trails, scribbled wildly across the blue. There were wide, diffuse ones made this morning; and thin, solid ones made within the last hour or so. Dog-fights had been going on over their heads all day. She could still smell traces of fuel. And the day wasn't over.

For weeks now, the Luftwaffe had just kept coming. Michal and his squadron were at daytime readiness almost permanently. So the four wizards were, too. They'd stopped going back to the cottage between battles – it was easier just to wait here, ready to leap up at a moment's notice and take their places around the Stone.

Maggie looked over at Alice and Vince. They looked pale – she didn't think they'd been sleeping any better than she had. Maggie wondered, not for the first time: *how long can we keep this up?*

It was what the whole country was wondering. The German bombers kept coming. The RAF kept shooting them down; but their pilots died in the process. When would it end?

And who would be alive when it did?

Maggie looked up at the blue sky. So far, the wizards had killed seven people. When she had nothing to do like this, she couldn't help thinking about them. The four men in the Dornier, of course. There'd been no time to think; she'd panicked, and they'd just blown the plane apart. The other three had all been Messerschmitt pilots. With the first two, the wizards had just pushed their planes to one side – lightly, they'd thought – but the pilots had never regained control. The third they'd rescued from the plane before it blew up, but they'd found out later his parachute hadn't opened. So that one wasn't really down to them at all. Was it?

They always tried to save the airmen, they really did. They'd perfected a technique of simply yanking the pilot out of the cockpit and letting him parachute away, because – as Alice pointed out – the pilot and the plane couldn't do much harm without one another. But everything always happened so fast. Sometimes all you could do was – lash out. When they thought about it later, it was always obvious how it could have been done better, but at the time...

She thought about Dad saying: 'What if they had a war and nobody turned up?' *But they have turned up. I'm sorry, Dad. But they're here.*

Maggie turned her head, looking for a distraction, as Alice sat up and reached out to run her hand across the Stone. The Ward Stone: the Guardian Stone. Alice always called it that now. She seemed to take comfort from the Stone's very presence. 'You know,' she said suddenly, 'the skull of Brandt should have been buried here. Not in London. Right here.'

Maggie looked away. No use pondering what should have

been done with the Skull when it was gone. Alice loved to discuss hypotheticals, but Maggie really couldn't be bothered. 'Have you thought any more about what you said last night?' she said, to distract her. 'About Mr Caplan?'

Vince stirred beside Alice. 'What's this?'

'I was wondering about speaking to Mr Caplan,' said Alice. 'About going to the temple with him and his family sometimes. The synagogue, you know.'

'Yeah?'

'Yes.' She swallowed hard. 'My father wants us all to keep quiet about the whole thing. Mother being Jewish, that is.' She thought for a moment more. 'But I don't think I shall, actually. Not any more.'

Vince grinned. 'Good for you.'

'He'd be frightfully angry. Father, that is. But…' she swallowed again, '…to blazes with him. To *hell* with him.'

Vince laughed delightedly. 'That's my girl.'

Alice laughed too. But then her smile faded. 'It's easy enough to say. But I don't think I'd have the nerve to actually *do* it.'

'I'll come with you, if you want,' said Vince.

'Will you? To a synagogue? You'd do that?'

'Course I would. Why wouldn't I go? I can go if I want. If they'll let me in.' He looked away. 'Why shouldn't I? Free country, en't it?'

Maggie laughed. '*You* shouldn't go into a church or a synagogue or anywhere else.' It came out harsher than she'd meant it to. 'You'd get struck down by lightning, godless sinner that you are.'

'Hark at who's talking! What do you and Michal do up here every other night, eh? Prayer meeting, is it?'

'Shoosh.' She reached over to poke his arm. He rolled away, laughing. 'Give each other holy communion, do you?' His voice rose to a mock-feminine falsetto: 'Oh Michal, bless me, bless me!'

'Shut up, Vince!' Maggie scooped up a handful of earth and threw it at him, quite hard.

'Stop it, you two,' said Alice. Vince subsided, still chuckling to himself. Maggie turned her head away and closed her eyes. She'd keep her eyes shut, and ignore the pair of them, pretend they weren't there. Just for a moment...

When she opened them again the light was dark gold. Night was gathering in the east. Bewildered, Maggie looked at the others, who were smirking at her. Vince said, 'Told you that would wake her up.'

Maggie looked around. 'What? What woke me up?'

Then she heard it again, faint but clear at the bottom of the Mound: the tring-tring of a bicycle bell. She smiled. 'He's here!'

Vince was already on his feet. 'Come on,' he said to Alice and Colin, 'let's leave her to her devotions.'

He winked and led the other two away. Maggie heard snatches of the lecture Alice started to give him for his irreverence: 'You shouldn't mock it, you know... it could even be considered a sacred thing, here in a locus of power...'

Their voices faded. Then Michal appeared, still in his uniform. 'Vince just called me Father Capek,' he said. 'Do you know what he was talking about?'

'Haven't a clue.' She held out her arms. 'Forget him. Come here.'

When she got back much later, the cottage was in complete darkness. Maggie tiptoed into the kitchen and slid off her shoes, finding her way by memory. If she could avoid the squeaky boards on the stairs, she could get up to bed without disturbing anyone –

'Bit late to be coming home, isn't it?'

Maggie nearly screamed. Gran was sitting at the kitchen table. Maggie heard the scratch of a match as Gran lit a candle. She was in her dressing-gown, a teapot and a half-empty teacup in front of her. Maggie said, 'Why aren't you in bed?'

'I could ask you the same question, my girl.'

'I was just… I mean…' Maggie was blushing, but then she raised her chin defiantly. 'I was out seeing Michal.'

After a long pause, Gran sighed. 'Sit down. Get yourself a cup, it's still warm.'

Maggie fetched a cup and helped herself to tea. She sat across the table from Gran, trying to look her in the eye. After another pause, Gran said, 'It shouldn't surprise me. Your mum and dad spent a lot of time together up at the Ward Stone. Your grandad didn't approve at all. Thought we should stop them.' Gran snorted. 'Just as well we didn't, or you wouldn't be here today.'

'Gran!'

'It's true. So I told your granddad that if *his* dad had stopped *us* going up to the Stone, back in our day, your father would never have been born either.'

'Gran!'

'Don't you Gran me. If you're old enough to do what I think you're doing with that pilot, you're grown-up enough to hear this. Things happen up at the Ward Stone, is all I'm saying. So you be careful, my girl. This isn't why your mum sent you back here.'

'She didn't send me here. I told you. She said I had to go to Scotland.'

Gran shook her head. 'And she knew you'd come straight back here the minute she said it. *And* she knew you'd bring the others with you. Don't look so shocked. She's a clever woman, your mother. And she knows her children.'

'That…' Maggie could hardly get the words out. 'That – scheming…'

'You watch what you say, now. She's still your mother. And she loves you, in her way. You be glad of her.'

'But she…'

'Now, then, that's enough. It's time for bed. Long day again, tomorrow.'

Maggie followed Gran upstairs. Her bedroom door creaked

when she opened it; Alice stirred, but didn't waken. Maggie shrugged off her clothes and slipped into bed. She heard Gran's bedroom door close behind her. The house was in darkness again.

Maggie stretched out and stared into the blackness. Her mother. Maggie had thought she'd gotten free of her. But it turned out she was still going along with her schemes, without even knowing it, like a stupid kid. That… *bitch*. Maggie clenched her fists and forced herself not to punch the mattress. How her mother must have laughed, when she'd gone off in huff like a sulky child, just as mummy knew she would. To hell with her. To hell with all of it.

Maggie slept.

When she woke, she knew something was different before she even opened her eyes. She was sitting up, not lying down; sitting on something with wooden slats, and she was bathed in warm sunshine. She could hear, distantly, good-natured voices calling to one another; an occasional car engine; somewhere, the thwack of a rope and the chant of little girls skipping. She could smell roses. Maggie could feel the extra warmth of a body beside her, hear someone breathing. She opened her eyes.

She was sitting in the middle of Wardston town square, on one of the benches under the statue of Queen Victoria. She blinked; she was feeling pleasantly dozy in the sunshine, so it took her a moment to figure out what was different in the scene in front of her. The flower beds around her were a mass of saturated colour, scarlets and golds and purples. The shops and buildings in her line of vision were spotlessly clean, and looked as if they'd just been painted. The mock-Tudor whites and blacks were so vivid it almost hurt to look at them.

The town square had never looked like this outside of a picture-postcard. It was Technicolor, like the colour parts of *The Wizard of Oz*. And the people – they looked different, too. Most of the women and girls were wearing dresses of bright pastel colours, or even snowy white, the most impractical shade in the world. But not one white dress was grey or stained, and not one of the frocks was crumpled, not even the ones worn by the little girls skipping. The girls looked like they'd been dressed up to have their photograph taken. After a moment, Maggie realised that one of them was the butcher's daughter, a child who invariably spilled something down her clothes within five minutes of putting them on; but she too looked immaculate, her frock gleaming white, her light-brown hair freshly combed and shining. There was no sign of her friend, Mr Caplan's granddaughter, though you rarely saw one without the other.

Maggie smiled. So it was a dream. That smell of roses would have given it away, if nothing else – the town square usually smelled of cars, baking bread, fish from the fishmongers and, in warm weather, as unwashed humanity. The rose scent was even more pungent now than in previous dreams, but it, was somehow part of the scene, like incense in church. Maggie watched the people going past a little longer, and laughed as she noticed something even more incredible than the colours: everyone seemed to be smiling.

There was a shuffle and a cough. Of course; there was someone on the bench with her. It would surely be Michal. She made herself turn to him slowly, savouring the moment. Then she blinked hard. 'Vince?'

Vince, who'd been staring around the square in bemusement, turned with a start. He was wearing unusually nice clothes – a white shirt and fawn flannel trousers – but there was nothing highly-coloured or immaculate about him. He was just Vince. And he looked just as surprised – and disappointed – to see her as she was to see him. 'Oh, hullo, Maggie,' he said. 'I thought you were Alice.'

Maggie tried not to smirk. She *knew* there was something between those two. 'No, it's just me,' she said. 'But I'm sure Alice is around here somewhere.' Michal too, she thought – it was her dream, she'd hardly leave him out. 'Colin too, I'll bet.'

Vince laughed. 'Probably. Even when I'm dreaming I can't get away from you lot.'

'When *you're* dreaming? This is *my* dream.'

'I thought it was mine.'

They looked at each other. Vince laughed again. 'Strange, eh?'

Maggie shrugged. Nothing to worry about: dreams were meant to be strange, after all. 'Want to go and look around?'

'Yeah, all right.'

As they stood up, Maggie was aware of a draught around her knees. At the same moment, Vince looked down at her and grinned. 'Hey, you've got legs!'

Maggie followed his gaze, and muttered a curse. She was wearing a short white dress, and satin shoes. For a moment, annoyance burned through the drowsiness: 'Why am I wearing a bloody *dress?*'

'Best watch your language, Mags.' Vince pointed across the square. The little girls had paused in their game to watch them. The sun was very bright on their pretty pastel dresses. When they saw Maggie looking, they waved shyly. Maggie waved back, puzzled; she knew all those kids, they usually ignored her and she ignored them. Vince, indifferent to the fact that she'd been forced into skirts, was already wandering away across the square as if nothing was wrong. She turned to follow him, but walked straight into someone. 'Oh, sorry.'

'That's *quite* all right, Miss Ogilvie. It was my fault.'

Maggie blinked. It was Mrs Chester, Charlie's mother. Now the woman was smiling. 'It was my fault, Miss Ogilvie. Please forgive me.'

Maggie looked at her, suspecting irony. There was no sign of it in Mrs Chester's face or manner. If anything, she looked nervous. '…Yes, of course,' Maggie said.

'So kind. And please give my very best wishes to Mr Walker, there.' She nodded towards Vince.

'I will.'

Mrs Chester remained standing in front of her, as if she were waiting to be dismissed. 'Well,' said Maggie, 'we must be going.'

Mrs Chester nodded, her smile still fixed in place. Maggie had to actually turn her back and walk away before the woman hurried off about her business. Maggie caught up with Vince, who was frowning. 'Was that old boiler actually being nice to you?'

'Yes.' Strange dream, indeed. Quite pleasant, though. And, well, she could suffer wearing a dress for once. 'Come on.'

They walked on. Pigeons fluttered hopefully around them; there was no sign of Simple Billy and his bag of bird-feed on the usual bench. They crossed the road; a car was approaching, but it slowed down courteously and the driver waved for them to pass. They stepped onto the pavement outside the bookshop, and Maggie stopped in confusion.

The bookshop wasn't Caplan's Books; it had a different name, spelled out in shiny gold lettering: *English Books*. The window displayed books that must surely be for children: the cover illustrations were of bright, smiling blonde families in green meadows, like pictures from Sunday School texts. Before Maggie could look more closely, a man appeared in the bookshop doorway. 'Miss Ogilvie! Mr Walker! How can I help you?'

It wasn't Mr Caplan, or one of his family. It was a big, beaming, fair-haired man with rosy cheeks; Maggie hadn't seen him before. She said: 'Where's Mr Caplan?'

The man frowned. 'I don't know who you mean, Miss.'

'Mr Caplan. He owns the bookshop. Do you work for him?'

'No, Miss.' He looked apprehensive. 'This is my bookshop, Miss. It's *English Books*.'

'But you…'

'Mags.' Vince nudged her. 'Leave it. Come on.'

He was right; it was just a dream. She followed. They passed the news vendor, with his placard bearing a headline: *Country Booms With Record Harvest!* Maggie frowned: she knew the harvest wasn't a record. She fished in her pockets for some coins. 'One paper, please,' she said to the news vendor. 'Vince, have you got any change?'

The news vendor said hastily, 'No charge for you, Miss,' and handed over the paper.

'Well, I could get used to all this,' said Vince as they walked on. 'Getting a bit of respect for once in our lives.'

'True.' Maggie was scanning the paper. The first page was taken up by the headline, and by a photograph: a group of blonde land girls standing proudly beside a haystack. She turned the page, and there it was: record harvest, there in black and white. 'Vince, this is a very strange dream—'

Vince laughed. 'You're telling me.' He reached over and tapped his finger at the top of the page. Maggie looked where he was pointing. It was the date. It said: *August 18th, 1941.*

'I don't think this is just a dream, Mags,' Vince said, surprisingly calmly. 'I think this is the future.'

'Maggie! Alice!'

Alice woke up suddenly when Colin burst into the room. It was early morning; too early even for Colin's Gran to be awake. Maggie lay inert beside Alice, sleeping so soundly she hadn't even stirred when Colin rushed in. Alice sat up: 'Colin, what is it?'

'It's Vince,' Colin said. He sounded close to tears. 'I can't wake him up.'

Maggie leafed through the rest of the paper. It must be a misprint; maybe the other pages would have it right? But they all said the same: *1941.*

'Just a minute,' Maggie said. She turned and went back to the news vendor. He was serving someone else, but he broke off as soon as he saw Maggie. 'Can I help you, Miss Ogilvie?'

'This date.' She held out the paper. 'Is it right?'

The man looked. 'Yes, Miss. It's the eighteenth all right.'

Vince was at Maggie's shoulder. 'She means the year. Is it 1941?'

The news vendor looked from one to the other anxiously. 'Of course it is, Mr Walker.'

'Thanks.' Maggie grabbed Vince by the arm and walked him away. When they were alone she said, 'We're a year in the future.' The warmth of the sun, and the heavy scent of roses, were making it difficult to think. 'How can we be in the future?'

'Jannah told me once she could see the future,' Vince said. 'Maybe she's doing this.'

Maggie paused. 'If it's Jannah, we can't trust her.'

'They murdered her mum and dad.' He shook his head, as if trying to clear it; perhaps he was feeling sleepy too. 'Maybe she wants to get her own back, so she's helping us?'

'But you heard everything she said. Back in Westminster Abbey. She's a Nazi.'

'Maybe she en't one no more.'

Maggie frowned. 'Do you think Nazis can just – not be Nazis any more?'

'Yeah, why not?' Vince said quickly. 'People can change, can't they?'

'I suppose so.' Maggie looked around the square. There were quite a few differences, she could see now. Suddenly, something struck her that should have been apparent at once. 'There's no one in uniform,' she said.

They both looked around. Maggie made herself concentrate. Something was very, very important. 'The shelter's gone,' she said. 'There are no sandbags. There's no sign of the war at all.'

They stared at one another. 'Vince,' Maggie said eventually, 'if this is the future, I think the war's over.'

Vince's smile was so wide he was actually handsome. 'Did we win?'

They must have done, or surely everyone wouldn't be so happy. Maggie thought of a way to check; she turned to look at the town hall, at the flags flying outside it. But it was all right – the Union Jack was still there. There was another flag beside it, but she knew that wasn't unusual – on the very rare occasions Wardston entertained foreign dignitaries, the town hall always flew the visitor's flag out of courtesy. But the British flag was still there. Maggie didn't recognise the other one; but the point was, it wasn't a swastika. She giggled. 'I think we did.'

Vince gave a big shout, caught her up in his arms and spun her around. Maggie let him. *Peace.* This was only 1941; so the war would be over and done within a year, maybe much less. They'd be safe. All of them. *And we're going to win...*

Vince set her down – rather heavily, Maggie wasn't a skinny girl – and for a moment, just a moment, she thought about kissing him. But he was looking over her shoulder, a slight note of worry in his eyes. She turned; he was looking at the unfamiliar flag beside the Union Jack. 'What flag's that?' he said.

'It's all right,' she assured him. 'It'll just be a visitor's flag.'

'Oh yeah, yeah.' He smiled again, but the worry was still there. 'What is it, though?'

They looked. The flag bore a black circular design on a background of white. A circle within a circle, with twelve crooked lines radiating out from the centre.

Maggie had never seen it before. 'I'm not sure. Alice would know.'

Vince's face brightened at her name. He looked around eagerly: 'Where *is* Alice?'

'At the cottage, probably. Or at the Stone.'

'Let's go and find her. And Colin. Come on!'

He took her hand, and they ran across the road into the brightly-coloured town square. It was pretty. Everywhere seemed to be adorned with big red roses; the statue of Queen Victoria wore a garland of them. This would explain the heavy floral scent in the air. The roses were growing in flower beds too, trailing down from hanging-baskets. Maggie stopped to look at a bed of them... there was something... no, it was gone. Maybe it would come to her.

They crossed the square. There were a few other changes, Maggie noticed. Not important, surely, just different. Several of the shops had new names, and apparently new owners. The flower shop, formerly owned by a man Maggie didn't know, had closed down altogether. The sweet shop, previously run by Mr Cromwell, a surly man with strange political views and a deep hatred of children, had been taken over by a plump blonde woman who smiled at them as they passed. She certainly looked a lot nicer than Mr Cromwell. But Mr Cromwell had always been there, and, for a moment, his absence made Maggie uneasy. And there was still no sign of Simple Billy...

Surely it was nothing, nothing at all. Then something occurred to her. 'They grow on bushes,' she said.

'Eh?'

'Roses. They usually grow on rose bushes.' She pointed at the flower beds. The big red roses were sprouting straight out of the ground, like daffodils. It looked…odd.

Vince shrugged. 'Must be a new breed or something.'

'Must be.' Then yet another stranger greeted them warmly, deferentially, on the way past. Everybody loved them; and the war was over. 'Let's go and find the others!' she said.

Alice said firmly, 'Vince is probably just tired, Colin. You should leave him in peace.'

'He isn't. He isn't just sleeping, Alice. It's like he's…'

He looked at Maggie. Alice realised she had never, ever, seen Maggie oblivious to Colin in distress. But Maggie was still asleep. Colin reached out and shook her by the shoulder: 'Maggie?'

Maggie didn't stir.

Chapter Eighteen

The Gothi

The New Forest, Southern England

Miriam Ogilvie stood by the Rufus Stone and waited. She rested her fingertips on the Rufus Stone's flat, three-sided top; she thought she could already feel power there, feel her fingertips prickling.

She watched as the others approached across the clearing. There were twelve of them; they walked slowly, one from each point of the compass. Their long white robes swished through the last remnants of ground mist. The robes' gilt embroidery glimmered in the morning sun.

Vivian was crossing the clearing from the east; Laura and the major on either side of her. Miriam couldn't help smiling as she watched the other coveners approach. They all carried themselves with the immense dignity of many years in the Craft; not one of them was under sixty. These old men and women were the elite of British witchcraft. They wore nothing but their loose-fitting robes, and their white hair hung loose and unadorned about their shoulders; but they walked across the grass like kings and queens.

They stopped three yards from the Rufus Stone, just before the Circle. Miriam had cut it into the turf earlier with a ceremonial sword, and filled the circular groove with salt. As one, all twelve of the coven bowed to Miriam. Miriam lifted the athame, the double-sided dagger, above her head. The twelve coveners concentrated on it, on the light glinting off its tip.

At last Miriam spoke. 'Salt is life. Salt is pure. Salt heals. Come into this circle of salt, and be healed. Be purified. Be born to a new life.'

The coveners responded: 'So may it be.'

The athame's blade began to glow. Miriam pointed it at the eastern edge of the Circle. The white salt began to shine, blue-white like snow in bright sunshine. One by one, the coveners stepped into the Circle, and proceeded solemnly inside it until they were all standing evenly-spaced inside the circumference. Miriam made a slashing motion with the athame. 'The Circle is closed. Let it not be broken until our magick is complete.'

'So may it be.'

Their voices were steady, although they all knew that some of them might not leave the Circle alive. Miriam turned to the Rufus Stone. It was their altar today, but it held no furnishings: no candles or chalices or images. *Silly toys*, the *gothi* children had called them; ever since that night, Miriam had been unable to draw any force from even the most sacred of artefacts. She would have to hope that here, in this place of power, such things would be unnecessary: that what came from within would be enough. Miriam stretched out her arm and touched the tip of the athame to the Rufus Stone. 'Here do I direct my powers, to call upon the great Power. Goddess and Lady, hear me.'

'So may it be.'

Miriam's whole arm was tingling. The magick was coming through. Miriam said: 'Queen of Light and Darkness, help us in our purpose this day.' She was silent for a moment. At this point, they would usually pledge to harm no one. Ill-wishing always came back on the wisher; no one here had ever used magick to bring harm to another person. But today was different. Miriam felt the others stir uneasily, although they'd known in advance that she would omit the pledge. Miriam said: 'Goddess Within and Goddess Without, come to us and help us.'

Magick was tingling through all of them now. Each of the coveners closed their eyes and focussed on Miriam's voice, as she began to sing:

'Goddess of Night and Day,
Maiden and Mother and Crone,
Venus and Hecate we call you,
Mary and Cerridwen we call you,
Astarte and Kali we call you,
Great Mother of All, we call you.
Lend us your strength,
Lend us your wisdom,
Send us your help this day:
Show us the one we seek.
Dark One, come to us.
Bright One, come to us.
Dark One, come to us…
Bright One, come to us…'

The twelve coveners joined in the chant. *Dark One come to us, Bright One come to us…* over and over again. It was the simplest chant any of them had ever used; there was no Latin, there were no Archangelic Names, no props and no formal rituals. Nothing but their most heartfelt and desperate need. *Dark One come to us… Bright One come to us…*

The Cone of Power was beginning to form. It rose, a shimmering transparent wall, sloping from the circumference of the Circle to meet in a point far above their heads. Magick enclosed them like a tent. They all focussed on a space just above the Rufus Stone.

A hot breeze whipped around the Circle as an image began to take shape. Out of a hard white light emerged a very well-known face, shouting and snarling at an invisible audience. A face with black hair and a small moustache. Miriam stopped the chant; after one more repetition the others did too. They focussed all the power and concentration they could muster upon the image above the Rufus Stone.

'Adolf Hitler,' said Miriam. 'You shall not come here. These shores are forbidden to you. You shall not come here.' The others took up the new chant. *You shall not come here…*

Gran shook Maggie, quite roughly. Maggie rolled limply from side to side. Gran checked her pulse and her breathing; both seemed quite normal. It was as if she were just asleep. But she wouldn't wake up.

'Is there any change?' Alice had appeared in the doorway.

Gran shook her head. 'What about Vince?'

'He's just the same.'

Gran nodded. 'I'll telephone Dr Braithwaite. It's probably nothing.'

It didn't look like nothing. Gran was getting briskly to her feet. She glanced at the window – there was a thin sliver of bright daylight where the blackout curtain had come loose. Gran said to Colin, who was hovering anxiously at her elbow, 'Let some light in, would you dear?'

Colin pulled the blackout curtains away from the window as Gran left the room. Sunlight flooded in. Alice sat on the bed, looking down at Maggie, who seemed pink-cheeked and healthy. Colin said, 'Alice?'

She looked up. Colin was staring out of the window. Alice went to stand beside him and followed his gaze. The bedroom faced south-east, over the Channel. Alice looked out at a beautiful summer morning, still a little hazy but promising fine weather. Except, that is, for a mass of black in the east; a heavy dark cloud.

Alice said reassuringly, 'It's just a storm coming in.'

Colin had seen storms coming in. 'I don't think it is, Alice.'

Gran appeared in the doorway. 'The telephone isn't working,' she said. 'Colin, will you run down to Dr Braithwaite's?'

Colin nodded and left the room. Gran came to stand beside Alice. 'Do you think all this is… is…'

'Magical? I don't—'

They heard a thump from the bottom of the stairs; then Colin, laughing. It was too high-pitched to be his normal laugh. Alice and Gran ran onto the landing and down the stairs, where Colin was lying on the floor in the hallway. He was trembling violently.

They knelt down beside him. Gran lifted his head into her lap. 'Colin?'

Alice checked his pulse: too fast. 'I think it's just one of his turns,' she said. 'He'll probably be all right soon, but—'

Colin opened his eyes. Gran cried out in shock: they were a bright, glowing blue. He turned his head to look at Alice. 'Hello,' he said. It was a female voice, with a German accent. Alice's head began to throb. 'Hello, Alice.'

Gran looked imploringly at Alice. 'What's happening to him?'

Colin grinned. 'We are coming to see you, Alice,' he said. 'We are coming now.' Then his eyes closed, he shuddered, and lay still.

Gran looked at Alice. 'Run for the doctor. Quick.'

'I can't.' Alice's face was white. 'I have to get to the Ward Stone.'

Maggie and Vince stood in the cottage gateway. They had enjoyed the walk here, past the harbour that smelled of flowers rather than engine oil and fish. Behind them the sea was a tropical turquoise, the beach golden-white. There was no barbed wire, and no sign of any mines. It was all beautiful. But the cottage was gone.

The only traces of it were the wall and the empty gateway. Where the cottage and the garden had been there was a field of red roses. Their perfume was very strong. Maggie looked around, bewildered. 'Where's the cottage gone?'

'Dunno.'

'And where's my Gran?'

'Gone somewhere else, I suppose. Don't fret, Maggie. We'll find her.'

'Yes. I suppose you're right.' Gran must have moved house, that's all. Maggie remembered talking to someone – she couldn't remember who – and saying emphatically that Gran would never move. It was a bit… worrying. But she said, 'We'll ask someone.'

'We'll ask whoever's up on the Mound,' said Vince.

Maggie nodded. There was someone up there, all right. She was sure of it. 'Let's go up then.'

'Right you are.' Vince reached down and picked one of the roses, and handed it to her with a flourish. 'Here y'are, milady.'

Maggie giggled and tucked the flower down her cleavage. He really was sweet. And the rose smelled so nice. Strong, but nice. There really was nothing to worry about. 'Thanks, Vince.'

They followed the spiral path to the top of the Mound.

The soft murmur of voices reached them before they got to the summit. They'd been admiring the clear azure sky, empty of clouds and of vapour trails, so they didn't notice the change until they were right at the top of the Mound. When they did, Maggie gave a little cry of surprise.

The Stone was gone. In its place was a structure of white marble, shining and beautiful against the blue sky. Maggie's first thought, stupidly, was that it was a bandstand – it was the right size, round and open and supported by fine columns. It wasn't a bandstand, of course: it was like a little Greek temple. It was pure white, except for black markings on the floor which Maggie couldn't quite make out.

There were people in the temple. Young men – boys, really – in white shirts and light brown trousers. Eleven of them. They stood in a circle, evenly spaced, although there was a gap as if someone were missing. In the centre of the circle was a marble throne, raised on a stepped pedestal. A figure in white sat there, quite still. It was a woman or a girl, in a long white veil – not a translucent veil like a bride's, but thick and concealing, like a beekeeper's. The veil moved very slightly as she breathed; otherwise she could have been a statue.

The boys looked up at Maggie and Vince's approach. Some of them stared at Maggie's legs, at the flower jammed between her breasts; one of them said something, and the others sniggered. But then the tallest looked at them severely, and they fell silent at once. The tallest boy left his place in the circle and came to meet Maggie and Vince. He was blond and very good-looking, a lot like Arthur. He turned a warm smile onto Maggie. Then he bowed his head and clicked his heels in a smart military salute. It should have made him look like a complete ass, but somehow it didn't. He really *was* like Arthur. 'Welcome, Fräulein,' the young man said. 'I am Albrecht.' He turned to Vince: 'And welcome to you, brother.'

His accent was light, but very obvious. When Maggie and Vince took a step backwards, he held up his hands. 'Please do not be alarmed. We wish only to talk to you.'

'You're Germans,' said Vince.

'Yes. And we hope to make peace between our two countries. We know that you can… influence your leaders. I think you are a man of peace, brother.' He turned again to Maggie. 'I know that your father was such, Fräulein. In his name, will you hear us?'

'What's all this?' Maggie waved a hand at the marble temple. 'Where's the Ward Stone?'

'It is safe, Fräulein. It is a precious historical treasure. We are treating it with the greatest care.'

'But – it ought to be here.'

'Forgive me, Fräulein, but this place is special enough. The Stone is not necessary. It is the place that counts. It is the ground.'

'What about my Gran? Her cottage is gone. Where is she? What did you do with her?'

'Do with her? We did not *do* anything with her.' Albrecht sounded so shocked that Maggie believed him. 'She is an old lady, a fine old English lady worthy of our respect. She simply no longer belongs here. She has been given a better house in the village.'

'But she lives here.'

'She is an elderly lady, Fräulein. She has kept this place for so long. Is it not time she retired? Has she not earned her rest?'

'Well, yes.' That sounded very sensible. 'But...'

'Please, Fräulein. All your questions will be answered. But first, hear us speak.'

Maggie looked at Vince. He shrugged. 'Can't hurt to listen.'

'All right.' They ought to be reasonable, after all. It was hard to be hostile, in the warm sunshine, smelling the heavenly scent of the rose tucked into her dress. 'But tell us, please – is this really the future?'

'It is *a* future, Fräulein. One of two possible futures. The other is very terrible. We wish at all costs to avoid it.' He smiled, and gazed lovingly around him, and gestured towards the village. 'But you have seen what may be. Is it not beautiful? Is it not perfect? Wouldn't you want the whole world to be so? That is our goal: to make the whole world as perfect as this place.'

'We thought you wanted to invade us,' said Vince. 'We thought you wanted to wipe us out.'

'No. We don't want that.' Again, Albrecht was so emphatic that Maggie believed him. 'We want to be your brothers. We want you to be at one with us. Come, please. Come and see.'

They went up the shallow steps into the temple. Albrecht pointed to the floor. A black design was set into the white marble: a circle within a circle, its spokes crooked lines. The same design printed on the flag in the town square. 'What *is* that?' said Vince.

'It is the Black Sun.' Albrecht's voice was reverent. 'The sun-wheel, the symbol of purity and the unity of all good people. It is divided into twelve, as you see.' Now they saw that each boy stood on the edge of the design, exactly where the central lines met the outer circle. Except there was a gap in the ring of young men, and one line was not occupied. Albrecht, anticipating their next question, said: 'But, as you see, we have lost one of our number. And we should like you, brother, to take his place.'

'Me?' said Vince.

'Of course. Will you not step forward? You are special – the people of the village know it. So should you. Come, take your rightful place.'

'What about Mags?'

Some of the boys sniggered again. Albrecht said, 'This is a circle of men, brother.'

'Who's that, then?' Vince pointed to the white-draped figure on the marble throne, who had not moved or spoken.

'She is our Lady.' Albrecht's voice became adoring. 'Our power, our life, our inspiration. As your lady here is to you, I am sure.'

Vince looked at Maggie, trying not to laugh. 'Umm... yeah.'

'Don't make your mind up about this yet,' Maggie said, irritated. 'Wait till the others get here.'

'Do you let this woman speak for you?' one of the other boys cut in. His voice was correct and toneless; his face was impassive. He was talking to Vince as if Maggie wasn't there. 'Do you not speak for yourself?'

Vince stared at him coldly. 'No need to be rude, pal.'

'Forgive him,' Albrecht said hastily. 'This is Petr. He means no disrespect, he only has great hopes for peace and unity.'

I'll bet, Maggie thought. She said, 'We should wait until the others get here before we decide anything. Alice and Colin. And I want Michal to hear this, too.'

The other boys laughed aloud. Albrecht smiled politely. 'The Polish pilot? But my dear Fräulein, this is none of his concern. After all, he will not be here for much longer.'

'*What?*'

Vince snorted. 'You've done it now,' he said to Albrecht.

'What do you *mean?*' Maggie was beginning to dislike this drowsy feeling. She felt it was making her…miss things. 'Where will he go?'

'Why, back to Poland, of course. Where he belongs.'

Maggie shook her head. The scent of the rose was suddenly too strong. 'He belongs here with me!'

'Forgive me, Fräulein, but has he said that he means to stay with you?'

'Of course he…' She trailed off. 'Of course that's what he means…'

'He knows his own place. That is how the future must be. Every man in his own proper place.' His voice was gentle. 'That is why the other… two cannot be here either.'

'Alice and Colin?' Vince's eyes narrowed. 'Why not?'

'They will have their own place. Somewhere else. Everything shall be as nature intended.'

The rose's perfume really was too strong. Maggie pulled it out of her dress and threw it aside. 'Colin's my brother, his place is with me! That's natural!'

Albrecht sighed. 'Alas, no. I commend your loyalty, Fräulein, but that will not be possible.'

'Why not?'

Petr interrupted: 'You must know why not. Because the boy is defective.'

'*What?*'

Albrecht sighed. 'He only means—'

'This place is for those perfect in blood. Or at least...' Petr eyed her coldly, 'as perfect as may be found. The power does not run true in your brother. He has *seizures*.' He made the word sound filthy. 'He could not perform his duties reliably.'

Albrecht interrupted, 'We should not wish him to come to harm, after all. You know how he suffers when the gift is upon him. He would be better off... elsewhere. And would you too not be better off? If you did not have to care for him? After all, you are not your brother's keeper!' He laughed, but when he saw her face he added hastily, 'But of course, your wishes would be honored, Fräulein. Many special privileges would be accorded to one as valuable as yourself. You may keep your brother with you if you desire.'

'Keep him with me? He's not a pet!'

Vince interjected softly, 'And what about Alice?'

There was another silence, chillier this time. Eventually Albrecht said, 'It will not be possible for her to be here. I am sorry if that disturbs you.'

'Why can't she be here?' No one answered. Petr looked away, disdainfully. Vince said to Albrecht, 'Why can't Alice be here? Come on, blondie, spit it out. Why not Alice?'

'I regret that her blood is compromised.'

'You mean she's ill?'

'No. Not – exactly.'

'Then what?'

'Because she is a – Jew.'

Kestrel Squadron sat outside the dispersal hut in the oppressive heat. A few of the pilots held open newspapers or books, but there were no cards or chess-boards in front of them. No one was even trying anymore. Kiddy Jones had fallen asleep: any moment now he'd wake with a cry, then go back to sleep again. He'd been doing it all day. Most of the pilots just stared into space. Or they watched Michal pacing up and down. Eventually Penry-Smith said, 'For God's sake sit down, Michal. You're giving us all the heebies.'

Michal paused, but kept looking at the skies. The light was a strange yellow. 'Something is—'

'—is coming. Yes, you've said. It's a storm, Michal. Good bloody thing too, the Hun don't like flying in electrical storms any more than we do.'

'It is not just a storm.'

'What is it then?'

Michal shook his head. He'd never found a way to tell Arthur about Maggie and her friends; he certainly couldn't tell the whole squadron. 'I do not know.'

Penry-Smith groaned impatiently. Arthur interrupted: 'I hear you and Harry brought in a German pilot yesterday, Penry?'

'Oh, yes.' Penry-Smith brightened up a little. 'You should have seen the poor bugger. He came down in a farmer's field just after the muck-spreading. So he had a nice soft landing, but he got a bit of the old *ordure* on him, didn't he?'

'Covered in shite,' agreed Williams.

'Exactly. So anyway, some local chaps were passing too, and they were all set to beat the snot out of him, but he whiffed so much they didn't want to go anywhere near him. So we—'

The phone rang in the dispersal hut. Kiddy Jones woke up

with a shout. Michal was already running towards his plane when Owens rang the bell and shouted, 'Squadron scramble!'

Michal was the first to reach his Spitfire. But he stopped to look back, in spite of his rigger and fitter staring at him impatiently. He was looking at Arthur. The strange light had caught him, giving his blond head a golden nimbus like a halo. Or a crown. Michal was remembering the bright aura he'd seen around Arthur, when the witch-sight was on him. *He is special*, Michal thought. *He is going to...*

But he didn't know what. Then Arthur had pulled on his leather helmet and mask, and he looked just like everyone else. When Michal's rigger said, 'Sir?', Michal climbed into his Spitfire.

This was their second sortie of the day, but still they were airborne in minutes. Adrenaline was overriding exhaustion, as it always did. Control was as prompt as ever, too; the squadron were still climbing, about to enter thick cloud, when the voice spoke in their ears. 'Kestrel Leader, this is Wardston. Take vector three-five-zero, Kestrel. Angels twenty-five.'

Before Arthur could reply, Michal interrupted: 'This is Blue Two. Repeat, please – we are to head *away* from Wardston village? Over.'

'Confirmed, Blue Two. They're coming from the north. Bandits a hundred plus. Over.'

There was silence as that sank in. A hundred enemy planes, or more. But Arthur's voice was enthusiastic. 'Understood, Wardston. A nice big target, lots to hit. Are we to have any company besides the Luftwaffe, Wardston?'

'Affirmative, Kestrel Leader. Jacko and Edey Squadrons are on the way too. Hurricane squadrons, so watch your fire.' There was a pause, then: 'Blue Three, try not to shoot the Hurricanes; they don't like it.'

'Wardston, this is Blue Three,' said Penry-Smith. 'Didn't know you wanted to be a comedian, Wardston. Don't give up the day job. Over.'

Michal's voice broke in again. 'Wardston, confirm please – there are no enemy sightings over Wardston village?'

'Not a thing, Blue Two. Just bad weather. Have you spotted something? Over.'

'No,' Michal admitted. 'No sighting.'

It didn't feel right. But if the village were under attack, he would surely be hearing Maggie's voice by now. And he wasn't getting a thing from her. She must still be asleep. It must be peaceful there.

The squadron swung around to the north, away from Wardston.

Chapter Nineteen

The Gathering Storm

Within minutes, Alice had pulled on some clothes – any clothes – and run out of the cottage. Gran came to the door and watched her go, a small figure pounding her way up the spiral path to the top of the Mound.

Gran went back inside and looked at Colin. He was like Maggie and Vince now: sleeping. But not waking up. Anything could be happening to them, anything.

They needed a doctor. Gran checked the telephone – it was still dead. So she pulled on her headsquare and hurried off to the village.

She was right outside St Michael's when the church bells began to ring. They had been muffled since the outbreak of war. They were only to be rung if there was an invasion.

Gran could see into the bell-tower. The bells were ringing wildly, but no one was pulling the ropes.

Maggie and Vince stared at Albrecht. 'Because she's a Jew?' echoed Maggie. 'Alice? So what if she is?'

Albrecht looked pained. 'I see that your education has been neglected, Fräulein. You have been much deceived. Jewish blood is the root of all treachery. Your... friend cannot be trusted. She cannot be in this place.'

Vince made a choking noise and doubled over. Maggie thought he was going to be sick; but then she heard the noises, and realised he was laughing. Albrecht looked puzzled. 'Brother?'

'Oh, good one, good one.' Vince straightened up. 'You really had me going there. All the bright colours, and the people being nice and that. You nearly had me fooled.'

'I beg your pardon?' said Albrecht.

'Is that the real reason Alice en't here? Is it really' cause she's Jewish? Or is it just 'cause she'd see through you in a heartbeat? Smart as a whip, that girl. Young Colin too – he's quiet, but he always figures out what's what when it really matters. Me and Mags here, we're a bit slower on the uptake, en't we? Well we are,' he added when Maggie looked at him indignantly. 'But we get there in the end. And I'm on to you now.'

Albrecht was staring at him in consternation. 'What do you mean, brother?'

'I mean, I know your game, mate. I know what this is. I've heard it all before.' He took a deep breath. His voice deepened into a rough bellowing chant. 'Jews *OUT!* Darkies *OUT!* *Eng*land *for* the *Eng*lish! *ENG*LAND *FOR* THE *ENG*LISH! That's all this is, isn't it?'

'I don't—'

'You make it look nicer, but you're no better than my stepdad, useless tosser that he is.'

Albrecht frowned. 'You do wrong to speak of your father that way, brother.'

'He en't my bloody father. And I en't your brother.'

'You are indeed not our brother.' Petr's disdainful voice broke in. 'You are weak and ungrateful. You were raised by a good man, one of the cause's footsoldiers—'

'Footsoldier, is he? Why don't he fight other soldiers, then?

Instead of sneaking around at night beating up old women?'

Petr smiled. 'You know all about that, don't you?'

'Please, brother,' Albrecht interrupted. 'Look at us. And look at yourself. We are one race. You *are* our brother. You have nothing to fear from us.'

Vince shrugged. 'Well, I'm in with you now, I grant you. I'm all right now. But that could all change, couldn't it? I never knew much about my real Dad. What if it turns out someday that I've got a Jewish granny or something?' He laughed harshly as their faces froze. 'That would be different, wouldn't it? See me in a whole new light then, wouldn't you?'

'Brother—'

'Or what if I go to the hospital and they find I've got a hole in my heart or something? What if it turns out I en't *perfect*? Or what if I have a kid, say, and he has fits like Colin? Or if he turns out like poor old Simple Billy?'

'Then he would be sent to a special place—'

'Where?'

'I beg your pardon?'

'If the whole world's to be like this, where would you send him?'

'I don't...'

'Where's left? All them missing persons from the town square, where would they be going? Where will you send old Caplan and Simple Billy and the rest of them?' He laughed again at Albrecht's confused face. 'You poor stupid bastard, you've never even thought about it, have you?'

Petr interrupted: 'Of course, if you proved to be so *sentimental*, you would be allowed to keep your child with you.'

Vince stared at him. 'You're a bloody liar. These others, they're daft enough to believe all the bollocks you've been told. But you don't, do you? You *know*.'

Petr smiled thinly and looked away. Albrecht said desperately, 'Brother—'

'I *en't your brother*.' He turned to Maggie. 'Come on, Mags, let's go—'

There was a rustle of silk. The figure on the marble throne was getting to her feet. She held out a dainty white hand. Silver mist began to form at the tips of her fingers. Vince looked at her suspiciously. 'What's she doing?'

'Showing your *friend* here who you really are,' said Petr.

The girl in the veil made a circular motion. The silver mist began to form into a circle before her, like a shield. The mist solidified, until it looked like a shining mirror. Maggie said to Petr: 'What do you mean, who he is? I know who he is.'

Albrecht looked grim. 'I regret you do not, Fräulein. He himself has forgotten. We must remind him.'

The silver mirror-shape flickered, and began to show moving figures, like a cinema screen. Sounds came from it, too. Half-a-dozen voices chanting; and screams, a woman's screams. The figures came into focus.

Vince had gone white. 'Stop this,' he said.

Alice, puffing for breath, reached the top of the Mound. She looked out over the sea. The black storm front was getting closer.

Alice put her hand on the Ward Stone. It reassured her. She could feel the power there. It wasn't a fraction of the power all four wizards together could draw on, of course. But it might be enough. It would have to be.

Alice watched the storm coming closer. She heard the church bells start to ring.

'Stop it,' Vince said hoarsely. 'Don't!'

No one listened. They were all watching the scene in the mirror. It was a street, outside a corner shop. It was night-time: obviously before the war, because street-lights lit the scene very clearly. Broken glass was all over the pavement. Half a dozen men – boys, some of them – were gathered around a struggling figure on the ground. A big man in a black shirt was leaning over, tugging. The men around were chanting: 'Jews OUT! Jews OUT!'

The figure was a woman, Maggie saw, an old woman. The big man was pulling her along the ground by her hair. She was screaming, and he was laughing.

'Oh God,' Vince said. He turned away from the mirror. 'Oh God no.'

One of the chanting figures was familiar. He was about three years younger, no more than thirteen, but it was clearly Vince. The big man was the man Maggie had seen hovering over Vince: his stepfather.

Petr was saying: 'The woman and her family were Jews. They replaced a local shopkeeper, a man of good Aryan blood. He had gone out of business. *She* had made that happen, of course. The shopkeeper complained to the local footsoldiers of the cause. They took action, as you see.'

'Vince?' Maggie said.

There were tears in Vince's eyes. 'She was just an old woman,' he said. 'He did that to her. And she died, Maggie. She had a heart attack and she died. And I did *nothing*. I just stood there.'

Maggie didn't know what to say. 'Oh, Vince...'

'I did nothing, Mags.' Vince shut his eyes, and tears spilled down his face. 'I was scared. I just stood there.'

Maggie turned angrily on the *gothi*. 'What do you think you're doing? Stop this!'

Albrecht looked away. Petr said, casually: 'Now do you see? Blood calls to blood. He is one of us.'

'You – vicious little bastard!'

The boys laughed and made a high-pitched 'Oooo-oooh!' sound. Maggie turned back to Vince, whose eyes were still closed.

'Vince? Vince! Open your eyes!'

'I can't,' whispered Vince.

Maggie looked again at the screen. 'Vince, you've got to look. You were just a kid, Vince. *Look.*'

Vince slowly opened his eyes. He watched the image of himself. The younger Vince looked very young indeed. He was crying. Vince turned to Maggie. 'She died, Maggie…'

'You didn't do that.'

'Yeah, I did. I did *nothing.*'

Petr said: 'You did nothing because you knew what your stepfather did was right. You may have been too squeamish to do it yourself, but you knew.'

'Shut up, you!' snapped Maggie. The boys laughed again. Petr said scornfully: 'Hold your tongue, you silly bitch.'

Albrecht frowned but said nothing. Vince lifted his head. 'Don't talk to her like that.'

'Vince.' Maggie grabbed him by the shoulders. 'Vince, listen. You were a kid. You were just a scared kid. *Look* at yourself!' She took hold of his chin and twisted his head towards the screen. 'Just *look!*'

Finally, Vince looked. He watched for a full two minutes as the image repeated, over and over. Maggie watched him take in how young the mirror-Vince was: how he was crying like a child, because that was what he was. 'Just a kid,' Vince said faintly.

Petr was frowning now. 'You may have been young, but you still knew—'

Maggie snapped, 'I said shut up.' She turned to Vince again: 'You're not like that any more, Vince.'

He shook his head slowly. 'I'm still scared, though.'

'I know. We all are. But you've got to stay with us. You've got to help us now. You – I mean – you wouldn't want them doing that to my Gran, would you? Or to Alice?'

He blinked hard. 'Alice…?'

'I know you feel bad, but we've got to—'

Petr interrupted: 'Still letting a woman tell you what to do?'

'She said shut it, you little turd.' Suddenly Vince sounded a lot more like Vince again. 'You deaf or something? And *you*.' He wiped his face angrily, and turned to the white-draped figure holding the mirror. 'You can put the newsreel away, sweetheart, we've all seen it.'

Albrecht took a step towards him. 'You may not speak to our Lady that way!'

Vince laughed. 'You know, I think I *may*.'

Petr was smiling unpleasantly. 'Would you like us to show the *newsreel* to your friend, Alice?'

Vince flinched, but set his face hard. 'Do what you like, pal. I'm gonna tell her anyway. If she hasn't worked it out already. Told you, she's smart as a whip.' He turned to Albrecht. 'So I'm sorry, old matey, but I'll be declining the offer to join your happy little band. You can stick it where the sun don't shine. Come on, Mags, let's go.'

'Oh, but you must not *go*.'

The voice came from the middle of the circle: from the girl in the white veil. The girl tipped her hand, and the mirror vanished. She turned to Vince and Maggie. 'You must not go yet. Not before we have been properly introduced.'

Maggie wanted to clap her hands over her ears. The voice sounded like two voices, speaking slightly out-of-sync. It was the most horrible thing she'd ever heard. 'Vince,' Maggie said, 'I think we should go. Now.'

Albrecht said, 'You may not leave.' He was gazing at the veiled figure as if she were the most beautiful thing in the world. 'Freya commands you to stay.'

Freya. 'Vince,' Maggie said, 'we need to go!'

'Think you're right.'

Vince grabbed Maggie's hand. Albrecht stepped forward, snapping a command to the other boys. But before Maggie knew what was happening, Vince had pulled her out of the marble temple and was running across the grass. Maggie heard Albrecht shout, felt hands catching at her dress; she heard fabric tear, but didn't try to stop. Vince was pulling her towards the edge of the Mound. But it was the *wrong* edge, the east one, where there was no path but only a steep drop onto rocks. '*Vince!*' Maggie shrieked.

But he had already dragged both of them over the edge.

Albrecht watched the two British wizards vanish. He sighed heavily. 'We tried,' he said. He turned to Freya, and knelt. 'I am sorry, my Lady. They would not listen to us.'

Freya said, 'There are other ways to make them listen, my Albrecht.'

She waved her hand. The *glamour* spell dissolved around them. Albrecht closed his eyes.

When he opened them again, he was back in the cockpit of his Messerschmitt, looking down at the cliffs of Dover.

Maggie screamed as she fell forward over the steep rocky east face of the Mound, and closed her eyes. She couldn't breathe, and drew in a great gasp of air—

Then she opened her eyes, and she was lying in the cottage, in her own bed. Colin was sitting beside her. 'You're awake!' he said.

Maggie sat up. Somewhere above she heard a great thump. Then Vince's voice, shouting from the attic room he shared with Colin: 'Maggie?'

'Down here.'

Hammering footsteps overhead and on the landing: then Vince burst in, wild-haired and wild-eyed, still wearing Dad's old pyjamas. 'You all right?'

'You pulled me right off the Mound, you idiot!'

'That answers my next question. I weren't dreaming.' He looked around. 'Where's Alice? And your Gran?'

'They're not here,' Colin said. 'Gran must have gone for the doctor. I think Alice has gone up to the Stone.'

'That's where we ought to be. Get dressed, Mags, I think something funny's going on—'

'What's that noise? Listen!'

Vince shook his head. 'It's just the church bells ringing, it's…' His eyes widened. 'Oh, hell.'

The invasion. Maggie ran to the window and threw it open. The sound became louder: bells, ringing wildly as if someone were swinging on the ropes. The light was yellow and livid. Dark storm-clouds were coming in off the Channel: not drifting on the wind, but rolling and boiling forward as fast as galloping horses. Something was flying just ahead of it, something like dark birds or black planes…

Colin and Vince had followed her to the window. 'What the hell's that?' said Vince.

'I don't know. But you were right, we need to get to the Stone—'

'Maggie!' Colin tugged her away from the window and pointed into the room. The three-panelled mirror on the dressing-table had gone silvery and opaque. Mist swirled inside it. Two points of blue light were forming. Vince pointed a shaking finger. 'That looks like—'

'Does it look like little *me*?'

The voice came from Colin, but it wasn't his voice. It sounded female. Maggie and Vince looked at Colin and – they couldn't help it – backed away from him. His eyes were neon blue. 'Hello, Maggie. Hello, Vincent,' he said. 'We have not met. You left so suddenly.'

A girl's voice, with a German accent. It was teasing, almost flirtatious; it grated like fingernails down a blackboard. 'I think you were very *rude*, you know. To leave so suddenly. We were not properly introduced. I am Freya.'

'What are you doing to my brother?' Maggie ran to Colin and grabbed him by the shoulders. 'Leave him alone!'

He looked up at her, his face twisted into a simpering grin. 'I do not think so. I have come so far to visit you, after all.'

'What do you want?'

'Why, to meet you. All of you. I should like you all to come to the town square, where we can become properly acquainted.'

Maggie looked at Vince. 'We need to get up onto the Mound. Help me with him.'

They both went to lift Colin, but he pushed them away. 'Ah, I feared that an invitation would not be enough. Look.'

The grey mist in the mirror was swirling and changing. It transformed into a picture, an image of a familiar scene. The town square: the bench and flowerbeds in front of the statue of Queen Victoria. Gran was sitting on the bench. She was slumped over, as if she'd fainted where she sat. People were running past, not stopping to help her.

'There.' A giggle came out of Colin's mouth. 'Come to the square now, all of you, or the first blow that falls will be on your dear grandmother. Don't keep me waiting! I am not very patient, you know!'

The mirror-picture swirled, then faded and cleared: the mirror was just a mirror again. Colin's eyes fluttered and closed, and he slumped, unconscious, into Maggie and Vince's arms. They lowered him to the floor. Maggie pried open one of his eyelids; his eyes had returned to normal. Maggie shook him. 'Colin, wake up!'

Colin didn't stir. Vince scooped his arms under him. 'Help me,' he said. 'We need to get to the Mound.'

'What? You heard! We've got to go to the village!'

Vince shook his head. 'We can't fight them from there, Mags. We've got to get to the Ward Stone.'

'But my Gran!'

'They're trying to split us up, Mags, we all need to be together!'

'Then come with me!'

'…I can't.' He stood up. 'I'm sorry. I need to find Alice.'

'Vince!'

'I'm sorry.'

And he was gone. Maggie screamed, *'Vince!'* but his only response was the door banging shut.

Maggie shook Colin again, but he wouldn't respond. She'd have to go alone. 'I'll be back,' she told Colin. She pulled on a few clothes and ran, out of the cottage, towards the village.

It was the proudest moment of Albrecht's life: flying in, with the other *gothi*, on the wings of the storm. Each of the boys piloted a black Messerschmitt: difficult to see against the dark clouds, until sheet lightning lit the sky. The pictures on the Messerschmitts' tails were garish even in low light; in the lightning's glare, they moved as if they were alive. All the paintings showed the great beasts of holy Germanic legend: the giant wolf Fenris; the ravens of Odin, and the storm-giant Thiassi in the form of an eagle. On Petr's tail fin, the Midgard Serpent writhed and dripped its poison. Only one tail fin was blank. Freya had wiped clean the picture on Manfred's plane, when she discovered he'd been cowardly enough to pack a parachute. He would have to do something spectacular today, if he wanted to earn back his sacred image.

Albrecht's plane was foremost. On his tail fin, the golden-haired Valkyrie swooped into battle. But, for him, even she paled into insignificance; because behind his cockpit rode Freya, sitting astride the Messerschmitt as if it were a flying horse. Her blue eyes glowed brighter than the plane's navigation lights. Her white dress and blonde hair blew in the wind behind her; neither the slipstream nor the freezing gale troubled her in the least. She sang as they went, a great battle-song by Wagner, and Albrecht could hear its blessed sound quite clearly above the blast.

Behind the *gothi* flew a squadron of Stukas. The pilots were well-trained, and they'd received strict orders to obey the Messerschmitt pilots in everything. Albrecht had been disappointed by their reaction; like the men at the Wewelsburg aerodrome, they had not seemed at all grateful for the honour they were receiving. They were officers of the Luftwaffe, however, and they would obey their orders whatever they thought of them.

The Messerschmitts reached the British coast, and the storm clouds broke over Wardston like a wave.

Chapter Twenty

Freya

Fifty miles north of Wardston, Kestrel Squadron climbed through the thick cloud. Outside the cockpit, Arthur could see nothing but blank grey. He looked to left and right; he could just see Michal's and Penry-Smith's navigation lights. 'Turn up all your lights, gentlemen. Reduce speed and stay close.'

They flew on through the cloud. It was little better than flying at night. Arthur switched constantly between checking his instruments and scanning the sky ahead. Damp was seeping into the cockpit, but he took no notice. The dark mist was hypnotising in its monotony it was easy to imagine patterns and shapes that weren't there. He had to focus on spotting what actually was. Although they all knew that if another aircraft was coming towards them at any speed, they'd never see it in time.

Sometimes the mist thinned and they emerged into a gap: sunshine and blue sky, towering white cloud formations all around, with even a hazy glimpse of the ground. And no enemy aircraft, not so far. Then they'd plunge back into the grey again. Arthur spoke into the radio, just to let the others hear his voice: 'Wardston, this is Kestrel Leader. Nearly at angels twenty-five, Wardston. No sign of bandits so far. Over.'

'Understood, Kestrel Leader. Radar says there's a hundred of them, Kestrel, they're there somewhere. Out.'

The mist was turning white. Then they were clear of the clouds, climbing into unbroken blue. The squadron evened out at 25,000 feet in bright sunshine. The twelve Spitfires were as colourful as toys in the unbroken light. Now the cockpit was dry, ice-cold. Arthur felt a surge of elation. This was why he'd wanted to fly in the first place. To be up here in the flawless blue, looking down at a landscape of thick white cloud. Flying so high, they were above even the weather. How did the lines go? *Angels alone, that soar above, enjoy such liberty…*

All right, enough of that. His oxygen must be up too high, it was making him think in poetry. He adjusted it and said, 'Keep your eyes peeled, gentlemen, they're here somewhere.'

He looked around, above and below, knowing the others were doing the same; he squinted carefully into the sun. They had a clear view for miles; but so far they seemed to be alone in the sky. 'Wardston, this is Kestrel Leader. No sightings of enemy planes in this location. Over.'

'Kestrel Leader, this is Wardston. You should be right on top of them by now. Over.'

'They have not been here,' Michal said. 'No one has been here.'

Arthur saw what he meant. At this altitude, anything with an engine would have left a vapour trail. A hundred planes would have left a mass of trails, but there wasn't even one. 'Wardston, there's no trace of them.' He had a thought: 'Do we have visual confirmation of them, Wardston? Were they ever sighted from land? Over.'

After a pause, Control said: 'Kestrel Leader, this is Wardston. Negative, there was no confirmation from the Observer Corps. But the radar definitely spotted one hundred plus bandits, Kestrel. At angels twenty-five. Over.'

'This is Blue Three,' said Penry-Smith. 'Unless they're one hundred plus invisible bandits, Wardston, they're not sodding well here—'

'This is Red Two.' It was Harry Williams. 'Sighting. Four o'clock low.'

Arthur stared into the cloud until his eyes watered. 'I can't see anything, Red Two. Are you sure?'

'I'm sure. Down in the cloud. Flash of sun. Reflected off of glass.'

'Follow me down, Kestrel.' Arthur still hadn't spotted anything, but maybe they needed to get closer. He half-rolled away and down, and the others followed.

A thousand feet later, Kiddy Jones said: 'I see it! Twelve o'clock, low!'

Arthur saw it too. Glints of light, winking here and there through the cloud. Sunlight reflecting off Plexiglass cockpit hatches; it couldn't be anything else. 'I see them too. Wardston, this is Kestrel Leader. Unknown craft still in cloud cover. Moving to intercept. Over.'

'Happy hunting, Kestrel Leader. Out.'

Kestrel Squadron went into a shallow descent, keeping pace with the winks of light through the white mist. Now they could see long grooves, six of them, being traced along the surface from inside the cloud. The other planes' propellers and engine exhaust were disturbing the cloud above them, drawing lines in their wake. Kestrel Squadron eased into place, just above the exhaust trails. There was a break in the cloud a couple of miles ahead. 'Stand by, Kestrel Squadron – prepare to dive.'

The cloud thinned into tatters of mist, and twelve dark shapes shot out into the sunlight. Arthur shouted, 'Hold your fire! Hold your fire!'

Alice watched the storm clouds roll overhead. *That's weather control,* she thought. *We can't do that. I didn't think anyone could do that...*

Lightning flashed, although the sun was bright. The air was still and close. They were on their way. And she was alone—

'Alice!'

'Vince?'

Vince half-ran, half-climbed to the top of the Mound. 'Alice, I'm here.'

Alice looked at him, and started to laugh. 'What are you wearing?'

Vince looked down at himself. He'd managed to pull on some trousers on the way up, but he was still wearing the top half of his pyjamas. 'I got dressed in a hurry,' he said. 'Didn't realise it was supposed to be formal wear. I'll go and change, if you like—'

'Don't you dare go and leave me!'

'I was joking, Alice. I en't going nowhere.'

She felt like falling into his arms and sobbing. Instead she said, 'Where are Maggie and Colin?'

'Colin's having one of his turns. Maggie's gone to the village. Those bastards have got her Gran.'

'She should have come straight here! She can't fight from there, it's not a locus of power!'

'I know.'

'And we need to be together! We're not strong enough on our own! Oh, *Maggie!*'

'It's her Gran, Alice.' He took her hand. 'And we're together. We'll be strong enough.'

He placed their joined hands onto the Stone.

Maggie was running past the church when the air raid siren began to wail. She saw figures outside the bell-tower: the vicar and the verger, staring in dismay at the moving bell-ropes no one was pulling. When they heard the siren they hurried to the big church doors and wedged them open; the crypt was a designated air raid shelter. The vicar spotted Maggie and started waving at her to come inside. Maggie shook her head and ran on.

The sea front was nearly deserted. The agitated sea was almost black, reflecting the low dark clouds. A wind was coming in off the water, not cool and refreshing as it usually was, but warm and damp. The fishing boats in the harbour bounced and tugged at their ropes. Beyond the harbour Maggie could see the soldiers wheeling out the ack-ack gun, surrounding it with sandbags. She turned up Harbour Lane, which was full of people making for the shelter in the church. They were carrying babies, cats, antique clocks, bags and cases; one big suitcase scraped Maggie's shin as she pushed past. Someone said: 'Margaret Ogilvie, you're going the wrong way!' but most people ignored her. They had the same wild, unthinking look she'd seen in the soldiers at Dunkirk. Maggie pushed past them and came to the town square.

The square itself was empty. There was a scrum of people outside the town hall, shoving to get in; the town hall's cellar was a designated shelter too. When they'd pushed their way inside, no one else showed up to swell the numbers. Everyone must be at home; most people in Wardston had Anderson shelters in their gardens, or big metal Morrison cages under the stairs. Maggie glanced inside the public surface shelter; as Dad had always predicted, no one had chosen to use it. She now seemed to have the square to herself. Gran wasn't on the bench in front of the Queen Victoria statue. Maggie was about to check the other side when a small figure in white walked out from behind the statue.

From a distance, the girl looked quite normal; but Maggie knew in an instant there was nothing normal here. It was as if there was an immense electric charge coming from the small white figure. Maggie's hands prickled; her hair tried to stand on end. There was a metallic smell, or taste, like biting on metal foil. She thought there was a buzzing sound somewhere, that was too high or too low to hear properly. Pressure built behind Maggie's eyes, the beginning of a headache.

The girl walked towards her, tripping lightly in dainty white high-heeled shoes. The veil was gone. She was wearing a clinging, silky white dress that accentuated how terribly thin she was. Her hair was long and bright gold: not blonde, but gold, like metallic wire. Her skin was white as chalk or salt. There were round patches of pinkish-red blush on her cheeks that looked like make-up, but weren't. Her lips were a bright red cupid's bow; they weren't made-up either. Her eyes were acidic blue, like neon. When the girl walked through the statue's shadow, Maggie could see that her eyes were glowing.

The girl smiled. Or rather, the corners of her mouth turned up; she didn't look capable of anything as human as a smile. 'Hello, Maggie,' she said. Her voice seemed to come from two directions at once. It was sickly-sweet, like artificial sugar. 'My name is Freya.'

'Where's my Gran?'

'Oh, still at the doctor's house, I think. Trying to persuade him to come out of his shelter and visit you.' She laughed, a sound like cheap tin bells. 'Trying quite in vain, I think! He is far too cowardly to come out in a raid!'

Maggie moved sideways, so she could see around the statue. There was no sign of Gran. 'Gran, are you there?'

'You do not believe me?' Freya gave a little pout. 'I am hurt. But I should not be surprised, because I have been quite naughty. I told you a little lie.'

'My Gran's not really here?'

Freya spread her arms wide to indicate the empty square. 'The picture in your mirror was quite false, I'm afraid. I am Freya. Do you really think I need to make war on old women? That would be dishonourable. It would upset my dear Albrecht so. But you... I see you have been naughty too. Where are your friends?'

'I... they couldn't come.'

'Would not come, you mean. That does make me a little cross, you know.' Her eyes flared. Amber sparks crackled in her hair. Maggie took a step back, and Freya laughed again. 'Oh, but *you* are here, so I shall not be cross with you! Why, I hope you and I may be friends! That I may be a kind older sister to you!'

Maggie's head ached. She could hardly look at Freya. 'Is this what it does to you?' Maggie said hoarsely.

'Whatever do you mean?'

'Is this what it does? The magic? Does it do *this?*'

'The magic? Ah, you mean the power of the Aryan Race-Soul.'

'The what?'

Freya tut-tutted. 'I see you have been kept in ignorance. The power – the magic, as you say – comes from the blood of the Aryan Race. The master race. The Germanic race!'

'I'm not German.'

'Oh, but you are! You must be descended from German stock, or you would not have the power! True, your blood has been mixed with... other races. Lesser races. But you can be redeemed!' Freya's eyes blazed. Her face was enraptured. 'You can mate with men of good blood! Your children can be almost perfect!'

'I've got a boyfriend already,' Maggie said.

'You mean the Pole?' The smile vanished. 'Yes, I know about him. And I know that you have *given* yourself to him.' The doll-face sneered in distaste. 'Your womb may be contaminated now, but perhaps it might be cleansed—'

Maggie couldn't bear it any more. 'Were you a girl once? A

normal girl?'

'Oh, yes! I was just an ordinary girl, like you!'

'Were you called Freya then?'

'No.' Maggie thought the blue glow dimmed for a moment. 'I was – *she* was named Lise. But she was ordinary. She was weak. But then the power of the Race-Soul transformed me! I have become a goddess!'

'So you're Lise? That's your name?'

Freya took no notice. 'Look at me! Am I not perfect now? Am I not everything the human race should be? You too can be this way!'

Maggie stared, and realised Freya – or Lise – was utterly mad. And she loved her madness, hugged it to her, and wouldn't let it go. 'What do you want? Why did you come here?'

'In part, to ask you to make peace. As my dear Albrecht told you, you can influence your leaders. Encourage them to see the error of their ways. With – direct intervention, if necessary.'

'What's the other part?'

'Why, to help you, of course! I can make you beautiful! I can make you perfect, just like me!'

'No!'

'Come now, don't be shy. Let me help you!'

Freya took a step forward. Maggie backed away. 'Don't touch me! Don't! Don't do that to me, don't!'

Freya stopped. 'You are ungrateful,' she said. 'And weak. I offer you godhead, and you snivel like a coward.'

'I don't want godhead! I just want you to leave us all alone! Please!'

'That is not an option. You have seen the glorious future we offer. How beautiful we can make this village. How perfect—'

'It wasn't perfect. Not for me. My brother, my boyfriend, my friends. I want them with me.'

'You reject our future? Then there is another possible future.

Would you like to see it?'

'No, I—'

Freya raised her arms. The sky went dark, and they were surrounded by fire.

Alice felt Vince squeeze her hand tightly, as eleven black planes emerged from the stormclouds. They swooped towards the Mound. Alice whispered, 'What are they?'

'Messerschmitts.' Vince snorted. 'Painted black to make them look scary.'

'I don't think that's all they are,' said Alice.

They watched the planes approach, and stop directly over the Stone. Just stop: hovering in mid-air like a hunting falcon. Vince exclaimed, 'They can't do that. Planes can't do that!'

'They're not just planes,' said Alice. 'I think it's *them*.'

'Hold your fire!'

The pilots of Kestrel Squadron took their fingers off the firing-buttons, and steered into a climb behind Arthur. Just in time, they'd spotted the red-and-blue circles – RAF roundels – on the planes emerging from the cloud. As they swooped away, Scots Eddy said: 'That's Jacko Squadron.'

'Bloody Hurricanes,' said Penry-Smith. 'They get everywhere—'

'Maintain radio silence, Kestrel. Wardston, this is Kestrel

Leader. The planes are ours, repeat, the planes are ours. Believed to be Jacko Squadron. Over.'

'Kestrel Leader, this is Wardston. The bandits must be in the clouds, Kestrel, there's nowhere else. Over.'

Michal said, 'We must go back to the village.'

Arthur ignored him. 'Wardston, there's nothing in the clouds—'

'Kestrel Leader, this is Wardston.' There was new urgency in the voice. 'Set new course, Vector three-one-oh. Fifty plus bandits at angels ten.'

'There will be nothing there,' Michal said. 'We must go back to Wardston.'

'Wardston, this is Kestrel Leader. Setting new course. Confirm... Blue Two, what are you doing? Michal!'

Michal had dropped out of formation. He swung away and down, and vanished into the cloud.

Chapter Twenty-One

The Lebensrune

The black Messerschmitts were moving again. They were flying in a circle, a hundred feet above, like vultures. Alice and Vince kept their hands pressed onto the Ward Stone. Vince pointed at the planes and said, 'What d'you think those symbols are? On their sides?'

Alice frowned, but when she spoke her voice was steady. 'One of them's the Black Sun. The other one's a rune.'

'What's a rune?'

'A magical symbol. Icelandic. They're very old. The Nazis use them.' She made a derisive sound. 'Not properly, of course. They use a cockeyed system called the Armanen system, dreamt up by a mad German anti-Semite called von List. It has nothing to do with the original Scandinavian rune-poems—'

'Alice. What does it mean?'

'That one? It's the *Todesrune*. It means Death.'

'Course it does.' Vince watched the black planes circle. 'Wasn't going to mean health and long life, was it?'

Alice's eyes widened. 'Vince! You're a genius!'

'Am I?'

'Health and life! The *Lebensrune!*' Alice dug her hand into the ground and pulled up a clod of earth. She began to daub a long vertical line onto the side of the Ward Stone. Vince watched in amazement. 'What're you doing, girl?'

'The *Lebensrune*. It's the opposite of the *Todesrune*. It means Life. And it means Protection.'

She added two angular lines at the top of the first one, and stepped back to show him. It looked like a stick-drawing of a fork to Vince; then he saw it was an inverted version of the symbol on the Messerschmitts. Somehow, that was fitting. 'So what do we do now?' he said.

'Focus on the rune.'

They joined hands, and placed their other hands on the Stone. There were only two of them. Vince thought, *can we do this... don't think that way, concentrate.* He made himself still, and drew on the power.

Voices and thoughts flooded in. *We can beat 'em... If we all do our bit, we'll come through... We've not been invaded in a thousand years, they're not going to get us now...*

As the black planes descended, the rune began to shine. The ley line under their feet lit up.

'Adolf Hitler. You shall not come here! You shall not come here!'

Miriam thought: *It's no use.* It had been over an hour, they were all beginning to tire, and the Cone of Power wasn't making the slightest impression. Miriam had hoped they could make some physical impact on him, even kill him. The magick might have rebounded and killed everyone in the Circle too, but they had all been ready to take that risk.

But in the event, they couldn't even make him hear them. The white light around him formed a barrier they couldn't cross. He had magical protection.

Miriam stopped chanting. One by one, the others did too. The image of Hitler faded away. When there was silence, Miriam began: 'Goddess and Lady, we depart in peace—'

A rush of warmth went through them, making everyone gasp. Shining paths appeared across the grass, intersecting at the Rufus Stone. Another image flared into life: two people beside a low standing stone. Miriam knew them at once: Alice Carrington and Vincent Walker.

Quickly Miriam said: 'Thank you, Lady, for this vision. Let us see. Let us help. Let us be part of what happens…'

All the while Miriam was thinking: *Where's my son? Where's my daughter?*

Maggie stood in the town square as the *glamor* spell swept over her.

The air raid siren was wailing. Suddenly it was night, but the sky wasn't dark. Searchlights swept to and fro across it, lighting up metallic shapes. The sky was full of planes. Rows and rows of them. Bombers.

Maggie looked around. Half the buildings around the square were burning. The others had already collapsed, spilling bricks onto the road and the square. The butcher's, the florist, Mr Caplan's bookshop; there was nothing left of them to burn. The town hall's decorative façade was a black silhouette against the fires inside, flames leaping behind all its windows. A fire engine stood outside; firemen had turned a hose onto the blaze, a thin stream of water. It seemed to be having no effect.

The bombs were still falling. Maggie could hear the whine of them descending, explosion after explosion. The air was hot and choking. It smelled of fire and gunpowder, and tasted like burning fuel. Drifting ash and sparks blew all around her.

From the other side of the square she heard a great boom; she looked around to see a huge ack-ack cannon recoiling on its big wheels. Men in siren-suits and tin helmets crowded around. The ground defences were returning fire. Maggie thought: *Go on! Get them!* But there was no sign the planes had been hit. Now she could hear the whine of something falling, loud and close. The pitch rose and rose; she saw something long and thin tumble towards the ack-ack gun. She screamed a warning, but it was no use. The explosion tore the gun, and the people, apart.

'How do you like this future?' Freya was standing quite calmly amidst the slaughter. 'It is not so pleasant, is it? Would you like to see a little more?'

She made a sweeping gesture. Immediately it was day again; and the bombers were gone. Maggie started to cough. Choking, she looked around.

Everything was gone. The air was hazy with thick dust, which turned the light sepia and made visibility poor; but for as far as Maggie could see, every building in town had been flattened. The ground was a strange grey-brown; dust and ash, Maggie realised. The square stank of ruptured sewers and burnt wood and another smell, like meat gone off in hot weather. Some of the things lying in the dust were bodies, she realised. Some had been covered with blankets; most had not.

Maggie felt a surge of hope when she saw people in uniform moving amongst the bodies. A man and a woman, with red crosses on their clothes. They went from body to body, obviously searching for signs of life, which they never seemed to find. They were the only ones moving; they were the sum total of the help that had come for the people of Wardston. Maggie wondered why some other town, Deal or Dover, hadn't sent ambulances and firemen and nurses. Then she thought: *What if all the other towns are just the same? What if there's no one left to help?*

Maggie fell to her knees. It was a battlefield. But this wasn't the Front, it was a village. These weren't soldiers, they were civilians; some of them were children.

She thought: *That's it, then. We have to surrender. Whatever happens, it can't be worse than this. Whoever they take, at least someone will be left alive.* This wasn't war; it was the end of the world.

'Well, Maggie?' Freya still stood unmoved amidst the wreckage. 'Do you prefer this future? Which one shall it be?'

Albrecht tried one more shot, swooping down at the Stone and the two wizards. He was a good shot; he had been diligently practising marksmanship, as well as basic piloting techniques, over the last few weeks. He had tried to get the others to do the same, but they still had more enthusiasm than actual skill. Most of them had exhausted their ammunition already; they'd seen too many heroic Party films about fighter pilots, and didn't realise how few shots the guns actually carried. But it wouldn't matter, surely; their magical abilities would be all they needed.

So far, however, neither magic nor firepower had solved this problem. He fired a half-second burst, more to study what was happening than with any actual hope of success. And once again, the tracer fire sparked in the air a few feet from the two wizards and the Ward Stone, and simply rebounded as if it had hit bulletproof glass. Once again, the boy Vince and the girl Alice were completely untouched. The boy threw Albrecht a mocking salute as he flew overhead.

Albrecht zoom-climbed away, looking back thoughtfully over his shoulder. Was there something drawn onto the Stone, something faintly glowing? That gave him an idea: 'Brothers,' he said, cutting into the radio babble of frustrated cursing from the other *gothi*. 'Concentrate with me. We will use the Eye of the Übermensch, as our Lady Freya has taught us.'

Obediently, the other boys fell silent. He felt their concentration focus; a moment later he was looking at the world through what the British wizards called witch-sight. Twilight descended; the other *gothi* were fiery torches in the cockpits of their dark planes. Albrecht looked down, and inhaled sharply.

He could see the protection now. A glimmering, translucent dome neatly covered the Ward Stone and the two wizards. Lines of power ran under their feet. And on the Ward Stone itself, a symbol of golden light burned against the Stone's rough surface. The *Lebensrune*. Very clever. And it was the Jewish girl, Alice, who had done it. She must have some good blood in her, after all.

But she was going to meet her match. 'You see, brothers,' he announced. 'The *Lebensrune*, the sign of birth and life. The *Lebensrune* is a feminine rune, brothers. A German warrior fights against other men, not women. This battle is not for us.'

They all murmured agreement. Yes, that must be it. They weren't really failing, they were hampered by their noble respect for Womanhood. 'What about that Stone?' asked Manfred. 'I thought we had to destroy it.'

'We can leave that to our Lady, brother,' Albrecht assured him. 'This fight is for Freya.'

'Well, Maggie? What shall it...'

Freya paused. She cocked her head to one side, as if a voice were whispering in her ear. Then she smiled. 'Ah,' she said. 'It seems I am needed elsewhere.'

She raised her arms again. The *glamor* spell melted away. Maggie sobbed with relief as the old town square reappeared. The siren was still wailing, and the sky was black; but the square was undamaged.

Freya lowered her arms. 'You must excuse me for a moment. I know; why don't you wait for me here? In that little house?' She pointed at the surface shelter. 'Now don't run off anywhere. I shall send some friends along, to make sure you stay put.'

'Wait—' began Maggie. But Freya turned her back in a swirl of skirts, and rose into the air. Maggie watched the thin white figure rise straight up into the low clouds. She stood up, unsteadily, taking in the square, complete and intact as it ought to be. Now what? *Gran*. At the doctor's house, Freya had said; was it true? She should –

Another wailing siren joined the air raid warning. Higher-pitched, more urgent. She'd heard it before. Her knees almost gave out again as she remembered: Dunkirk. Soldiers jumping out of the boat to get away. She remembered the word they'd used: *Stuka*.

A dive-bomber. Its siren was getting louder. It was coming here.

Maggie ran to the surface shelter. It had brick walls, but just a sheet of corrugated iron for its roof. But there was nowhere else. She pushed open the metal door and hurled herself inside. It was dark, and stank of urine, but she didn't care. She kicked the door closed and crouched in the corner, arms wrapped around her head.

Then she heard another wailing sound. It wasn't regular and rhythmic; it wasn't mechanical at all. It sounded like a cat, or a distressed baby. It was coming from outside the shelter. Maggie pushed the door open, knowing she shouldn't; Dad had always told her, *If you can see the explosion, it can see you.* But she had to see what was making that noise.

There was a boy standing in the middle of the square, howling. *Colin?* No, she didn't think so – this was a much bigger boy, although he was wailing like a toddler. Before she could see who it was, the boy crouched down and pulled his jumper up over his head, muffling the sound but not cutting it off. Maggie immediately saw why; something had come out of the clouds, over the roof of the town hall. It was a small plane, so small that for a moment she hoped it was a fighter, a British one. But then she recognised its lowered wheels, its little fat ankles. It was a Stuka. Maggie called to the boy: 'Over here! Quick!'

He didn't move; he couldn't have heard her. She looked up at the Stuka, which was aiming right for the square. In fact, Maggie thought she saw it adjust its course slightly, as if it were aiming at a new target. As if it had seen the boy in the square, and was aiming for him. It was deliberately targeting a child, just because he was there.

Maggie thought: *I don't bloody think so.* She left the shelter and ran across the square to stand over the boy. Her hair was unravelling from its plait. The Stuka had just cleared the roof of the town hall, still on target. Maggie screamed, *'Leave us alone, you bastards!'* and brought her hand down sharply. The Stuka's nosecone jerked downwards. The tail fin flipped into the air, and the plane spun nose-to-tail straight towards the statue of Queen Victoria. Maggie saw frantic movement inside the cockpit. Then she couldn't help flinching as it slammed down onto the statue's bronze head.

The crash was so loud it hurt her ears. The boy at her feet, still hiding inside his jumper, screamed again. Fire bloomed in the wreckage. And Maggie thought: *It hasn't dropped its bombs yet.* She grabbed the boy's arm and dragged him towards the surface shelter. He was a solid weight, and she came very close to letting go and running to the shelter alone. But then he got the idea, and started running with her. It was all so horribly slow. *Any moment, any moment now…*

There wasn't even time to go inside; Maggie dragged the boy behind the shelter, threw him down and put her hands over her ears. Then the explosion came, a hurricane of noise. Maggie screamed, but she could barely hear herself. Leaning against the wall, she felt something thud into the other side of the shelter, making the whole thing shudder. There was a timpani of metallic sound as debris rained down on the corrugated iron roof.

It seemed to go on forever. In fact, it was only a few seconds before Maggie could hear her own voice, screaming and then tailing off into coughing as the air filled with dust. She stood up, and nearly looked around the side of the shelter; then she remembered some bombs might not have gone off yet. She turned instead to the boy, who was coughing beside her, and pulled his jumper off his head. It was Charlie Chester. Of course, it would be. She'd risked her life, and killed a man – no, two men, Stukas had a two-man crew – for bloody Charlie Chester. 'Charlie,' she said, raising her voice above the whistling in her ears, 'Why the hell aren't you in your shelter?'

He just stared at her, like a panic-stricken rabbit. 'I just… I wanted… to see the b-b-bombers…'

'You stupid little twit, Charlie. Honestly, Colin's got twice your common sense and he—'

Colin.

She'd left him lying in the cottage, unconscious. With an air raid on. She hadn't even carried him to the Anderson shelter, she'd just left him on her bedroom floor. Maggie went to the corner of the shelter and looked around the square. The statue and the Stuka, tangled together horribly, were belching smoke that made her cough all the more. The benches were on fire, and there was blackened wreckage everywhere. But there was no sign of any other bombers. 'Charlie,' she said, 'get into the surface shelter—'

She looked at the shelter, and changed her mind. It was leaning away from the direction of the explosion; it looked like a strong wind would knock it down. 'Charlie, go to the town hall shelter. I've got to go.'

'Don't leave me!'

'Now, Charlie!' She hauled him to his feet and shoved him towards the town hall, then set off at a run. She went to cross the road, and skidded to a halt as the fire engine screeched around the corner in front of her, bell jangling, heading for the blaze in the square. As soon as Maggie stopped, someone cannoned into her. It was Charlie, grabbing hold of her arm. 'Don't leave me, please don't leave me!'

Maggie swore and was about to pull away, when they heard the descending wail of a Stuka. It seemed far away, but what direction was it coming from? Impossible to tell. Maggie understood now why Charlie had just stopped and pulled his jumper over his head; she wanted to curl up in a ball and close her eyes. Instead she caught Charlie by the wrist and said, 'Keep up or I'll leave you behind,' and began to run.

They ran up the wide Dover Road. More Stuka sirens were sounding, far away and close up. Charlie screamed as the thump of an explosion, somewhere to the west, shook the ground. Maggie kept running, although her knees weakened. Even the ground was unsafe. The buildings that had been the background of her life for years, they could fall and crush them at any moment. There was nowhere, nothing safe. The scream of the bombers was everywhere and all they could do was run.

Charlie looked back, and shrieked and fell to his knees, pulling her down with him. She yanked her arm away; then she saw what he'd seen. Two Stukas, flying so low they barely cleared the roof of the town hall, were heading straight for them. Freya had said: *I shall send some friends along to make sure you stay put.* They were coming for her.

All right then. Maggie went to stand in the middle of the road. She shouted at Charlie, 'Get under cover,' but she never took her eyes from the bombers. Her fists clenched, and her hair blew up around her. *Come on then, you bastards…*

But as the Stukas flew across the square, they suddenly swerved, one to each side, and zoom-climbed away. Maggie stared at them. With all the noise of sirens and engines and explosions, she hadn't heard the other engine behind her. She didn't notice until the other plane flashed by overhead, and swooped after one of the Stukas. It was a Spitfire.

Michal!

Maggie. He'd heard her. *Get to your shelter.*

I need to get to Colin. Then the Mound!

Go, then. Hurry!

He had already closed in on the Stuka. Maggie didn't hear him open fire, but she saw the Stuka jerk and wobble. 'Come on, Charlie,' she said, and started to run.

Kestrel Squadron looked around in silence. The sky was completely clear. There wasn't one aircraft in sight, let alone fifty.

'Wardston, this is Kestrel Leader.' Even Arthur was starting to sound irritated. 'Still no trace of bandits. What's going on, Wardston? Over.'

'Wardston here. Kestrel Leader, we can't explain it. The whole radar system's gone haywire. It's showing enemy planes everywhere, but the Observer Corps says there's nothing there.'

'This is Kestrel Leader. Are there any over Wardston village? Over.'

'Wardston here. No bandits detected in Wardston vicinity, Kestrel Leader. The radar's showing nothing, and the Observer Corps can't see a thing in the storm...'

Control's voice dissolved in a burst of static. Arthur said, 'Wardston? Come in... come in Wardston...'

Nothing. A crackle, then silence.

After a pause, Arthur said: 'Kestrel Squadron, this is Kestrel Leader. New course, Kestrel. We're heading back to Wardston.'

Chapter Twenty-Two
The Battle of Wardston

Alice and Vince watched the black planes circle a hundred feet above their heads. There was no engine sound. They'd already spotted that the Messerschmitt's propellers weren't spinning. The 109s were circling too slowly – an ordinary plane would have stalled at such a low speed – but they kept going round and round, like horses on a carousel. The death rune and the Black Suns were vivid against their red circles, and the planes' tail fins were brightly painted with garish pictures of wolves and eagles and ravens and other creatures, which moved as if they were alive, writhing in the livid yellow light. Flashes of lightning pulsed inside the dark clouds. The air was hot and close; despite the thick clouds, there was no trace of rain. 'What d'you think they're doing now?' Vince said.

'Looks like they're waiting for something.'

Vince nodded. There was nothing to do but keep their hands on the Ward Stone, and watch the black planes. Eventually he said, 'Alice.'

'Yes.'

'I used to be in my stepdad's Fascist gang.'

'I thought you probably were.'

'You did?'

'Yes. But you're not in it now, are you?'

'No!'

'Well then.'

'Alice, I…'

'Quiet. What's that?'

Someone was singing, a reedy soprano that cracked on the high notes. Something white appeared in the circle of Messerschmitts, and floated down towards them. Lightning flashed: Alice and Vince had to turn away, rubbing their eyes. When they opened them again someone was standing in front of them. 'Bloody hell,' said Vince.

'Ah, Vincent. It was so naughty to run away when I wanted to chat with you!'

Vince stared back in horror. The girl was the ugliest thing he'd ever seen. She looked famished: the elegant white dress, which should have been figure-hugging, hung on her loosely. The scrawny, blue-eyed creature simpered, then twirled around on the spot. 'Here I am without my veil, Vincent. I am so keen to talk with you!' She paused for him to offer a compliment, as Albrecht would have done; when he kept quiet she said, 'Do you like my boys' little black planes? Do you like the pretty pictures on their tails? It is very fine German art, is it not?'

'I'm more of an Impressionist fan myself,' said Vince.

'Oh, you!' She actually giggled. 'You are so naughty!'

Alice said: 'Who are you?'

The smile vanished. 'I am Freya, goddess of the German people. I am their hopes and their dreams and their fears.'

'Whoever you used to be, Freya is killing you.' Alice looked her skinny body up and down. 'The magic's burning you up.'

'Why do you care?'

'I don't. But I'm telling you. There'll be nothing left of you, very soon. If you don't get rid of Freya.'

'There will be nothing left of *you*, I think.'

Alice looked at Vince. 'Stay focussed on the rune. Don't let the protection fail—'

'You mean this?' Freya lifted a thin hand. Her eyes glowed like electricity. 'This will not protect you from *me*, I'm afraid.'

Alice and Vince pressed their joined hands onto the Ward Stone as hard as they could. The *Lebensrune* lit up for a moment. Then the light dimmed, and went out. Alice cried out as the rune turned to fine powder and drifted away.

Freya sighed. 'I told you. I am goddess of the German people, and the *Lebensrune* is mine. Now. Stand away from that Stone.'

'We're not afraid of you,' whispered Alice.

'I think you are.'

Alice straightened her shoulders, squeezed Vince's hand, and began to chant. 'Before me, Gabriel. Behind me, Raphael. To my right, Michael. To my left, Uriel...'

Freya sighed again. She strolled to the Stone and put her hand on it. Vince and Alice gasped as witch-sight flared around them. Freya was a blaze of fiery light towering over them. The ley lines had begun to glow a dark golden-orange under her feet. Vince felt the power going out of him; he saw too that the lines were drawing the amber light out of Alice, into themselves, and then into Freya. He looked at his own hand; the light in it was dimming, ebbing back inside the lines of his own body. Freya shone brighter than ever, as she drew off all the power and left Vince and Alice with nothing.

Vince kept his and Alice's hand pressed onto the Stone. Then he felt Alice's hand go limp, and pull away from his own. He heard Freya laugh: 'Oh, Alice, what a dreadful *mess* you are in!'

The witch-sight vanished. In the daylight, he saw Alice's legs give way, as blood poured from her nose and ears, spattering her clothes and staining her blonde hair. Vince ran to her and eased her down to the ground. He pinched her nostrils closed, but blood kept seeping between his fingers. *'Alice!'*

He heard Freya call something in German. Then she said to him, sounding bored: 'You really ought to get out of the way, Vincent.'

Freya was gone. Vince paid no attention. He was holding his hands over Alice's ears now, trying to keep the blood in. 'Alice… wake up, Alice…'

He heard the Stuka's wailing siren, but he didn't look up until the bomber was nearly above them. He waved his hand at the Stuka, but nothing happened. The power truly was gone. So he did the only thing he could – he half-lifted, half-dragged Alice away from the Stone, onto the path and under cover.

The Stuka dropped its bombs, and blew the Ward Stone to rubble.

'This is Kestrel Leader. Reduce altitude, gentlemen, let's get under this.'

Arthur had to shout above the sound of hail battering on the cockpit hatch. The Spitfire bucked and lurched through the black cloud. Lightning flashed; for a split second he saw Penry-Smith's plane in vivid detail, then he was back in the gloom. Thunder growled. Then there was another booming crash, followed by another. Arthur said: 'Sounds like some action, gentlemen. Looks like bad weather isn't Wardston's only problem today. Stand by.'

The cloud thinned for a moment, and suddenly they were out in bright sunshine. Arthur's eyes watered under his goggles; he blinked rapidly. They were a mile or so from the airbase, almost on top of the Mound. The strange black cloud hung over the base and the village. Dark smoke was rising over Wardston. Planes were swooping and diving through the smoke; there were flashes of fire, not lightning, but explosions on the ground. Nearby, a Stuka was zoom-climbing away from the Mound.

Behind it, circling, was a squadron of black Messerschmitts with red markings. At least they looked like Messerschmitts. But they hovered in mid-air, as motionless as hot-air balloons. Penry-Smith's voice spoke in Arthur's ear: 'What the bloody hell are those?'

'Wardston, this is Kestrel Leader.' Control hadn't answered for quite some time, but Arthur made his report in case they could still hear. 'Sighting of Me109s over Wardston. Also what looks like Stukas over the village. Moving to engage.'

'They can't be Me109s,' said Penry-Smith. 'Since when could 109s just hang there like that?'

'Radio silence, Blue Three. We're splitting up, gentlemen. B-Flight, head for the village and sort out those Stukas. Watch out for friendly planes, I'm guessing Michal's having his fun over there already. A-Flight, let's get these Me109s.'

'Kestrel Leader, they're not like any Me109s I've ever seen—'

'Whatever they are, Penry, they're bombing Wardston Mound and we're going to shoot them. A-Flight, follow me down.'

Six of the squadron peeled off, heading for the village and the Stukas. The remaining five – Arthur, Penry-Smith, Williams, Scots Eddy and Kiddy Jones – swooped towards the Mound.

Freya landed lightly on the Mound amidst the remains of the Ward Stone. She prodded a large piece with her toe. Nothing. The power was gone.

She turned towards the path, where she could hear Vince's voice calling: 'Alice!' Then movement above caught her eye. Five Spitfires were diving towards them.

Freya cried out, so that her *gothi* could hear. Albrecht and the others heard her voice quite clearly. *My warriors! At last! You can prove yourselves in battle!*

Arthur watched the circle of black planes stop revolving. Then each one swivelled so its nose was pointing towards them. All the while they hovered in mid-air like hawks. Arthur's scalp crawled. *What in God's name are they?* He tried to hold his voice steady. 'Well, gentlemen, it looks like the Bosch have invented something new. Let's see how it stands up to the Spitfire, shall we—'

The radio crackled. Then a voice said: 'Hell-o-o-o-o!' It wasn't one of Kestrel Squadron, and it wasn't Control; no one else should have been able to come through on this frequency. 'Hello-o-o-o-o Tommeee! We can see you!'

'Jesus Christ All bloody Mighty,' said Penry-Smith.

Arthur said, 'This is Kestrel Leader. Who is that?'

'Hello, Kestrel Leader!' It was a German accent. It sounded very young. Behind it other voices were laughing; giggling, in fact, like children. 'Mr English man! We have come to take your country, please!'

More sniggering. Penry-Smith said, 'Christ, they sound about twelve!'

'Good morning, Kestrel Leader.' This voice was serious; a little older, although still very young. 'We have come to engage you in combat.'

'Kestrel Leader here. Who are you?'

'I am Albrecht von Irmer. We are the *gothi*.'

The word meant nothing to Arthur. He found himself gently speaking. 'How old are you? Why have they put you in those planes?'

Now the voice sounded offended: 'May the best men win, Kestrel Leader.'

The next part was in German, too rapid for Arthur to follow, although he picked out the words for *rise* and *glory* and *destiny*.

The black planes moved, forming into a V behind their leader. When each was in place, they came at Kestrel Squadron, faster than Arthur had ever seen any plane move. He could hear more excited laughter. Then yells of triumph, as the black planes zoom-climbed past the Spitfires.

Arthur said, 'Stand by.' He knew he had to do this. But when the black planes flashed past, and every Spitfire pilot opened fire except Arthur, his trigger finger froze: *They're children*, he thought. *They're children...* He heard startled yelps and shrieks as the other Spitfires' shots connected. He flinched as a terrified scream, high-pitched as a girl's, was suddenly cut off when one of the black planes exploded in a fireball.

There was a horrified silence. Arthur thought: *We're in trouble. We've never been in worse trouble.* He spoke quickly, hoping the

Germans would find it hard to understand: 'Prepare for evasive, Kestrel. Follow me.'

He swung into a climb, a thousand feet above the Mound, the other four Spitfires behind him. The top of the Mound was scorched and smouldering, he saw. A woman in a white dress stood on the blackened earth. A few yards away on the path, someone – a man or a boy – was cradling someone else in his arms. Arthur glimpsed a skirt, long pale hair, and blood. They'd attacked a civilian. A girl. It might even be Maggie's little friend, Alice. Arthur's heart hardened. 'Stand by, Kestrel,' he said. 'Follow—'

The radio erupted with angry German. Several shrill voices were shouting and cursing all at once. The older voice was trying to recall them to order, but they weren't listening. Arthur looked back and saw the black planes swing into a turn; they could move impossibly quickly, he saw, but their turning circle was still fairly wide. The black Messerschmitts were now hurtling towards them, in no particular formation. Arthur knew they couldn't outrun them. 'Follow me, Kestrel,' he said, and swooped into a dive.

Kestrel Squadron followed. The black planes followed too, closing the gap rapidly. Boyish curses and sobs still in his ears, Arthur dived as steeply as he dared. He was over fields now, brown ploughed fields. He saw people pointing upwards, running out of the way. When Arthur was no more than two hundred feet from the ground he said: 'Starboard turn. Three! Two! One! Now!'

He swung to starboard, turning as tightly as he could. If one of the other Spitfire pilots had misjudged even slightly, they would crash and that would be it. But the others turned with him, as perfectly choreographed as a flock of swallows. The black planes behind scattered, some turning to left or right, some flipping over and flying upside down. Two didn't stop in time. One skimmed along the turned earth, bouncing through the fields, dragging a long groove behind it before it crashed into a dry-stone wall. One simply slammed into the ground and burst into flames. Neither pilot cried out.

Arthur wasn't finished yet. 'Keep going, Kestrel,' he said. The other Spitfires followed him into the tight turn. By now they were so close to the ground they sent some low trees hissing and nodding. One of the black planes had turned to starboard, and was now in their path. Arthur heard some fast, panic-stricken German and knew it came from the man – the boy – in front of them. He thought of blood on long light-coloured hair; but he still couldn't bring his thumb down on the firing-button. He didn't rebuke the other four, however, when they opened fire. He called, 'Pull up,' and the Spitfires zoom-climbed. The panic-stricken German voice was cut off, and the black plane ploughed into the ground.

Now there was radio silence apart from some very quiet sobbing. The older voice – Albrecht, he'd said his name was – spoke again, strong and reassuring. It was exactly the tone of voice Arthur would have used. As Arthur climbed, he watched the black planes draw together. They were forming up behind one in particular, he noticed. The rest of Kestrel noticed it too. 'That one's the leader,' Scots Eddy said, 'the one with the woman on the tail fin.'

Arthur looked; Eddy was right. The planes didn't have ident numbers, just strange symbols on the fuselage; but they did have elaborately decorated tail fins. They all bore paintings of animals, except for the plane the others were flocking to; its image was a golden-haired woman. Arthur said, 'Yes, that one's Albrecht.' He didn't have to say anything else; they all knew he meant, *target the leader*.

Then Penry-Smith said, 'Jesus Christ, look at that.'

One of the black planes, one with what looked like a raven on its tail fin, had only one wing. The other was a ragged stump; it must have been so badly holed by their fire that it had just fallen off. But the plane was still flying. It seemed completely unaffected. Now Arthur noticed something else; only one or two of the other planes' propellers were turning. Their engines weren't running, but they were still in the air.

'Mother of God,' Penry-Smith said. 'What the hell are those things?'

No one answered. They evened out at two thousand feet, watching the black planes. The Messerschmitts weren't coming towards them; they were hovering again. They had all swung around to face the same direction – towards Kestrel Squadron – but still they didn't move.

Arthur listened to the voice, Albrecht's voice, over the radio. Arthur couldn't make much sense of it: something like *Eye of the Super-human*. But then Albrecht began speaking slowly and carefully: *KS D*. He repeated it. Arthur thought: *KS D. That's a plane ident number. That's one of ours. That's—*

Then Eddy's plane, ident number KS D, vanished in a white-hot explosion.

My God, Eddy... But there was no time. Arthur looked at the black planes, but he couldn't see any special weapons, any cannon. He hadn't seen any fire connect with Eddy's plane. It had just – blown up. No, he mustn't think like that: something in those black planes had killed Eddy. 'Kestrel Squadron,' he said, 'Break formation, evasive flying, but follow me.' *Let's find out what they're firing and blow it sky-high.*

Arthur swung around, aware of the others falling or climbing away. He began to loop and dive, swaying and turning, knowing the others would be doing the same. Over the radio he could hear childish laughter and cheers of triumph; the German boys were celebrating killing Eddy. It was stomach-turning, but it might keep them diverted for a while. He dived towards the black planes, looking them over, hoping to spot whatever it was they were firing: their secret weapon.

He heard Albrecht's sharp voice: the laughter and cheers died away as he recalled the others' attention. *Yes, Albrecht*, thought Arthur, *We'll have to get rid of you, pronto.* Albrecht was speaking slowly and carefully again. He was spelling out more letters. *KS.* Arthur went cold. KS for Kestrel: another ident number. Albrecht concluded: *E. KS E.* Harry Williams.

Arthur shouted, 'Harry, get out, it's you! Get out!' At the same time he flung his Spitfire into a dive, straight at the leading black plane. Arthur bellowed at the top of his voice as he plunged towards the black Messerschmitts. *Not Harry, you little bastards, not him too.* He had no real plan, just a vague hope that they might stop whatever they were doing and scatter. Sure enough, a few of the 109s leapt aside as if they were on springs. It gave Arthur a moment to glance back at Harry's plane. The engine was on fire; Harry had pushed back the hatch. As Arthur watched, Harry flipped his Spitfire over; he must already have undone his straps, because he fell out. In seconds, Williams' parachute was open. *Good for you, Harry.*

He looked forward again. Albrecht hadn't panicked; his plane had stayed motionless. Arthur could hear Albrecht speaking calmly, spelling out another ident. *KS A.* Arthur's.

Arthur aimed directly at Albrecht. He could feel the cockpit getting warmer. There was no fire; the whole plane just seemed to be heating up. 'Kestrel,' he said, surprised by how calm he sounded. 'It's some sort of heat weapon. Get back and report it.'

Penry-Smith said, 'Arthur, we can't—'

'That's an order, Penry. Out.' He was only a thousand yards from Albrecht now. *I'll take a few with me, at least.* The cockpit was stifling. He bellowed again, and swung into a steep dive.

He was only a few hundred yards away when Albrecht's plane simply dropped out of the way, and he heard the German boy cry: 'Nein, nein! Halt!' At the very young voice, Arthur's finger faltered on the firing button again as he shot over the black Messerschmitts. He wouldn't have hit them anyway, he told himself, the black plane had moved too quickly. Even if the boy hadn't been begging him to stop...

But as he swung into a turn, he heard Albrecht still talking: 'Nein, mein gothi, nein.' *No, my gothi* – the name he'd used before. The boy hadn't been speaking to Arthur at all, but to his comrades. And now he was telling them: 'Nein, nicht den…' *No, not that one.* There was more, Arthur didn't catch all of it, but the sense seemed to be: *Not that one. Not him.*

In their cockpits, Albrecht flew on in the twilight of witch-sight, the Eye of the Übermensch. He was aware of the others in their planes around him, balls of yellow light in their cockpits: he could hear them exclaiming, demanding to know why he'd stopped them destroying an enemy target. But he wasn't listening. He was gazing at the leader of the British squadron swinging away in his Spitfire. He was seeing him truly, through the Eye of the Übermensch. He saw how brightly the man shone, like a noonday sun among stars. Albrecht knew just what that meant.

This was their King. Who else could shine so bright? He was their Leader, the true, natural Leader of the British. Here, in a humble fighter squadron. But then, where else would he be? Where else but here, at the forefront of the battle?

The King of the British. Albrecht knew there was another who claimed the title. He knew that just as the fraud Winston Churchill called himself Leader of this country, there was some fool in a London palace who was known by the name of King. But such a one could never truly call the title his own. That name couldn't belong to an old man hiding safe in a bunker, while others fought and died. What sort of a King was that? This, this was he.

Albrecht had to stop himself exclaiming for joy. He was humbled by the blessing he'd received. He found he even wanted to speak to the man, to the British Leader. He wanted to tell him what an honour it was that he, Albrecht von Irmer, would be the one to kill him.

Chapter Twenty-Three

The Sacrifice

Gran stared at Dr Braithwaite. 'So you refuse to come with me, then?'

The doctor flinched as another explosion shook the ground. He clearly wanted to shut the front door, whatever side of it she was on. 'Mrs Ogilvie, for the last time, we can't go out in an air raid! Come into the shelter with us!'

Inside the house, Mrs Braithwaite ran down the stairs with a sobbing child in her arms. 'Stephen,' she screamed, 'we need to be in the shelter! Now!'

'Mrs Ogilvie, please! Come to the shelter!'

'You do what you like.' Gran shook her head and turned away up the doctor's front path. 'I'm going back to my grandchildren.'

Maggie ran on through the streets of Wardston. Charlie dragged at her arm and whined, but she ignored him. There was another dull thump, and the ground shook again. Another bomb.

A Stuka siren wailed. Charlie screamed and pulled them both to a halt. Another Stuka had appeared below the black clouds. But then Michal's Spitfire was there, swooping towards it, and the Stuka turned aside and fled. Maggie watched the Spitfire give chase. *Michal, be careful!*

Stukas. She could hear his scorn. *Good at making scary noises. But not good at fighting Spitfires.*

She laughed. 'You cocky sod.'

'What?' said Charlie.

'I wasn't talking to you. Come on, if you're coming.'

They emerged onto the sea front. The hot, humid wind was blowing more strongly off the black choppy sea. Lightning flickered. Maggie jumped at the boom that followed, but it was the soldiers' ack-ack gun outside the hotel. She hoped they were hitting something that wasn't Michal. Charlie tugged at her arm. 'Where are we g-going?'

'You're going to the shelter in the church crypt. Come on.'

She pulled him away. They ran uphill to the church gate. The bells were still jangling wildly. There was a black-clad figure hurrying along the path towards them: the vicar, in his long black cassock and a tin helmet. 'What are you children doing?' He pulled open the gate and said to Charlie, 'Young man, you bring your young lady friend inside right now!'

Charlie turned to Maggie and patted her arm condescendingly. 'It's all right now, Maggie,' he said, loudly enough for the vicar to hear, 'you're safe now. I've brought you to the church, you don't have to be scared anymore.'

He smirked as the vicar put an approving hand on his shoulder. Maggie looked Charlie in the eye. 'You're a little shit, Charlie,' she said, and shoved him into the arms of the Vicar. Ignoring the shouts behind her, she ran on towards the cottage.

She gave a great cry of relief when she reached the cottage and saw it was still standing, undamaged. And she cried out thankfully when she saw the small figure at the cottage gate. 'Colin!'

'Maggie.' He suffered himself to be hugged for a moment, then wriggled free and stared up at the Mound. His eyes were huge behind his glasses. 'We need to go up there, Maggie,' he said. 'I think something awful's happened. And there's a dog fight…'

Maggie jumped as an engine roared overhead. But it was a Spitfire: not Michal's, she thought it might be Arthur's. For the first time she saw the black Messerschmitts, criss-crossing silently against the dark sky. Colin was right. There was something terribly wrong. She thought: *Michal. I'm at the cottage. Something's going on.*

I am on my way.

Maggie took Colin's hand and ran up the path. They were halfway up the Mound when they heard gasping sounds, turned the corner, and saw the worst sight they'd ever seen.

Freya watched the battle from the top of the Mound. She was frowning. She was no longer annoyed by Vince's sobbing: he was now out of earshot, he had taken the girl Alice away somewhere, Freya didn't care where. She was displeased at the progress of the battle. Four of her *gothi* had sacrificed themselves gloriously – she was already planning the wonderful funeral rites she would arrange for them – but so far only one of the enemy was dead. *Albrecht,* she called. *My Albrecht—*

He answered at once; she'd never heard him sound so thrilled. He was so excited he spoke out loud: 'Look, my Lady! Look! Do you see him? Truly see him?'

Freya called down the witch-twilight, and looked through the Eye. She caught her breath when she saw the Spitfire Squadron leader. *I see him.*

'Lady, he is their King!'

A great Leader, certainly…

'My Lady, this is fated! Even his name is right! His name is Arthur!' Albrecht laughed delightedly. '*King* Arthur!'

Of course. They all knew the stories, naturally, of Britain's great heroic king. How he died when Camelot fell; how his kingdom was taken by the Angles and the Saxons, the Germanic invaders from the east, when his precious royal blood was shed on the ground. *Albrecht,* she said. *You must sacrifice him. Sacrifice this new Arthur.*

'It shall be my honour, Lady! Mine and mine alone!'

Sacrifice him here. She spread her arms wide across the blackened top of the Mound. *Only here. When we spill the British leader's blood on their most sacred ground, history will repeat itself. The German people will take this land and make it their own, as they did before. We will be victorious.*

'It shall be done, my Lady.'

And, my Albrecht?

'Yes, my Lady?'

The Polish pilot is on his way here. Kill him.

'Yes, my Lady Freya. With your permission, we shall first deal with these other British pilots.'

Of course.

Freya watched as the black planes formed themselves into a V, an arrow pointing at the Spitfires. One of them, the man Arthur, had left the other two behind when he dived at Albrecht. The other two were flying side by side, only yards apart. Freya smiled, as one of the Spitfires exploded in a fireball, and the blast threw the other one into a downward spin.

Maggie tried to turn Colin's face away. But he wriggled free and ran forwards. 'Alice!'

Vince was half-carrying, half-supporting Alice. They were both covered in blood. Vince was sobbing. Alice's face was grey, what they could see of it; blood covered her mouth and chin. Maggie thought she must be dead, until Alice coughed spasmodically, spitting more blood onto herself and Vince. Vince saw Maggie and shouted, 'Help me!'

Maggie ran to them. Vince, Maggie and Colin gathered around Alice, cradling her. Vince was saying, 'I can't stop the bleeding. I can't. It won't stop. Do something! Do something, Maggie!'

Maggie grabbed Vince's hand, and used his fingers like a vice to pinch Alice's nostrils closed. 'Hold them shut like this.'

'I already tried that, it—'

'Just do it!' Maggie tore a strip off the hem of Alice's skirt, wadded up the fabric and pushed it into Alice's ear. 'Hold that in place,' she told Colin. Alice moaned as Colin pushed down on the pad of material. Maggie tore another piece of fabric, crooning to her: 'Sorry, I know, it hurts, sorry, it'll be okay in a minute…'

She pushed the impromptu dressing into Alice's ear. It was soaked through in seconds. 'Come on,' muttered Maggie, 'come on…'

Alice opened her eyes and smiled.

'Penry! Penry!'

Arthur tried to keep the tears out of his eyes. He watched the Spitfire spiralling down to earth. He called again: 'Penry!'

At last a faint voice answered. 'Here, Arthur. Don't worry, old boy, I've got them surrounded.'

'Penry! Bale out, for God's sake!'

'I'm a bit stuck, old man. Hatch won't open. They got Kiddy, did you see?'

'I saw.'

'Rotten luck, eh?'

'Yes, Penry. Rotten luck.'

'Well. Ta-ta then, Arthur…'

'Penry? Penry!'

No answer. Arthur looked up so he wouldn't have to watch him hit the ground. He swung around to face the black planes. He could hear the German boys laughing; then Albrecht's voice interrupted, and they were silent. Arthur flew towards them; he didn't know what he was going to do. He should probably run for it, but they'd catch him anyway. As he approached the Mound, the cockpit began to heat up again. The black planes sat motionless in the air in front of him. He prepared to fire.

Just in time, he saw the Spitfire behind them and took his thumb off the firing button. At the same moment, one of the black planes exploded; the pilot's shriek was cut off abruptly. The Spitfire darted overhead and climbed away. Arthur's cockpit was almost unbearably hot now, but he laughed. 'Morning, Michal.'

'Hello, Arthur…'

Michal fell silent as a babble of angry German broke out on the radio. Arthur said quickly, 'They can hear us. No idea how.'

'Because they are using magic, Arthur.'

'Didn't catch that, Blue Two.' It had sounded for all the world like *They are using magic*. 'Come again—'

'Arthur! Bale out! You're—'

Arthur's engine burst into flames.

Michal watched Arthur sliding back his plane's hatch. The flames were already high enough to lap into the cockpit. *Come on, Arthur, come on…* Michal had heard the German boy say *Arthur*, and say *The honour shall be mine alone*. He didn't know why, but they were gunning for Arthur. *Bale out, Arthur…*

The burning Spitfire flipped over, and Arthur tumbled out. As soon as he was clear, Arthur tugged at the cord and his parachute opened perfectly. Michal breathed out again. They were only at two thousand feet, so Arthur should be safe on the ground in minutes. It looked like he'd come down close to Addison's farmhouse, so he could run for cover there. In the meantime, Michal just had to hold off those Messerschmitts. They hadn't moved since he'd blown up their comrade: they were still hovering in mid-air.

Michal made a wide turn and examined the 109s. There were six of the black planes now. Going by the black wreckage scattered around the area, there had been quite a few more of them to begin with. The paintings on the tail fins writhed and leered. One of the planes flew with only one wing; not one of the propellers was turning, so either they'd run out of fuel or stalled the engines, or they'd never bothered to use the engines in the first place. As Michal watched they swivelled around, pointed towards him and suddenly started forward, faster than arrows.

The movement was smooth and mechanical, but the pilots' conversation was chaotic and human. They were all trying to talk at once. Either they'd forgotten he could hear them, or they assumed he didn't speak their language. Michal, whose German was almost as good as his English, listened carefully. There was nothing that really mattered: a babble of threats and insults, mostly directed at him. Good: they were disorganised, so if he kept his head there was always a chance. Michal steered towards them, ready to zoom-climb over their heads before they knew what was happening.

Then Albrecht's voice cut in: 'Forget that one. It's the other that matters.'

Another boy said: 'Lady Freya said we should kill the Pole.'

'Later. He's not important. It's the other one. Can't you see what he is? Bring him to that Mound. It must be done there.'

Arthur. Michal changed his course and flew straight at the leading black plane. If he could bring down the leader, the rest would forget about Arthur. Michal opened fire.

Sparks danced along the leader's port wing, which exploded into fragments. Michal aimed more carefully, focussing on the 109's cockpit, and fired another burst. But this time nothing happened, and he heard the *clunk-clunk* sound that meant he was out of ammunition. At the same moment he heard Albrecht say, 'Get that one out of the way,' and something invisible hit his plane astern, jolting his head violently to the side, and sending Michal's Spitfire spinning away.

Maggie thought: *Michal!*

He'd been hit. He was spinning out of control. She took Colin's free hand, and pressed it down on the blood-soaked pad in Alice's ear. 'I've got to help Michal.'

Vince looked at her. 'But Alice…'

Maggie was starting to think nothing could be done for Alice. But she said, 'Keep her like that,' and stood up. She'd have to do this alone; but she could see Michal's plane now, that would help. She concentrated, and gently – if she did anything too quickly it would be like throwing the plane into a wall – she slowed down the spin. Slowly, slowly…

Alice opened her eyes. She was watching Michal too.

Albrecht called down the Eye of the Übermensch. There was the man Arthur, the King, the Leader: a ball of white-gold flame, parachuting down towards a farmer's field. Albrecht watched him in admiration. He didn't like having to shoot any man while he was helpless; killing this one would be a pity indeed. But it had to be done. And, he told himself, if this Arthur knew what a glorious new order his death would usher in, he would surely sacrifice himself gladly.

Albrecht began to draw Arthur away from the fields, towards the Mound.

At last, Michal's plane was steady. Maggie prepared to turn back to Alice. *Michal, I've got to—*

What's this? What's this?

It wasn't Michal. It was Freya. *Dear me, Maggie, I thought I asked you to stay put? How rude of you to run away like that!*

What did you do to Alice?

Why, nothing. A bodily weakness. She is flawed.

Maggie tried to shut her out. *Michal?*

I am afraid not. I cannot have you talking to him, not at the moment. I cannot have you doing anything.

Maggie suddenly felt heavy, as if her clothes were made of lead. She slumped to the ground. She must be able to do something, something… she saw a pebble on the path, the tiniest thing, she could move it easily. She reached out. But the magic was gone. Maggie could hardly move, and her power was gone.

'It's her,' Vince said. He nodded towards the top of the Mound. 'She's up there. She's smashed the Ward Stone. She's drawing off all the power.'

Michal opened his eyes. He must have blacked out for a moment; the light still seemed dim. He felt woozy. He was still dizzy from the spin, maybe he even had a touch of concussion. But he'd felt a lot worse. Automatically he checked the controls; incredibly, the engine hadn't stalled and the Spitfire was still running smoothly. He'd been lucky. No, not lucky – *Thank you, Maggie.*

No reply: he couldn't get anything from her. *Maggie?*

'She can't hear you.'

Usually Michal would have jumped out of his skin. But at the moment it didn't seem at all unusual that someone was right behind him. It must be the concussion, he thought. He turned his head to look, and blinked hard. 'Alice?'

She smiled. She was sitting right behind him, as if the Spitfire had turned into a two-seater. There was a light about her, soft and golden-white. Everything about her shone. He'd never noticed before how pretty she was, although her smile was a little sad. 'Hello, Michal.'

'What are you doing here, Alice?'

'I've come to show you something. I can't stay long, I have to go soon.'

'Where are you going?'

'I don't really know yet. But look, Michal.'

She pointed forwards. He looked out into twilight. It was witch-sight. The land and sky were a grey mass. But somewhere below was a shining light, hanging in the sky as bright as the Bethlehem star on a Christmas card. He looked carefully; there was a grey-white mass just above the light. A parachute. He realised who the light was. 'That is Arthur,' he said.

'Yes, it is. But look there.'

Michal saw the black planes, and the pilots glowing in the cockpits. The *gothi* shone golden-yellow like other people, although they were shot through with streaks of an ugly greyish-purple, the colour of a bruise. The black planes were circling above the Mound, Michal saw. And Arthur was drifting towards the Mound. No, not drifting: he was being pulled towards it. 'What are they doing?' Michal said.

'They're going to kill him,' Alice said.

'I shall stop them —' Michal remembered: he was out of ammo. 'They can't...'

'They will.'

Michal watched the planes. Shapes outlined in fiery light writhed on the tail fins. One was a woman with yellow hair and livid blue eyes; the rest were beasts, snakes and carrion birds and wolves. Especially wolves, with their devouring mouths gaping. Michal looked at Arthur hanging there defenceless. He looked at the brightness of his light. 'We need him, don't we,' he said. 'We will all need him. *They* will need him. Maggie, and Colin. And – everyone.'

'He's going to do something extraordinary,' agreed Alice.

'Unless he dies here.'

'That's right.'

'And I have no ammunition. There is nothing I can do.'

Alice didn't reply. Michal realised there *was* something he could do.

'Withdraw,' Albrecht told the others. 'Watch from above. This is for me to do.'

Petr – who, Albrecht couldn't help but notice, had managed to keep quietly to the rear for most of the day – said: 'Surely the glory of this should be shared, brother? Should not we all—'

They all flinched as Freya's voice blared in their heads: *Do as he says! This honour is for Albrecht alone!*

Without another word the others climbed up and outwards, retreating to several thousand feet above the Mound, where they circled slowly. Freya herself, who had been standing amidst the rubble of the Ward Stone, rose gracefully into the air, her white clothes billowing around her. Nothing must be in the way, not even her blessed person. Albrecht gently, reverently, drew the parachutist into place; a thousand feet above the Mound, slightly to the north so that he would be drifting over exactly the right spot when Albrecht opened fire.

His blood must fall where the old Stone stood, Freya told Albrecht. *Precisely there, on the locus of greatest power. Do not fail, my Albrecht.*

Albrecht would not fail. He was filled with holy awe, but his hands were steady as he swung his plane away and launched into a smooth, controlled dive.

Arthur watched the black Messerschmitt approach. Everything seemed to be happening slowly. He was aware of the warm sunshine, the cool breeze, the green landscape and shining sea below. He could smell wild flowers. Here it was. At last. The day he'd always known was coming. It had come to his father at the Somme, and his father before him in Pretoria. Arthur came from a long line of heroic deaths; he had the feeling it had all been planned, somewhere. It wasn't fair.

He didn't shut his eyes. If Albrecht was going to shoot him in cold blood, he could look at his open eyes while he did it. At least Harry Williams was safe, he thought. And Michal, of course. Michal. Where *was* Michal…?

Arthur looked up. 'Michal! No!'

Michal stopped climbing, and evened out. Alice had told him exactly how it should be done, how he should be placed. If he chose to do it. 'It's your choice,' she'd said. She was still sitting behind him; he could feel her hand resting on his shoulder. It helped.

Michal found exactly the right place, and launched into his dive.

Maggie thought: *She's dead.* The bleeding had almost stopped. Alice's eyes were open now, and staring. Maggie wondered if she should close them. But when Vince gave a harsh sob, they flickered briefly towards him; then she was staring up again. Her gaze wasn't fixed: she was watching something. Maggie turned and looked up.

'*Michal!*'

Albrecht saw Arthur look upwards, and start to thrash and wave his arms. Albrecht frowned; he had thought this great man would die with more dignity. Then he realised Arthur was looking at something, gesturing towards someone; shaking his head, *No, no.*

Albrecht saw Michal's Spitfire only seconds before it hit him. A pilot's quick reactions might have saved him, but Albrecht wasn't a pilot. He was only just starting to move when the Spitfire's wing cut through his cockpit.

'Michal! Michal!'

Maggie began to scramble uphill. She didn't use the path, she crawled and climbed over rocks and grass. Her hands and knees were scraped raw, but she didn't notice. *'Michal!'*

Maggie?

She heard his voice. He was alive.

Freya had been watching Arthur when it happened. Waiting, in the magical twilight, to see his blood spill onto the Mound. Would the power be obvious to her? Would she see their victory begin, right then and there?

She didn't notice Michal until he'd killed Albrecht. She felt Albrecht's moment of surprise – there wasn't time for real fear – and then he was gone. She called, *Albrecht? Albrecht!* but he didn't answer. He had never failed to answer her. He was gone.

Somewhere inside, Lise wailed with grief. But Freya's voice dominated; Freya's scream of cheated rage overpowered everything else. Her Albrecht. Her loyal knight. Her truest, most precious servant and most fervent admirer. Taken from her – stolen – by a sneaking, cheating Pole!

She saw the girl Maggie climbing the sides of the Mound,

reaching out her arms. Freya looked at the Spitfire. It was falling to earth. One of its wings had broken off, it couldn't hope to fly, but it was otherwise quite intact. Freya looked through the Eye, and saw the glowing light inside. There seemed to be two lights, in fact, the pilot's and one behind him, outside the cockpit, something white and translucent. Freya didn't care about that, though. The Pole was alive – injured, judging by how the light was dulled, but very much alive. And Maggie, his lover, was trying to save him.

Freya, still hovering above the Mound, drew on all the power she could. She took all of it. She watched Maggie stumble and fall, barely able to move, unable to work magic. Maggie started to scream: *'No, don't! He's alive! Please! Please!'*

Freya laughed, and set the Spitfire alight.

'Freya, no, please! I'll do anything! I'll make peace, anything! Freya! Lise, don't!'

The man in the parachute, Arthur, was still descending towards the Mound. Freya waved her hand and pushed him away. She would retrieve him later, and sacrifice him herself. But first, she would watch the Spitfire fall.

This is how it feels. It's like this.

The engine had cut out, so Michal fell in silence. He could see flames all around, but couldn't feel them. Perhaps Alice was doing something to keep the pain away. He could still feel her hand on his shoulder. It didn't matter if she was really there or not.

He thought: *I love you, Maggie*, and hoped she could hear.

His plane smashed into the ground, just where the Ward Stone had stood.

Chapter Twenty-Four

The Morrigan

Alice sighed and closed her eyes. Vince, his finger pressed to her wrist, felt her pulse stop.

Michal.

Maggie was still running uphill. She'd heard the crash, and heard the wreckage burst into flames. But she kept going. She was a wizard, so was he. Anything might be possible, anything.

Michal?

Freya watched Maggie scrambling up the side of the Mound. The stupid girl didn't seem to realise he was dead: she was still floundering uphill, bleating his name. Ridiculous. *Oh, oh, poor you!*

Freya said. *Your poor brave man is dead! What a pity!*

Maggie ignored her, but Freya knew she could hear. *What will you do, Maggie? Do you not know he's dead?* Freya began to laugh. *Just like your dear Daddy! He's dead!*

The surviving *gothi* boys joined in. The Pole who'd killed Albrecht was dead, and his woman was howling over him. It was a glorious victory. Albrecht would have said it was dishonourable to mock a beaten enemy, but Albrecht was dead. Maggie looked so stupid, grovelling in the dirt like that. They laughed and laughed.

Maggie, on her hands and knees, reached the top of the Mound. The heat hit her in the face. Orange flames engulfed the black wreckage. The air was thick with oily smoke. Maggie didn't care. She must be able to do something; he couldn't be dead, not just like that. *Michal?*

Maggie walked forward. The heat singed her clothes and her eyebrows, but she kept going. *Michal!*

Miriam Ogilvie watched, with the other coveners, as her daughter walked towards the fire. They'd seen all of it: Alice Carrington's death, the pilots, everything, and there had been nothing they could do. Now Miriam did the only thing left to her. She slammed her hand down on the Rufus Stone, and said: 'My life for hers.'

One by one the others did it too. *'My life for hers.* 'They had to turn sideways so they all fitted around the Rufus Stone. But soon their right hands were all touching the iron and stone surface. *'My life for hers.'*

Laura wailed as Vivian collapsed over the Rufus Stone, bleeding from her ears and nose and mouth. But no one moved, and they didn't stop chanting: *My life for hers.* Vivian slid to the ground, her eyes wide and empty.

A pulse of white light went through the ley lines under their feet.

Freya paused as the ley under Maggie's feet flashed white. For an instant a figure made of pale light stood behind Maggie, a large stocky woman in some sort of uniform; the figure threw both arms around Maggie, and vanished. Now the pale light was all around Maggie, like a second skin. Maggie took another step forward. She was almost in the fire.

For a moment, Freya was worried. But then she realised what the girl was trying to do. She thought she was some great Germanic heroine, a character from one of Wagner's operas, throwing herself onto the funeral pyre of a dead warrior. Her, a stupid British girl, with her dead Pole. It was too funny. *What are you doing? Do you think you are Brunnhilde? Do you think your dead Polack is Siegfried the Hero? Oh, you silly, silly girl!*

Maggie walked into the fire.

Maggie felt the ferocious heat, but it didn't touch her. She pushed aside a sheet of burning metal, and her hand was unscathed. She looked into the orange flames and stepped onto the place where the Ward Stone had stood, the exact spot where Michal had fallen to earth. *Michal!*

She couldn't see much. She couldn't see, at least not clearly, what the crash and the fire had left of him. But she knew the truth, then; if only because she was standing on the locus of power, the most powerful spot in the country, and she still couldn't hear his voice. He was dead. She could still hear the *gothi* boys laughing, hear Freya's jeering voice: *Do you believe me now? Or do you still think he can hear you? Oh Michal, oh speak to me, Michal! Oh, you are just too amusing, Maggie!*

Maggie had been unable to breathe since she'd heard Michal's plane crash. Now, her feet planted on the site of the Stone, she started to draw in a deep, shuddering breath. Witch-sight came instantly; the ley lines under her feet blazed white-hot. The spiral path shone like a white flare. She saw that, all across the countryside, the lines were lighting up, the minor paths and the broad thoroughfares. The power of Michal's self-sacrifice was filling them all with blinding white light.

Maggie drew in a breath. From all along the lines, everywhere in the land, they came to her: those whom the leys had kept, over thousands of years; they came to her, and made her their own.

She was a girl from the east coast, raped and tortured by invading Norsemen. She was a monk in a northern island monastery, watching the Scandinavian raiders burn a thousand years of writings in the library. She was a woman watching the Norman army butchering her sons, before they raped her daughters. She was a man in Cornwall, fighting in vain to keep the Spanish troops from destroying his village and burning his crops. She was a boy on the south coast abducted and enslaved by Roman soldiers. She was a man from York, beaten to death by Border Scots; then she was a woman from the Borders, beaten and raped by Englishmen who told her it was justice.

She was all of those things, and many more. Sometimes the invaders came from beyond the sea, sometimes they came from elsewhere on the coastline. She was a woman from Newcastle, taken and enslaved by pirates from southern England. She was a boy from a time before anything was named, raped and hanged by men from a settlement a day's voyage away. All of them, in their thousands, flooded into her.

She could hear jeering laughter. She could see the one she loved burning. She understood that they had always come, the invaders. They had come to the peaceful farms and the fishing-grounds and the people who tended them. They had farms and fishing-grounds of their own, but they chose to come anyway. And they took everything. They murdered and they raped and they burned, and they kept the land for themselves or they simply went on their way, and they laughed. Sometimes they came sober and self-righteous, but usually they laughed.

They were laughing now. They had killed him, *and they laughed*. Did they really think they could kill *him*, and LAUGH?

Maggie closed her eyes. When she opened them again, they were wholly black. Her hair whipped up behind her. Fire leapt all around her, flames thirty feet high. She opened her mouth wide, and let out her breath in a howling scream of rage.

Miriam Ogilvie stared at the coveners and said, 'My God, the Morrigan,' and collapsed over the Rufus Stone.

On the path, still leaning over Alice's body, Colin opened his eyes wide. 'The Morrigan,' he said.

She opened her eyes. Fire was all around her. The ley lines blazed white, and she heard everything that passed along them. She heard someone saying her name: *The Morrigan*. She'd had another name once, but not anymore. Not now *he* lay burned and dead at her feet. She was the Morrigan.

They were still flying above her, the tormentors, circling the Mound. They were still laughing. She let out another scream, a scream of a thousand voices. *Do you think you can do this, and laugh? Do you think you can LAUGH?*

They had stopped laughing now. They knew something was wrong; some of them began to turn away, to try and escape. But they were too late. She breathed in again, here on the spot where *he* had died, and she drew all the power into herself, everything that had been trodden into the leys for tens of thousands of years. She drew the energy from the earth and the air. She left them with nothing.

Suddenly the *gothi* were just powerless boys in planes they didn't know how to fly. They cried out as their plummet to earth began. But that wasn't enough. *He* had burned, and so they would too. She reached out and drew down lightning from the black sky, and set their planes ablaze. Now she could hear them screaming as they fell. She could have destroyed the planes instantly; it would have been merciful but she was the Morrigan, and mercy didn't interest her. She made certain her voice was the last thing they heard: *BURN! BURN LIKE HE DID! DIE! DIE! DIE!*

Now she could forget them. But wait; she needed one of them alive, as a messenger. She chose one of the falling planes at random: one with a snake painted on its tail fin. She snuffed out the fire and spoke to the pilot.

Petr sobbed with relief when the cockpit flames went out. But then the witch-sight came down, and the face of the Morrigan appeared to him. He screamed, wet himself, and closed his eyes.

But it made no difference. Her face was still before him, in the darkness. It was pale and slack and empty, like the face of a corpse. It was still the face of the red-haired British girl, but now it had flames for hair and eyes like a blackout. Petr screamed, 'Don't kill me! Please! I can tell you things! I have information!'

The Morrigan opened her mouth, which was red and wet as a wound. Her breath reeked of gas and burning metal and rotting bodies. She spoke with a hundred voices, with the wail of a Stuka, and the scream of the dying, and the whistle of falling bombs:

GO BACK TO YOUR LEADER! TELL HIM I AM AWAKE NOW! TELL HIM THIS LAND IS MINE! MINE! MINE!

'I have information! The Führer and Himmler! I know what they're going to do! With the Jews and the gypsies! I know! I'll tell—'

The Morrigan didn't know what the snake-boy was talking about, and didn't care. She told him: *GO!* and hurled him away, beyond the sea, back towards his own land. Then she lost interest in him. She looked down from the Mound, down at the twilit country, at the network of burning lines that covered the land. She found the girl, the one in the white dress. There were others nearby too, a boy and a young man leaning over a dead girl, and a man floating to earth on a parachute; they flinched, without knowing why, as the Morrigan's gaze swept over them. But the Morrigan had no interest in them. She focussed on the girl, who was lying at the foot of the Mound curled into a foetal ball. This was the one who called herself Freya. She had killed *him*. She had laughed. She would burn too.

The Morrigan raised her hand, and made lightning stab down from the sky. It should have turned the girl into a human torch; the Morrigan was looking forward to seeing that. But the girl just curled up tighter. The Morrigan looked more closely. There was a golden glow around the girl. She had some form of protection. The girl was repeating something, over and over. She was saying: 'Führer, my Führer, given to me by God… Protect and preserve my life… You saved Germany in its hour of need… I thank you for my daily bread… Be with me forever, do not desert me, Führer, my Führer, my faith, my light. Hail to my Führer!'

The Morrigan laughed. The girl was praying to that ridiculous Führer of hers, as if he were a god. Her faith in him was protecting her. The Morrigan stretched out to strip that protection away, it would have been easy – but then she had a better idea. The boy in the snake-plane had said: *I know what they're going to do, the Führer and Himmler.* The snake-boy was long gone, away across the sea, but the Morrigan didn't need him to tell her the future. She knew someone else who could.

The Morrigan reached out along the ley lines. She could go anywhere that war had been, and war had been everywhere. Quick as a thought, she found the one she was looking for.

Jannah.

Jannah lay on the bed in her dark little cell in London. She opened her eyes when she heard the voice. Witch-sight bloomed around her. She waited.

Then the face of the Morrigan was in front of her. Jannah recoiled; when she saw traces of Maggie's face in the horror before her, she closed her eyes. But her voice was steady: 'What do you want?'

Show me the future, Jannah. Hitler's future. Jannah spat on the floor when she heard the name. The Morrigan laughed. *Show me what he means to do. With the Jews and the gypsies. Have you seen that future?*

'Yes.' Jannah had had a great deal of time, alone in her cell. She'd seen a lot of things. 'I have seen it.'

Show it to me, Jannah.

'Why should I?'

An image of the Freya-girl, praying to the noble Führer she believed in so fervently, flashed before Jannah's eyes. The Morrigan said: *So I can show it to* her.

Jannah said: 'What will you do with her, when you have shown her?'

I'll send her home, of course. Back to her beloved Führer.

Jannah smiled, and showed her the future.

Faster than light, the Morrigan was back with the girl in the white dress, and poured all the Führer's future into her head.

In an instant, the girl saw all of it. The lines of people, shot and buried in the trenches they'd been forced to dig. The vans, packed with men, women and children, the exhaust fumes pumped inside. And the specially built shower-chambers, the gas, and the ovens. Every bit of it.

But it was the sight of the Führer's own last days that started the girl screaming. The Führer, hiding scared in a bunker in Berlin: hiding like a coward, while boys and old men fought to protect him. While his enemies advanced on him regardless. Then the Führer's suicide, alone in a small stuffy room.

Alone, that is, but for his woman. Eva Braun. The woman he'd kept for years, while he professed to celibacy. His whore. In his last hours, after the hasty ceremony there in the bunker, his *wife*.

Freya and Lise screamed together: 'It isn't true! It isn't true! You're lying! It isn't true—'

But she knew it was. The Morrigan laughed again, and thought how best to send the girl home. She plucked one of the boys out of his burning plane, tossed him carelessly aside and dropped Freya into the cockpit. Then she threw her like a discus, over the sea, towards Berlin.

When the Morrigan was gone, Jannah lay back and watched the future unfold. A new future: the old one was melting and changing. Something had made it different. Someone who was due to die had lived; someone else had died instead. The invasion now seemed a lot less certain. Jannah watched something new happening, something that was less than twenty-four hours away.

She watched a naked man snoring on a luxurious bed. He was probably the most famous man in Europe, but he looked pale and flabby and unremarkable. His plump blonde mistress sprawled across him. The sheets tangled around them were silk: only the best in the Kaiserhof Hotel, the finest hotel in Berlin. And only the very best here in the private suite, the rooms reserved for the Führer.

Outside the bedroom, elite SS guards kept careful watch through the night. They were highly trained, and utterly dedicated. No one could have got past them, it was agreed afterwards. No one.

But suddenly there was someone, something, in the room. A blazing amber light like firelight. A white face, metallic yellow hair, blue eyes glaring like neon. A figure in white, leaning over the bed, shrieking like a banshee: 'Traitor! Traitor! Traitor!'

The man and woman awoke, screaming. In seconds the guards were pounding at the door, but it wouldn't open. The blonde woman clung to the man; he pushed her away, howling like a child. He cowered as the shrieking figure thrust its face into his, and the blue eyes blazed even brighter.

Jannah watched as Freya tried to burn the Führer in his bed. She couldn't succeed, Jannah saw regretfully; there was a hard white light around him, shielding him from harm. Eventually the apparition screeched in frustration, threw itself across the room and crashed through the window out into the night. The Führer shouted for his guards as an air raid siren began to wail.

Jannah watched Freya tear a city block apart. Jannah understood: Freya couldn't hurt the Führer, so she would destroy his city instead. Jannah saw the destruction and death, heard the official pronouncements about air raids. It seemed the British air force were to get the blame: a cowardly night-raid on innocent civilians. Shocking.

And when it was all over, she saw Lise. Just Lise; there was no sign of Freya now. She saw Lise crouching catatonic among the ruins, oblivious to the medics who loaded her carefully into an ambulance and took her away. Her brown eyes were dull and empty, her yellow hair turned pure white.

She always did want to be whiter than everyone else, Jannah thought. For the first time in months, Jannah began to laugh.

The Morrigan threw the Freya-girl away across the sea, then forgot about her. Her feet were still firmly planted on the Mound, but she travelled freely along the ley lines, faster than electricity. Everywhere she went, she heard the voices of her people.

She heard a father, planning how he would gut the Germans with a kitchen knife before they touched his daughters. She heard a mother and father, talking about poisoning their children rather than leaving them to the invaders. She heard a man who'd fought in the trenches, rejoicing in the chance to kill more filthy Jerries. She heard children, and adults, watching with excitement as airmen fought and died over their heads. She heard the thoughts of a man who hoped that the Germans would come, so he could kill a man, to see what it was like. She heard a woman wishing the bombs would fall on the family across the street, because it would serve them right. She heard people, so many, hearing the siren and thinking: *Not me or mine, please, not us. Someone else, not us.* All of them, all that fear and love and hate and glee, it poured into her and she fed on it.

Most of all, she heard the voices of the bereaved; those who'd lost *him* or *her* to a bomb or a bullet. And they all sang one song: *Kill the Enemy. Kill them all.* They were the Morrigan's people, and she revelled in them. She laughed as she roamed the lines, faster than thought. In an instant she could rise high above the earth, and look down through the witch-twilight at the network of shining ley lines that criss-crossed the countryside. She could see the new band of white light, the line of protection pulsing outwards from the Mound, surrounding the whole island. She could see it all. She was the Morrigan, and she was free, and this country belonged to her.

There was one voice that kept calling, though. She couldn't think why, there was nothing in it to interest her, but she couldn't help hearing it. It sounded like a child, a little boy. He was saying: 'Maggie? Maggie, can you hear me?'

The Morrigan didn't know any Maggie. But the voice was persistent. 'Maggie, wake up, please, Maggie.'

The Morrigan didn't want to listen. There were bombs falling somewhere, planes being shot out of the sky. That was where she belonged. But now there was another voice. 'Maggie? Maggie, love?'

It sounded like an old woman. 'Maggie, love, it's Gran. Can you come towards me, please, love? Can you come out of there?'

An airbase to the south was under attack. Men were killing each other, they were dying in flames. That was real, the Morrigan thought. It was the only true reality. But that voice still tugged at her: 'Maggie, pet, we love you. Please come back to us. Please.'

It sounded on the verge of tears. Tears were the Morrigan's business, but these made her feel – wrong. 'Please, Maggie, don't you leave us too. We need you, love.'

'Maggie, you listen, girl.' Another voice now; an older boy. 'You need to come out of there now. We can't lose you, too.'

A name came into her mind: *Vince*. This was Vince. He was saying, 'You know I can always find things, Mags. And I've found you now, haven't I? You can hear me, can't you? Nod your head if you can hear me!' The voice echoed: *Nod your head if you can hear me! Nod your head if you can hear me! Nod—*

The Morrigan nodded her head. Her head, it didn't feel right. Her face was too hot. In fact, she was too hot all over. There was a fire, she thought. Fire was part of the Morrigan, but this was making her uncomfortable. She raised a hand and snuffed out the flames. The voice – *Vince* – said, 'That's better. You come on out of it, Maggie. You've got your Gran and Colin all worried here.'

The old woman's voice again: 'Maggie, it's Gran.' *Gran.* That was right. 'Come a bit closer, pet, come to Gran, won't you?'

The little boy's voice: 'It's Colin, Maggie. It's okay.'

Colin. Of course, Colin. Her brother. She remembered a condescending voice saying, *After all, you are not your brother's keeper!* But she was, wasn't she? If not her, then who was? He was just a little boy, and Mum didn't... Mum...

She stopped, confused. She felt cold now, and her face was wet. She could hear a hissing noise, then a low grumbling... Bombs! Gunfire! But no. No... just distant thunder. It was raining, she realised. The storm had broken. She was standing in the rain, getting all wet. She could feel it now, soaking through her hair and her clothes. She heard Vince say, 'Come on, Maggie, you silly moo. We can't be standing on the Mound in the pissing rain all day, can we?'

Now the other voices were scolding him, but she was thinking: the Mound. That was where she was. Things had been happening all around her. She remembered burning: planes burning, voices falling and screaming. Most of those voices were silent now, but one was still there, still sobbing. It was a boy, she thought; she reached out to find him. She found he was hanging from a parachute. He had been burned. The parachute had been burned, too; spots of it were burnt right through, and now the whole thing was ripping apart. The boy sobbed louder. He was crying for his mother. He didn't sound much older than Colin. She found that she knew his name – Manfred.

The boy's parachute disintegrated, and he began to plummet. Without thinking she caught him and slowed his descent, so he drifted to earth lightly. Then, because he was in pain and he wouldn't stop crying, she made him fall asleep. There. That was better...

Something had touched her hand. Her hands were cold and wet, she realised. But another hand, warm and firm, was taking hold of hers. The boy, Vince, said: 'That's it. Take a step forward, all right? Just the one, Maggie.'

Maggie? Who was that? She took a step forward, then another. That seemed to be right, because Vince was saying, 'That's it. One more now, Maggie. Mind how you go, it's slippy. Good girl,

337

Maggie. Now, can you open your eyes?'

Her eyes were closed, she realised. Did that mean she was Maggie? No, she was... didn't she have another name? But Vince was saying, 'Yep, Maggie, that's you. You with your eyes shut, you're Maggie. Open your eyes now, Maggie.'

She thought: *That's me. I'm Maggie.*

Maggie opened her eyes.

She was standing on the Mound in the pouring rain. Colin and Gran were standing in front of her; Vince was beside her, holding her hand. He was saying, 'There she is, now. She's back.'

'Colin? Gran?' Maggie said. 'What's happened?'

Gran looked as if she'd been crying. 'Don't you remember, love?'

'No. I mean, I remember...fire. I was walking towards it. I don't remember after that. But before, before that there was...there...'

She remembered. She tried to turn around, but Vince caught hold of her, and Gran and Colin stepped forward and held her tightly. 'No, love,' Gran said. 'He's not there. Don't look there. He's gone.'

'Michal...Oh, Michal, Michal...'

She fell to her knees. They all knelt with her, in the rain and the mud. They put their arms around her. Maggie put her head on Colin's shoulder, and cried.

Epilogue
The Sweetheart Pin

Never in the field of human conflict has so much been owed by so many to so few.

Winston Churchill

September 1940

It was the first day Maggie had woken up without eyes red and swollen from crying. It was so early even Gran wasn't up yet. When Maggie got downstairs, Vince and Colin were already in the kitchen. 'We're going to have visitors today,' Colin said. 'Three visitors.'

The other two didn't argue. They got dressed and went out. The sun was bright, but the air was sharp and crisp. Autumn was coming. Without having to discuss it, they headed up the Mound.

The top of the Mound had been cleared. The signs of burning were all gone; the whole site had been re-landscaped, and fresh turf laid down. The green of the turf was almost hidden, however, by the carpet of wreaths and flowers. Colin, Vince and Maggie had to pick their way through the bouquets that had been laid around the new Monument, which stood exactly where the Ward Stone had stood. Its official name was the Wardston Monument, but Maggie already thought of it as the New Stone.

She looked at it now. The New Stone was much more sculpted than the previous one. A solid oblong pillar of white granite, it stood on a granite plinth on a huge granite slab. Marble would have been fancier, but granite would last much longer. This new stone would stand for as long as the old one. Black letters were welded onto the smooth grey-white surface:

SACRED TO THE MEMORY OF THOSE
WHO DIED AS A RESULT OF ENEMY ACTION
IN WARDSTON-UPON-SEA
18TH AUGUST 1940

WILLIAM RODERICK ANDERSON
ALICE MARIANNE CARRINGTON
MICHAL CAPEK
PATRICK DRAYCOTT
JANE GILLIES
NICHOLAS KENNETH JONES
ELIZABETH CATHERINE LARKIN
EDWARD ALASDAIR PATERSON
AGNES MARGARET SIDNEY
GEOFFREY JOHN WINCHESTER

THEY THAT WAIT UPON THE
LORD SHALL RENEW THEIR STRENGTH;
THEY SHALL MOUNT UP WITH WINGS AS EAGLES

Maggie and the boys picked their way through the flowers, the formal wreaths and garden roses and the loose bunches of daisies. Most of the village came here regularly. No one seemed to wonder why the monument had been put up unusually swiftly; bombed-out families in London were living in tents, but nobody questioned why erecting the Wardston Monument had been given such high priority. Maggie supposed all communities thought their dead were more important than anyone else's.

They reached the paved area in front of the monument, a single large slab of granite. The workmen had received precise instructions, from the highest level, and had worked in absolute secrecy. So hardly anyone knew that under the thick granite, under the foundations reinforced with concrete, were two plain coffins.

Maggie knelt down and pressed her hand against the granite slab. 'Hello, Michal,' she whispered. 'Hello, Alice.'

Vince and Colin did the same. They came here every day. They'd never bothered to visit the military graveyard, or Alice's family's crypt. The coffins there, although much more ornate, were both empty.

After a few moments the three wizards stood, and went to sit on the steps of the Monument. They waited for their visitors to arrive.

They heard a car door slam at the bottom of the Mound. After several minutes, they heard laboured breathing. A large man appeared at the top of the path, wheezing slightly from the climb. They gaped at him. Vince said, 'Is that…'

It was. Winston Churchill made his way through the mass of flowers. Impressed in spite of themselves, the three wizards rose and went to meet him. He was carrying a huge wreath of poppies. 'Good morning,' he said.

They murmured a reply. Churchill removed his hat. 'May I?' The wizards stood to the side. Churchill, hat held to his chest, bowed towards the Monument and carefully laid his wreath on the granite slab. Then he bent down, and pressed his hand against the slab, as if he expected it to be warm.

After a moment, Churchill straightened up and turned to them. Maggie braced herself for a stream of consoling platitudes. But instead he said, 'I've come in person to ask for your help. I should like you to come to London.'

Vince's face lit up, but Maggie shook her head. 'We belong here,' she said.

'I think you'll find that your work here is done.'

Maggie folded her arms. 'We need to protect the Mound. It's a power spot.'

'Surely the Mound is already defended, Miss Ogilvie. By *him*.' He nodded towards the granite slab. 'The new sacrifice. The new Skull of Brandt. Isn't that right?'

'*You* believe in all that?'

'I am not certain. But I have no intention of disinterring Flight-Lieutenant Capek to find out one way or the other. Or Miss Carrington, since you found it necessary to keep her here too.'

There was a question in it. Vince said, 'Her family didn't appreciate her while she was alive. They en't getting her back now—'

Maggie nudged him. 'It's necessary. If we're defended by Michal, then we're defended by Alice too.'

Churchill shrugged. 'It would seem we're defended by something. My people have confirmed that Adolf Hitler has cancelled his invasion plans.'

They looked at him in astonishment. Vince said, 'I thought he was hell bent on invading?'

'He was. Now he is not.'

'Why?'

'That is unclear. There are many good practical reasons, of course. Most of them involve the English Channel. But sources close to the Führer have told us he believes our country is protected by demons.' He looked hard at the wizards; his gaze came to rest on Maggie. 'She-demons, apparently.'

They stared back levelly. 'Fancy that,' said Vince.

'Indeed. Apparently, a young man in a Messerschmitt told his superiors he was driven away from British skies by what he described as a demon. A red-haired demon, he told them, which left him badly burned. It seems the Führer was disposed to believe him, because he himself had encountered a similar creature. A blue-eyed she-devil, or so he said.'

'That Adolf,' said Vince. 'What a loony.'

'Quite. And now he has resolved that Germans will not set foot in this country until it has been cleansed.'

'Cleansed?'

'Yes. With fire.'

The three wizards looked at each other. Churchill said quietly, 'His new policy is to bomb our cities until we capitulate. Until we dispense with our protections, supernatural and otherwise, and invite his forces in. We are no longer at immediate risk of invasion. But invasion is not the only way to bring a country to its knees.'

Maggie turned away. This was where she belonged, she was sure of it. But London. Those crowded streets. *Cleansed with fire.* When she stayed silent, Churchill said: 'Did your mother tell you we are still searching for your father?'

Maggie turned to him. 'She told us. Is there any news?'

'Perhaps.'

There was a long silence. Eventually Maggie said, 'So if we come to London and help you, you'll keep on looking for our Dad?'

Churchill shrugged. Maggie shook her head. 'You're a real bastard, aren't you?'

'I suppose I have to be, Miss Ogilvie.'

Maggie looked at Vince and Colin. They both nodded. 'All right,' Maggie said. 'We'll help you if you promise you'll keep on looking for him.' She stepped onto the granite slab and held out her hand. 'Promise it *here*. On their graves. Right here.'

Churchill stepped onto the granite. For a moment, Maggie thought the sun must have slid behind a cloud; the light dulled, and a shadow formed behind Churchill, a dark smoky shape like a big dog or a wolf. She blinked; the sky was bright and clear again, and the shadow was gone. Churchill shook Maggie's hand. 'Then we have a deal,' he said. He stepped back onto the grass and put his hat back on. 'I'll let your mother give you the news. Good morning to you all.'

He had the grace to go away without another word. They heard a murmur of voices on the path below. They waited. A minute later Miriam Ogilvie emerged, carrying a bouquet of white roses.

Colin cried, 'Mum!' and ran to her. Vince wandered tactfully away. Maggie approached her mother slowly, trying to hide her shock. Miriam looked ten years older. Her hair and make-up was immaculate as ever, but her face was lined and she moved stiffly. For the first time, she looked old. 'Mum, are you all right?'

'Maggie.' Miriam hugged her briefly. Maggie could feel that she'd lost weight. 'Of course, I'm just tired.'

Colin was tugging at her arm. 'Mum, what about Dad?'

Miriam smiled. 'You mustn't get your hopes up too much. But there's a man in a hospital in Dunkirk who was brought in the day your Dad…went missing. He's been unconscious ever since. He fits your Dad's description.' She cut off their questions, 'That's all we know so far. But it means there's a chance, doesn't it? Now.'

She turned to the monument, and laid her bouquet beside Churchill's wreath. Maggie recoiled as she caught the flowers' scent. The strong perfume made her stomach turn. Miriam looked at her hard. 'Are *you* all right?'

'I've gone off the smell of roses, that's all.'

'Is that so?' She sighed. 'I'm sorry about your young man, you know. And your friend.'

'Mum.' She had to ask. 'Did you know they were going to die?'
'Not them specifically, no.'

'But you knew someone would. Someone would be *sacrificed*.'
'Yes. I knew that.'

'Did you ever think it might be us? Me and Colin?'

Miriam's voice was barely audible. 'Yes. I knew it might be you.'

If she'd tried to deny it, Maggie would have hated her. As it was, there didn't seem to be much point. Miriam was what she was. Instead Maggie said, 'I'm sorry about your friend Vivian.'

Miriam looked up sharply. 'Are you?'

'Yes. Of course. I mean I hardly knew her, but...'

'No. I suppose you didn't. Well now.' She raised her voice to include Vince in the conversation. 'You three are coming to London, then?'

Vince wandered back over. 'Yeah, we're coming. Mr Churchill was very persuasive.'

'He is persuasive, isn't he. That's why I sent him to ask you, rather than doing it myself.' She looked at Maggie and smiled. 'I was afraid you'd just say no if I did the asking... What is it?'

They were all staring at her. 'You *sent* him?' Vince said. 'You *sent* Winston Churchill?'

'Well, yes.' She frowned. 'He didn't say anything wrong, did he? I mean he...' She looked mildly offended as Maggie, Vince and Colin exchanged glances and burst out laughing. 'And *what* is so funny?'

'Nothing, Mum.' Maggie got herself under control. 'Have you seen Gran? Does she know you're here?'

'No. I'll go and see her now.' She turned to go, and realised no one was following. 'Well, are you coming?'

'We're waiting for someone else first, Mum,' Colin said.

Miriam looked as if she were about to argue, but then nodded. 'All right. I'll see you shortly.' She hugged Colin, and leaned over to kiss Maggie on the cheek. She frowned, and looked Maggie up and down. '*Are* you all right? You look...'

'I look what?'

'...No, no. It's nothing.' She nodded goodbye to Vince, and disappeared down the spiral path.

The three wizards resumed their seats on the monument. After a moment Vince said, 'She *sent* Winston Churchill.' They all spluttered with laughter. They hadn't laughed for weeks; Maggie had to admit it felt good. Vince shook his head: 'She's some woman, your Mum. Whatever she wants us to do in London, at least it en't going to be boring.'

'She's never boring, I'll give her that.'

They waited. The sun was warming up, although there was still a chill in the air. Maggie thought she heard a car door slam, but decided it must be someone else. He wouldn't come by car; he'd come on foot or by bicycle. Like Michal always had.

Michal. Maggie closed her eyes. One day she'd be able to stand here on the ley lines and summon up the past, and hear the *tring* of his bicycle bell and watch him hurry up the path. One day she'd be strong enough to see him floating down on his parachute, and watch herself running to meet him. Maybe one day she'd be able to watch all that, and it wouldn't break her heart.

They heard footsteps on the path. They all got up, smiling with genuine warmth, as Arthur came into view. He picked his way through the flowers. He was in uniform, neat and handsome as ever, but Maggie thought he seemed different: not quite so shiny, somehow. He had a scar on his right cheek; the parachute landing hadn't been gentle. His face was thinner, paler; his eyes had dark shadows, and didn't beam with quite so much general bonhomie. His hair had been combed, but a strand had escaped over one ear. At last, Maggie thought, Arthur had begun to look *interesting*. At the moment he was frowning at the bouquets around his feet: 'I didn't bring any flowers.'

'I think we're all right for flowers, mate,' said Vince.

'So I see. I meant to bring some anyway. Before I go.' He looked up. 'I've come to say goodbye. The squadron's being posted elsewhere. We fly out this afternoon.'

'Where are you going?' said Colin.

'I shouldn't tell you. Careless talk, and all that.'

Maggie sighed. 'You're going to London. That's where the

bombers are going, isn't it? Telephone my Gran when you get there, and leave her an address. We'll keep in touch.'

He smiled. 'Yes, I'd like that.' He cleared his throat. 'Maggie, could I have a word?'

The two of them left Vince and Colin sitting on the Monument, and walked to the east side of the Mound, overlooking the sea. Maggie said, 'How's your friend Penry-Smith?'

Arthur's face brightened a little. 'Much better. Sitting up in bed. Making a confounded nuisance of himself, according to the nurses. Takes more than a few burns and broken bones to slow down Penry.'

'Will he fly again?' she asked, since that was what pilots always wanted to know.

'Eventually.'

They reached the edge of the Mound. Maggie saw Arthur scan the skies, out of habit; but everything was quiet. Then he fished in his pocket, and took out a little jeweller's box. 'This is for you. Michal – Michal wanted you to have it.'

She opened the box. Inside was a brooch, shaped like an eagle with its wings spread wide and a little crown on its head. The RAF symbol. It looked like the badges the pilots wore, but it was smaller and more delicate, and it was made of solid gold. Maggie drew in her breath. 'It's…'

'It's a sweetheart pin,' Arthur said. 'Men in the services give them to their wives, you know. Or their girls. He wanted you to have one.'

Maggie lifted it gingerly out of the box. It was probably the most expensive piece of jewellery she'd ever touched. 'It's beautiful.'

'Michal wanted you to have it. He saw other men getting them, you know, for their sweethearts and all. He was determined you should have one. He said, I'll get one for Maggie, one of the best ones. Here, try it on.'

He helped Maggie fasten the pin to her jumper. The little eagle flashed in the sunlight. Arthur was still talking. 'He wanted you to know how much he thought of you. Men, you know, we don't always say these things until… well, we don't always say them. But he loved you. Anyone could see that. He loved you very much.'

But he died for you, Maggie thought. She looked at Arthur's shadowed eyes, however, and knew she would never say it. 'I loved him too.'

'Yes, I know that. I just wanted – I mean, he just wanted to be sure you knew.'

'I knew.' She smiled at him, touched by the sweetness of the lie. Because it was a lie, almost certainly. Michal couldn't have afforded something like this brooch. He wouldn't have thought to buy it for her even if he could, and she wouldn't have thought to want it; Maggie never wore jewellery. No, this was Arthur's doing.

She had a sudden suspicion, and looked at him hard. He looked back, his gaze straight and honest now he'd stopped fibbing, concerned and slightly puzzled. No, Maggie decided; no. This wasn't a come-on; he had no ulterior motive. Arthur was taking care of her because she was Michal's girl: the last thing he could ever do, for Michal. 'Thank you, Arthur. I know he loved me. I'm even more sure now.'

'Good. Good.'

'And Arthur, he… he thought the world of you, you know. You were his best friend. He loved you too.'

Arthur had been gazing out to sea. Now he turned to her, and she thought she'd never seen such anguish. 'I loved him too,' he said.

'Yes, I know.'

'I mean I loved him. I *loved* him…and now he's…'

Maggie stared at him. She didn't know what to say. Did he mean what she thought he meant…? *Oh, Arthur, Arthur…* She'd heard it was a sin, of course. But she saw the tears come to his eyes and said, 'I know you loved him. I know.'

Arthur stumbled towards her. Maggie took him into her arms and held him as he wept, his body shaking. She let him cry himself out. 'I know, Arthur. I know.'

Eventually, he lifted his head and dried his eyes. 'I have to go,' he said.

She nodded. 'Don't be a stranger, Arthur.'

'Never.' He looked at her for a long moment, then kissed her lightly on the forehead and turned away. She watched him cross the Mound, and shake hands with Colin and Vince. He spoke quickly and quietly to each; she saw both boys straighten their shoulders, and smile, as if a burden had become a bit lighter. Michal had been right, she thought: it *was* a sort of magic.

When Arthur was gone, she went back to the monument and sat between the boys. They ought to be moving, she knew. Miriam would be waiting impatiently. They'd have to pack, and say goodbye to Gran. But still they sat, looking out to sea. Maggie looked in the direction of Dunkirk, and thought: *Dad. If it's you, wake up. Come back to us. Come back to Gran, because we're not going to be here. We might never be here again...*

She thought she felt something: a stirring, a familiar voice murmuring. A smell, of pipe tobacco and salt and diesel oil: Dad's smell. But she couldn't be sure. Might just be wishful thinking. She took a deep breath, and looked at Vince and Colin. 'Do you think we can still do this?'

'Do what?' said Vince.

'Magic. You know. Now it's just the three of us.'

Colin smiled. 'Four of us, you mean.'

Maggie and Vince exchanged looks. 'Colin,' Maggie said gently. 'They're not going to let Jannah come back to us.'

'Not Jannah, silly.' Colin reached over and patted Maggie's stomach. 'Us three and the baby.'

They were still standing on the Mound, shouting at each other, when the squadron of Spitfires flew overhead. The lead Spitfire dipped its wing in salute, but they were too busy arguing to notice. The ley lines thrummed with their voices. The squadron swung around to the east and headed for London.

Cathy McSporran's fiction has appeared in a wide range of magazines and anthologies such as Mslexia, Chapman, Nerve, Eclogia and From Glasgow to Saturn. She has been shortlisted for the Macallan/Scotland on Sunday prize, and was awarded the Constable Award by the Scottish Association of Writers. She has a PhD from Glasgow University's School of Creative Writing, and teaches classes in creative writing, poetry and Dante's Inferno in Glasgow's Open Studies department. Cathy's debut novel Cold City was published in 2014.